# The Awkward Girl

*A Novel*

*By Mary Rose Callaghan*

*Attic Press*
Dublin

*F I C*

*cop 1*

First published in 1990 by
Attic Press
44 East Essex Street
Dublin 2

British Library Cataloguing in Publication Data
Callaghan, Mary Rose
  The awkward girl.
  I. Title
  823'.914 [F]

  ISBN 0-946211-96-7

Cover Design: Paula Nolan
Origination: Attic Press
Printed and bound in Great Britain by
The Guernsey Press Co. Ltd., Guernsey, Channel Islands.

The publishers acknowledge the assistance of The Arts Council/An Chomhairle Ealaíon who grant aided this book. The author was assisted by the "Authors Royalty Scheme Loan" of The Arts Council/An Chomhairle Ealaíon.

M76

$5.95

*To Olwyn*

## Acknowledgements

Early versions of some of these chapters have appeared in the following publications, to which I make grateful acknowledgement: "Rita" as "Underwear" in *The Wall Reader and Other Stories*, Arlen House; "Deirdre" and "Jim" as "Two Daffodils" and "Dole Day" in *U magazine*; "Denis and Kitty" and "Peggy and Tony" as "Breakfast with Turgenev" and "How I Saved Fifteen Thousand Pounds" in *The Journal of Irish Literature*; "Mona" as "A Far, Far Better Thing" in *Image magazine*, Dun Laoghaire, Co. Dublin.

*I am the Duchess of Malfi, still.*

JOHN WEBSTER

# Contents

# I Rita

"Hello," Rita snapped into the phone, "this is the Superior."

"Are you the Reverend Mother?" a man's voice asked.

Parents, she sighed. "I am the *Superior*, yes."

"Ah! Alan Murray here. I'm the manager of the Dublin Roches'. Ah ... look, I'm afraid there's someone here dressed up as one of your nuns."

"If this is some sort of joke, I'm hang -"

"Oh, it's no joke," he said, laughing. "She claims to be Sister Margaret Mary O'Connor."

"But Sister *is* one of our nuns! Why do you think she's dressed up?"

"You'd better come in, so."

She kept her voice level. "Just tell me the problem. I'm far too busy ..."

"The problem," he mimicked icily, "is that Sister was apprehended leaving this shop with items of underwear she didn't pay for. And if you don't come in, I'll be forced to call the guards."

Her face felt on fire. "I'll be right in. Give me half an hour. But there must be some mistake."

"Good, I'll wait, so."

"Eh, - it might take longer. The traffic ..." She cleared her throat and continued firmly, "It must be some mistake. The convent will, of course, pay for anything Sister bought."

Click. The phone went dead.

Rita replaced the receiver and paused by the hall window-sill. Maggy May? The infirmarian. The little ones doted on the flabby old lay sister, trailed her everywhere. Only this morning when that spindly-legged child fainted at Mass, she was first over and carried her out, whispering wheezily, "That's my pet, my girl."

The convent buzzed at the faintest hint of gossip. Good thing she came to the phone herself. The less said ... and no recriminations. Maggy May would see a psychiatrist. But underwear?

It was a case of senility.

Car keys were needed now. Cheque book. Outside it was rainy and already almost dark. After ten years in the States, she'd never again get used to the twilight of Irish winters. Only a few hours of daylight. Lapland with those wintry trees. No time to go to her cell to change. Or get a coat. Luckily she had her suit on. She'd promised Mother General to wear the habit in public, but no matter. Heavens, it was nearly 1967. In Florida she'd gone around in shorts. But no one wore civvies here. At first they'd gaped at her jumpers and skirts, but now she was accepted as an oddity. No doubt because of her PhD.

As she turned abruptly, the green baize screen clattered onto the floor. Obscurantist, but the old nuns insisted on privacy. She lifted it, suddenly

7

queasy from the smell of floor wax. It permeated the house, along with incense, chalk and cabbagy dinners. The odious smells of an institution, she thought, seeing a child lurking at the far corner of the big hall.

Sally Ann Fitzpatrick. A trouble-maker from 6B.

What had she heard?

Rita crossed the flagged floor, noting the girl's too short uniform skirt, torn tights, unruly dark hair. "Why are you out of class?"

"I've a terrible headache, Mother." The girl was pale, her eyes red from crying. A bit of Sellotape held on one wing of her glasses. "Sister Margaret Mary's out, so I've to ask your permission to go to bed."

"Go to bed with a headache?" Rita mocked, searching the unhappy young face. "We're getting very soft!"

"But it's a bad headache, Mother."

"Have you taken aspirin?"

"After breakfast. And lunch. I've had it all day."

"Have you been wearing your glasses?"

Sally Ann nodded, pushing the broken frames up on her nose.

Rita glanced irritably at her watch: 3.10. Surely at seventeen the girl could take better care of her glasses? She was neurotic, an attention seeker, probably avoiding a test. "If it's not better by study time, go to bed then. Back to class now!"

"Please ..."

"Back to class this minute!"

The girl went away, sniffling. When she rounded the corner, the noise changed into loud sobbing. Rita hesitated. It sounded heartbreaking, but there was no way she could give in to that. As she hurried through the mossy gloom to the bursar's office, the noise faded. There was always some problem with Sally Ann. Lately she had affected a tragic pose - Hamlette. It was infuriating. She was always sulking. In the wrong place. You only had to tell her to do something and she'd do the opposite. And last week she'd almost knocked out Jane McMahon with a tennis racket. Rita had had to drive the child into Vincent's emergency. But thank God she was all right. Oh, it was an accident, but she'd given Sally Ann a stern lecture. It wouldn't have happened if she hadn't been disobedient. The courts were meant for netball now. It was typical of her to be playing tennis in December.

Then there was that silly fuss about her hair. She did Art as an extra and was always clashing with Clement, the teacher. The older nun insisted she should have it cut. It was in her eyes and she was "wearing it out" by pulling at it. Rita listened but refused to make her cut it, so long as she pinned it back tidily. She always tried to be fair to the children. Not one of the fascist dictators she had known in the novitiate. But the very next week there'd been another ridiculous row with Miss Murphy, the Irish teacher. The woman brought Sally Ann to her, complaining that she'd given cheek. Apparently, they'd had words about her choice of hobby for discussion at the Irish Oral exam. Sally Ann had chosen fishing - *Iascaireacht* - for which she's learnt all the vocabulary.

"But what's wrong with it?" the girl had pleaded.

Rita silenced her, although secretly wondering the same.

"But women fish," Sally Ann had argued.

"Do you?" Rita snapped.

"No, but ..."

"Then it's not really your hobby, is it?"

In the end Rita had ordered the girl to choose a more suitable topic. Something more feminine, like knitting or sewing. Even stamp collecting might do. It was ridiculously petty, she knew. And unfair. But she had to back up the staff. After all, she'd recently taken the girl's side about the hair.

Mother Clement, who doubled as a bursar, was dwarfed by a big oak desk. She was dressed in the Order's brown habit. "Is anything wrong?"

"No!" Rita met her watery gaze. I just want the car keys. Anyone out?"

"Only Margaret Mary." The older nun reached behind for the keys. "She went into town on the bus for her glasses."

"I'll be back in an hour. Give me the cheque book. Or do you have cash? About fifty pounds would be fine." Better too much than too little.

The little nun looked consumed with curiosity. "Wouldn't a cheque do?"

"Have you no cash?"

"Yes, but it's awkward. I've made out the lodgement slip."

"A cheque might be difficult. Give me cash as you've got it."

Clement's bloodless lips curved downward as she pulled out the desk drawer. As she rooted grumpily, Rita fiddled nervously with the brown ornamental puppy on her desk. Ridiculous, having to consult the bursar about every halfpenny. In the States, she'd dealt with all finances, picket lines, construction unions. The Irish were still in the Dark Ages, at least religiously. You'd think there'd never been a Vatican II. It would have no effect here, if Archbishop McQuaid got his way. He sat out in Killiney with his head in the clouds, unaware that his world was collapsing.

"Mr Felice paid Maria's fees this morning. In five pound notes!" Mother Clement laughed cattily, counting out the money. "Bet it's counterfeit. Italians look sinister, if you ask me."

No one is asking you, Rita thought. Idly she picked up the ornamental puppy. Yellow tears splashed down his cherubic brown face onto his chubby paws. I MISS YOU was in large red letters on the base. "Whose is this?"

Clement smiled slowly, her face transforming. "It's Margaret Mary's Gary, God bless him!"

Rita frowned. "Gary?"

Goodness. Not a statue of that stupid little yapper she'd insisted be put down? Perhaps she'd been too harsh. Was the pettiness of the convent getting to her? Making her inflexible? She could still hear Sally Ann's sobbing in her head. It wouldn't have hurt to be kinder to the child.

The older nun pushed ten fivers across the desk. "Margaret Mary dropped him. But I have a good glue."

"Oh ..." Rita put the ornament down.

"Is it a bill?"

But Rita wasn't to be drawn. She pocketed the money, letting the question float over her. Pope Pius XII glared suspiciously from his portrait on the wall. Surely it was time for a successor? There'd been two popes since - John and now Paul. Yet fifties attitudes still prevailed. There was an atmosphere of fear and mistrust in the convent. It needed fresh air, new ideas to blow out the cobwebs. But it was impossible to change others. You could only do something about yourself. Perhaps she should ask Clement to see to Sally Ann. "You might go over to 6B."

"Yes?" The older woman looked up, hoping for a clue.

"Never mind!" Rita glanced at her watch. With the girl in that mood, there might be another row. Clement wouldn't handle her properly. She'd dash over to the school herself and call Sally Ann out of class.

As Rita entered the classroom, the girls of 6B rose noisily to their feet. The Irish teacher turned from writing on the blackboard, her face reddening. "Yes, Mother?"

Rita signalled the class to be seated. "Miss Murphy, would you mind excusing Sally Ann Fitzpatrick?"

"Not at all. Sally Ann!" The teacher called to the back of the classroom.

Sally Ann got up sulkily. She was still pale.

Rita waited outside the door.

"How's the head?" she asked cheerfully when the girl appeared.

Sally Ann wore her martyr's expression. "Terrible."

"Take some more aspirin and go to bed."

"That won't do any good. It's probably a brain tumour."

Rita kept herself from smiling. "Well, go to bed. I'll have your supper sent up."

The girl turned back to the classroom door. "No, thanks."

God, she was infuriating. "If it's that bad, you should rest."

"I'd prefer to suffer." And she pulled open the door.

Rita was suddenly short of breath. "Come back here, Sally Ann!"

She closed the door, staring sulkily at her feet.

"Go to bed, this minute!"

But she stayed rooted to the ground.

Rita felt like laying hands on her. She wanted to drag her upstairs to bed. But she struggled to control herself. "Sally Ann, did you hear me?"

The girl nodded.

Rita kept her voice low. "Then why won't you obey me?"

Sally Ann looked at her defiantly. "You jeered me."

"I didn't jeer you."

"Yes, you did! In the hall."

Rita looked at her watch. She hadn't time for this nonsense. Clenching her fists behind her back, she said in a deadly quiet voice. "You have one second to get yourself up that stairs."

Sally Ann stood there.

"One second!"

The girl turned abruptly to the stairs.

Rita took several calming breaths. Stop getting angry. Stop it.

Speeding down the drive, she waved to the gardener hoeing by the massive gates. Hard to imagine he had chauffeured them everywhere in the novitiate. They were forbidden to go out by themselves. Still, happy days then, a gaggle of girls flapping round the grounds after tea, with rambling blackberries everywhere and angry swans attacking anything in trousers. Now the swans were gone: the male was eaten by a fox and the female pined away. And the novices were dwindling to two a year. The choir had given up singing the *Benedictus* in chapel, and sickly rows of new houses were sprouting on the lower hockey field.

After the village she accelerated for the long stretch before the shopping centre. Friday evening's mad rush would delay her coming back. Tonight she must phone her father about his arthritis. It was worse recently, but he never complained. On her last visit home, he had brushed her concern off. "Ah, don't worry about me, child. Amn't I almost with herself?"

Rita had looked away. The hypocrite! After the life he had given their mother.

Later that evening he had said gently, "Child, would ye not wear the veil?"

She couldn't answer.

Oh, why did he still upset her? He didn't drink now. And her brother said he boasted that she was Superior of the Irish Mother House at thirty-six. Had rebuilt the convent in Florida. And had taught the professors in Florida State, getting a PhD. Her brains were something to boast of. Hmm ... no matter. She could never forgive him her childhood. Never. She could see him now, red-faced and eyes bulging.

"The bitch is gone! Gone! Left me with six brats! And I didn't want one of ye! Not one of ye!" He swerved drunkenly, children and dogs scattering.

Poor Mama, married to that.

Then sober breakfasts when he had to be up to teach, the children eating in strained silence with him shakily sipping tea. But someone would always be picked on before the day was out.

"Look at this room! What, cheek me? Get me the strap!"

Then screams followed by the swish and smack of leather.

11

Once he had caught her chatting to a college boy and had dragged her home through the town, crying.

"Hussy! Is this what the nuns teach you? Is this what they do with my money? My eldest daughter going to the bad! Over my dead body! My dead body!"

Rita braked for the lights at the end of George's Street. Going to the bad? Honestly. Oh, if he'd been drunk she could forgive that beating. But he was on the dry for Lent. He had no control, that's all, picking all Mama's tulips after her funeral and strewing them on the ground.

"Twenty-nine! Thirty! Thirty-one! Only ..." He fell on the earth, clawing it.

Whitefaced, Rita had gathered the wilting heads. "Mama's tulips! Mama's ..."

"What? Here! Give me those!" He grabbed the flowers, scrunching them into the earth. "Look! Take a good look! That's where your mother is!"

When Rita said she was entering, he muttered, "One less to feed!" And didn't look up from his newspaper.

"But who'll make the porridge?" her little sister had whined.

Later she found her brother crying in the garden.

"I'm not going far. Now stop! Please stop! There'll be holidays. And you can visit."

A giant Christmas tree flood-lit the pillars of the Bank of Ireland. Childhood. Christmas lights. Funny how it all came back. The square in Ballaghdereen. Cluttered country shops. As children, they had made the most of their presents. Unlike today's young. The big event was Midnight Mass, then walking home through the inky night. *Come Follow Me and I will be thy God*.

She felt nothing in the chapel now. Nothing moved her, not even the books she read. Nothing. Still, she worked on her Wallace Stevens book, joined a women's political group, humoured the old nuns. And she slogged for the Honours Leaving Class, helped them understand poetry. No one had bothered over her. Her father had once slammed shut her copy of *The Wasteland*, shouting, "Poetry? Ha! It doesn't even rhyme!"

So much for a country schoolmaster. What did he recite in his cups?

"Alas for the rarity,
Of Christian charity ..."

How did the rest go? He always finished with a flourishing, "Under the green sod lies!"

At O'Connell bridge she waited for the guard's signal to move on. It was nearly an hour since the man had phoned. Being Superior was exhausting. She was always running. Adjudicating quarrels. It drove her crazy. Anyway why should she be pestered about Sally Ann's headache? Why couldn't Patrick cope with it? She was Mistress of Upper School. Rita sighed. Now she felt guilty for getting angry with the girl. Hmm. Adolescents and their moods. But had she been wrong about Gary? Was Maggy May having some sort of breakdown because of her harshness? The old woman had loved the stupid mutt but he yapped at everyone else's ankles. One bite meant trouble. And who had to face the parents? *Who?* Oh, an amiable dog that would stay outside might've been different. She was running a boarding school after all, not a menagerie.

Then the reprieve.

In the bus on the way to the Dog's Home, Maggy May had met Mrs Farrell, who agreed to take him. Now they phoned each other daily. Or if Mrs Farrell was on holidays, the convent was flooded with telegrams:

NEW DOGFOOD SUITS

HAS FOUND LITTLE FRIEND

IS ENJOYING SEA AIR

Weird. Just weird.

Once she had met Maggy May at the phone.

"Ah, Mother, the Lord punishes those He loves," the old woman muttered. "Poor Gary ..."

Rita nodded dismissively, crossing the hall.

But the old nun grabbed her arm. "They left him alone all day yesterday. God help him! I knew he'd be desperate, so I waited outside."

"In this weather?" Rita kept a straight face.

The old woman shook her head, going behind the screen. "But didn't he see me? And bark through the window! Ah, the Lord punishes!"

Town was crowded. Christmas lights winked magically on the trees lining the centre of O'Connell Street. Clery's looked like something out of Fairy Land with a Santa in the window. Why didn't Maggy May get her underwear there on account? The old nuns weren't used to modern shops, still wore the habit, couldn't adapt to being ordinary people. And couldn't even have the pleasures of ordinary people.

Oh, she'd been wrong about Gary.

And she was in the wrong with Sally Ann - infuriating though she was. The girl looked ill and was probably unhappy about something. She was motherless with a neglected look. She'd been the victim of last year's fashionable illness - appendicitis. At least five girls had come down with it. Odd, the way symptoms ran through a school. Mass hysteria. One sheep over the fence, all sheep over, Rita had thought at the time. But Sally Ann's case had been genuine. The father had muttered something about an infection. Possible complications later on. He was a doctor with a busy Dun Laoghaire practice. And the vaguest man. His wife had died young, leaving him with two children to bring up. Sally Ann had come to the school in first year and, according to the other nuns, had always been a problem. Obviously she was suffering from the loss of her mother. You didn't get over things like that. There was a younger boy in school somewhere in the country. He and Sally Ann ran wild during the holidays, she had heard. No supervision. Sally Ann seemed to do all the cooking and minding. It wasn't fair, weighing her down with responsibilities. Why couldn't the father employ a housekeeper? You never saw a poor doctor in Ireland. He should at least replace Sally Ann's glasses. Rita had written to him, but received a reply she couldn't read. Perhaps she'd ring him. No, it might bring his wrath down on the daughter. Last year he'd been summoned to the school about her report. It had taken several phone calls and messages through Sally Ann to get him there. Rita was only trying to involve him in his daughter in a friendly way. She'd tactfully tried to point out that Sally Ann had trouble concentrating and that perhaps this was a psychological problem. But he wasn't interested in this theory. In his grumpy way, he seemed fond enough of Sally Ann, referring to her as "Cordelia". But he hadn't a good word to say about the son. Rita was going to ask if he were the bastard Edgar, but had lost courage. He'd gone on and on. He'd thought he could depend on Sally Ann, he said, but she'd been a grave disappointment because of her poor results in Latin. How would she now be able to study medicine? Rita had asked politely if the child wanted to study medicine. But he hadn't heard this, he was too busy complaining at length about "the tedious generation". Children didn't survive that. No wonder the girl looked unhappy, didn't work. Associated with that clique of troublemakers in 6B. She was easily an A student, but lazy and inconsistent. She needed someone to sit on her, more than anything, someone to take an interest. Tonight I'll talk to her about moving up to 6A, for English at least. That way I can keep an eye on her.

She parked behind Roches Stores and weaved her way through the crowds to the Henry Street entrance. "Oh, come all ye faithful ..." a group carolled in the distance. "Oh, come ye, oh, come ye to Be-e-the-le-hem." Mothers with wailing children pushed parcels in prams. Girls linked happily. Street traders shouted and waved balloons. Everyone hurried. Rita had her nieces and nephews to shop for, but was this getting and spending all it meant? And what was the store manager's name? He had sounded so sure of himself. Rita suddenly felt sick with nerves. The children, even the parents, were in awe of her. But a store manager? Who insisted Maggy May had stolen?

A sales assistant pointed her to a door marked, "Manager". She knocked and almost immediately a burly young man came out, looking enquiringly at her smart tweed suit.

"I'm Mother Rita Hynes," she said, walking in.

Maggy May sat in a corner, bent over a hanky.

Briefly their eyes met.

"I was expecting a nun!" He laughed, offering his hand.

"I am a nun." Rita shook hands limply, taking in the several pairs of frothy panties on the green formica-topped desk. A skimpy bra cascaded down one side.

He pulled out a chair, "Sister, a seat! Ha! You can't tell who anyone is these days."

"Thank you, I'd rather stand." Rita opened her handbag. "How much do these come to? We have to get back."

He waved away the uniformed figure appearing in the doorway. As the door shut, he pointed again to a chair. "A seat, Sister!"

Rita remained standing, eyeing him obstinately.

He smiled back with his mouth.

She put two five pound notes on the desk. "This should cover it."

"Ah, I'm afraid it's not so simple." He held up a pair of panties. "Sister was apprehended leaving the shop with these items."

Rita felt herself reddening. "I'm sure she meant to pay for them."

He dropped the incriminating garment onto the table. "Hmm! ... Well, I'm not so sure. She didn't have the money. And she could hardly wear them."

Rita ignored his fat smirk.

He planted his palms heavily on the desk and leant towards her. "In this shop we fight a constant war against shop-lifters. I prefer the word 'thieves'. And when we catch them, we make it hot. Hot!" He gestured towards the old nun. "Sister here is a *nun*! She should know the difference between right and wrong!"

Maggy May began to sob.

Rita looked over helplessly.

"It's surely not just a case of right and wrong," she said after a second.

"What did you say?"

"That some things aren't just a case of right and wrong."

His eyes were an incredulous blue. "But if *nuns* do it!"

"She's not different because she wears a uniform."

"Ah! So you admit she's not different from other people."

"Yes - yes, I do!"

"Well then!" He folded his arms triumphantly. "Why should she be treated different?"

"I - eh -"

"Take yourself now. You don't want to be treated different."

"Why do you say that?"

"Well - your clothes." He glanced appraisingly at her suit.

Rita looked away, flustered.

"Can't you see she's an old woman?" she said after a second.

"Hmm! We have them all ages. All ages!"

Rita groped for the chair and sank into it. He sat down too and, folding his arms, stared at her quizzically. Maggy May wheezed noisily.

A newspaper lay folded on the desk. Headlines flashed into Rita's mind's eye: NUN CAUGHT SHOP-LIFTING! JUDGE CAUTIONS CONVENT! Mutely she fingered the money. It'd be awful. Awful. There'd be courtrooms, clamouring parents, the Bishop. Oh God, she must think of something. Say something! Quickly she caught the manager's cold blue gaze. What was keeping him? Why not call the guards and be done with it?

He sighed, picking up the phone.

She braced herself, looking supportively at Maggy May. I'm behind you, she wanted to say. You're not alone.

There was an awful silence. Awful.

"Send in a bag and a receipt for four pounds fifty pence," he said at last. He replaced the receiver, sternly eyeing Rita. "You'll take charge of Sister? You'll guarantee this won't happen again?"

She put five pounds on the table. "Yes! Of course!"

When the uniformed guard came in with the bag, he told him to bring back the change. Then slowly, carefully, he folded the garments and put them one by one in the bag. "I wanted you to realise the seriousness of the situation."

"Yes!" Rita snapped. "Yes!"

"I know she's a nun, but next time ..."

"Yes!" Hastily she pulled Maggy May up and steered her out to the white light of the shop. It was closing time, and a cluster of sales assistants stared as they made for the door.

"Sister! Sister, your change!" The guard caught them in the street outside.

Numbly Rita pocketed the money.

They walked on.

Suddenly the older nun stopped. "Mother ..."

Rita pushed her gently onwards. "You don't have to say anything."

"I - I just couldn't stop thinking of him ..."

Rita sighed guiltily. "Yes, Gary, I know."

The old woman smiled sweetly. Ah, no, Mother. Not Gary. A boy I knew. Long, long ago."

"A *boy* you knew?"

"Ah yes, Mother ..." The old eyes hazed over. "We'd go up the fields together ... and once ..."

"What are you saying?"

Maggy May shook her head. "It was a terrible sin."

"What?"

"We did it."

Rita felt hysteria bubbling inside her. In a minute she'd lose control. "What are you saying?"

"He went away to England afterwards." Maggy May smiled dreamily. "There was a big family."

"Stop it! Do you hear me? Stop it!" Rita shook the old woman's arm. "You'll never go out alone again! Do you hear me? Do you hear?"

Rita plunged frantically into the crowd with the old nun tottering after. She had to get home. It seemed miles to the parking lot. Miles. At the car she fumbled shakily for her keys and, glancing over the top, saw Maggy May pale and hunched in the rain. Dear God, what was the point of being in a convent? Of slogging for other people's children? If she made an old woman cry?

"What was his name?" she asked when they joined the snake of traffic sliding homewards through the dark.

## II Deirdre

"Do you want to wait on?" the barman called across the great counter.

Reddening, Deirdre looked up from her evening paper. "Uh?"

"Do you want to wait on, or do you want to order something?" He wiped the counter top deftly.

"I'll wait ... uh ... if that's ... uh." She bit the inside of her lower lip.

"Righto," he said, giving her a curious look.

Deirdre studied the paper sightlessly. She hated sitting on her own in a pub, and there was nothing left to read except the small ads and the death notices. Surely he didn't object to her sitting there, not drinking? She'd read that some Dublin pubs didn't like women. But, sure, there were women's voices coming from the other room. Why couldn't Sally Ann, if she was going to be this late, have agreed to meet in a café?

She folded the paper neatly and placed it on the table before her. Her hands lay moistly in her lap, the fingers red and stubby, but looking better now that she'd finally given up biting her nails. Well, except when she met new people. That had been her big dread about coming to Dublin. But, on her second lunch hour from the Grafton Street branch, who should she meet but Sally Ann? She was dressed completely in black. The hair was different, frizzed out, sort of Afro. And no glasses. But it was Sally Ann all right. The same old Fitzer, her best friend, ambling down the other side of the street, wrapped round a tall boy, with dark, crinkly hair. Deirdre remembered his hair and the curved slouch of his back as he waited with his hands in his pockets.

But half past eight. Where was she? What if she wasn't coming? The nerve! Fussily, Deirdre flicked a piece of fluff off her new skirt. No, Sally Ann would turn up. She just wouldn't do a thing like not come. Going home now would mean waiting in the cold for a bus. And she was beginning to like the warmth of the pub. But she was hungry. Missing her usual chop from the shop near her bedsit, she'd had a skimpy omelette in a place in Grafton Street. Not that she liked omelettes, they were just cheap. A pity she couldn't afford one of those delicious Rum Babas on the desert tray. Say, a bite of the Mars Bar in her handbag would keep her going. But she could hardly eat it here. Unless she slipped out to the ladies? No, she might miss Sally Ann.

After her meal, she'd used up the extra time window shopping. Now her whole evening was just wasted. Still, she'd only be sitting in at home. Even if Sally Ann came now, they mightn't get into the pictures. Or they'd have to join a queue with all the other pairs of girls you saw in Dublin. Maybe it was just as well. If she went home now, the Take-Away would still be open, and the landlady might invite her in to watch Kojak, offer her tea with homemade ginger cake.

The door flashed open, and a man left. Deirdre shivered as a blast from the December night penetrated her tights. She'd give Sally Ann another few minutes, then make a dash for the Take-Away. Have a nice ...

"Chérie! There you are! Hiding away in the corner!" Sally Ann plonked her basket on a chair, and, beaming through her smudgy mascara, leaned to kiss Deirdre.

"Uh ... I didn't see you coming in." Deirdre started. What if someone saw them kissing? People at the bank never did that.

"But Chérie, there's another door. Fabulous in here, isn't it? So genuine." Sally Ann threw off a raggy, black fur coat and squinted rapturously.

"Genuine?" Deirdre turned her head. Genuine what?

"Chérie, that ceiling. I could sit in here for hours, just gazing at that." Sally Ann giggled happily and flopped into the chair opposite.

Deirdre contemplated the clusters of plaster fruit on the ceiling. Nice. Sort of old-fashioned. But genuine? Sally Ann lolled facing her. She wore dirty blue jeans, rolled at the ankles to reveal thick red socks and shiny black high heels. What a get-up. Like a little girl in her mother's shoes.

Deirdre broke the silence. "Don't you still have to wear glasses?"

"Contacts! I had a hell of a job getting the old man to fork out. But he did!" Sally Ann flicked out her curls and stretched her legs under the table, taking up all the room. "What are you drinking? Nothing. Never mind. They'll be over."

"Well, I ... eh."

"You'll love Dublin, Chérie. Devastating place. This pub, for instance, reeks, I mean absolutely reeks, of atmosphere. I wanted to come in here last night. But Colm! Do you think he would? It was Horse Show House again."

"Was that Colm I saw you with?" Deirdre managed to interrupt.

"Saw me with? When, Chérie?" Sally Ann blinked her blackened lashes.

"Last week. When we met."

"Oh. Then." Sally Ann tapped her chin with a badly nicotine-stained index finger. "Now, let me see, who was I with that day? Hmm, confusing sometimes, keeping track. Yes, that probably was Colm." She smiled quickly. "Did you like him?"

"Well, yes, I ..."

"I'm living with him. Of course, he's brilliant. But a Philistine about Art. Walks round with his head in the air. Totally, I mean totally intellectual." Sally Ann sank suddenly into deep thought.

"Well ..." Seeing the far-away look in Sally Ann's eyes, Deirdre broke off. If he was her boyfriend, what was he doing then with that other girl? Last Saturday, after looking round the boutiques, she'd cut through the Green and seen him dawdling with another girl. She'd followed, a few paces behind, to make sure it was him, then passed them out as they dangled arm in arm over the bridge. It was him, she remembered his hair and dark good looks.

"Always joking me about being a film snob," Sally Ann said abruptly. "What?"

"But I'm a good influence on him. Yes, I am. Do you know, I refuse, absolutely refuse, to go to Clint Eastwood."

"Oh," Deirdre said. Clint Eastwood?

"Yes, I'll only go to French films. I think ...," Sally Ann's eyes focused impatiently on the bar, "I'll go over and get us a drink. What will you have?"

"Pineapple juice," Deirdre said, taking in the multi-coloured scarf Sally Ann wore tied round her tight, black polo-necked jumper.

"Oh, try something stronger," Sally Ann coaxed.

"No, I don't drink at all," Deirdre said quickly.

"Just as well, Chérie. You might get addicted." Amusement flickered in Sally Ann's eyes as she walked jauntily off to the bar.

Addicted indeed! Chérie! And those jeans were too tight. Still, they suited her in a way. Even in a school uniform, Sally Ann managed to look ... what was the word? Distinctive, maybe. Certainly unusual. But she seemed changed. The black jumper was too dark for her. It looked weird with her blackened eyes. She was like someone in mourning.

"Here we are!" Sally Ann's high heels clicked as she came back with a pineapple juice and a pint of Guinness. "I'm trying to train myself to like this stuff. Wine of the country, and all that."

"You should let me pay. After all ..."

"Oh, fooh! As I was saying, it's crazy to drink anything else when there's a natural drink available. Given to nursing mothers and all that. I used to take nothing but double Crème de Menthe with ice. But that's a little affected, n'est-ce pas?"

"Er," said Deirdre.

"Oh, my God!" said Sally Ann, suddenly clutching her side.

"What is it? Are you all right?"

"Yes, I've just ovulated."

"Oh," said Deirdre. There was an awkward silence. "Oh, do you ever see anyone from school?"

"Och, that place was a jail!"

"The other day I thought I saw Mother Rita on a bus."

"Oh, her., Jesus I'd forgotten her. She was a bitch."

"Oh, I don't know," said Deirdre slowly.

"I do," said Sally Ann, gazing pensively upward. "The cow confiscated my art books. Not enough fig leaves in the pictures I suppose."

"Well, she was strict all right, but she liked you, everyone did."

"Do you think so? Sally Ann looked at her eagerly, then said slowly, "Oh, I wasn't very popular with the nuns."

She picked up her pint and looked at it distastefully. "Rita made my life hell in sixth year. God, I had to report to her every night. She was demoted you know."

"That must've been after I left. I left after the Inter, remember?"

"Oh, yes, I'd forgotten." Sally Ann sipped her Guinness. "Ugh. I'm bracing myself to throw this back."

"I wish you'd have let me pay. You're not working yet."

"Oh, I get the occasional few bob for my writing efforts."

Gosh, Sally Ann a writer. "Do people," said Deirdre slowly, "actually pay you for writing?"

"Oh, now and again," Sally Ann shrugged. "I report for a Maoist paper - *The Irish Student.*

"I'd like to read your articles."

Sally Ann frowned, and then fished a paperback out of her basket. "Have you read duh Beaver's memoirs?"

"No, the whose?"

Sally Ann passed the book over. "Duh Beaver."

The second volume of the memoirs of Simone de Beauvoir. Had Sally Ann forgotten all her French? See moan de Bowvwar, surely?

"Satyr and she would ..."

"Who?"

"Satyr. Jean Paul Satyr. Well, Sartre then."

How silly, Deirdre thought.

"Satyr and she would go round the bistros in Paris, and all that. It must have been *too*, really just *too!*"

Bistros, weren't they places for soup? And *too*? Too what?

"And when they visited the different parts of France, such as the provinces, they'd taste all the local wines. But they liked the working-class places best. Do you ever go down to the quays here? You should. I mean to. It's an education in itself. But Colm, of course, it's always the plastic lounges of the petit bourgeois for him. Funny, when he's a Maoist. I'm one too." She flicked through the tattered paperback reflectively. "As well as politics, I'm into all things French. Wine, sex, snails, everything. Shall I lend the book to you?" She put the book back in her basket. "Well, what film are we going to?"

"There's a Peter Sellars at the Savoy."

"Peter Sellars? Wouldn't that be a comedy? I never think the subject is serious enough in comedy. Like to try some of this?" She held out a small casket with brown powder in it.

"Is that ... is that dope or something?"

"No," said Sally Ann darkly, "that's snuff." She shook a little powder onto the side of her hand and sniffed. "Try some. Don't be afraid."

"I'm not afraid," said Deirdre hastily. "I'm off everything like that - since Lent."

"Pity, it's marvellously relaxing." Sally Ann sniffed again, then her nose began to twitch. "Oh, dear! Ah-ah-ah-tishoo!"

"Are you all right?"

"Of course, I'm ... ah-ah-ah-tishoo!"

"Do you want a ...?"

"Ah-ah-ah-tishoo!" Sally Ann shook her head and brushed the tears from her eyes with the sleeve of her jumper.

"Are you sure you're ...?"

"Of course, it always affects you like that. You just have to get used to it. A Politics lecturer gave it to me. Well! I think we should go to the True-Foot film at the Astor. He's fantastic on triangles. He made *Jules and Jim*. You'll really like him. Give us a look at the paper." Sally Ann snatched the paper, and rustled through for the cinema pages.

"I think we're a bit late," said Deirdre. True-Foot? An Indian?

"Yes, the last show is nine-twenty. We'd surely make that. What time is it anyway?"

"Nine!" Didn't she realise she was so late?

"Good, that's settled then. You'll love True-Foot. His stuff is always about ménage à trois, and all that."

"Oh," said Deirdre. "I've heard of him." Humph, she thought.

"I assure you it's an education in itself." Sally Ann sipped her drink slowly. "Ugh. Colm refused point-blank to go with me. Says he wants value when he goes to the pictures. Plenty of blood and guts. Ugh." She paused reflectively. "And his latest kick is to go round quacking when I say anything even slightly uplifting."

"Quacking? Like in - quack-quack?"

"Yes." Sally Ann leaned forward confidentially. "Unfortunately I told him that Satyr's party piece in the thirties was an imitation of Donald Duck. And last night in the pub he really embarrassed me. I tried to tell him about this novel I've just read, *Le Grand Meaulnes*. I'll lend it to you. Marvellously rich and strange. Well, anyway, last night I started to tell him about it and he went 'Oooogh, oooogh!' And I said, 'What are you doing?' And he said, 'That's your novel - The Great Moan.' And I said, 'Well, Sartre liked it.' And that's when he got up and began flapping his elbows and hopping round the pub on his haunches, and going 'quack-quack-quack-quack'. Then of course all his intellectual friends burst out laughing ..."

"That must've been embarrassing," said Deirdre. Then when Sally Ann didn't answer, she said, "Do you remember the time we won the 3D Netball cup? It was a near thing, wasn't it?"

"The 3D Netball cup?" Sally Ann said slowly, bewilderment somewhere in her hazy eyes. Then jerking upright, she said quickly, "Yes, it was a near thing. Though, mind you, I'm not always so easily embarrassed. But later when we were walking home, I said, 'What about joining the Film Society,

Colm?' Just like that, you know, casually, and he began quacking again in the street. Of course, the people with us howled, like the idiots they are. Big joke! Oh well, enough of that." She looked quickly at Deirdre. "Do you know I discovered a marvellous cure for constipation!"

"Oh," Deirdre said, startled. "What?"

"Anal sex. It really works, Chérie."

"Oh." Deirdre's face set stonily. God, was that what they expected of you in Dublin? Violently red in the face, she stretched for her pineapple juice and sipped it in silence.

"Do you have a boyfriend?" Sally Ann was the first to speak.

"What?" Deirdre looked at her nervously.

"Are you going with anyone?"

"Oh, yes," Deirdre lied. "A boy at home."

"Best place for him. Frankly, men bore me. All wet from their mother's milk. But still if you wanted to get fixed up, the people in our house are giving a party, and you might like to come. If you wanted to."

"Oh, I would! I'd really like to." Deirdre's eagerness suddenly faded. "I wouldn't have to do anything, would I?"

Sally Ann waved a hand. "Of course not!"

Deirdre sighed with relief. Now she was sounding like the old Sally Ann. Are there many living there?"

"Yes, it's a commune of Maoists. They're all bores really. Except Colm! ... But it might be nice to meet someone while you're in Dublin ... Duh Beaver and Satyr were separated for long periods. They never got married at all. Did you know that?"

"Eh, no."

"Yes, and once they even had a triangular affair. Satyr wanted to be free. Let me see ... maybe I can find the bit." She retrieved the book and leafed through it. "Yes, he wanted to be free to 'experience life and give it expression'. Good way of putting it, isn't it?"

"I suppose so," said Deirdre. "Give what expression?"

"Well," Sally Ann shrugged, "life, of course. Reality and all that. But the affair with Olga led to complications." She shook her curls darkly.

"Is that what Colm and you are doing?" Deirdre said suddenly.

"Finally they decided it just wouldn't work. There were blistering scenes, wrenching for everyone concerned." She looked up suddenly. "Sorry, what did you say about Colm?"

"Nothing," said Deirdre. "I just thought you and he might be doing that."

"Doing what?"

"Oh, you know, experimenting with other people, managing au trois. Like Jean Paul Sort."

"Oh, no. Not yet. I wouldn't say we'd get to that stage for a while yet. Still ..." Sally Ann regarded Deirdre pensively. "It'd be perfect. You could

23

be Olga."

"Olga?"

"Why not? You and I have a relationship, and the three of us - why not? Oh, I'm not talking about now, but sometime."

"I don't think so," said Deirdre, reddening again. "It'd be an occasion of sin."

"Oh no, it'd be perfect. We could try. You never know till you try." Suddenly the eagerness drained out of Sally Ann's voice. "You just said something about Colm?"

The three of them? What was Sally Ann saying ...? "Oh, did I? Oh yes. I saw him last Saturday morning with another girl, in Stephen's Green."

"That must've been someone else," Sally Ann said flatly.

"Yes," said Deirdre innocently, "it definitely wasn't you."

"Well," said Sally Ann finally, "it was probably his sister."

Nervously she pushed back the cuticles on her nails.

"No, it couldn't have been his sister."

"Brothers and sisters don't always look alike."

"That wasn't what I meant. No," Deirdre insisted stubbornly, "it couldn't have been his sister."

"Oh," said Sally Ann, eating her nails energetically. "What time is it now?"

"Ten past."

"Ten past what?"

"Nine!" Didn't she realise they were going to the pictures in a minute.

"Have to go to the loo." Sally Ann stood up abruptly, fumbling for her purse. "Back in a tick, Chérie."

Deirdre watched Sally Ann swagger to the back of the bar. Had she been tactless? No. A thing like that wouldn't take a feather out of Sally Ann. Not the way she went on, about sex and all. But why was she so changed? Wasn't there more to talk about besides films and things in books and Maoism? What was that, anyway? When they first met, they were two daffodils in the school play. It was nice then. They were both eleven, and every day after tea they'd play behind the tennis courts. Deirdre would be Black Beauty, Sally Ann steering her through various adventures. Sometimes they'd imagine another book, but mostly it was Black Beauty. For four years they'd been best friends. Then Deirdre's father had died and she'd had to go to a Commercial College in Galway. It was the Summer after the Inter. When Sally Ann heard, she came for a visit. They'd cycled all over Mayo. Sally Ann ahead, clutching her wide straw hat, swerving from side to side.

"We'll write! We'll always keep in touch! Always!" Sally Ann waved frantically from half-way out the carriage window.

Bereft, Deirdre had stood awhile on the empty platform. After that she hated stations. And she hated the Commercial College in Galway. School

24

had been so much nicer. After lunch on Saturday washing your hair. Learning useful things like recipes for Lentil soup, or notes on the character of Prince Hal. Even Latin, even Geometry theorems hadn't been that bad.

Deirdre drained the last of her pineapple juice. She had hardly seen Sally Ann after that summer. In spite of the pledges they'd made. Once she'd visited school. Someone jeered her about doing "ticky tack". There'd been an outburst of giggles. But Sally Ann glared, and everyone was quiet. No bitter bread of charity for Sally Ann. Her father was a doctor. She'd gone to UCD. And was now in her second year.

A boy snatched Deirdre's empty glass. Then he stooped towards Sally Ann's unfinished, not even half-finished Guinness.

"She's coming back!" Deirdre cried. Her eyes snapped up to the clock, high up on the wall, near the plaster fruit. Sally Ann had been gone almost ten minutes. Was she sick? Fainted in the Ladies? Drowning in the lavatory? Slipped and broken her back? Oh Jesus, Mary and Joseph, why had she been so mean to Sally Ann? Grabbing her handbag, Deirdre dashed towards the back of the pub.

The sign, "Ladies", arrowed down the stairs. Deirdre bustled down them two at a time, and then stopped dead. Who was crying? Spinning round, she gaped up. At the top of the stairs, Sally Ann was hunched and shaking over the phone. Was she all right? Those noises? Was she on drugs? Was it the snuff?

"Quack, quack, quack," Sally Ann's voice quavered into the phone. "Quack, quack ..."

She replaced the receiver, and taking out a rumpled hanky, savagely wiped her eyes, messing her mascara. Then, she walked blindly back to the bar.

"Sally Ann," Deirdre whispered, stumbling up the stairs after her, "Sally Ann!"

# III  Paul and Colm

I think of Paul whenever I'm in Earlsfort Terrace now. Sometimes I even imagine him still standing in the Main Hall, homespun and slightly balding, his big red hands deep in his pockets. As always, he's apart from the other males who cluster by the notice boards, smoking or eyeing the talent - any female, bar nuns, crossing to the office or to the annexe for coffee. Our college, by the way, is like a railway station at rush hour. Day or night, people hang around, waiting. We're nicknamed "The Tech on the Terrace", because of our situation, I suppose, and our shabbiness compared to Trinity, Dublin's older university. But we don't feel inferior. Cherry blossoms cheer us up in Spring. And we have year-round ducks in nearby Stephen's Green. Hopkins taught in our mausoleum. And we can boast of being founded by Newman and the alma mater of Joyce. The Literary and Historical Society where he read his famous paper on Ibsen is still in existence. And Newman has a house called after him. In first year English, we read his dull prose, learning that he intended our university for the Catholics of Dublin. And there's evidence of this in the clerics who still blacken the place like crows. They flock in daily from the seminaries, disappearing harmlessly into cloakrooms in the bowels of the building.

I digress, but in a way it's all relevant. Paul and Colm and I and even Tom Mansfield, the clerical swot, were in a certain place at a certain time, University College, Dublin, in the late sixties. And, although we didn't realise it at the time, something happened which affected our whole lives. Imagine a drab tutorial room at the end of a drab corridor in Earlsfort Terrace. It was a Tuesday afternoon in October, 1968, and the second History tutorial of our second year. Three of us waited for Professor O'Dea to discuss the problems of the fourteenth century church. Paul, I remember, was late that day. We had been on several dates - to a Synge play and some French films - so he was the only member of the group I knew. As the professor was late too, I probably sat there hoping the others wouldn't talk to me. I didn't talk much in those days. Besides Paul, I had made hardly any friends in first year. Mostly I hid behind a book in the Ladies Reading Room and even crossed the Main Hall by going up one stairs and down another. I was terrified of men looking at me. There was even a student revolution I didn't notice. My only concern was passing First Arts, which I did, barely - thanks to grinding by a certain nun in school, Mother Rita, whom I've never had the manners to even thank. My father, a widowed doctor, urged me to study Medicine so I signed up, dropping out at the sight of dogfish. He was puzzled at my wanting something as useless as a BA, but I walked in realms of gold. I had yearned for college and saw knowledge as an ocean in which to immerse myself. I soon discovered that, like the ocean, my ignorance was boundless.

At last, the professor popped his head around the door. "Second Arts General?"

We nodded and he swept in, carrying a briefcase. He was a typical intellectual, Irish variety, and wore a shabby elbow-patched sports jacket with baggy cords. Also he was dauntingly tall with floppy grey hair and a red, whiskey-veined face, and penetrating blue eyes which perused you through steel-rimmed spectacles.

He sat in front of us, rooting impatiently in his briefcase. "Eh - Mr Connolly?"

Colm put up his hand.

"This is excellent, Mr Connolly. I want you to read it to us later."

Colm shambled up for his paper, brushing his unruly hair with embarrassment. He was lithe, dark and handsome with the rumpled look of either a busy or sloppy person. I didn't know him yet. I just knew he was brainy and spent most of his time on the barricades for this cause or that, and then sailed effortlessly through exams. I'd often seen him reading in the library without taking a single note, while I always ended up with reams. Paul told me he was a founder member of SDA - that's Students for Democratic Action, the group that organised last year's so-called "Gentle Revolution." Also I'd seen him on the front page of *The Irish Times*, being pushed off the road by a garda on a Civil Rights march in the North. To me he was the epitome of glamour. The odd thing was him being in our group. "General", I should explain, is the polite word for "pass". I was doing pass because of my poor first year results, but we were considered the absolute pits by all departments. It was their policy to fail as many of us as possible - the place, after all, was crowded.

The other odd thing was us having MacDarragh O'Dea.

I mean, a world-renowned scholar should have had an honours group. You've probably heard of his book about the Irish monks at the court of Charlemagne - I forget the exact title. We Irish, by the way, kept the flame of knowledge alight in Europe's Dark Ages. I learnt later we were to have had the usual underling doctoral student, but the poor fellow had some sort of crackup. So the famous professor had taken us over at the last minute.

As he shuffled through his papers, I quaked inwardly. Mine had to be next. Tom Mansfield was getting his, but Paul wasn't in yet. lately I'd lost all confidence in myself. Oh, Mother Rita, that nun in school, always read out my English essay, but everyone in college was miles more intelligent. I mean, I actually mispronounced John Donne's name at a tutorial and said he was the epi*tome* of something. Everyone gaped, so I never went back. I got through the year without writing a word - except at the exams. I had fancied myself a French speaker, but at registration a lecturer had babbled uncomprehendingly at me, so I did Latin. You didn't have to speak a dead language, and I could read it almost fluently. I found the lectures beneath me, of course - and, of course, almost failed. Philosophy, my third subject, was OK. But History was a complete jumble. For one thing, I had no historical background. I had just read that, to understand the present, you had to know about the past. But I understood neither, I was clogged with facts. Clogged. They absolutely froze my brain, so I daydreamed at lectures, and on hearing the word "watershed" imagined a shed with buckets of water. Or a dyke. Oh, it occurred to me that this was a weird metaphor for Catholic Emancipation or Luther nailing the thirty-nine theses on the Wittenburg church door, but I didn't look up the word. It's a "line separating two rivers' basins; a divide". And I know now that, as there are turning points in history, things happen in life by which we are changed.

But I was explaining what happened at the tutorial.

"Eh - Miss Fitzpatrick!" Dr O'Dea was peering at the corner of my paper.

Nervously I raised my hand.

"Yes ... indeed ..." He cleared his throat. "We can all learn from Mr Connolly's essay. Especially *you*, Miss Fitzpatrick!"

I felt myself redden. I'd spent hours on the essay. Could it be that bad? Reclaiming it, I noticed a red line drawn through the first page. And the second. And the third.

"I couldn't give you a mark, Miss Fitzpatrick."

I was in total shock.

"*Why*, do you think?" His thin voice had a trace of his Cork origins.

"Eh ... I ..." Numbly I turned to the last page, hoping for some sort of a clue. But there was only a scribbled UGH! And the red line was drawn through every page. I wanted to die.

"Why no mark, Miss Fitzpatrick?" His blue eyes were merciless. "Read us the title of your essay!"

There was an awful silence.

I was aware of Colm's heavy breathing beside me. Everything else had turned the vile green of the walls.

"What's the title of your essay, Miss Fitzpatrick?"

I could barely see. "Eh - 'The Most Important Movement in the Fourteenth Century Church'."

"Good girl. Now read us your first paragraph."

I kept my voice steady.."All history is a nexus; especially that of the fourteenth century church. There were many different events in that time which were interdependent. At a first glance, it would seem that the residence of the papacy at Avignon instead of at Rome for over seventy years would certainly be the most important movement. But was it so important? Was it an unmitigated disaster to the church? I think not. I would analyse the word *movement*. In the fourteenth century, there was a new element of thought among laity. Dante was the first lay critic of ecclesiastic affairs ..." Somehow I got through it. " ... The seeds of the revolt which was to follow in 200 years were sown. This was perhaps a very important movement, if not the most important."

I stopped. "Eh - that's the first paragraph."

The professor was looking boredly out the window. "And quite a plausible one. A bit unsophisticated here and there in your use of the first person, but decent enough." He sighed, staring at his nails. "Now, what would this paragraph lead a person of ordinary intelligence to expect?"

"Well ..." My mind refused to work.

"What thesis have you set up, Miss Fitzpatrick?"

I studied the first paragraph again.

The professor sighed impatiently.

Then Colm whispered behind me, "The new element of thought among the laity."

"I didn't ask you Mr Connolly."

"The new element of thought among the laity," I repeated parrotly.

"Good girl! But what are your next six pages about?"

"The Avignon Papacy."

"Yes! You set up an argument which you completely ignore. You go off on a slovenly tangent. Presumably you knew more about that subject?"

I nodded weakly.

"But you could've used your information intelligently. How, Miss Fitzpatrick?"

I prayed for him to stop. It was like some sort of inquisition.

He sighed impatiently. "We're waiting, Miss Fitzpatrick."

There was another awful silence.

"She could argue the Avignon Papacy was the most important movement." Colm broke the silence at last.

The professor glared at him coldly. "Thank you Mr Connolly. Now, Miss Fitzpatrick. Tell us how you'd make the case for the Avignon Papacy being a *movement*?"

I searched my essay for a clue.

He went on relentlessly. "Did the Avignon popes bring about any changes?"

"Well ... all the abbeys began paying the popes."

"Good!" He spoke slowly, as if explaining something to a child. "By about 1363, every major benefice, that is every bishopric and abbey, became a source of papal income. So we could argue it was a time of papal consolidation?"

I nodded.

"And could this be described as a movement?"

I nodded again.

"Good!" He pushed his spectacles up on his nose. "So we have our argument! The Avignon Papacy was a time of movement towards centralisation. A time of stabilisation. What else contributed to this?"

I cleared my throat. "Well - eh - on the whole - mostly - they were good popes. They ordered the friars back to the monasteries. Wandering friars were a social problem at the time."

He nodded encouragingly. "They were indeed. Did the popes initiate any other reforms?"

"Eh ... they all favoured the inquisition."

He raised one eyebrow. "Is that a recommendation?"

"Well, they were pretty conscientious."

Everybody burst out laughing.

I realised the stupidity of my statement. But the laughter was mortally wounding. Just then the door opened and Paul came in. As I've said, he was from Wicklow and had an agricultural air about him. His forehead was high from losing his hair, and he was spotty and sleepy-looking from being up all night - he worked as a night telephonist to pay his way through college. He was a mature student of twenty-five or thirty, and years older than Colm or me.

As he went to the back of the room, the professor snapped, "You there! What's your name?"

Paul reddened. "Brady, Paul A."

"Why are you late?"

Paul went into a seat. "Eh - ."

"*Why* are you late?"

Paul shrugged one shoulder. He had a way of walking with one shoulder awkwardly higher than the other. "Couldn't get a bus, Professor."

"What bus?"

"The 8 from Dun Laoghaire."

"Surely that's a good route?"

"There was a bit of a go-slow." Paul laughed nervously. "CIE."

I knew he had probably overslept.

The professor thumbed irritably through his papers. "Did I get your essay?"

Paul shifted uneasily. "Your box had been emptied so I gave it to the secretary."

"When did you go to my box?"

"Eh - I think it was last Friday."

"If you'd gone to my box last Friday, you'd have found it full."

"Oh, it might've been Saturday."

"It was full then too. And on Monday. And Tuesday. I suggest you didn't go to my box at all."

"Actually, I mightn't have. I gave it straight to the secretary."

"I suggest you're lying, Mr Brady!"

"No - I'm not."

"You are, Mr Brady!"

Paul could hardly breathe. "I - gave it to the secretary."

"You did? Well! Let's go and collect it then." The professor pushed his chair back and stood up.

We gaped at each other. Just gaped.

Paul looked as if he was going to cry.

"Oh, well, Professor, you see ..."

"We'll collect it now, Mr Brady. *Now!*"

The professor strode purposefully to the door, pulled it open and waited for Paul to follow him. Then he marched him out. We heard their footsteps all the way down the corridor to the department office.

We sat in stunned silence.

Colm broke it. "Phew, what a Nazi!"

Even Tom Mansfield looked upset.

"It's just like school," I whispered at last.

Colm put his head in his hands, moaning, "Stupid Brady. He's lying."

"How do you know?" I asked.

"He told me he couldn't finish it. He hadn't time."

Tom Mansfield tidied his notebooks primly. "Well, he shouldn't have lied then."

"Ah, shut up, fuck face!" Colm growled. "You try staying up all night!"

Just then we heard the footsteps coming back. Professor O'Dea came in first, giant-like, followed by Paul. He looked sort of shrunken and slunk to the very back of the room.

The professor fiddled irritably with his glasses. Then he fumbled madly through his papers. "Read us your essay, Mr Connolly."

Colm began in a deep gravelly voice. "The most important movement in the fourteenth century church was the revolution of John Wycliffe. This Englishman was a teacher at Oxford when ..."

He stopped.

Loud sobs came from behind us.

Paul was crying.

I had never heard a man cry.


Paul never came back to the tutorial. And we didn't think anything of it. The place, as I've explained, was a railway station where people came and went. Anyway, I was madly in love with Colm by now and had no time to think of Paul. After all, I didn't owe him anything. He'd given me a taste for French films OK, but so what? I saw him once in the Main Hall lingering the way men did. By then I'd shed my fear of crossing it, along with my pleated skirt, glasses and straight hair, and went to talk to him. He shifted nervously as I approached. He looked spottier than ever and badly in need of a shave.

"What've ye done to yerself, Sally?" He ogled my newly permed curls and my Levis.

I ran my fingers self-consciously through my afro. "Do you like it?"

"It's great! Just takes a bit of getting used to. I liked your tartan skirt."

"That's old hat."

"You're gorgeous anyway, Sally. Too gorgeous to be cooped up here. Come out to the hills."

There was drink on his breath.

"I've to finish an essay."

"For O'Dea?"

"Yes." I could've said something consoling about his débacle, but didn't. "We're awfully lucky to have him."

He loosened his grimy white collar. "Yes, indeed."

"He has an international reputation." I echoed Colm.

"Come out to the hills with an old tramp, Pegeen."

This was a joke between us. He came from Wicklow like Synge whom he adored, so he often called me Pegeen Mike. And himself an old tramp. As I've said, our first date had been to a Synge play at the Abbey. I had sat on my hands all through for fear he'd try and hold them. Afterwards he kissed me goodnight at the bus-stop. I know it's weird, and I'm an exception to the whole world, but I loathe kissing. I really do.

"I can't - my essay."

He picked at a pimple. "Well, come for a coffee. I'll buy you a cream bun."

"I really can't."

"You're turning me down, then?"

"No! I - I just don't believe in personal relationships." Again I was echoing Colm who believed love to be a bourgeois invention.

Paul looked as if he'd been slapped.

I felt myself redden. "Look, I'll go some other time."

So we made a date for the pictures next week.

I didn't turn up.

And a few days later I received an anonymous verse in the post.

*When by thy scorn, O murderess, I am dead*
*And thou think'st thee free*
*From all solicitations from me*
*Then shall my ghost come to thy bed.*

It was from Paul. We had first met at the back of an English lecture on John Donne. He'd asked my name and I'd said it. Then he'd said, "Brady, Paul A." Then I'd laughed. And we got talking about Donne, his favourite poet. Although I knew hardly anything about him, I said he was mine too. You'd never think it, but Paul was a wizard on poetry and literature, as well as films. He worshipped Art.

I've no excuse for my behaviour. I should've said no first thing. Or else gone. I know that. I liked him OK. I just couldn't imagine anything else. Anyway, I was obsessed with Colm since the day he came to my rescue at that tutorial. For him I had vowed to conquer my fear of sex - the only problem was he never asked me to the pictures or "tried" anything. We were never alone. I suppose it was too bourgeois. And to be honest, I was relieved. Although I had become a Maoist for him, I couldn't shed my terrible hang-up. Luckily we did everything in a group. My old friends didn't recognise me. I saw History now, not as something to guide me through life, but as class struggle. Something which had never struck me before. I had just accepted my family and friends as middle-class, but now everything was different. My friends were the masses, and my enemies all those in league with imperialism - "the war-lords and bureaucrats, the comprador class, the big landlord class and the reactionary section of the intelligentsia attached to them ..."

Colm had given me a copy of Mao's *Quotations*. He'd also invited me to meetings and helped me with the next essay for Professor O'Dea.

"You'll have no trouble if you write like this, Sally," he said, handing it back.

"Like what?"

"You can write. All you have to do is think clearly."

I realised that up to now I'd been afraid to think. I'd worked OK, but in the wrong way. I'd spent hours in the library, hours, copying out chunks of books and stringing them together for an essay. I now tried to arrange my thoughts into a coherent argument. And then another misfortune turned to my advantage. Thanks to my awful Latin results, I was forced to continue with Philosophy. At first I believed myself condemned to a Limbo of clerics, because nearly everyone else in the class was in religious black. But when we read Plato's *Republic*, I realised Philosophy was the poetry of life. All Art was decadent. Ideas would reclaim our fallen nature, and politics were ideas in action. Aristotle said happiness was the final end of man, and Mao that happiness could only be brought about by the triumph of the proletariat. How had I lived so long and remained so ignorant? Colm said it was my upbringing, and his word was gospel. As well as Mao, he was for Trotsky, Jesus Christ and Che Guevara. And against everything else - from the university curriculum to Vietnam to the Archbishop of Dublin. Especially the Archbishop. Sometimes he'd collect me from the library to occupy the Pro-Cathedral or else for a sit-down outside Mountjoy. At the first hint of a famine in Africa, we'd be fasting on O'Connell Bridge to collect money for hunger. A new age was dawning, and we were bringing it about. In Rome, Vatican II had radicalised the church, and we did our bit, liberating our college library so that women could wear trousers - we all wore them in one day, so what could they do? I mean what? Even degrees were part of a decadent system. Colm was only doing one to please his mother - but only pass, he wouldn't stoop to honours. He was the son of a wealthy solicitor who disapproved of his radicalism. So he lived in a commune of squatters and supported himself by working for the Labour Party.

Housing was one of the issues of our day.

While thousands went homeless, capitalist speculators bought up old houses around the city and neglected them until they had to be condemned. They were then bulldozed, and offices or flats were built on the grounds - flats for the rich, I need hardly say. It was a crying shame. A Georgian city was tumbling around us. The derelict mansions were usually guarded by patrol dogs to prevent squatters. But people still broke in. One man was thrown into Mountjoy and his wife and children put on the side of the road. So the Dublin Housing Action Committee - a pressure group formed to bring the problem to the notice of the government - organised a march to Mountjoy in his support. "We should support whatever the enemy opposes and oppose whatever the enemy supports" was one of Mao's maxims. And the enemy was capitalism. I mean, I had relations all over the city with houses full of empty rooms. It was difficult for a person of my idealism not to point this out to them. Even my father had a garage. Why couldn't he convert it into a flat for some homeless person? And why did he have to charge his patients? I had become a zealot for change. A zealot. And there was no way I'd miss the march to Mountjoy.

There was to be an all-night vigil at the prison, so I brought my sleeping bag. We met at the Dáil and marched through the darkening city over O'Connell Bridge to the north side. Colm was unperturbed, but I felt shy at first. In the streets people hurrying home stopped to read our placards: RELEASE JIM HUGHES! and FAIR HOUSING and ONE FAMILY ONE HOME. As well as students, there were workers with families and children - all arm-in-arm. The feeling of comradeship made me forget myself. I was mad with happiness. All my life I'd been blind to injustice, but now I saw.

At the prison gates, men made speeches from the back of lorries. They condemned the social system and our uncaring government which had betrayed the ideals of Connolly. Capitalism was the cause of all ills, and Socialism the cure. Colm was making a speech, and as he clambered up on the lorry the crowd cheered.

He wore his red anorak which contrasted with his olive skin. And when he held up his hands for silence, the crowd cheered.

"Comrades!"

They cheered louder.

At last he got a word in.

"Comrades ... Comrades, we meet tonight to protest against the unlawful and unjust imprisonment of a member of our committee ..."

There was another raucous cheer.

"Jim Hughes, along with his wife and children ..."

Just then there was an altercation at the back of the crowd. I turned to see the guards roughly dispersing the people. They resisted, and soon everyone was linking arms and singing, "We shall overcome ... We shall overcome ..."

I sang too, but very nervously.

As more people were hauled off into a big black van, the others sat down on the pavement.

"Sit down, Sally Ann!" Colm called to me as he jumped from the lorry.

At that moment two burly guards grabbed him and hauled him off.

I watched, my legs like jelly. Suddenly I got a mental image of my father's tired face. He was old before his time with work, bringing us up and paying for my younger brother in boarding school. Also my college fees. I saw myself behind bars and him reasoning with me.

So I picked up my bed and walked. Away.

Colm was arrested and beaten up by the guards. I told myself his family were wealthy and could bail him out, while my father couldn't. And what would happen to my part-time job? I earned a pound a night over the weekend at a Dun Laoghaire restaurant for pocket money. If my name got into the paper, I'd lose it. Then how could I go to college? I told myself all this, but it was no use. Like Saint Peter in the garden, I had denied my love at the first test.

But Colm didn't blame me. As always, his father bailed him out. Oh, there was the usual family row, but it ran off him. Things like that just didn't worry him. I think he sort of gloried in strife. One evening about a week later, he walked me to the station and showed me his bruised stomach. "I can't be caught again. Not till after this case."

Gently I touched his blackened rib-cage. I had never seen such bruises and was amazed at the brutality of the police.

He closed his eyes. "Phew!"

"Sorry!"

"No, do it again!"

"Do what?"

"Touch me."

I did.

He pulled me to him, kissing me. "Give, Sally! Give!"

I tried to. But we were outside Westland Row station and had to stop.

"Come back to my place! I've got a hard-on."

I glanced nervously at his crotch. The thought of anything sexual gave me terrible butterflies. I could manage kissing boys in the pictures, because they paid and expected it.

"Eh - my father's expecting me home," I lied.

The truth was he probably wouldn't notice if I disappeared.

"Would you come tomorrow? For the weekend?"

I nodded and ran blindly into the station. I got into the train in a daze.

As it pulled out, he appeared on the platform, screaming, "Do you know where the house is?"

"Yes!" I tried to open the window.

"I'll be home by teatime. Come then!" And he waved me out of sight.

I told my father a school-friend had invited me for the weekend and packed a small case. Colm and some other Maoists were occupying a house in Sandymount. They hoped to found a commune and had squatters' rights while the case was being tried in court. The house was halfway down Serpentine Avenue in its own grounds. A sign on the gate said BEWARE OF DOG. I pushed it open and crept cautiously up the spooky tree-lined avenue. There was no sign of life, but triffid-like branches clawed my face. The house stood forlorn in a jungle of weeds at the end. The plaster facade had once been pink, but now was diseased with brown patches of damp. Missing slates left large holes in the roof. Gutters sagged limply, and a downpipe dangled like a broken limb. The downstairs windows were bricked in, and the hall door was padlocked.

Could Colm really live here?

I knocked, but no one came.

Was it the right place?

I tried again.

Finally I walked around the house, past a weedy tennis court to the kitchen door. I knocked again, and this time heard footsteps.

"Who is it?" an Englishy voice asked suspiciously.

"Sally Ann Fitzpatrick. A friend of Colm Connolly."

The door inched open, and a pale skinny boy peered out. He had thick blond page-boy hair and wore a beret like Castro. "I'm Tom. Who sent you?"

"Colm invited me."

He jerked his head, indicating I was to enter.

We passed through a dank and dilapidated kitchen to the hall. There was rubble everywhere, and wallpaper hung in strips from the walls to the ceiling. The smell of must was terrible. Floorboards were ripped up, and only odd rails remained of the bannisters. I followed him up the rickety stairs, asking chattily, "Is Colm in?"

"Not yet!" Suddenly he pointed to missing floorboards. "Mind yourself there!"

I followed. One false step and I was a goner. "When are you expecting him?"

He shrugged. "You never know with Colm."

"Are you at Trinity?" I asked on the first landing.

"I was."

"Oh. You got your degree then?"

"I left. It's an imperialist institution."

I had to admire his courage. Although I'd opened my mind to other things besides exams, I was still hooked on getting a degree. I longed to be an intellectual like Simone de Beauvoir. I even had fantasies of going

36

on to someplace like Cambridge. It was so silly when I couldn't even write an essay.

We went up another flight, coming at last to a large, cluttered room which seemed to be the field of occupation.

There was a worse smell here: a mixture of cooking, dirty socks and rank bedclothes. In the murky light, I could make out a table with a basin-full of dirty dishes. Coffee cups and beer bottles littered the room. In one corner there were stained mattresses and by the blackened grate a lumpy couch.

He pointed to it. "Take a pew. Colm should be back soon. I'm typesetting the paper."

I looked at the squalid table. "Will I wash up while I'm waiting?"

"Whatever you like!" he called from the hall. "There's water in the kitchen. You'll have to heat it on the fire."

The fire was almost out. So I threw on some coal from the bucket and carried the kettle back down the stairs. I knew squatters couldn't be choosers, but why didn't they wash up in the kitchen? It had a sink big enough to bathe in.

As I ran the water, something moved in the corner.

A mouse?

I couldn't see anything, so I threw a piece of wood in the direction of the noise. To my relief, a tiny dog ran out the door - a chihuahua, one of those lap dogs women have.

"Here! Here!" I called, as I quite like dogs.

But it was gone. So I carried the filled kettle back up the stairs.

Tom was still typing in the other room. While the kettle boiled, I went in saying, "There was a lovely little dog downstairs."

He stopped typing. "A dog?"

"Yes, in the kitchen. A little chihuahua."

He roared laughing. "That was probably a rat. The place is infested."

I said nothing. I mean, rats *really* horrify me. At least the idea of them. I don't think I'd ever really seen one before as I'm a city person.

Just as I finished the dishes, another squatter came in. She was a tall, burly girl dressed shabbily in jeans and a man's grubby raincoat.

I said hello, and she nodded curtly in recognition, then took some groceries out of her pocket: a tin of baked beans, a packet of sausages, and rashers.

She looked at me coldly. "Who are you?"

I felt very awkward. "Colm - eh - invited me. I'm from UCD."

She said nothing.

"We're in the same History tutorial."

Grumpily she put the pan on the fire. "Pity he didn't let us know."

"Oh, I'm not very hungry."

"We take it in turns to cook."

Just then Tom came in the door with a manuscript. "Take a look at this, Rosemary."

While she read it, he ignored me. Then there were noises downstairs and the sound of someone coming up. I fervently hoped it was Colm.

It was.

"Sally! You made it!" He came in the door, wearing his rumpled suit. Then, forcing a smile at the others, gave a Nazi salute. "Heil, comrades!"

They didn't look up from the manuscript

"This is Sally Ann Fitzpatrick. Eh - Sally, this is Tom and Rosemary."

"We've met," I said cheerfully.

They just nodded curtly in my direction.

He rubbed his tummy hungrily. "Sally's staying for the weekend. What's for tea?"

They were both glaring at him.

He took off his tie and stuffed it in his pocket. "Well, there's *enough* for her, isn't there?"

Tom broke the silence. "I suppose we can *all* have less."

I was definitely *persona non grata*.

Somehow we got through the meal. Mostly Colm talked to me, and they munched silently. Afterwards he brought me for a pint in Horse Show House, his favourite haunt.

"They're pissed, 'cos I didn't ask them if you could stay. They have all these blasted Nazi rules," he explained. "Ignore them."

I sipped on my Guinness. To me it tasted like rusty water. I didn't really like it, but everyone else did. And I feared being different. I feared everything: Rosemary and Tom, the rats, but mainly sex. It loomed ahead like some great ordeal. How would I manage? And would it hurt? I mean, I'd never even used a Tampax. I couldn't get it in. I was sure I hadn't an opening down there.

"Colm, I think I'll go home."

"Because of those creeps?"

"No, I - I'm scared."

"Of what?"

"I dunno ... pregnancy!"

He took a condom from the hanky pocket of his suit. "I've taken care of that."

I was falling into an abyss.

We sat in the pub till closing time and then went back to the house. There was no one around, and we went straight up to Colm's room on the top floor. It was a little less squalid than the rest of the house. On one wall was a large poster of Fidel Castro and on the other a photo of James Larkin with his arms upheld. I recognised now Colm's stance on the truck as imitating the Irish Labour Leader. In one corner there was a mattress with a cheerful duvet quilt.

"Sit down." Colm put on a record of Bob Dylan, and as it whined out a song, "It ain't me, Babe ...", he pulled me down on the mattress and began kissing me passionately.

I tried to kiss back. After a while he opened my blouse and put his hand inside my bra.

Oh God, I thought, this is it!

"Take it off, Sally."

I obeyed, and he kissed my breasts. My nipples actually became pronounced. He seemed to be in a trance. Then he pulled off his trousers and underpants. I had never seen an erection. Never. And the sight of it, dangling like another limb panicked me completely. I jumped up and pulled on my clothes.

"What is it?" Colm put his arms around me.

"I'm sorry. I've got to go home!"

He was trembling. "*Please* don't go, Sally."

"But I can't." I was crying and frantically pulled on the rest of my clothes. I know I was acting like some terrible teaser of men, but couldn't help it.

Resignedly he put on a towel dressing gown. "You've missed the last bus."

"I'll walk."

"To Monkstown?"

I pulled on my coat.

"Stay, Sally!"

"It's not fair to you."

"I'm all right. If you like, I'll sleep on the floor."

I began crying. "I'm sorry."

"I shouldn't have pounced on you."

"Do you think I'm peculiar?"

He sighed, putting an arm around me. "No, you're just not ready for it."

Then we heard a noise on the stairs, and someone knocked on the door. "Are you still up Colm?"

It was Rosemary.

"I've been up for some time," he answered sarcastically.

"But are you up *now*?"

"Sort of. Why?"

Her voice was insistent. "I wanted you to look at something."

We were both in stitches.

"Can it wait?" he asked in a level voice. "I'm not up anymore."

I put a pillow over my mouth.

"I don't know what's so funny!" Her anger seemed to burn a hole in the door.

We slept that night like brother and sister. I awoke first and lay staring at Colm's handsome sleeping face. He had very dark skin for an Irish person and looked almost Italian. I wanted more than anything to be *engagé* with him. To rid myself of my terrible virginity. But I couldn't. And I don't know why to this very day. How could everyone else in the world enjoy sex and not I? What was wrong with me?

We had tea and toast for breakfast. Colm brought it up to his room and then went into his job at the Labour Party. I said I'd go home, but he persuaded me to stay for the weekend as arranged. I had my café job that evening, so he said we'd go for a walk on the strand that afternoon.

At about ten o'clock I went downstairs for some more tea. Rosemary and Tom were checking sheets of typing at the table. They didn't look up as I came in. The dishes were strewn around the room again, and again I offered to wash up.

"Will you see about the evening meal?" Rosemary looked up wearily. "We take it in turns to shop and cook."

I nodded cheerfully. But I've only a pound till tonight. I get paid on a Saturday."

"Oh, you don't need any money!" She laughed sarcastically.

Tom looked up. "We usually just liberate it."

"You mean you shoplift?"

He nodded.

"But that's theft!" I was horrified.

"So is all property," he quipped.

"I can't." I was Oliver fallen among thieves. I mean, what if I were caught? My father would disown me.

Rosemary stood up and reached for a book on the shelf. "I think you should read the rules to our new member. She seems to be full of bourgeois shit."

"I'm not. I just can't steal."

Tom leafed through the book - the *Quotations of Mao* - saying, "We're in a disorganised state now. But we operate on strict Maoist principles. I'll just read you what he says on discipline. 'One: The individual is subordinate to the organisation. Two: The minority is subordinate to the majority. Three: The lower level is subordinate to the higher level.'" He looked up. "All three apply to you. But if you don't want to stay ..."

"I do! I'll do it!"

They smirked at each other.

I knew Mao had also said the soldiers of the revolution shouldn't steal. But I desperately wanted to stay. To be with Colm and bring about the Utopia he talked of. I decided to chance it. After all, I was a Maoist now and no longer middle-class. All property was probably theft. I had once read a magazine article that people shoplifted by hiding a bag under a coat. So I shortened the strap of my shoulder bag and concealed it under my anorak. Then I walked casually to the big supermarket in Sandymount Green. I thought my chances would be better in a big shop like that.

As usual, I picked up a basket going in. I had a pound so I could buy a few cheap things to allay suspicion. I decided on dishwashing liquid and a bag of potatoes. Next I lingered by the meat counter, fingering the packets of meat. A sign warned SHOPLIFTERS WILL BE PROSECUTED, but I ignored it. Checking that no one was looking, I slipped two packets of steak into my bag.

No one had seen me.

I dawdled to the cheese counter. "How much is the Danish Blue?"

"10/6 a pound", a whitecoated boy said.

"It's a bit expensive."

"I can cut you a quarter."

"No thanks."

I went casually to the check-out. There was only one woman in the queue ahead of me. Trying to ignore my thumping heart, I put my basket on the counter. The woman moved on, and the checker emptied my basket, ringing up the prices.

"18/11, please."

I paid and put the items in a plastic bag.

I was at the door when a voice called, "Miss! Miss!"

I stopped, frozen with fear. A future of imprisonment flashed before me. My father's tired face. Should I try and outrun them? Then a hand tapped my shoulder.

I turned.

The shop manager held up a brown woollen glove. "Did you drop this, Miss?"

It was mine.

I took it. My heart racing, I walked numbly out of the shop and around the corner. Once out of sight I ran all the way back to the house. It had been so easy. And I felt a strange exhilaration. I now understood the thrill of the criminal life.

That afternoon on Sandymount Strand with Colm, I mentioned that I'd got steak for tea. To my surprise he offered to reimburse me for what I'd spent. So I told him of the morning's conversation with Tom and Rosemary and my adventures in the supermarket.

He gaped at me. "What? They told you we stole everything? Well, that's not our arrangement! We have a kitty. We all put in money. I've put in some extra for you!"

He was absolutely fuming. And I was speechless.

Colm suspected they'd told me to shoplift as a way of making me leave in disgust. To them I was full of bourgeois shit. And an "uptight virgin." But this made Colm more determined for me to stay. So I did. I'm vague about exactly how long. I was so happy. My father says one of my mother's maxims was "*Know* when you're happy". According to her, this was the secret of life. And now, although I couldn't talk to her, I lived in the knowledge of happiness. My relationship with my father was OK. I suppose it was like any girl's with her father. I mean, he gave me money if I needed it, but he didn't talk to me at all. I think he probably didn't even notice I was living away from home. But now everything was different. I had Colm to talk to. On walks. At demonstrations. And often till the small hours in his little room.

To avoid Rosemary and Tom, we often ate out in Gaj's Restaurant in Baggot Street. I loved the cheerful kitcheny look of its pine tables and chairs and gingham tablecloths. We met other students there and often writers and intellectuals. And when the restaurant closed, we would sometimes go to a flat for late night coffee. As Colm's girlfriend, everyone deferred to me in a way that was new. I now had status. I existed because someone loved me. Or so I thought.

One evening along with some others we were in Gaj's, discussing plans for a fast on O'Connell Bridge to aid the victims of some war in Africa - I forget where - when Paul came in. he looked really bad - pale and unshaven. And downright dirty. I saw him queue for food, but said nothing to Colm who was deep in argument with someone.

"No, Sally and I'll take the shift from eight till noon. Then you two. And Mansfield's actually volunteered."

I watched Paul sit at a corner table. I was glad there was no room at ours. What would I say to him? But I felt very badly about my behaviour, and something made me nudge Colm. "Paul's come in. Will we ask him to join us?"

Colm looked round quickly. "No, he's got really weird lately."

"What do you mean?"

Colm tapped the side of his head. "Nuts!"

I sat with my back to Paul while the others argued loudly. There was no way Paul could avoid hearing or seeing me. Then Colm went to phone someone, and I decided to go and talk to Paul. Ignoring a friend was too much. Even an ex-friend.

But when I turned round, he was gone.

His food was untouched so I felt sure he was in the loo. But no. He never came back. He must have seen us and fled.


After our first débâcle, Colm hadn't tried to make love again. Just living with him helped me conquer my weird fear. So on the night of our second Sunday together, we were kissing each other goodnight, when I suddenly said, "let's try it again."

He hesitated. "Are you sure, Sally?"

I nodded, feeling the dread of someone taking a high dive.

It hurt a bit when he penetrated me, but I felt no desire. Nothing. I didn't seem to have a hymen, so there was no blood either. As he moved up and down inside me, I felt only discomfort. In a few minutes he was finished.

"Oh, Sally," he sighed.

Nothing had happened. Nothing. What on earth did people make such a fuss about? Then as he pulled out of me, I felt wavy sensations.

"Wait!" I whispered.

There were more sensations inside me. And the next thing I was a woman. I giggled with relief. He started too. At that exact moment, there were loud voices in the garden. And the sound of something crashing.

Colm pulled out of me. "Christ, what was that?"

The crashing got louder, and someone spoke through a megaphone. "This is the guards! The house is being demolished! All trespassers must vacate the premises immediately!"

Colm jumped out of bed. "Get dressed! They're pulling a fast one and demolishing the house!"

We both scrambled into our clothes and ran down the stairs to the kitchen door. Luckily the fuss was at the front of the house, and we ran out the back through the garden.

"It's jail if I'm caught, Sally. Hurry!"

I tripped, twisting my ankle painfully.

"Come on!" He pulled me up.

"I can't. You go ahead!"

At that moment a vicious police dog pounced on me. I screamed. Colm ran in terror through the trees. A burly guard pulled the dog off me, grabbing my arm.

They found marijuana in the house. All the others had got away, so I was charged with possession of drugs and trespassing. I spent the night in Sir Patrick Dun's Hospital guarded by police. Also I lost my contact lenses.

People sympathised with my father over his wild daughter, but he stuck by me. He hired a solicitor and a barrister to speak for me, and I got off with the Probation Act for a first offence. For months I hobbled around on a broken ankle. But the pain was nothing to the pain inside me. Colm wrote that it would only do my case harm to be associated with him and that we shouldn't see each other for the moment. He never even comforted me. I saw him once in college with another girl and ducked into a classroom. Later I heard they got engaged. I was afraid to go back to Professor O'Dea's tutorial where I'd meet him for certain. I retreated back into my shell and the Ladies' Reading Room and avoided the Main Hall and Annexe. I wanted to leave college completely, but my father wouldn't hear of it. I was abandoned and betrayed. I was Christ weeping in the garden, an outcast whom nobody loved.

Now I realised how badly I'd treated Paul. If only I had another chance. If only he'd ask me again to do a strong line. Or go out to the hills. Or even for a cup of coffee and cream buns in the Annexe. I looked for him in all the usual college haunts, but to no avail. I knew he'd forgive me, if only

I could ask him. So I stalked Gaj's Restaurant, knowing he sometimes ate there. But I never saw him. Never. I called at his digs, but his landlady said he'd left Dublin. He'd always been secretive about his sister in Wicklow, so I couldn't find out anything for sure from her. I didn't know who she was. Finally I rang the operator in the telephone exchange, and someone there at last said he'd left for England.

But he hadn't.

And I have more.

Soon after the Christmas holidays, I was slinking through the Main Hall when someone called, "Sally Ann!"

It was Colm.

He was standing talking to the college chaplain, Father O'Connor, a tall young redhead. Fear suddenly choked me, and I pushed my way blindly through the crowded hall. If only I was nearer to the safety of the Ladies' Reading Room.

But halfway down the corridor, Colm caught me.

"Sally! Wait!"

I hurried on.

"No! Wait! Please!"

People were looking, so I had no choice but to face him.

"Did you hear the news?" He looked ashen-faced, and before I could answer blurted, "Brady's committed suicide!"

"Wh-what?"

"He was pulled out of Lough Dan this morning."

I looked at him, stunned.

"Maybe he fell in?" I said at last.

Colm shook his head. "There were stones in his pockets."

I felt I was going to faint. "I was very unkind to him."

Colm suddenly reddened. "We all were. Remember O'Dea's tutorial? We should've walked out, but we just sat there! Why?"

The memory of the tutorial will wound me forever. As much as my not turning up for that date. Oh, I don't flatter myself that Paul drowned himself out of unrequited love or anything like that. He had problems, and I didn't help him. None of us did. And he was to suffer even more indignities at the hands of others.

Father O'Connor drove Colm and me down to the funeral the next morning. We had to go over a bleak mountain in the rain, and it was just ten o'clock when we arrived at the mean little church on the outskirts of a Wicklow village. Surprisingly there was only one other car, and men already were carrying the coffin up the steep hill to the graveyard. We hurried after them.

"I thought there was to be a Mass," Father O'Connor said breathlessly to the men at the graveside.

They looked at each other, and went ahead lowering the body with

44

ropes.

"Who's performing the burial rights?" Father persisted, puzzled.

As one of the men started shovelling in clay, the other muttered grumpily, "The parish priest is afraid of scandal, Father."

"Scandal?" The priest looked amazed.

"He's a manifest sinner, Father."

"A what?" Colm said.

"It's a term from Canon Law", Father O'Connor said.

Now the men were both shovelling. I stared into the deep grave. One day I would lie in one. But in the meantime was I worthy of life?

"Stop!" Father O'Connor shouted. "I'm going to ring your parish priest."

They did, leaning lazily on their shovels. The priest ran down the hill to the church. In a while he came back, his young face set in anger.

"He quoted Canon Law at me", he said to Colm and me.

"What about Vatican II?" I said. "Hasn't it changed everything?"

"Christian burial can still be denied at the discretion of the individual PP" Father O'Connor explained. "Let's say the Our Father."

As the men filled in the grave, we said those ancient words, begging forgiveness of God as we forgave others. I was sorry I couldn't remember John Donne's poem about Death being not proud. But really death was proud and won in the end. Here was the final end of man, despite Aristotle, Marx, Mao, the lot. What did anything matter? Paul had needed us and we failed him. Our college days were the best of times, and the worst of times. We were meant to be the "gentle" generation, the harbingers of change, of the Brave New World. We would support any foreign cause, but had stood by when one of our own was humiliated.

# IV Jim

The birds awakened Jim.

"Nora," he whispered to his sleeping wife. "Nora, wake up!"

She groaned, rolling to her side of the bed.

He plumped his pillow and sat up. Outside the birds chattered away. There was the occasional cough of a car engine. Then the clink of milk bottles. Normally he was up by now. But that was before he was laid off from his temporary job at the Post Office. Oh, there was a chance he'd eventually be taken on permanently, but in the meantime this was the life. He squinted at the alarm clock. 7.10. By this time he was usually halfway up the Glenageary Road. Probably stuffing the usual bundle of bills into the flats at 122. Peculiar place that, tenants always on the go. Letters handed back, marked "Not Known Here", or "Please Forward". Well for them. Wonder what the flats rented for? Too much.

The purple and gold-starred wallpaper of his mother-in-law's spare bedroom glimmered in the half-light. Horrible. Yet, she'd done it up specially for them. But those colours made the room even pokier. What with their bed and the baby's cot, you couldn't swing a cat. But even this bed wasn't big enough for some people. He curled round his wife, fondling her behind gently.

She flung his hand off. He blew into her freckled face. She wrinkled her nose and turned away. He reached inside her nightgown.

"Jim!" She flung his hand away again. "I'm jaded."

"Ah, come on! You can sleep later!"

"You know, I can't! And stop it! You'll wake the baby!"

But the baby was breathing steadily, his little back rising then falling. He pulled off his pyjamas. "Come on, Nora!"

"Not now!" She was suddenly wide awake.

"What's wrong with now?" He kissed her eagerly.

She pushed him away, whispering at the wall. "Mammy!"

"Ah, to hell with Mammy! Nora! Please!"

"Sssssh!"

"Mammy!" he shouted through the paper-thin wall. "Mammy! Can you hear us?"

The baby started crying.

"Now, look what you've done!" As she got out of bed, the crying got louder.

He covered his head with the pillow. It rose to a crescendo. God, there was no peace! He was going deaf. He grabbed the blanket and slammed out to the bathroom. He stood naked over the toilet, drowning the floor. The Mammy would scream when she saw that, but he didn't care. She could clean it. Or else Nora could. Serve her right. She took her mother's side in everything. And she'd gone off him since that purple frog was born. The kid took up all her time. She was always tired and didn't seem to do anything but breastfeed, day and night. It drove him mad with jealousy to watch the kid sucking her breast. What about him? They had no communication anymore. There was nothing to talk about since she wouldn't read. He tried giving her novels. But the Dennis Wheatley was lying half-read on her bedside table and she'd never even opened the Conrad. And now she wouldn't even have sex.

In the hall they passed without speaking.

"There now", she soothed, carrying the baby downstairs.

He slammed the bedroom door shut and threw himself back onto the bed. Kids were awful. Christ, why had no one ever told him?

He grabbed the pillow again, muffling the crying. He'd been led a dance OK. Marry me, Jim! I love you, Jim! And now what? Mammy before breakfast! Well, he'd show them! Tonight he was getting plastered with the boys. He'd drink twenty pints, like Kevin once did. Kevin would get him home. He had avoided the pitfalls. "Play it cool", was his motto. Had all the women he wanted. Last week he'd sauntered up to that blonde mot at the bar. And the next thing, *she* was buying *him* drinks.

There was a low muttering coming from downstairs. Then his mother-in-law's voice pierced the ceiling like a saw. "What was all that shoutin'?"

The baby drowned his wife's reply.

He pictured her rocking him back and forth, her red hair on her shoulders. Oh, he shouldn't have frightened the poor little bastard. Well, not quite a bastard. He stared dismally around him, then pulled the eiderdown over his head. He was a prisoner for life. When he'd met Nora, he'd been doing the Leaving at Killester Tech at night. He wanted to go to the university. Get some kind of degree. Then get out of Ireland. Travel to some remote place. Have the life of adventure he'd always read about in Conrad and Dennis Wheatley. He'd be like Marlow. It had all started with Captain Marryat's *Mr Midshipman Easy*. God, what a book. Maybe he could write a novel, charting his own adventures. Like Dennis Wheatley. Or maybe the definitive work on Livingstone. Yes, that sounded OK. But for that he'd have to do research in Africa.

That was a dream now. He'd never write anything. Nora had seen to that.

Through the jungle darkness, he crawled on his belly like Alan Quartermain. Light peeped in the distance. Yes, he'd pitch camp there. Pick up some natives. Read his piled-up post. Fling back Nora's letters with a scrawled "Not Known Here". Of course, she'd probably follow him to the bush with the baby. "Sorry, Mees, we no see Bwana Jim two year now", a black boy would tell her. She'd cry, of course. Then the baby would start up. "Try that way!" the black boy would say, pointing toward the Nile, the heart of darkness in the centre of the bed.

Someone prodded his back. Nora was sorry. Well, she should be.

He threw off the eiderdown to see his mother-in-law standing over him with a mug of tea.

"You?" Quickly he covered himself.

Her bulging eyes didn't even blink. "Take this!"

He did. But instead of going, she stayed at the end of the bed. Her platinum hair was in plastic rollers and her chin jutted like Woody Woodpecker. A gaudy pink dressing gown covered her gaunt body.

"The gas is comin' today", she snapped. "Make sure you get back early with yer dole money. I'm not forkin' out again!"

He sipped his tea. Thank God, Nora wasn't skinny. And didn't wear rollers. The woman was made of plastic. She put plastic on the cushions, plastic strips on the carpet, plastic flowers in the sittingroom. They ate out of plastic dishes and had to look at a dish of plastic fruit.

"Did you hear me?" she screeched.

He nodded.

"I'm not forkin' out again."

When he didn't answer, she flounced out of the room. He fixed her back with his index finger and fired. Bang. Mercy killing. God, she was like something out of a play. You could laugh at mother-in-law jokes. But it was another thing when you found yourself with one. Maybe they should just rent a flat. Not wait for the corporation house. Get away immediately. No, they couldn't afford it. They could hardly afford to live.

He lay there feeling depressed, then looked at his watch. Come on, Jim! He finished his tea and hauled himself out of bed. Then washed, dressed and hurried from the house.

Halfway to the dole, he began to feel better. Poor Nora. She hadn't wanted to live with her mother. Christ, she'd always wanted to get away from her. Now she was landed right back under the thumb. Never mind, they'd leave as soon as he got a job. In the distance, the sea was a brilliant blue. Summer was coming. He'd teach the baby to swim. You just threw them in, he'd read, and they swam to Wales. Like little fish.

The Dun Laoghaire Labour Exchange was conveniently beside the pawn shop in George's Street. Already a line of men stretched raggedly to the corner. His friend Kevin was near the top. He was an unemployed mechanic with the wiry dark good looks women went for.

Jim slipped in beside him. "You're up early for a change."

"I'm off to Greystones for the day. There's a practice rugby match there. Old Belvedere are playing. Why don't you come?"

"Thanks, but I've to get back. And there's the bus strike."

"Ah, come on! We'll hitch down. It'll be gas."

The door opened and the line moved slowly. While Kevin joked with another man, Jim remained silent. He'd never been to a rugby match. Only football. Kevin was interested in all sorts of sports. It'd be fun all right, but there was no way he could go. It wouldn't be fair to Nora. She'd only think he was still annoyed about this morning.

"What's the use, if you can't enjoy life?" Kevin said when they stopped again.

Jim said nothing. Kevin didn't understand marriage.

At the hatch he handed in his card. The girl counted out his money. Thirty pounds, forty pence.

Jim took it, feeling himself reddening. "There's - meant to be extra. The wife's had a baby."

The girl studied his file. "There's nothing about a baby here. We have a note of your marriage two months ago. But nothing about a baby."

"Oh, he's proved himself!" Kevin butted in from behind. "I'll testify to that."

There was a giggle along the line.

The girl coughed. "You'll have to see the supervisor."

"But I did. Last week."

The girl went away. In a few minutes she came back. "We'll have it for you next week."

Kevin got his money without a hitch. Outside he said, "Come on, Nolan! The mot'll live without you for a day."

Jim shook his head. "Sorry!"

"Put yer foot down from the beginning!"

"I - can't."

"God, she has ye henpecked!"

Jim turned away. Did Kevin really think that?

"Henpecked!"

"OK. I'll go!"

They headed for the Bray Road. After all, Nora hadn't even bothered to say goodbye when he was leaving the house. She probably sent her mother up to taunt him about the gas money. That old hag never stopped reminding him how much she was helping them. She talked about nothing but money. And Nora didn't stand up to her. Allowed herself to be bullied to avoid rows. Yes, it'd do her good to worry. Do them both good. Maybe they'd appreciate him then.

The first lift was from a taciturn truck driver who left them at the Wexford turning. They waited for an hour there before deciding to walk on through the town of Bray. It bustled with shoppers and activity. At the other side they stopped at a garage. Except for another girl hitchhiker it was deserted and had signs hanging from the pumps: NO PETROL.

"That's a bit of all right!" Kevin eyed the girl professionally.

Jim glanced over. The girl had black curly hair and gold granny glasses. She wore a yellow anorak and black jeans. And a red bandanna around her head. Probably some sort of hippy. He'd definitely seen her round Dun Laoghaire. She had a nice little arse on her, but Kevin would grab anything that was going.

"How are you, love?" Kevin called.

She waved, but didn't come over.

"That's a stuck-up piece!" Kevin joked. "I'd like to get her down on her back."

Jim ignored him. Kevin was often too crude.

Kevin went over to the petrol pumps. "Arabs holdin' the fuckin' world to fuckin' ransom."

Jim smiled to himself. Kevin's language got choice when he started philosophising. "What about CIE?"

"What about them?"

"The bus strike's holding us to ransom."

"That's a fuckin' just cause."

Jim said nothing. He was looking at the girl. She was much slimmer than Nora. Nora had a nice arse when he first met her. But she'd put on weight with the baby. Now she could only think of things like gas to dry his clothes. But how would she dry them now?

"Did ya hear me, Nolan? CIE's a fuckin' just cause."

Jim nodded. So was Nora's gas. He should never have come. He'd been mad to give in to Kevin's taunting. He didn't even like football.

"It's about time you fuckin' wised up, Nolan."

"What do you mean?"

"To the fuckin' cause of the workin' man. Did you read that life of Connolly I fuckin' lent you?"

Jim nodded. "It was good."

Kevin sat on the curb. "It was fuckin' marvellous. You're wrapped up in your own fuckin' problems. You've got to think globally."

"What do you mean?"

"I mean the fuckin' world situation! It makes our fuckin' problems fuckin' pifflin'." Kevin leaned back, his head supported by his hands. "Nothin' seems fuckin' worth doing. I'll never understand how people can have fuckin' kids!"

"It happens - you meet the right girl." Jim looked regretfully over at the girl. Would he have any chance of getting off with her?

"Not me!" Kevin shook his head. "No, sir! Not with the fuckin' holocaust comin'."

A truck roared up. The three of them thumbed frantically but it passed.

"Waitin' long, love?" Kevin shouted.

The girl came over. She was carrying a sketch pad in a basket and seemed oblivious to the coming holocaust. "About half-an-hour. I'm trying to get to Wicklow."

Jim thought her accent posh.

Kevin went into action. "For a dirty weekend?"

The girl looked alarmed.

50

"He's only messing," Jim said.

Kevin smirked. "Any crack down there?"

She shrugged. "Dunno. I'm only going for the day."

Kevin winked at her. "To see a fella?"

"Yes, in a way. I'm visiting his grave."

The boys looked at each other.

"He committed suicide," the girl went on, "in college."

Kevin snorted. "Fuckin' eejit! Are you in college yerself?" He glanced at the sketchpad. "Art College?"

"Oh, no! I've finished. I did arts. Now I'm unemployed."

"That makes three of us!" Kevin sidled up to her, putting an arm around her shoulder. "Listen love. I'm Kevin and this is my pal Jimbo ..."

"I'm Sally Ann Fitzpatrick."

"Why don't we travel to Greystones together? Have a drink there?"

"Three's a bit awkward, she said. "You'd be better sticking together."

"You two go on," Jim said. "I should get back."

But Kevin glared him into silence, turning to the girl. "Three's fine. You thumb. Jim and I'll hide by the wall. then when someone stops, we'll run out."

Sally Ann shrugged. "OK. But I won't bring you any luck."

Just then a red sportscar screeched to a halt beside them. A girl with long blonde hair pushed open the passenger door. "I'm going to the Burnaby."

Her voice sounded rich and she wore riding clothes. The rich looked so healthy, Jim thought. Their skin kind of glowed. Must be the right vitamins or something.

Kevin leaned over the car. "That's great."

She took a riding hat off the front seat. "I can only take two. One of you'll have to squeeze in behind."

Jim stood back. "Sally was here first."

But she stepped to the back of the pavement. "That's OK. Go ahead!"

Kevin winked meaningfully at his friend. "In you get, Jimbo."

The blonde driver relented. "Oh, well, we're not going far. The three of you can squeeze in."

Kevin had now switched his attentions to the driver. He chatted her up as the car jerked forward and roared up the hill to Greystones. Jim found himself curled into the back with Sally Ann. He couldn't believe his luck. Several times their thighs touched, causing him interesting sensations. He'd try inviting her for a drink when they stopped. Then who knows what might happen. Nora would never know. How could she?

She held onto her bandanna. "It's a strong wind."

Jim put an arm around her. "It's great!"

He could hear almost nothing of Kevin's conversation. Just as well. God, this was the life! He'd never been in a sportscar before. Fields flashed past. At the top of the hill, the driver ground the gears for the descent. He could see the harbour through a hedge. The sea was a blue band. He never wanted to stop.

But she stopped at the Harbour Bar.

Kevin got out, turning to the driver. "How about a drink?"

To Jim's amazement, she agreed. She hopped out of the car with the litheness of a greyhound. Kevin ogled her clinging white jodhpurs. He was almost drooling.

Sally Ann climbed out, lingering hesitantly.

Jim smiled at her. "What about you, love?"

She shrugged. "Why not!"

Jim swallowed. God, now he'd have to pay.

But inside the pub, he said to her, "Sit down there, love."

Then the two men took orders.

Miss Jodhpurs wanted a gin and tonic. Sally Ann ordered a glass of Smithwick's.

"Have a pint", Jim urged.

But she shook her head. "A glass is fine."

The two men gave the order at the bar, adding two pints of Guinness for themselves. When the barman turned his back, Kevin whispered to Jim. "Let me handle this."

It was Kevin's boast that he never paid for a drink.

As they took their glasses, he said "Put that on the slate, pal. We'll be back for more."

The women were chatting at the table.

"So you have your own horse," Sally Ann was saying.

The glamorous one flicked back her hair. "Yes. I stable it at a riding school - the Bel-Air Hotel."

"Where's that?"

"Ashford."

Kevin sat beside her. "Could we go there for a dirty weekend? Get that into you!"

She giggled sexily and he sat with an arm poised on the back of the seat. They immediately started up a flirtatious, jokey conversation.

Jim took out his tobacco and rolled a cigarette. He offered it to Sally Ann. "Smoke?"

"No thanks."

Then he offered it to the other girl.

She declined, waving her manicured hand.

"So you have an arts degree," Jim said to Sally Ann. "I always wanted to study that."

"You still could."

"Ah, no. I have commitments" He couldn't tell her he was married. "Parents."

"Oh! ... But people manage. The person whose grave I'm visiting was a telephone operator at night."

"If he's dead, that isn't a recommendation!"

She sipped slowly. "No. But you could do a night degree."

"Hmm ..." He changed the subject. "Have you ever heard of Conrad?"

"Everyone's heard of Conrad."

Jim swallowed. Not where he came from. Nora thought he was talking about a friend. "He's my favourite writer."

"I like *Youth*."

He hadn't got around to that yet. "Ah, but *The Nigger of Narcissus* is great. Or *Lord Jim*. I mean what a story!"

"They're not as interesting as 'The Secret Sharer'."

"Who wrote that?"

She laughed. "Conrad! You haven't read everything by your favourite writer!"

Jim felt himself redden. "I have, mostly."

"It's a novella. Remember, he introduced the doppelgänger?"

"The what?"

"The doppelgänger! That's a double. The alter ego."

Jim had never heard of the term.

"In literature, that means a double who experiences things for you. In the story the fugitive does the growing up for the young captain."

Jim took a gulp of his drink. Christ, she really knew her stuff. He'd never met anyone who could talk about Conrad.

"You've got good taste. My father likes Conrad too."

This cheered him up. "Do you like Dennis Wheatley?"

"Who's he?"

"Ah, you must've heard of *The Prisoner in the Mask*. Or *The Second Seal*."

She stared into her glass. "I haven't. He must be some low-brow bestseller type."

Jim felt himself getting angry. What did she mean low-brow? Only last week he'd found an article on Dennis Wheatley in the Dun Laoghaire library. As well as being a brilliant author, he was on Churchill's staff during the war. "He's a great writer - renowned for historical accuracy. You must have heard of *The Satanist*."

She shook her head. "Sorry."

He tried again. "Well, what about Captain Marryat?"

"Now, he's a poor man's Conrad. But pretty good, I'll admit."

Jim stared at her. A poor man's Conrad! Did she think he was poor or what? An inferior?

"For me Kafka's the greatest", she said heedlessly.

Jim had never heard of him.

"He was a sort of pre-existentialist."

He knew this term, but he didn't want to make a fool of himself again.

So he fell into a grumpy silence. At least Nora didn't think he was an inferior.

She gave him an odd look. "You know, 'angst' and all that."

He didn't answer.

"You should read the bug story - 'Metamorphosis'."

Sulkily Jim tuned in to Kevin's chat. He had all the luck.

"How about a drive down to Glendalough" he was saying. "A toss in St Kevin's bed. Then finish up with a nice meal in the Delgany Inn."

The girl raised an eyebrow in amusement.

Jim kept a straight face. Who was paying for that? It sounded much more interesting than the other one's blasted existentialism. Kevin was the man to pick them. He'd succeeded in getting his arm around the mot. It was a treat to see him in action. She was lapping it up. And every so often let out a burst of laughter. It was a rich musical laugh.

But then he whispered something Jim couldn't hear. She shook the ice in her glass. Then suddenly downed her drink and got up. "Sorry, must dash!"

Kevin looked flummoxed. "You mean, you're going?"

She looked at her watch. "Have to. Sorry!"

"Ah, have another!"

"Sorry." She flashed a diamond-ringed finger. "I'm engaged."

Kevin ran after her. "I didn't know anyone did that anymore! Anyway, that's half the fun!"

But she wouldn't wait.

Jim sipped his drink. Kevin had backed the wrong horse this time. It was consoling that he didn't always win.

"I'd better be off too." Sally Ann said.

"Ah, wait. Have another."

Kevin came back, looking as if he was going to cry with disappointment and went straight to the gents. When he came out he looked sharply at Sally Ann. "Will you have another, love?"

"She will!" Jim laid claim to her. "We're going to a rugby match. Would you like to come?"

She shook her head. "No, but thanks. It's really nice of you."

What did she mean? It was really nice of him. Did she think she was too good for him?

The two men went again to the bar.

"I was hoping to stick Miss La-de-da for the drinks." Kevin snarled.

"Well, you didn't succeed!" Jim whispered. "And we can't do it to her."

"Why not?" Kevin laughed shortly.

"It wouldn't be fair."

"What's fair? You'll never get a ride out of her. She was comin' on the intellectual. No good in a woman!"

The word "intellectual" mortified Jim. She had shown him to be an ignoramus.

"You know my motto." Kevin taunted. "Love them and leave them!"

Jim obstinately reached into his back pocket for his wallet. But it was gone. Frantically he tried his other pockets. "No, lost. Jesus."

"You search the bar! I'll try and stop the car!" Kevin ran out the door.

Jim combed the area where they were sitting. But it wasn't there either.

"Was there much in it?" Sally Ann was crawling around the floor on her hands and knees.

"My dole money. I have a wife and child."

"Gosh, I'm sorry."

Frantically he ran through the bar to the road.

"Wait! Maybe I can borrow some from my father!"

Outside the sportscar was gone. Nowhere in sight. Kevin stood on the other side of the road.

"Did you see the number?" Jim called.

"No! But you might have dropped it on the road. Or in the lorry. Come on! Let's get away from here."

Jim walked over. "But what about Sally?"

"What about her?"

"We didn't pay for the drinks."

"You know my motto."

"But ..."

"Love them and leave them!"

Just then a car came and Kevin thumbed it down. Jim hesitated. He looked back to the bar and saw Sally Ann standing in the doorway. He should go back. But hadn't she ridiculed him? Maybe she needed a lesson. The car stopped and they got in. Jim sat in the back with his head in his hands. Jesus. Now what'd they do for the week's money? Nora would cry. And her mother would scream. He'd have to go to the pawn shop with his good suit. Then he might never be able to get it out. What if he was called for an interview?

The rugby club was just outside the town. It consisted of a clubhouse and a field beside a road. Buses were parked nearby and a straggle of supporters lined the edge. The match was about to start, but Jim had no interest in it. He could only stare miserably in front of him. Nora always called the day before the dole her "waiting day". It was the day they had to go easy, sometimes eating nothing but porridge. Now she'd had two "waiting days".

"What'll Nora say?" he muttered miserably.

"Here", Kevin took out his wallet. "Take a tenner!"

"You can't spare it!"

"Take it, and stop worrying!"

After about ten minutes, Jim said, "I'm off".

"Don't be mad! You've come all this way." Then Kevin let out a cheer as a goal was scored. "Christ, did you see that!"

The rest of the watchers roared in appreciation.

Jim watched without enjoyment. A sense of dread sat in his stomach like lead. How would he face his mother-in-law with no money? He'd never live it down.

During half-time, people spilled carelessly out onto the road. There was a sudden screech of brakes.

Then a thud.

There were screams of alarm. People ran over.

Jim followed them.

In trying to avoid one of the spectators, a motor bike had hit a wall.

A crowd had already gathered around a young man who lay on his back with his eyes closed.

"He went right down on his head!" someone said.

"It's what comes of not wearing a helmet."

Jim saw he was only a boy of about sixteen. He had lank blond hair and a school scarf. Blood trickled from his mouth, but otherwise he looked as if he were sleeping.

The bike was a tangled mess.

A medical student came over and declared him dead. Nevertheless, someone covered him up to the chin with a coat.

It'd been so simple. A thud. He'd never even opened his eyes.

People stood about on the road, waiting for the ambulance. It came finally, and the body was loaded gently onto a stretcher. A garda car screamed up and took names and addresses. Jim avoided talking to them. He wasn't in the mood. Anyway, he hadn't seen anything.

Then the match went on, as if nothing had happened.

Jim just stood there, watching it mechanically. He seemed to have lost all will-power. He felt stunned by the accident. "He's dead meat" was all Kevin could say.

Kevin wanted to go drinking afterwards, but Jim didn't stay. He started walking out of Greystones towards Dublin. After a while he got a lift. Then another. All the way home he felt terrible. It had been the worst day of his life. The poor fucker's death had depressed him terribly. In a way it made all his worries seem pointless - unemployment, losing the money, his mother-in-law. Christ, death was so near. To everyone. Yet you never thought of it. What was that poem, he'd read in the Protestant Church? Last Sunday Nora and he'd been out walking the baby - walking was the only entertainment they could afford. They'd come across this church with the door open. Nora hadn't wanted to go in, thinking she'd be excommunicated or something stupid like that. But he'd persuaded her it was OK. All that was changed now. There was a new spirit of ecumenism in the air. Still, she'd been reluctant. Inside it was sort of musty and full of memorials to the dead of both wars. Then they'd come across a plaque on the wall.

*Remember man as you pass by*
*As you are now so once was I*
*As I am now so shalt thou be*
*Remember man eternity.*

Normally he hated poetry. He couldn't see anything in it. But that was the most touching thing he'd ever read. He'd learnt it by heart and copied it into his notebook as soon as he got home. He kept a notebook for interesting passages from books. Who could have written it on that plaque? Some poor fucker from another age. Yet he'd felt connected to this person. "Remember man ..." You forgot, that was the trouble. You forgot and most of the time acted like a shit. It was shitty to leave that girl to pay in the pub. He should have gone back. Said he'd lost his wallet. Offered to wash the dishes or something. And it was shitty bullying Nora about sex. And being jealous of a tiny baby. Nora and the baby were the only things that mattered. What if you died before you realised something like that? Like that poor boy.


The two women waited in the speckless kitchen.

He knew they'd been fighting.

Nora eyed him mutely. Her hair was newly washed, her eyes red from crying.

"You took your time!" the older one snapped, her hair still in curlers. "Where's my gas money?"

Jim put his tenner on the table. "That's all I have."

She looked triumphant. "If ye've been drinkin' ..."

"I haven't. I lost it."

She started to dance with rage. "Yer a liar! A liar! He's been drinkin' Nora!"

Jim looked at his wife. "Can I've something to eat?"

His wife went nervously to the fridge and took out rashers and eggs.

"Don't you dare give him those!"

Nora took the frying pan from the rack and put it on the cooker.

"Well! You connivin' bitch! Put them back!"

Nora ignored her, putting rashers on the pan.

"Put them back!" Her mother's face turned an ugly red as she struggled to control herself. "I paid for that food! Yer not givin' him my eggs!"

When she got no reaction, she grabbed the box of eggs and threw them on the ground. Then slammed out of the room.

They looked at each other. Then at the oozing egg-carton.

"Good riddance!" Nora snapped tearfully.

Jim took her in his arms, burying his face in her hair. he loved the smell of shampoo. "I'm sorry!"

"I was worried."

"I know ... How's the baby?"

# V Doc

People always think doctors make wonderful parents, so I don't disillusion them. It's their aura, or their place in society and all that muck. Anyway, it isn't true. Our father, for one, feels a complete flop - not that he is entirely. He puts this down to his vast age of sixty-something and the generation gap. But the reasons are otherwise: mainly his refusal to talk to my brother and me.

Oh, he talked *at* us OK, but not *to* us.

There's a difference, I usually tell people. And while he always ignored our physical health to the point of death, he blindly dosed us with culture, novels, poetry, music, paintings et al. As children he even made us learn a poem a week which we had to recite on a Sunday evening in the drawing room.

It was absolutely Victorian.

Unfortunately nothing took. Not permanently. Oh, I could hold my own in any conversation about books. And I liked Simone de Beauvoir and Virginia Woolf. But I now considered literature obsolete compared to film and was lately only interested in Modern Art. While my younger brother Tim is obsessed with cartoons and pop music.

It's the natural result of force feeding.

But my father doesn't see it like that. He complains non-stop about his loutish children, warning all who will listen about the evils of a late marriage. He was forty-four when he married my much younger mother. And they had ten delirious years until one Christmas Eve long ago she died. From cancer.

It left a terrible gap. I mean, it was all wrong. My father had expected to die first. But for her sake he tried to make us happy. And we tried to be happy. And basically we were, considering. But despite your man Tolstoy's generalisations about all happy families being the same, we were unhappy in our own peculiar way.

Christmas was our time of trial. I always ended up not talking to Tim. And my father wanted to murder us both - more than usual. Oh, he said, two weeks of dressing gowns, Christmas trees and chocolates got on his nerves. But although he never mentioned her, the real reason was my mother.

Take last year. one morning in the aftermath of the festivities, my father arose from the breakfast table, glaring at my brother Tim. "The windows are filthy!"

Tim was in pyjamas, harmlessly chewing muesli. Although only seventeen, he was taller than a man, with long black hair like a Rolling Stone. And as usual insulated by a Walkman. The Hoover was at his feet - this was his dog. We called him that because he ate everything in sight:

curtains, cushions, shoes, even golfballs. Once he had irritated the neighbours so much, he'd been put on tranquillisers. They say dogs reflect the psyches of their owners. Ours was quite mad but Tim loved him.

"An absolute disgrace!" snapped my father.

This brought a puzzled growl from the Hoover. He was a golden labrador with worried brown eyes and now rested with his head on his paws. I was in my dressing gown and deep in *The Irish Times*. I looked up, resenting this dawn raid on my sleepiness. It was hard enough to be cheerful in the morning.

My father rubbed the window pane with his hanky. He was dark too with a look of the greying Robert Donat. And, as usual, he was fully dressed in his one three-piece striped suit and puffing angrily on his pipe - it's odd to see a doctor smoking. Breakfast was a meal he always insisted on, which meant I had to get up to cook big, greasy fries - another oddity for a doctor. But, like all men, my father's peculiar about his stomach.

"Filthy!" he fumed.

He's peculiar about a lot of things. Normally he keeps to his study reading, but, as I mentioned, Christmas brings out his maniac streak. It was then he always fussed about crazy things like cleaning the insides of presses.

So I thought this was just his yearly tantrum.

He waved the hanky at Tim, who was still oblivious to all sound. "Well? ... Well, young man?"

This brought more growls from the dog.

"He can't hear you", I suggested tactfully.

My father coughed on some smoke. "He'd better!"

I nudged Tim.

He removed his earplugs obligingly.

And the Hoover's ears cocked too, ready to spring to his defence.

My father waved the hanky. "Look at this dirt!"

"Hmm ... Probably tobacco smoke", Tim muttered in his deep gravelly voice. Then he replaced his earplugs.

The dog settled back to snooze. But Tim had incensed my father, as did any reference to the evils of tobacco. He had now taken up battle position with his back to the Aga and was angrily emitting large mushrooms. "Take those mufflers out of your ears!"

This made the dog growl. I nudged Tim again.

He obeyed, giving me a look which meant the old man had finally "flipped", gone senile, which was his greatest fear for my father. My brother spoke a sort of *lingua franca*: things are cool, brill, brillo, neat, OK, AOK, ace, wow, or fab.

My father pointed his pipe stem at him. "I'm addressing you, sir!"

The Hoover was now all ears.

Tim shovelled in more muesli. "Me?"

"And don't speak with your mouth full!"

Tim chewed on.

"Well?" ranted my father. "Well."

The Hoover echoed him with barks.

"Well, *what*?"

Another yelp.

My father was now breathing heavily. "Enough of that puppery!"

Tim was an angry red now, but he reassured the Hoover, grabbing him back by his collar. "It's OK! Quiet! Look, what's up Doc?" He always called our father this.

"The windows are filthy!"

"So *what* if they're filthy?"

"So *when* are you going to clean them?" My father's voice was low and menacing.

Tim shrugged. "I had plans for the day, but I can scrap them."

"Good! You can do the bedroom windows too! Get the ladder out."

"Dad, we could hire a window cleaner," I suggested.

Then my father turned on me. "You're willing to pay for one, of course!"

I went back to my paper. "He might fall off the ladder."

My father's eyes narrowed into angry slits. "Stop interfering, Sally Ann!"

"I wasn't!"

"And don't answer back!"

This renewed shouting brought growls from the Hoover. But I was sick of being treated like some sort of kid. I really was. "I have a right to speak."

"Go to your room!"

I looked at the ceiling. The Hoover started barking, but Tim calmed him.

"Go to your room!" screamed my father.

When I ignored him, he stepped towards me.

At this my brother jumped up, towering threateningly over my father. For a second they were eyeball to eyeball. Then my aged parent raised his hand.

I jumped between them, receiving the blow intended for my brother.

The dog started barking again.

Clenching his fists, Tim started shadow-boxing. "Step right up and fall right down!"

This was a saying of Poopdeck Pappy, the Pride of the Pacific - Popeye's father. I pushed him away.

"I can take him, Sally! Step right up and fall ... !"

"Go away!" I shouted.

The dog yapped hysterically. "Say the word, Sal!"

"Just go!"

"OK!"

"And take the Hoover!"

"OK! OK! And he grabbed the dog, dragging it barking from the room and calling, "Cool it, Doc! OK?"

At least it was quieter. But my father's breathing sounded dangerous. "The pup! ... The pup!"

I was in tears. "Dad, he's not a pup."

"No! He's a cur!"

"I'll clean the windows. Tim wouldn't be safe on a ladder."

"A lazy cur!"

"Remember the time he fixed the tap?"

My father said nothing.

"The house took weeks to dry out. I'll do the kitchen windows this evening. And we'll get someone for upstairs."

My father still said nothing. He just sat down and moodily tried to get his pipe going. So I went to get dressed for work.

"Come back!"

"Dad, I'll be late for work."

He laughed shortly. "You wouldn't know the meaning of the word! Neither of you would!"

I kept cool. "That's hardly fair."

"You must be the most highly qualified waitress in Dublin."

"I'm working in the gallery now."

"You're still no better than a servant. Why can't you use your degree? I've brought up a couple of layabouts! Freaks!"

"Freaks?"

"Look at your brother's hair."

I sighed inwardly.

"I've made an appointment with his Dean of Studies. He can make him cut it!"

I'd had enough.

"Or he's going back to Rockwell."

This was a religious jail my brother had run away from. He was now a day boy in Blackrock. "Dad, Tim's OK."

He pointed his pipe stem at me. "That dog's going out of the house!"

I just looked at him.

"Is he on drugs?" My father perused my face.

"Of course not!"

"What does he do in his room all day?"

"He draws cartoons."

My father laughed shortly. "He's insane! It's both inherited and induced. You realise your great uncle died in an asylum?"

As long as I can remember this was our father's comment on any aberrant behaviour. He seemed to expect us both to explode with madness.

"Dad, Tim's very talented."

He bit his pipe. "Hmm, cartoons will take you a long way!"

I'd really had enough. "He could be a millionaire ..."

"Good! Then it won't be my task to feed him."

"You shouldn't hit him."

"I should've done it years ago!"

"Well, it's too late now."

Of course, it was OK to hit a woman. But without a word of apology, my usually mild-mannered father pocketed his pipe and slammed out of the kitchen to the surgery at the front of our large and shabby house.

I thought once Christmas was over he'd lapse back into his usual indifference. The windows were forgotten about OK. But now he quarrelled at every opportunity. He gave away my brand new guitar for a jumble sale, saying he thought it was junk. He nagged Tim non-stop and kept threatening to have the Hoover put down. He even put an ad in the paper, offering to give him away. Some people came, but luckily the dog got hysterics and they fled in horror. It was crazy. Having ignored us all his life, our father was now coming the heavy.

I'd always been a referee between Tim and him. I felt responsible for my brother. After all, I had almost brought him up. In school, when he was little, I'd always be sent for, to help him find his football boots. He could never find anything. But the other boys would always be coming back in by the time he was ready. Maybe I was too impatient. Once I hit him. If he had problems, it was probably my fault. He did spend all his time in his room now. But who would blame him for wanting to avoid my father? Luckily he had school to save him. My gallery job had come just in time for our father's personality change. But I didn't have to be there till eleven and was driven crazy with his morning nagging, about me being "little better than a servant" when he'd paid out "good money" for a BA. Blah, blah, blah.

Since college, I'd worked in a succession of restaurants. For heaven's sake, there were no jobs. And my father had all these middle-class notions about his daughter 'serving' people. But didn't a doctor serve people too? I mean, look down throats. Into ears. Or worse. To avoid rows, I refrained from pointing this out. But there was no pleasing him. I had become his butt. Oh, he had the decency not to mention my criminal record for being caught in Colm's house. I have to admit he was good about that, bailing me out with the line he'd quoted to me in all the griefs of childhood, "I am the Duchess of Malfi, still". Then, he'd insisted I stay in college. But now for no reason I was a bad example to my brother. Did he deserve a child like me? Hadn't he worked like a slave to bring us up alone? Was his waiting room ever empty?

True, even if he forgot to send out bills, my father worked hard. He was known all over Dublin as a soft touch. Every malingerer in search of a cert ended up in our waiting room. He did house calls every morning and often on Saturday and Sunday. He got up at night for people. And in his spare time he'd even written a history of Dun Laoghaire. So we were probably a great disappointment to him. After all, neither of us read much. Or could take over his practice.

But I couldn't help being unscientific. And Tim was artistic. Apart from not getting into Medicine, he'd faint at the sight of a thermometer.

My father's latest kick was nursing. We were both to train in one of the big English hospitals. So we'd be able to get pensionable jobs, and, unlike him, be able to retire. I was to pave the way for Tim, who could follow after his Leaving and be a psychiatric nurse. Maybe some day he could manage a hospital for the disturbed. It was daft, considering I was a terrible hypochondriac. I'd only to talk to a patient on the phone, or read one of the medical journals which avalanched through the letter box to imagine symptoms. Last year alone I'd had rheumatoid arthritis, mitral valve prolapse, cancer of the shin bone and the latest, gum cancer.

I got a gum boil at which the dentist had just shaken his head. He wouldn't give me a diagnosis. And when I'd asked my father if it was cancer, he'd yelled at me. Yelled, reminding me of our mad great uncle. That's another oddity about doctors: they're kind to the whole world, but impatient with their own. I said once that now they were discovering that many illnesses were psychological. "They've always known that," he retorted, "'physician' means healer of the soul." He told me then that many of his patients had nothing wrong with them. And that Time cured most things. I couldn't agree with this. I mean, *he* was a case in point.

So the fear about my gum took root. On top of this, things were going badly with my job.

It was only temporary, a fill-in for my American friend, Kathy who had gone home for six months. But at least it got me out of the house and away from my father. And I was earning twenty pounds a week on top of the dole. So I'd never been richer in my life. And, although the gallery owner, Kingsley Kelly, was difficult, and had only reluctantly agreed to me, I felt it was OK now. The bus ride in from Dun Laoghaire was great. And I loved the walk up O'Connell Street to the gallery in North Great George's Street.

The gallery occupied the ground floor of one of the big Georgian houses in that seedy street. The high ceilings and tall windows were wonderful for light. Also it had dividing doors between the huge front rooms. And the whole street had a sort of faded charm, an old world elegance, that was part of our history. Belvedere College was at the top. And Mahaffy, the famous Trinity College preservationist, had once lived there. As had John Dillon, the patriot and friend of Parnell. As I mentioned, the street had now fallen on hard times, but there was a fight by the Georgian Society to save it. In which my employer Kingsley Kelly was very involved. He had completely done up his house and treated it for damp and all that.

Kingsley was an Irish art critic who had been to school in England. So he was rather theatrical with a pale floppy face and mournful, doggy, blue eyes. He was also puffy and bald with two wings of greying hair. He had a girlfriend called Anabel who lived with him in an upstairs flat. She was darkly glamorous and complemented Kingsley's velvet evening jackets, the gallery's thick pile carpets and hushed air of money. Their aim was to make Dublin, through the gallery, the mecca of the western avant-garde art world - sort of a rival to Edinburgh. (We'd even shown a woman who painted in menstrual blood.) And my job was generally to assist: make coffee, hoover, send out invitations, and in between just sit there, looking nice.

One morning soon after the row with my father, I came in late. I think I missed a bus or something, but, as I was never late, I didn't worry. I just said good morning cheerfully.

Kingsley had opened up the gallery and was frowning at the bundle of half-done invitations on my desk. As usual, he wore a striped grandfather shirt and white button-on collar and tie. He didn't return my greeting.

I sat down. "Sorry I'm late."

He still frowned, wrinkling his bald patch. He held up one invitation and raised his eyebrows at me. "Could you possibly write a little more legibly, Sally Ann?"

I felt myself redden. "Eh - yes. I suppose I can. Can't you read it?"

He pursed his lips, looking ruefully down at me. "It's legible all right. It just doesn't have any *tone*."

"*Tone*?"

He looked mournful. "Kathy had such a beautiful Italic script."

I was completely flustered. "She had a special pen. An Osmiroid. I could get one."

He flung down the invitation. "Do that! And then address the envelopes again. Remember, these are very important people, Sally Ann. *Very* important people."

"Will I get the pen now?"

He glided to the door. "Yes! Take it out of petty cash." Then he paused, turning to stare at my legs. "And Sally Ann ..."

"Yes?" I was walking towards him.

He was still staring at my legs. "Could you wear something a little longer?"

I stopped in my tracks. "Eh - yes. I - I have a midi skirt."

He raised his eyebrows again. "That sounds lovely. Remember, the gallery has a certain tone!"

I nodded.

"A tone!" he whispered, forcing a smile at me.

I tried to hide my embarrassment. "Do you need anything else?"

He shook his head and glided on.

I went to Easons for the pen.

I was fed up. I really was. At twenty-three, I felt about ten. Also I'd thought my green suede mini skirt and black top and tights were *it*. Just *it*. God, it was the mid 70s. His girlfriend Anabel wore minis. So why did he pick on me? And when I'd visited Kathy in the gallery she always wore denim jeans and a man's tweed jacket.

But I did the invitations again. Later I studied the list of VIPs. It included a number of politicians and business people. I suppose they were important. And it was important to make a good impression, but it caused me a lot of extra work. The opening was in two weeks, so they had to be sent out quickly - that night, in fact. The gallery had just had a real coup in its next show: Jan Wessell, the internationally famous Dutch conceptual artist, had agreed to an exhibition of his sculpture.

They weren't the usual statues, but post-object. I mean, it was the *idea* more than anything else. Jan Wessell had made his reputation in New York by exhibiting a battered old van with a wild dog inside - to represent the two poles of civilisation. Another time he'd lain in a coffin with candles around him. I suppose this was to make people think of death and that. I don't know, I was just glad we weren't doing anything like that. Our exhibition was to be inanimate - a collection of stones which the artist had gathered around Wicklow. The man was an absolute genius. He had suffered appallingly in the war from the Germans, and recently he'd come to live here to avail of Haughey's new tax deal for artists. The show would be great for the gallery, and greater still: the artist himself was to open it.

The preparations for the exhibition were endless: wine, food, more invitations for the press, radio and TV.

But the day came at last.

I wore a new blouse with by midi. Also I invited my father - so he'd see I wasn't a servant and to impress him with my job. He accepted, hiring a locum for his surgery and buying a new white shirt and striped tie. He arrived early, so I took his shabby camel coat and got him a glass of wine from the flitting waiter. Then showed him into the gallery.

He looked at the bare walls, then at a line of stones down the centre of the room. "I thought it was a sculpture exhibition, Sally Ann."

"It is", I whispered.

"But they're stones!" he shouted.

I nudged him. "Shh! I know!"

He sipped his drink, his eyes amused. "Why didn't you tell me? I could've brought some."

"It wouldn't be the same."

He sipped more wine. "And why not?"

"They wouldn't be Wessell's."

My father sipped again. "No, they'd be stones."

"*Please*, Dad!"

He smiled at me, the first time since Christmas. "All right! I promise not to say another word."

And he drifted off into the crowd.

I watched him stop at another pile. Then went to the door to give out programmes.

The gallery was really filling up. The VIPs were a motley crew. Despite Kingsley's decorum about clothes, only one or two were in evening dress. The rest wore jeans and ordinary clothes. All immediately made for the drinks being served by a waiter behind a table at one end of the gallery.

Jan Wessell came in with a harem of women. He was a bronzed weasely man dressed in the usual denims and bomber jacket with a white aran sweater inside. Also he wore an aran tam o'shanter - he had a thing about oiled wool. And instead of a scarf, he wore a snake.

I had heard he did this, but didn't expect it now.

I recoiled in horror, and it brought a gasp from the crowd.

People sort of backed away from him.

Kingsley and Anabel came hurrying over.

"Sally Ann!" Anabel, ravishing in strapless black, blinked her furry lashes at me. "Could you take Mr Wessell's things?" She had a shrill English accent.

"His things?"

Kingsley wore his black velvet jacket and red cummerbund. "Offer to take the - eh - snake, Sally Ann."

Then Jan Wessell unwrapped his scarf.

I just gaped at the slimy thing, its tongue darting viciously.

But luckily he rescued me. "A chair, my cheeld. A chair vor Cocoa."

"A chair? Of course!" And I got one from behind my desk.

"Ye can leave it dere. Goot!" The snake sort of poured itself revoltingly into the chair. He patted it. "Cocoa, stay dere!"

"What an original statement a snake makes," Anabel fawned over the famous artist.

"Ah, no. Cocoa ees chusst a pet." Jan Wessell smiled benignly.

"Wine for Mr Wessell!" Kingsley snapped at me.

"Red or white?" I enquired politely.

He asked for red, and I got a glass from the waiter.

Then, as Kingsley and Anabel chatted to the artist, I went to see if my father was all right for wine.

"I'll just coast on my pipe, my dear." He looked in the direction of Jan Wessell, chuckling. "Is that your famous artist?"

I shuddered. "Did you see the snake?"

This transported my father into more chuckles. And at that moment I had one of those epiphanies Joyce was always writing about. I realised my father was giddy with happiness because I'd asked him here. Had we both shut him out? Thinking he wouldn't be interested in our lives? If he didn't talk to us, we didn't talk to him. A relationship takes two. But how do you change things?

"Ah, good evening Dr Fitzpatrick." Kingsley glided over. "I'm delighted you could come." Then, turning to me, "Sally Ann, Jan requested a blackboard. Where is it?"

"Did he?" It was the first I'd heard.

"Why didn't you get it?"

"Oh - sorry!"

Kingsley had an angry red blotch on his pale cheeks. "I pay you to see to these things!"

"You can't trust staff, dear", Anabel shrieked. "How many times have I told you!"

I looked at her nervously. She said stawff instead of staff.

Jan Wessell had never requested a blackboard, and I don't know why I didn't just tell Kingsley this. Say it right out. Aggressively. But instead I just stood there, apologising. Then I hit on a brilliant idea. "I can borrow one."

Kingsley raised his eyebrows. "At this time of night?"

"There's a convent next door."

"Well, try them!" And he stalked off.

A flustered young nun opened the huge convent door to me. She agreed to lend a blackboard so long as I guaranteed to have it back before the morning. Together we went down to the basement for it. Then, as it had an easel, she helped me carry it to the street and next door to our gallery. I asked her to stay and have a glass of wine, but she wouldn't.

We set it up at one end of the double room in front of a circle of chairs on which people were already sitting. Then Kingsley gave a short introduction. And Jan Wessell began his lecture.

He looked even smaller now, swamped by his white aran sweater and still wearing his tam. "People always ax mee to expleen my work. Vell, in dis exheebition of de stones, I breeng de nature into de gallery. Und by breenging nature into de gallery, to breeng it to you. De nature dat ees all around you in dees country ees var more beauteous dan anyting you veel ever see in de gallery. Und so, de nature ov my work ees vot I call de social sculpture."

My father, who stood with me at the back of the crowd, gave me a knowing look. But everyone else listened politely as the artist took a piece of chalk and turned to the blackboard.

He drew two circles, one large and one small. "Now in dis small circle we 'ave de eenspiration." He drew arrows to the large circle. "Und in dis beeg circle we 'ave de people." Then he drew another arrow from the people circle to the inspiration circle. "Art ees de flow from one to de oder." Then he drew a lot of wavy lines between the two arrows. "See de flow from one to de oder. Und so, vat am I saying?" He looked expectantly at the crowd. "Vat am I saying here?"

No one said anything.

"Pleese, vat am I saying?"

I looked at my father.

He was clenching his pipe between his teeth, staring in the direction of the snake.

It was gone from the chair!

And slithering across the floor.

"God", I muttered, frozen.

My father pursed his lips in amusement.

Kingsley was across the room looking at Jan Wessell with a kind of rapture.

No one else had noticed.

"Vat am I saying here now?" Jan Wessell tried to get some reaction from his audience.

But still no one spoke.

Then Kingsley raised his hand. "You're suggesting that art is a democratic activity."

Then Anabel said, "Anyone can become an artist."

"Ah yes!" Jan Wessell's face lit up, and he held up his arms like the Pope. "Dat ees it! You are all de arteests! An arteest cannot hog de inspiration, zo to zay."

The snake had now disappeared under the circle of chairs. I signalled desperately to Kingsley, but he was still gazing adoringly at Jan Wessell.

Suddenly a woman screamed.

There was a mad rush and scraping of chairs.

I just stood there, frozen.

Kingsley came fussily over to me. "What is it?"

"The snake's escaped", I gasped.

He put his hands to his head in desperation. "Well, do something! Don't just stand there!"

I looked under the chairs.

Then Jan Wessell's voice came over the crowd. "Now vat ees all dis fuss? Pleese keep de seats. Cocoa veel harm no one."

By now everyone was in the front room.

And the snake had coiled calmly in one of the vacated chairs.

"Do something, Sally Ann!" Kingsley hissed.

I gaped at the monster.

"Eh - Mr Wessell," I shouted over, "Can we put Cocoa in the loo?"

He came to my rescue. "Cocoa in de loo? Vat are you saying? Cocoa veel be vith mee." And he came over, picked up the wriggling monster and threw it nonchalantly around his neck. "Eet's all right now. Come back now! Come back!" And he made signals like a traffic guard.

Reluctantly the people dribbled back into the rows of chairs. And Jan Wessell finished his lecture.

Afterwards Kingsley tried to get the audience to ask questions, but they were too thoroughly dampened by the sight of the snake - although the party livened up when drink was served again. It was meant to be over by seven, but at eight was still in full swing. So Kingsley ordered the waiters to collect the glasses and serve no more drink. This worked, and people began to go in dribs and drabs. Then, as arranged, Kingsley and Anabel took Jan Wessell and his party to dinner at the Lord Edward, leaving me to get rid of the rest of the people and tidy up.

"See, you're a servant!" my father grumped. He had put on his coat and scarf and was helping me gather the remaining glasses and ash trays.

I sighed wearily. In his worn camel coat, he looked like a giant teddy bear.

"And as for that snake charmer!"

I was tipping ashtrays into a black plastic bag. "Dad, he's a world famous artist!"

"Who says so? Here, let me help." And he held open the bag. "Just tell me who says he's an artist."

"Qualified people."

"Kingsley Kelly, I suppose?" My father laughed shortly. "He's really qualified."

"He's a Renaissance man. And an art critic for the *Sunday* ..."

"He's a charlatan. Everyone's an artist - what rubbish! It's typical of your generation to expect fame without work."

"Dad, please! ... Just -"

"Why didn't he bring you to dinner too?"

"Because I'm ..."

"A servant!"

"An employee! You don't have to bring your employees to dinner." I was now running the carpet sweeper over the thick carpets, getting really irritated with my father. What had persuaded me to invite him here? He never did anything but grumble.

He went to wait for me in the hall, saying, "I'll take you to dinner."

"You can't afford it."

"Yes, I can. Get your coat, we'll go to the Lord Edward."

He stood there, smiling at his brilliant idea. Suddenly my irritation with him went. He was right about the way Kingsley treated me. I just wouldn't admit it. "Well, OK ... but we're not going there."

"Do as you're told for once!"

"Somewhere else, Dad. Please!"

He thought for a minute. "The Gresham then. Hurry and get your coat."

"I have to give back the blackboard first."

I rubbed off Jan Wessell's scribbles, totally ignoring my father's accompanying sighings and mutterings of "Nonsense ... Utter nonsense." Then we hauled it together next door where the same young nun allowed us to leave it in the hall. She said the pupils would bring it back to the classroom in the morning.

Then we walked down to the Gresham.

We got a table without any trouble. My father has a great sense of occasion. I suppose it's his aura, or something to do with being a doctor, but waiters always flock to him. He would've made a good courtier in olden times, he was always so deferential to women. He even held my chair.

As we studied the menu, I watched him across the table. He'd had his only suit pressed and with the new shirt and tie looked quite distinguished. Why hadn't he ever married again? Surely Dublin was full of single women and widows. Life must've been lonely for him, especially as he had no relationship with us. Why was that? He had no trouble talking to the rest of the world.

He put down his menu. "What're you having?"

I studied the pastas. "Spaghetti."

"Oh, have a steak or something."

He looked at me over his reading glasses. "The food here used to be good!"

"No, I like spaghetti." I never knew what to have, so always had the cheapest.

He was looking sadly around the room. "Things never stay the same."

"Did you come here with Mum?" I suddenly blurted, breaking all our family's unwritten code of not talking about my mother.

He dived back into the menu. "Have the roast beef."

This was typical of him. Just typical.

"I'd prefer the spaghetti, Dad. And salad to start."

"All right ..." He was now looking at the wine menu. "And I think ... a Beaujolais."

The waiter took our order, and we sat in our usual Trappist silence. So I studied the only other couple in the room. My father took out his pipe and filled it. "Do you mind if I smoke, my dear?"

"Of course not."

"Well, you know your brother."

I smiled. "He's not here."

"By the way, I'm sorry about your guitar, my dear."

I'd never known him to apologise. "That's OK. You didn't know."

"I should've asked."

"It wasn't your fault. Anyway, I'm not very musical. The teacher gave up on me."

71

He put his pipe on the table and rummaged in his pocket. Then he took out a small package and handed it to me. "I nearly forgot. I got you this, my dear."

I peered at the package. "What is it?"

"A small act of reparation."

What was he talking about?

"Open it, my dear."

It was a gold watch.

"Weir's will change it if ..."

"God, it's gorgeous! I wouldn't change it! Thanks Dad." I looked at him, puzzled.

"I'm - sorry for that blow, my dear."

I giggled - I do this in all life's serious moments. "You shouldn't have ..."

"I certainly should! It was the act of a cad."

I put on the watch. It had Roman numerals and a brown crocodile strap. He'd obviously paid a fortune for it. "It's beautiful."

The waiter came with the wine. My father tasted it, nodding approval. "That's nice and dry."

The waiter poured mine.

"It is dry," I agreed, sipping some. Actually all wine tasted more or less the same to me. I didn't care, so long as it was alcoholic.

My father lit his pipe. When he'd got it going, he looked slowly around the room again. "They've certainly changed this place. There used to be a piano over there ... You asked about your mother. I did bring her here." He looked right at me. "We came here the night of our engagement."

Now it was my turn to be speechless.

My father went on in a low deadpan voice. "We met in December and got married in January. Your mother kept on her teaching at first - but then she got pregnant with you. You were born the next winter. We didn't go out much after that - except for a Sunday walk. I used to carry you on my back. Once I carried you to the top of the Sugar Loaf."

"I remember."

"You couldn't."

"I do."

"You couldn't." He smiled maddeningly. "They were - very happy years. Of course, I shouldn't have married. I was too old.

"Dad, that's ridiculous!"

He knocked out his pipe. "Your brother was right to call me a randy old goat."

I sighed. "That's only because you gave him those condoms."

It was my father's greatest fear that one of us would make him a grandfather. So, although a faithful Catholic, to prevent that dread event he'd supplied us both with contraceptives: condoms for Tim and spermicidal jelly for me. At one stage he even suggested Tim have a vasectomy. It was mad. Tim had no girlfriend. And I could hardly drown with no water. I had read that frigidity comes from an unresolved relationship with your father. But I didn't know how to overcome this.

"No, I shouldn't have married", my father said, brooding. "Look at you."

"What's wrong with me?"

He sighed. "I wanted this to be a pleasant evening, Sally Ann."

For courage, I downed my wine. "Just tell me what's wrong with me."

He fell into silence, then said sadly. "You were very clever as a young child."

I didn't answer. I knew what was coming: how I'd failed him by not being a doctor.

The waiter brought my salad and my father's soup.

"You wanted one of us to do Medicine."

He tucked his napkin into the top of his waistcoat. "No, it's not that. I realise that Medicine's not your bent. You're just too good for that ruffian, Kingsley Kelly and his ridiculous gallery."

"It's just a start."

"To what?"

"To - some sort of career in the arts."

"Hmm ... well, I always thought your paintings very nice."

I just looked at him. Why had he never said?

"I hoped you might do something in that line." He sighed heavily. "It's different for Tim."

"Why?"

"A woman will only have to support herself."

"Dad, Tim will be OK."

My father shook his head. "I can see the writing on the wall."

"What writing?"

"It'll be my task to feed his family - in my dotage."

I said nothing. There was no point in arguing. Or reminding my father that Tim didn't seem interested in girls. Never mind marrying.

"Of course, I blame myself entirely", he went on.

"For what?"

"For my children."

I sighed. "Oh, Dad, you're not Jesus Christ."

"Please don't blaspheme!"

"Sorry. I only meant you're not responsible for the sins of the world. Tim, me, my guitar."

"Hmm! ..."

He looked somewhat appeased. Between courses, we lapsed into another silence. I desperately wanted him to talk more about my mother. So I sat there, gauging the right moment to ask again about her. You had to pick your moment with my father.

When we had started our main course, I tried again. "It must've been awful for you - when mum died."

He gave me his panic-stricken look and finished chewing some food. "It was - a great loss to me ..."

"Me, too."

"I know, my dear."

"I suppose boarding school was ..."

"It was the best solution at the time." He put down his knife and fork and looked worriedly at me.

"I know."

"I thought you should be with women. Was it that bad?"

I shrugged. "It was OK - you did your best."

I knew talk of the past was upsetting him, so I changed the subject. But the rarity of any communication with him put me into a high gear and I couldn't sleep that night.

I tossed and turned, thinking of my mother's death. How could such a young woman die. Actually school was fine. My big hang-up is I forgot her so easily. It hurt me that I had so few memories. One was of me being in bed and waiting and waiting for her to come back from town in time to say goodnight. I didn't think she'd come, then she did. "I'm so glad you were awake and we could chat", she said. Then once I made her cry. God. I did something and she corrected me, so I kicked her. That haunted me - to have made her cry. Then I remember feeling odd at her funeral, sort of dislocated. I seemed to be watching myself. And I wondered how the people there could smile when I had lost my best friend. Of course, I was only eight and didn't understand they were greeting their friends outside the church. And it's normal to smile then, but I thought they were laughing. But I could feel nothing. Nothing.

And I knew nothing would be the same again. Overnight everything changed. My father became a recluse. Tim went to stay with an aunt. I was sent to boarding school where no one deferred to me - as the elder at home, I'd always considered myself grown up. But suddenly, like Gulliver I was surrounded by giants. The nuns and senior girls seemed huge. Even my father, though tall, was diminished by the vast high ceilinged convent parlour. At first I looked forward to his Sunday visits. But when he came, he never hugged me. He'd just sit on one of the hard chairs, telling me how much the school was costing. Then he'd quiz me about what I'd learnt that week. I'd have to recite "Frère Jacques" or "How They Brought the Good News from Aix to Ghent" - wherever the hell that is. Then I'd recite my tables, and he'd spend the rest of the visit firing questions at me: "Twelve twelves? ... Nine nines?"

It was crazy.

I remember thinking my father was so old. Why hadn't he died? And why wouldn't he go, so I could get back to the other girls. Having no mother was a sort of status symbol among them. I was different. I didn't want their pity, but I liked being different. Although I had no best friend, there were interesting things to do in school, even new words to learn - words like refectory, dormitory, recreation, infirmary.

How could I have forgotten my mother so easily? Why didn't I have more memories? I mostly remembered her being sick and having to tiptoe past her room. A woman at a counselling session in someone's house told me it was probably still stuck in my subconscious. That when I was eight I blocked the emotion. And that's true. Because I began sleepwalking in school. And wetting my pants. Which caused me terrible embarrassment. Terrible. Oh, one nun was kind about it, but one was a sadist. An absolute sadist. And I'd get weird fainting illnesses and spend weeks alone in the infirmary doing jigsaws. Or sums out of Holmes Comprehensive Arithmetic. After all, I was wasting money by being sick.

For my first year I was the good child. But then things changed. I made friends with a new girl, Brigid Dalton. We'd sit writing letters to each other at recreation. Once I wrote:

Dear Mrs Dalton,
    Brigid is very bold. She has broken ten chairs, twelve desks. And on top of this has spilled ink all over the good floor. Please take her home. We can't have her in this school much longer.
        Love,
        Reverend Mother.

Well, a novice confiscated it. And I was in disgrace. I got "Indifferent" at Weekly Notes and lost my Pink Ribbon - that was a satin sash you got for two "Very Goods" in succession. Losing the ribbon broke my heart. I didn't understand what I'd done wrong. And no one explained. The loss of my mother hit me then. She had always explained things. Now there was no one. The incident made me close up, I'm sure. It set me on the downward path. From then on I started looking for notice. I got into more and more trouble and was eventually expelled. I begged to go to a day school, but my father immediately sent me to another boarding school which took junior boys. And Tim joined me when he was five. In my second last year there, Mother Rita came back from America. Oh, I know I'm always talking about her, but she saved me. She talked to me. She told me her mother had died too, and she understood ... she understood.

So I started improving. I got my Leaving, and then went to college to study History, which was my way of trying to reclaim the past. But you couldn't change anything. My mother was part of History now, and I could hardly remember her face. So that night I fingered her wedding ring which my father had given me and I always wore, realising my father was right in his stoical pride. It was awful for him. And awful for my mother, having to leave us. But stoicism was all we had. And I would try and make a job of my life.

When I arrived at work the next morning, Kingsley had already opened up. Seeing me, he snapped, "Where's the blackboard, Sally Ann?"

I took off my coat.

"I brought it back."

"You what?"

"I rubbed if off and brought it back."

He sat down putting his head in his hands. "Oh, my God!"

"What's wrong?"

His eyes were dead and cold, and he spoke in a mechanical voice. "Put your coat back on."

"What?"

"Put your coat on and go." Then he stood up, shouting madly, "You're fired!"

I obeyed, terrified of him.

He stalked to the hall door and pulled it open. "And never come back to the Gallery!"

"Would you not tell me what I've done?" I asked on the outside steps.

"You've destroyed a work of art! A work of art!"

"The scribbling on the blackboard was *valuable*?"

He nodded, speechless.

"But it belonged to the nuns!" I argued. "I had to bring it back."

He just slammed the door in my face.

I went home in tears.

How could I have done it?

Of course, my father laughed to scorn the idea of the blackboard being art. But I knew otherwise. I even thought of writing to Jan Wessell and begging him to scribble on another blackboard. But I didn't know his address and was too depressed to even try.

Now I was back answering my father's phone, and listening to his patients' symptoms. So my own returned. The lump in my gum had spread to my neck, and I was sure it was Hodgkins' Disease. But, as always, my father dismissed me with a callous joke about being dead in six months. And a reminder of our mad great uncle.

His humour didn't help. It just depressed me more and more, plunging me into the certain knowledge of death. Once, over lunch in Mooney's of Abbey Street, I confided my fears to my friend Denis.

He was Adonis-like in his blond good looks, but married.

He peered at my neck, feeling it. "It's there all right. What does your old man say?"

I shrugged. "That I have six months."

Denis stared at me. Then he put his arm around my shoulder. "That's no help, Sally Ann."

Suddenly my abysmal failure at everything brought tears to my eyes.

"My father doesn't care at all. He just picks rows."

Denis gave me a squeeze. "I care, Sally. I do. My God - I'd really miss you if ... You're *sure*?" He pulled back, looking intently at me, then saying bossily, "Well, you can't just sit at home. That's the worst thing for your condition." He frowned for a second. "I always thought you'd make a good journalist."

I wiped my eyes on my sleeve. "Did you?"

"Yes. You wrote articles for Colm Connolly's *Irish Student*. Remember?"

"Oh, they weren't very good." I had only done them to impress Colm, but I didn't say that. Denis was a real writer who had published short stories in *St Stephen's* and *The Dublin Magazine*, and was now working on a novel. "I can't write."

"If you can speak, you can write. Will you have another Smithwicks?"

I nodded, and he went to the bar.

Coming back with two more pints, he said, "You know, Sally Ann, I can arrange some work for you. Seamus Daly, the new editor of *The Catholic Trumpet* is looking for an arts assistant."

I sipped my pint. "What'd I have to do?"

"Some art and drama criticism. The odd book review."

"Thanks, but I couldn't."

"Of course you could!"

"But I've never done anything in the line of acting or plays. How could I criticise others?"

"It's easy. If in doubt, attack!"

"Oh, Denis!"

He waved me into silence. "Name any Dublin critic."

"Well ... Kingsley Kelly."

"Has he done anything? Had an exhibition?"

I shook my head. "I don't think so. He knows a lot though."

"Well, go through all the papers. I'll bet you'll never find a critic who's also an artist. The two callings are different, Sally Ann."

So I agreed to go for an interview the next day.

*The Catholic Trumpet* was a right-wing weekly which was under a new left-wing editor. The office was at the bottom of Gardiner Street, on the top floor of a gaunt Georgian house. A secretary in the outer office announced me, and I went into a back room. Seamus Daly was there, typing madly. He was a heavy man with rolled shirt sleeves, a red face and thick grey hair. He nodded at me without stopping typing. "Take a seat, I'll be with you in a minute."

I sat down, looking around the untidy and cluttered room. There was a smell of sweat and cigarettes. It looked like a poor paper, but it was a start. Maybe one day I could transfer to one of the bigger dailies. Of course, I'd have to join the NUJ.

"So, you're Denis's friend?" The editor swung round, facing me glumly over his desk.

I nodded. "We were in college together."

I expected him to interview me and had brought clippings from my student efforts. But Seamus Daly didn't want to see them. To my surprise, he just rooted in a pile of letters on his desk. "Let me see ... There must be something here for you." Then he handed me a card across the desk. "Write me five hundred words on that."

It was an invitation to a Paul Henry opening at Trinity. "When do you want it?"

"Wednesday's copy day. Can you have it before noon?"

I said yes and he went back to his typing.

That was all. I'd got the job. And was walking on air.

The opening was a grand affair. In my new blouse and midi, I went along to the New Library at Trinity. The party was already in full swing so I lingered at the door. But I was now a critic and as good as Kingsley Kelly, so why be shy? I went in, but guess who was the first person I saw?

Kingsley.

He was standing near the entrance with Anabel.

I fled.

The next day I viewed the exhibition privately. And I spent a couple of days slaving over the review. It appeared in the next week's *Trumpet* under the subheading,

## COLOUR BLIND

The Paul Henry Exhibition is being held at Trinity College Dublin and then moving to the Ulster Museum, Belfast, where it can be seen until January 12th.

Clearly no Irish artist could be so well known to the Irish in reproduction as Paul Henry. The blue mountains and lakes of the West, the romantic cottages, the Rousseau-like peasants working in the fields are all familiar to us. To be honest, we are sick looking at them. The muddy blue Paul Henry used is not even an accurate depiction of the West. It is interesting to note that it is a well-established fact that he was red-green colour blind. Can a colour blind person be an artist at all? He painted mostly at dawn and during the hours before sunset, but his work does not even reflect the light effects of these times of day which can often be very unusual. His colours are like mud on the whole.

In the catalogue, George Dawson states that he was much influenced by Van Gogh. Certainly his figures resemble Whistler's in their stillness, but his work lacks the emotion with which Van Gogh used paint and colour so that his landscape took on movement. Is there any real comparison? I think not. One is an artist of world class, the other a dauber.

Van Gogh's Cypress Trees flare up into the sky like black flames, whereas there is no sign of any movement in Paul Henry's work. The clouds are like slabs of concrete; here one thinks of other landscape painters like Constable where the clouds sweep across the sky. The figures in such paintings as The Potato Diggers are also caught in a static position; his fishermen are eternally looking out to sea, and it is easy to make the comparison with the far superior figures of Jack Yeats. Paul Henry presents us with an image of reality which is stupidly romantic, he fails to portray the hard life of rural Ireland, which some of his peasants must have lived, the reality of hunger and emigration. He is a painter of visual perception in the nineteenth century tradition who fails to look beyond his subjects and find the essence or meaning of reality. Whose idea was it to mount this exhibition? Haven't we had enough of Paul Henry and his cottage art?

I was so proud of myself. I thought it was pretty good. But I didn't want to boast to my father about my new job. So I left the paper, lying casually on the hall table.

And, of course, he saw it.

"Who bought this fascist rag?" He flicked through it, coming into the kitchen.

I was cooking the supper. "The *Trumpet* has a new editor now, Dad."

"It's a fascist rag, and that's all it'll ever be!"

"Dad, you're living in the past. It's not fascist. Besides, I'm writing for it now."

He gaped at me. "You're *what*?"

"I'm writing for it. I have an article in that issue."

He searched through it. "Where?"

"On the Arts Page ... There. 'Colour Blind'."

I waited in a sort of nervous pride while he read it quickly.

"Well," he said finally in an injured voice, "I'm surprised at you, Sally Ann."

"Oh ..." I still expected he'd be pleased.

"You've become a Philistine."

"A Philistine?"

"Yes, I never thought you'd descend to criticising an artist like Paul Henry!" He flung the paper on the kitchen table in disgust. "And it's ungrammatical. In the second last paragraph you have semicolons where you should have full stops."

He slammed out of the kitchen to his surgery.

I reread my article. Semicolons instead of full stops? Why couldn't that be my style? And a Philistine? Why should I like Paul Henry? He was old hat. My father was too much, he really was. How could I ever succeed with him on my back? How?

I ignored him, continuing with my career as a Philistine. I did weekly articles on all sorts of topics: art shows, plays, books. I reviewed an O'Casey revival, slamming it. Hadn't we had enough of Dublin tenements? Why couldn't they put on *Who's Afraid of Virginia Woolf?* The editor never spoke to me. Or commented on what I wrote, good or bad. So I assumed it must be OK. Denis was my only critic. We met for the odd drink, during which he always enquired about my health. He also said I was doing well but should get more "chat" into my stuff. So I tried this in my next book review: *Da*, a published play by Hugh Leonard. It was a boring flop, I wrote, with a cold central character. And I wouldn't risk the hazards of the bus strike by going to see it - even if anyone were ever foolish enough to produce it. Then I added some "chat" about meeting a Jehovah Witness, hitching to see *Black Man's Country* by Des Forristal the previous week. Leonard wasn't worth a journey, I ended, and hopefully he would not bore us again, but stay buried between the boards of a book in some forgotten library, etc etc etc.

I was thrilled with myself. I was no wishy-washy critic.

Imagine my surprise when my father yelled at me after Mass the next Sunday. "Sally Ann! Will you come down here, please!"

I struggled out of bed.

My father was standing fuming in the hall. He waved the paper in my face. "I bought this outside the church. I've never read such drivel. I don't know how you ever got a degree!"

"What's wrong with it?"

He glared at me. "Come into my surgery."

I went, thinking him a maniac.

He sat at his desk, leaving me standing. "First, let me say this: if you *ever* do anything as good as Hugh Leonard, I'll be the proudest father in the world!"

"Dad ..."

"But in the meantime, I won't stand by and let him be abused by the likes of you."

"But ..."

"Just hear me out! What right have you to criticise others?"

I blushed. "I don't know."

"Have you ever written a play?"

I shook my head. "I've a right to my opinion."

"An uninformed opinion!"

I had never seen my father so angry.

"And what is the relevance of this bit: '... which I did last week when I saw Desmond Forristal's play, *Black Man's Country* ... ' Did you give that a bad review too?"

"No. It was OK. Fair."

He put his head in his hands. "Fair! *Who* are you to say? And just what's the relevance of your argument with a Jehovah Witness here?"

I felt utterly crushed. "I was told it needed chat."

"Who told you that?"

"Denis."

"A boyfriend?"

"No, a friend. You don't know him. He's married."

"You're not ... ?"

"No! Dad, he's a *friend*!"

"Well, if you insist on being a Philistine, you can at least be grammatical." My father took a pen from his inside pocket and, as I stood there, went through my article word for word, saying at last, "Now in future show me what you write."

But he needn't have worried because the next time I went in to the *Trumpet*, Seamus Daly wanted to see me.

"Take a seat", he said, as I came into his untidy, reeking office. He looked mournfully at me over his cluttered desk. "How are you feeling?"

I sat down. "Fine."

He shuffled some papers. "Look, you should probably be taking it easy."

"Taking it easy?"

"Well ..." He looked at me, then quickly averted his eyes. "Your condition ..."

"My condition?" Did he think I was pregnant? "I've never felt better in my life."

He looked puzzled. "But ... don't you have Hodgkins' Disease?"

"Hodgkins' Disease ..." I felt my neck, the truth suddenly dawning - Denis had believed my hypochondriacal fears. When I had forgotten them.

"Denis said you only had a few months to live."

I bit my nail. "Oh. Well - eh - it seems to have cleared up."

He rubbed his face in embarrassment. "You're work is - ah - fine. It's just that I want to employ someone more general. Someone full-time."

"Wouldn't you give me a chance?"

He shook his head. "I'm afraid it's not in my hands, love. I thought you'd be dead by now."

So I was fired again.

I didn't tell my father. I wouldn't give him the satisfaction.

I applied for a job as a hostess with Aer Lingus, but failed the interview for wearing Wellingtons. For God's sake, it was lashing rain. And I didn't realise it was the *real* interview. I'd been sent a cart to "call" to the Shelbourne Hotel. But it was for real. The row of interviewers just looked at them and then at each other. One man asked my name. And a woman smiled, saying sarcastically that I'd worn sensible footwear anyway. Then smiling, they said I could go. So I went, without giving my spiel about my hobbies or where I went on last year's holidays.

Next I got a job in Murph's Restaurant in Baggot Street. But the pay was awful, and I clashed with the manageress who said I was too careful. So I was fired again.

When you're sacked as a waitress, it's time to come to a realisation about yourself. Maybe my father was right about me being qualified for nothing. I wish I could say that things have got better with him like they would in a book, but we've relapsed back to our former Trappist silence. Oh, my poor father's like the old woman who lived in the shoe. He has two too many children and doesn't know what to do. And we're too old for boarding school now.

# VI Alastair

Holidays are hell. How is it, the worst things happen when you're meant to be enjoying yourself? Maybe it's from too much hope. I mean, the gap between illusion and reality. I don't know. Anyway, I lost Alastair when we went to France together. Which was the exact opposite of what I'd planned. Although we'd split up, I'd asked to go, hoping to change his mind. So he took me to visit some friends, and then camping. You'd think staying with friends might be difficult, but no. That was OK. It was the camping that finished us.

Our last day was the end. I had to get back to my Dublin job, so was leaving the next morning. We'd driven through Normandy all day and were dead tired. I'd wanted to stop hours before, but he insisted on sightseeing till after dark. We'd seen everything in the area except the American cemetery: the Sherman tank at St Mère-Église surrounded by tulips. Omaha Beach with its German bunkers stinking of urine. It was too late for the Cemetery at Collville-sur-Mer - which I really regretted. And, of course, the camp-sites were all full up, so we ended up persuading a farmer to let us use his field. Bloody hell. Just when I needed a bath.

Alastair drove the van slowly over the bumps. "Let's go on to Bayeux in the morning and skip the American cemetery."

He had a lovely Edinburgh accent. It was a reasonable request and I could've agreed, but didn't.

He parked in a corner of the field. "I don't know what you see in graveyards."

I didn't either. I suppose I'd just read so much about the war. Also it was a way of asserting myself. One of the girls we'd visited was so bossy, I decided I'd handled everything the wrong way. But I didn't argue as he pulled a ragged aran jumper over old jeans and jumped out of the van. He was tall, dark and woolly-haired with thick hornrimmed glasses. Ordinary-looking, really. But that's the reason I liked him - besides, I wore glasses too. He ran to close the gate. He's careful about things like gates, which was another reason. I suppose opposites attract.

I was meant to be getting the meal started while he pitched the tent. But as he spread it out by the van's headlights, I lingered by the passenger door. Everything looked eerie in the moonlight. Sort of lonely, yet beautiful. The traffic from the nearby road was muffled, and the farm house hidden by a clump of trees. It could easily have been haunted. After all, blood had been spilt there for centuries: Norman, English, German, American, French. And ages ago Caesar and the endless tribes of Gaul - I'd spent years translating those wars. Absolutely years.

"Pass the pegs, Sally!"

I flashed the torch into the back of the van. Light fell on old jeans, rucksacks, the primus stove, but no sign of the pegs. Then it hit me. I'd left them in the loo at St Lo. I'd gone there at the last minute. The loo at St Lo was almost a tongue twister, but he'd be too mad to appreciate that. He always got unbearable when hungry. And he'd have a fit now.

"Hurry up, Sally!"

I don't know why, but I kept looking. "They're not here."

"What do ye mean?"

"Ils ne sont pas ici."

"Oh, shut up! Your French is awful!" He came over and, grabbing the torch, rooted impatiently in the van. "I've to do everything myself!"

Snob, I thought, a first in French didn't give him a monopoly on the language, just a superiority complex. Everyone in France bowed before his fluency. It was crazy to be jealous, but I was. The farmer hadn't even minded being disturbed. "Eh, bien! Bon Dieu! Bon appétit!" The Frogs were sickening about their language. I mean, the hours, absolutely endless hours, I'd spent in the Dublin *Alliance* were to no avail. The day before, I'd finally got up the courage to say, "Café au lait, s'il vous plait". But the smirking waiter had answered in perfect English. It was maddening.

Alastair was searching the front of the van. "Dammit! They aren't here!"

"I told you ..."

"You're awfully good at saying that!"

I grinned nervously. "Sorry."

"And don't be facetious!" He flashed under the seats. "I saw you holding them at St Lo. They must be here."

Wearily I shook my head. "I left them in the loo."

"You *what*?"

"I went at the last minute. I must've left them."

"Well, why didn't you say?"

"I told you."

"Don't say that!"

I giggled - I do this when I'm nervous. "Sorry!"

"It's not funny!"

I composed my face, studying the ground.

Irritably he pushed his glasses up on his nose. "You let me search like an idiot! Where're we going to sleep?"

"The van?"

"You have it! I'm sleeping in the tent!" He flashed the torch at the hedge behind him and then further along the field.

"An accident, n'est-ce pas?" I pleaded.

He didn't answer.

And I didn't blame him. It was my fault. I'm definitely very irritating. I suppose I'm facetious too.

Alastair pulled a branch out of the hedge. "I'll try and use twigs. You get the meal on! Lucky it's our last night!"

His words were like lead in my heart. What was so lucky about it? He was leaving me to the Paris train the next day. So there wasn't really time for the cemetery - not if I wanted to see one of the world's wonders. Although I wasn't pretending, I was miserable about going back to Ireland and secretly hoped he'd stop me. It was my Casablanca complex.

I'd thought the country of the Impressionists, of those vaulted country roads and Proust's Balbec would be a rubicon in our relationship. How could we *not* fall in love?

But he'd said nothing about the future.

Not even at the Quatorze Juillet dance we'd stumbled on, then danced stumblingly through.

Things were definitely not going well. I have to admit finding the campsites disappointing. The toilets were holes in the ground and they were usually crowded with Germans and Americans. We might as well have been in Bray on a bank holiday. In comparison, Bray was almost depopulated. It'd been my idea to stay in the one place and meet French people. But even they were mostly rude or in a hurry, like that damn waiter.

As usual, I burned myself lighting the primus. I hated camping. There was sunburn cream, but where? Ici le problème. Or was it *la* problème. Ice was best, I knew from my father, but there was definitely none of that. So I plunged my hand into the cooling grass. The daisies were curled in sleep. Lucky things, able to exist without all our clobber. I often think I'll come back as a flower in the next life. If you think about it, reincarnation makes much more sense. The Buddhists were right. I was thinking of becoming one. I mean, what could be more boring than eternal life?

"The meal won't cook itself!" He was dragging a branch past.

"I burnt my hand!"

"You're always doing that."

"Sorry!"

"Is it bad?"

"No."

The pain was easing up. While he pared the branch and cut it into twigs, I put two fish on the pan. The eyes stared eerily up at me. I'd bought them that day in a leafy market with all sorts of stalls and live chickens running about. I remember wondering whose task it'd be to kill the bird if we bought it. Not mine. At least the fish were obligingly dead. In Ireland they had the decency to cut off their heads, but the French probably eat them. They eat the oddest things: frogs, snails, brains, et al. Yet when I said this to Alastair, he'd called me provincial. I suppose I was.

He was hammering loudly now. "That smells good."

The tent was nearly staked out. He was so damn efficient, I couldn't help regretting my imminent departure. But since college, I was only for holidays. Not for real life. The Irish sea separated us, since he was teaching in England. When we first met, only Stephen's Green lay between us. It had been bliss to meet halfway for coffee in Bewley's, then a matinee in the Green cinema. I get lonely thinking of the Chinese meals we had: Peking duck and Lychees for dessert. He was at Trinity for an M Litt, while I struggled with History essays in UCD. It was all Bertrand Russell's fault for saying on TV that you couldn't understand the present without knowing the past. Now I was an expert on things like Lanfranc, the Avignon Papacy and the Defenestration of Prague. But I couldn't manage a simple relationship.

Alastair, on the other hand, thought History bunk. Pointless, like turning pebbles on a beach. The past didn't matter, he claimed. Even our bodies changed every seven years. He was brilliant, so maybe I had a BA in turning pebbles. I mean, Aristotle thought History inferior too. It related what happened, not what *might* happen. Coping with the difference was my problem.

Still, the past's all you have. Alastair said I was the clinging type, and he was right. My problem was accepting everything he said, being his mattress as well as his mistress. The holiday had changed nothing in that line. Except I was less nervous about sex. I was coping. I'd read Edna O'Brien, so I knew it was difficult for others too. Although most people I talked to *said* it was the greatest thing since sliced bread. But I still panicked. I couldn't let go. Maybe it was being Catholic. But, crazily, I think it upset me that he used condoms. Despite my father I wanted to get pregnant. To love one person. But everything was so mixed-up. And when I wasn't anxious, I was jealous of his life without me. But love isn't angry or jealous. Still, how did other people manage? You saw them in college. Cooing in the library or over lunch in the Country Shop. They did a line for years. Then got their degrees and got married. How did they do it? My friend Denis was happily married. I'd even tried to make Alastair jealous of him by talking about him nonstop, but it'd had no effect.

"It's working!" Alastair called.

The tent was yellow in the dusk. Although I pretended to hate it, I'd miss it so much. It was our only home. Maybe I'd back down and stay? To hell with my job. Except he didn't mind me going. no, I had to show independence.

Just then the farmer appeared at the gate, flashing a light. "Ca va?"

I just stood there.

He flashed the torch at me. "Ca va?"

What should I say? Bien? Merci?

Luckily, Alastair went over.

"Bon appétit! ... Bon appétit!" came through the silence.

I buttered two slices of bread and put them on plates with the fish. They looked bon appetising enough. A change from the tinned food we'd been eating. That's another thing Alastair always said, you need variety in food, just as you need variety in people. A person wouldn't dream of eating the same food all his life, so why live with the same person? It was sickening. Oh, I know he wanted freedom. Lots of women. But I'd hoped he'd change his mind. I mean, looking back, it was crazy. But I was scared of being twenty-five with no one lined up to marry me.

I peered into the darkness. "It's ready!"

Alastair had disappeared.

"It's ready!"

"I heard you!" came from the tent.

He came over and hunkered down beside me.

I passed his plate. "They're very big."

"They look yummy." He wolfed down a mouthful. Then immediately spat it out.

I stared at him. Then at his plate. "What's wrong?"

"You didn't clean them!"

"Clean them?"

"Yes, gut them."

I peered at my plate. "But fish don't have guts."

"Of course they do!"

"But they're not mammals." It was stupid of me. When I bought fish at home, they were ready to eat. So I thought this was always the case - if you hadn't actually caught them.

"I'm going to bed!" He got up and scraped his plate into the refuse sack in the van.

He didn't have to do that.

Oh, there was cheese and bread, but I wasn't offering him any. I picked at my fish, avoiding the area near the head. It tasted OK, but I'd lost my appetite. Men were impossible. So demanding and precious. Why had he brought me to France, if he was going to be so awful about everything? I heard him pee in the ditch and then go into the tent.

"Come to bed" he called.

I was in no hurry. I stared miserably at my fish, thinking the poor thing should never have left the water. Then I went over and scraped it onto the field for the birds.

He looked through the flaps. "You're littering."

I didn't answer. I was too weary. Besides, his superiority was maddening. Matter turned to matter, didn't it? I went to the loo on the grass.

Inside the tent, I zipped myself firmly into my sleeping bag.

He leaned over. "Give us a kiss goodnight."

I turned my back. "'Night."

"Sorry I was grumpy."

I could've turned, but I didn't.

"Let's go to Bayeux tomorrow" he said. "Then I'll leave you to the train."

The word "train" finished me. Tomorrow I'd be on my own. Probably forever. "I'd like to see the cemetery."

"Seen one, seen them all."

"But it's the thirtieth anniversary of D Day."

"The tapestries are from the Middle Ages. They're one of the world's wonders."

I wriggled down into my bag. "There wouldn't be a world if the Americans hadn't defeated Hitler."

"They didn't do it alone. And I don't understand you."

That was true, but I didn't say so.

"Hitler was dead before you were born", he went on. "I thought you liked Art."

"I do. But I'd still like to see the cemetery." I was being difficult, but the cemetery had become a sort of symbol of my liberation, or something. Anyway, being agreeable hadn't worked.

He sighed resignedly. "OK. I'll leave you there and have a coffee in town."

"You won't come with me?" It was stupid but I panicked at the idea of going by myself. I was terrified some French person would speak to me.

"Sorry, don't like graveyards." He snuggled into me, patting my behind through the bag. "It's our last night, Sally."

"So what?"

"It'll probably be a while."

"I can last."

He turned away, angry. "I thought you'd got over your frigidity."

That got me. "My *frigidity*?"

"Don't pretend you enjoy it."

"I do! It's just ..."

"What do you want, Sally?"

"I want you to love me."

He sighed. "Go to sleep, for God's sake."

I curled up, crying to myself. I'd never be Mrs Macbeth now. It sounded so interesting - Mrs Alastair Macbeth. Looking back, I wasn't going about it the right way. But then, was it fair to call me frigid, when I thought I'd been so seductive?

After a while, I blew my nose noisily. "Last night was pretty good."

"Hmm ..." He was nearly asleep.

I shook him, whispering, "Macbeth shall sleep no more."

He groaned again. How could he sleep at a time like this? "It worked last night!" I said again.

"Yes, but not for you."

"It did."

"You didn't ... come."

"I did ... a bit."

88

"Go to sleep."

"But what about us, Alastair?"

"We have no great love affair."

He went to sleep, but I lay awake for hours. It was no use, he'd never love me. No great love affair. Why did he speak for me too? Once I'd shown him a poem I wrote, and he'd said I was no great writer. He was right there. What had your man, Yeats, said? There could only be perfection of life or art. Something like that. I had neither. I was born to blush unseen, beside the springs of Dove. Wherever that was. But why was love so hard? And if I was that hopeless, why did he have anything to do with me? Oh, the holiday had been my idea, but once he'd invited me to visit his parents in Edinburgh. I'd loved them. He had a mother at least. And a father who wasn't always having fits. It was all so normal. I lay there, telling myself there was no hope. After all, he'd broken it off with me three times, each time giving me a blasted poem to read. "La Donna something", by TS Eliot. Maybe it was a block, but I could never understand it. Why couldn't he speak, if he wanted to say something? Anyway there was only one thing I wanted to hear - "Marry me".

But he'd never say it now, I'd be gone tomorrow.

I don't know how long I lay awake. Hours. But I'd just fallen off when I awoke to a strange noise.

Someone was sniffing outside the tent.

I lay in rigid fear as the sniffing moved along the tent to my feet. Was it an axe-murderer? Or a ghost? After all, the ground here was red with blood.

I nudged Alastair. "Wake up!"

"Go to sleep!"

"But there's someone outside!"

"Nonsense!" He rolled over.

I lay very still. If I pretended to be asleep it might go away.

"Sniff! Sniff!" came from outside.

I thumped Alastair's back.

He jerked awake as the tent collapsed.

Outside a cow bellowed madly.


Alastair was right, my pilgrimage was depressing. Terribly. At first I followed a coachload of noisy Americans past sentries into the cemetery's entrance museum. It had US flags and photos of the different Second World War battles and a short movie. Nine thousand, three hundred and eighty-six men were buried there. And most had died on D Day: 6 June, 1944, all cut down like flowers. Even the Americans seemed daunted into silence. I definitely was: some had been nineteen, six years younger than I was.

Outside, rows and rows of little white crosses stretched endlessly over manicured lawns. I mean, you see heroic war movies with John Wayne, but nothing prepared you for those endless crosses. In school Mother Rita had read us poems about the First World War. Poems about poppies "In Flanders fields ..." growing between crosses "row on row". Except there were no poppies there. I thought of her in all the oddest situations. When I was leaving school she gave me a book of Emily Dickinson's poetry - she's an absolutely beautiful writer. Lines of hers just rattle round in my head.

*I felt a funeral in my brain,*
*And mourners, to and fro ...*

Alastair says quoting things is a sign of adolescence, but Mother Rita used to say poetry was useful furniture for the mind. Yet, she didn't make us learn poems by heart. We had to criticise them, intelligently.

I remember wandering up paths that day, to kill the time until Alastair came back. He was right, there was nothing much to see. Here and there the lines of crosses were broken by a star of David. At least they hadn't separated the different religions. They were all brothers in death. "For he today that sheds his blood with me shall be my brother." Laurence Olivier in *Henry V*.

Yet the brotherhood of man was rot. People never learn. Violence still solves everything. Hate rather than love. We're still barbarians beating the drums. I mean, it's all around you - Vietnam, Northern Ireland. Before the Troubles, I'd been shocked to hear that people were shot in Belfast in the fifties. And now they're shot every day. It's something I'll never understand. Bombed to bits. For Ireland, a dying country on a dying planet. What a fate. And what a fate to have had to run up Omaha Beach. To be blasted by bullets. When I'd paddled there the day before, I'd thought it just like Rosslare or Brittas. Except for the German bunkers peeping out of the dunes. But I could never run up a beach. Yet death was the one certainty. There were only two important things I heard someone say on the radio. "How well can you live, and how bravely can you die."

I sat on the grassy verge, aching all over. Alastair had got the tent up again, but I'd been afraid to sleep, imagining the cow would wander back. If you were afraid of a cow, how could you run up a beach? And die at nineteen? Without having loved? But Alastair thought I hadn't loved either at twenty-five. "If I speak in the tongues of men and angels, and have not love, I am a noisy gong or a clanging cymbal." But that was a different sort of love. Everyone wanted the other sort. The "wings on your feet" sort. Which was nothing to do with sex or having children. How had everything got so mixed up? Maybe in the future they'll be separate.

A dog yapped in the distance.

At first I could see nothing.

Then a high American voice shrieked. "Bridie! Bridie!"

And a small white Scottish terrier tore up the path. It wore a little red tartan body blanket.

"Bridie! Bridie! Come back here!"

The little dog ignored her and, reaching me, jumped on me hysterically. I soothed it. "Down doggie! Down, now!"

But it kept yapping.

The woman wobbled on high heels down the path. She was oldish with lacquered hair and dressed in a suit of the same red tartan as the dog. "Arrêtez le chien! Arrêtez le chien!"

I reached for the dog, but he scampered away over the dead.

"Mademoiselle! Arrêtez le chien!"

I had a thing about walking on graves. But I ran along the grass between the rows. The dog saw me and kept on running and yapping joyfully. At last I threw myself over a grave, grabbing his collar. Then brought him yelping back to his owner.

The woman took him in her arms, smiling at me madly. "Merci! Merci!"

"It was a pleasure." I didn't know the right French.

"I have to be so careful!" she said in a squeaky Southern drawl, clipping a lead to the dog's collar. "She's in heat."

I had to smile. "There's hardly any danger."

"There's always danger!" The woman looked around conspiratorially. "But my, we're speakin' English, honey. Isn't that a coincidence? Where are you from?"

"Ireland."

"Where in Ireland?"

"Dublin."

"Another coincidence! My second husband's third cousin lives in Dublin. You might know her. Miss Clarke."

I shook my head. "I don't think so."

"Are you Episcopalian?"

"I'm nothing, really."

"What a shame! Everyone has to be something. Miss Clarke plays the organ in the church. You ought to go hear her."

"Which church?"

"Have you heard of Findlater's church?"

I nodded. "If I'm passing I'll call in."

"You can say we met." She turned imperiously on her heel. "Which way are you going now?"

"To the car park. I'm meeting a friend."

Her blue eyes lit up. "Your beau?"

"Well ... yes." I backed away from the sniffing dog.

"Stop it, Bridie! Mine is buried here!"

"Gosh ... I'm sorry."

The woman's eyes suddenly filled with tears. "He was killed on Omaha

Beach. His grave is back there. I visit him every year. I was laying flowers there when Bridie ran away." She suddenly clutched my arm. "Would you like to see it?"

I nodded. I had plenty of time.

"Come on!"

With the dog between us, we walked back toward the entrance. The woman kept up a constant stream of chatter. "We were madly in love. Madly. But he was a musician, and my people were in law. They didn't think he could support me. We were going to elope - I was in college in Virginia, Sweet Briar College, have you heard of it?"

"No."

"He wasn't college-educated. War was declared and he was drafted. That was it."

She stopped at a Star of David. A single red rose lay on the ground before it. I read the inscription. *Philip Cohen 1925-1944.* "He wasn't very old."

"Soldiers never are. He used to call me from England every week. Then I heard nothing for months. There was great secrecy about the invasion. Then I heard he was killed."

"Running up Omaha Beach?"

The woman nodded. "He was Jewish, you see. That was the problem. My parents didn't approve, and I hadn't the courage. But he was so talented. He could sing. You've heard of Al Jolson?"

"Yes."

"Well, he did a marvellous imitation of him!" Then she started singing and doing a sort of dance with the dog. "You made me love you! I didn't wanna do it! I didn't wanna do it ..."

It was funny.

"Before he left he bought me a Scottish terrier for company. Just like Bridie here. So I've had one ever since. She's great company."

The dog pulled on its leash, growling.

"Now, Bridie, behave. We come here every year, don't we honey?" She picked up the dog and hugged it. "The war ruined Momma's life."

"But you married?"

"I sure did, honey! Twice."

"Did you have children?"

"I had four dogs!" She looked sadly at the grave. "But the love of my life is under that clay. Now, honey, I'd like to be alone."

"I'm on my way."

"And give my regards to Miss Clarke!"

I waved, making for the car-park. She was dotty, but I'd learnt something from her. You can meet strangers in the oddest places and learn things from them. I mean, there hadn't been time to divorce Philip Cohen. So, of course, he became her only love. An imagined love to be mourned forever.

The van was in the car-park and Alastair waved from the window. That's what I mean about him being reliable. He was always there.

He wore his woolly white aran. And smiled behind his glasses as I clambered into the van. "How was it?"

"It was great!"

"Hmm ... graves?"

"You should've come! I met an American woman. From Sweet Briar College. Have you heard of it?"

He shook his head.

"It's an interesting name, Sweet Briar."

He snorted. "It's awful!"

"I don't know ... Two opposites - briars have thorns, yet they're beautiful. She was a bit of a nut."

He drove out of the car-park. "You have a knack of attracting oddities! We'll just make the train."

I looked at him sadly. Maybe if he died, he could be my lost love. He'd enter another realm then, like Philip Cohen, or Paul Brady from college.

Alastair caught my look. "What're you thinking?"

I shrugged. Sometimes it's impossible to express your thoughts. "Nothing really. Just that woman."

He pointed to a brown paper bag on the dashboard. "I got you some fruit. And a yoghurt for lunch."

"I've no spoon."

"I've put one in the bag. Have you got your tickets?"

I patted my anorak pocket. I was touched by the spoon. "Yes."

"Passport and money?"

I nodded, looking through the window. I didn't want to talk. I was imagining myself dead and Alastair mourning me. The tent-peg wars would be forgotten. I could be the love of someone's life. But that kind of love was only an idea. It was nothing to do with now. Now had to do with commitment and decisions. "Life consists in action and its end is a mode of action." I'd learn that in philosophy. And Alastair was right about one thing: history is bunk. To survive you have to change all the time. You have to face things like people not loving you. Or taking trains in foreign countries when you don't know the language. It's like running up a beach in a way.

We waited together on the platform. He broke the silence. "It won't be long now."

I nodded nervously. I'd soon be adrift. "Tell me again how to ask if I'm on the right train."

"You'll *be* on the right train."

"I might want to check."

"Ici le train pour Paris?"

"Ici le train pour Paris?" I repeated.

He put his arm around me. "You're very quiet."

I nodded.

He looked pained. "Look, Sally ..."

I hugged him. "I know ..."

"You know *what*?"

"We've no great love affair."

"What do you mean?"

The train screeched into the station, drowning speech. I hugged him again tightly, controlling tears.

I got on.

He handed me my rucksack from the platform. "I'll write."

"Me too."

I blew a kiss from the open door.

Then I found a free seat opposite another girl. When I'd got the rucksack into the overhead rack, I asked, "Ici le train pour Paris?"

"Yeah," she drawled in American. "This is it, OK." Then she went back to her book.

As we pulled out, Alastair waved from the platform. I knew I'd never see him again and I haven't. But I kept the spoon for years. I don't know where it finally got to. And I don't know why I insisted on a graveyard instead of a work of art. I must be crazy. I used to blame myself for ruining the holiday. But maybe you invent choices if you don't have any real ones. And maybe you're not a person till you fail miserably. In a way Alastair's in that perfect world of the past now. Except there's no grave to mourn at.

# VII  Denis and Kitty

Scowling, Denis looked up from the manuscript. "Kitty, you're not listening to me."

"I am!"

"No, for some bizarre reason, you are crawling around under the table."

Shockingly, the child within her gave a kick. Oh dear, she thought.

"I realise," he said icily, "it's only a first draft. Nevertheless! Never-the-*less*!"

"Yes, yes," she said, scraping her ear on the side of the table as she clambered up.

"Of course," he continued, with emphatically sublimated suffering, "you may not want to hear it."

"Urk", said Macduff. "Urk."

"I do!" she said. "It's just Macduff. He dropped his bread and butter." Macduff snatched the bread and butter and stuffed it into his mouth.

"No, darling!" she cried. "Dirty!" Too late.

"What do you think," he mused, "of Duncan - for the new one, I mean?"

"No," she said firmly, "at school they'd call him Dunky."

"Umm", he said, stroking the manuscript. "I'll start from the beginning."

"Marmalade!" Macduff demanded.

"No marmalade", she said.

"Are we now ready?" he inquired with heavy politeness.

"Don't start from the beginning", she said. "You'd got to the place where she was going out of her mind."

He slammed down his coffee-cup. Slosh. Stain. "She was never going out of her mind. I didn't write that."

"Marmalade!" Macduff demanded.

"No", she said. "Hush, dear!"

"You might at least do me the courtesy of paying attention."

Macduff howled.

"All right, all right, just a minute." She hastily spread marmalade on half a slice of bread.

Denis lit a cigarette.

Macduff regarded the proffered bread without enthusiasm. Then he put his finger in the marmalade. Then he put his finger in his mouth.

Knew he didn't want it, she thought.

"I might as well go to work", Denis said, aggrieved.

Or keeping, as it were, a slack lower lip. Not bad. Should she tell him that? No.

"No", she said. "I'm ready." She pushed her uneaten cornflakes to one side, and planted her elbows in a dry place, and jammed her chin into her fists. "Ready!" she smiled. "Ready!"

"Please understand first-thing that I never wrote she was going out of her mind. If you can't take that in, there's just no use in proceeding."

"Oh. But I thought she was. I thought that was the whole point."

"God!" he said, contemptuously flicking his cigarette ash on the floor.

"Read it from the beginning", she urged. Macduff was now dunking the bread in the cereal bowl.

"I need some more coffee first."

"I'll make it," she said hastily.

"*I'll* make it," he said, stamping off. The implication being, I'll make it right. How could you make instant coffee wrong? She sighed.

Macduff was now stuffing the bread into his shirt pocket. Lay off Macduff.

"No, darling," she said. "No. Here, you go and play." With a grunt, she lifted him down.

"OK," he said happily. "Outside."

"No, over in the corner by your toy box."

"Outside!"

"All right, all right. Outside." Taking one pudgy little paw, she started to lead him out.

"Go by myself," he said.

"OK." She opened the door, and he toddled swaggeringly out. How could he toddle and swagger? He was so small. Outside in the garden was the pile of weeds and stones she had neatly raked together the day before. Macduff went straight to it and gave it a big kick. She sighed and reflectively licked his marmalade off her hand. She had spent three weeks preparing the ground for seeds. Now that they were in the country, why shouldn't they have plenty of homegrown vegetables? But Denis kept forgetting the seeds.

"Damn!" he said, and a lid clattered to the floor.

"What's the matter? I'll do it."

He came back to the table with a cup of coffee, and sucking his thumb. "I burnt myself," he said accusingly.

"Do you want some - ?"

"All I want is your undivided attention."

"All right." She sat down and sipped her coffee. Cold.

"Here's my idea. There was Sally Ann, see, all alone, in that horrible mucky flat of hers."

"Sally Ann? I didn't know it was about Sally Ann."

"It's *not* about Sally Ann! Just shut up for a minute."

"All right."

"I got the idea *from* Sally Ann. There she was, away from her tyrannical father for the first time. But then she lost her job. No dole money. And there she was, surrounded by weeping walls and creeping fungus, making one last desperate attempt, one superb struggle to liberate herself, to ascertain her identity, her quidditas."

"Her what?"

"Never mind! So one day she calls me up at the office. There's something in the chimney. This awful rustling, some bird maybe. Would I come over and get it out? And so I went over. Now visualise."

"The bird?"

"No," he said, "the manuscript wadded all over the floor, the ashtrays full ..."

"I don't think she smokes."

He sighed. "There's no need to be so literal! I am trying to convey an atmosphere!"

"Oh!"

"Visualise the ashtrays. The dirty coffee cups. And her struggling to get it out."

"The bird?"

"No, for Christ's sake, not the bloody bird! Her identity. In utter agony and bad grammar, she was grinding out what it all meant. In pain and squalor, she was giving birth to her personality. Terrific. And what do you think was the first thing she said to me?"

Kitty pondered on the question. Sally Ann was too impractical to help herself. She could be an awful messer sometimes. There was a pair of them in it.

"Well," Denis persisted, "what did she say?"

"Get the bird out of the chimney?"

"Just forget the bloody bird for a minute. She said, should she go to America? She'd met this American history lecturer who wanted to take her away and embalm her in the tombs of Baltimore or Maryland or someplace like that. What should she do? Should she go?

"Well, there were slugs in that flat."

"The flat was her. Her!"

Kitty sighed. Sally Ann was dying to get married and have children. But she didn't know how boring they could be. Or how much work. "I wonder whatever happened between her and Alastair Macbeth?"

Denis studied his manuscript. "He wasn't her type."

"He was practical. She needs someone practical. Remember when she was keen on Colm Connolly?"

"He was a turd."

"I think he gave her a nervous breakdown."

"Nonsense!"

"She changed when she met him."

"I didn't notice it."

"She was very shy in first year. Remember?"

Denis was looking reflective again. "What about Macbeth for the new baby?"

"He was a murderer."

"You're right ... It's not bad though."

Kitty changed the subject. "Whatever happens, I hope Sally Ann keeps up her painting and drawing. She'd make a good artist."

"She'd make a better writer."

Kitty smiled to herself. "I read some of her articles you brought home ... Everyone isn't a writer."

"True, but she could be a journalist. She could use her degree. Otherwise, what's the point in having it?"

Kitty smiled smugly. "You don't particularly like your law degree."

"Hmm!"

"And I hope you didn't butt in about the American."

He regarded her with scornful dignity. "I simply said - Sally Ann, if you can leave this, if you want to opt for an air-conditioned, wall-to-wall soul, then I have nothing more to say."

"And what did she say?"

"She said get the bird out of the chimney."

Kitty giggled.

"What's funny?" he said.

"Nothing!"

"Well," he said, "so I got the bird out of the chimney."

"Was that when you tore your jacket?"

"Just keep quiet. I got the bird out of the chimney and - the bird, the bird was dead."

"Oh."

"The bird," he repeated, "was dead."

"Oh. Then what?"

"Then nothing! I mean, then everything! That is my story."

"I don't get it."

He slammed his coffee cup down. "Oh, for God's sake! Look, the chimney was awful, see? Dirty, dank, like her flat, but the bird was at home there. Because it had to struggle, it lived. But take the bird out of the chimney, the bird dies. Get it?"

"Do you think Sally Ann will die in America?"

"God, how can you be so thick. It's symbolic, see. She's out of her milieu, evading her identity. Wham, symbolic death."

"Oh."

"I'd better read it to you."

"I should do the washing."

Macduff crawled happily over the doorsill with a fistful of dirt.

"I was only up half the night writing. So do you want to hear it or not?"

Macduff came over and dropped the dirt in the cereal bowl. "Story?" he said.

Seizing the opportunity, she picked up the glass. "Macduff, finish your milk."

"No! Story!"

"Finish your milk, and you can hear the story."

"No milk!"

"The temptation," Denis began sonorously, "loomed over her. Persistent. Pervasive. Palpable. Embalming the day, spreading its very inchoate sombreness, dankly and dourly, over her very thoughts. The temptation to stop. Cease. Desist from her lonely battle with words. The temptation that vibrated in her very mind with an almost physical pain. Suddenly it was too much, the very anguish of it all. Sullen. Stubborn. Inarticulate. Aghhh!"

"What, what?" she cried.

"He's dribbled milk on the manuscript!"

"Awwwooo," howled Macduff.

"Just a little, just a little," she said. "I'll wipe it off."

"Don't touch it!"

"Awwwooo," howled Macduff.

"Monster!"

"Don't yell at him, Denis. Come on, Macduff. We're going to feed the baby." She took the little boy by his milky hand. "And you can have a Smartie."

"Oh," said Macduff.

In a few minutes, she came back with the baby. "Hold him for a second, can you?"

He was scribbling. "Umm," he said, looking up vaguely. "What do you think of Othello?"

"No child of mine is going to be called Othello. Here." She gave him the baby.

"Watch the manuscript," he said, "watch the manuscript."

The baby gurgled.

"Coo, Banquo," he said vaguely. "Coo, Banquo. How's Daddy's boy?" He hugged the baby, then shifted him to one arm and returned to the manuscript. "The death of the bird was an omen," he muttered. "Sickeningly, belatedly, she knew that. And there was a void within her. Heavy. Dull. Torpid. Mute."

"Hush!" she cried, listening. "It's Laertes. He's crying. Run upstairs and see what he wants, Denis."

"I'm holding Banquo."

"Please!"

Looking slightly crucified, he got elaborately up and handed her the baby. She sighed. She cradled it in her arm, sat down, and began to spoon food into the baby's mouth. Oh, it would be the same today. He'd forget the seeds. But the next child would have an ordinary name, she was determined on that. Not after another Shakespearian character - except Antony would be OK. James, if it was another boy. After Henry James, she'd tell him. Or Evelyn, if it was a girl. After Evelyn Waugh.

Denis returned. "He's finished colouring. I gave him a magazine."

"I'll need to move the mattress down here. The doctor said be sure to keep him off the leg. Will you give me a hand getting it down?"

He looked up from the manuscript. "What? I'm late for work."

"It'll just take a minute."

Abruptly he jammed the pages into his pocket. "Must run, love. Bye, Banquo!" He went quickly out, calling up the stairs as he passed, "Macduff! Laertes! Be good! Mind Mammy!"

"The seeds!" she called.

Outside, the motor of the car roared up.

Banquo spluttered some food out on his chin.

"Mammy, Mammy," shrieked Laertes upstairs, "Lorry took my magazine!"


Red-faced, she looked up from the cooker as he clattered into the kitchen. "You forgot them," she said flatly.

"Forgot what?"

"The seeds!"

"Oops, sorry!" He banged his head comically several times with the heel of his hand, then bent down and kissed her on the forehead. "Well, how was your day? How were the lads?"

"No worse than usual. The doctor called and said Laertes could get up for a bit tomorrow."

"That's great", he said, and flopped down in his chair by the fireplace, kicking off his shoes and unfolding the *Evening Press*.

"How was yours?" she said.

"Rugged", he said. "Made some phone calls to clients and did a bit of writing on the story in the morning. Went out for an early lunch with Derek, and met Tony. Then went back to the office and made a few more phone calls and got a good hour's work done on the story."

"Oh," she said, "there's a letter from the States."

He looked up quickly. "From the States?"

"It's in the sitting-room on the mantlepiece."

He hopped up and went out. "Hullo, Laertes," he called as he passed through the hall. "Hullo, Macduff."

Then silence.

"Is it from Sally Ann?" she called.

Glowering, he came back and fell into his chair.

"Sally Ann?"

He went back to his paper. "Yeh", he said, disinterestedly.

"What's she say?"

"Nothing."

"She must say something."

"Just a load of rubbish. Read it!" He crackled his newspaper irritably and buried his head in it.

She wiped her hands and went into the sitting-room. He had wadded the letter up and tossed it into the grate. She retrieved it and smoothed it out.

Dear Denis and Kitty

I arrived safely. The flight was OK, except I was afraid to go to the loo. Every time I tried, the plane rattled. So I thought I'd be sucked through the bowl. And if it crashed, I didn't want to die alone. Or be caught *in flagrante delicto*! So imagine my state in JFK!!! I'm having a really marvellous time. Richard (Dick to close friends) met me at the airport. He took me to New York for a night and we stayed in the Algonguin Hotel. We had breakfast in bed the next morning and they put a daisy on the tray. Imagine! It was really marvellous to stay in the haunt of the famous literati: Dorothy Parker and Co met there in the thirties to talk at the Round Table. (You know that quip: "Men don't make passes at girls who wear glasses." Well, she said that. I always thought it applied directly to me. Now I'm hoping my luck with men will change. I'm hoping Richard will ask me to stay after the trip.)

That day we called on Donnelly, a friend, who is going to put on a play by Richard in New York. Imagine! Then the three of us went to the Museum of Modern Art. There are paintings there, paintings that you've only seen on postcards all your life, just hanging on the wall. I spent nearly an hour just looking at Guernica. It takes up nearly a whole room. The poster I had in my flat was only a postage stamp compared to it. Also I saw some Paul Klees - they're quite small. Then Donnelly brought us to a play Off-Off Broadway and guess who was sitting in the audience? Arthur Miller! I'm dead serious ..."

Suddenly Kitty started to giggle. She couldn't stop.

"What's the matter?" he said, peering in.

She spluttered and waved the letter. "So much," she said, "for symbolism."

# VIII *Donnelly*

Dear Dad and Tim

Sorry I haven't written. This'll be a good long one to make up. I'm really enjoying my visit. So much has happened I don't know where to begin. Athens, where Richard lives, is a nice little college town, full of such beautiful young students that I'm beginning to feel old. (I mean, they look so much healthier than we do.) Richard's apartment is in an old house on the main street. We stayed there for the first week, mostly playing tennis when he wasn't working. Or else we visited friends. So many people asked us to dinner just because I was over - Irish hospitality's a myth compared to American, it really is. They're wonderful people.

Now we're in New York where Richard's play is going on Off-Off Broadway - that's a local name for the small theatres dotted all over the city. (Sort of like Focus in Dublin.) And guess what? I'm to be house manager! Me? Me? I keep telling myself it's not really happening. But yes, your terrible dropout daughter has at last found a vocation. We arrived yesterday, taking the Greyhound bus straight after Richard's class to Port Authority where Donnelly, the director, met us - he's an old friend of Richard and always called that, never Joe. As they shook hands and chatted, I tried not to stare. The truth is, I'd never seen a Broadway actor before! Would you believe he's a vet of *Philadelphia Here I Come*? And now he's turned his hand to directing Richard's plays. Last year they won a prize for the best Off-Off. I don't know what I expected him to look like, maybe less rumpled, but he must've heard my thoughts, 'cos the next thing he was staring at me, like wondering who the hell I was. Then Richard introduced us, saying I could help with the house. I joked that I knew about acting from being a daffodil in the school play when I was eleven. But it fell flat, because he just nodded grimly, almost cracking my hand shaking it. Then grabbing my case and chatting to Richard, he plunged into the Port Authority crowd.

Somehow, between snatches of gossip about *Da* being a hit uptown and who was acting in what, I got separated from them. As Richard's tall white-haired figure disappeared up the escalator, I experienced panic at the thought of the white slave traders roaming the station. But Richard noticed me missing and, as the escalator disgorged me, grabbed my hand and said to stay close. When I coolly asked why, he said it was wiser, confirming my worst theories. So all the way to the car, I avoided eye contact with the passing faces - there's a great variety here: black, brown, yellow. So different from Ireland where everyone's boringly white.

The car turned out to be just as rumpled as Donnelly, 'cos we all had to climb in through the windows. I know what you're both thinking, but that's show-biz! New York style. Anyway it's quite in keeping with the roads here, which mostly have pot-holes. Honestly, it was like the bumpers in Bray, honking through the evening traffic to 22nd Street. We didn't even stop for something to eat, as the actors were waiting. But I was too excited by my first sight of the city to feel even remotely hungry. Dad, if I had the words, only the words to describe the sun sinking behind those canyons of skyscrapers! It was poetry, pure poetry. Maybe someday I'll write about it. For the first time in my life, I envied no man. It was like that line you're always quoting about "Ulysses and his windy plains of ringing Troy." This place is an experience and you must see it.

Even our theatre's on hallowed ground, around the corner from the famous Chelsea Hotel which has plaques to Laertes Thomas, Brendan Behan, Thomas Wolfe and Arthur Miller. Oh, Dad, to walk where they walked! Our street reeks, I mean absolutely reeks of atmosphere, with two truckloads of uncollected refuse! But that's NY. There are two other theatres on the street, one called *Time and Space* run by a mysterious feminist group who're never there, and the other called the *Borough of Manhattan Theatre* (BMT for short) run by friends of Richard who specialise in American plays. And believe it or not, there are residents of 22nd Street, mostly blacks on welfare who sit on the stoop of a very dingy hotel all day, throwing dice or drinking from bottles wrapped in brown paper bags. With little girls rope-skipping and little boys competing to see who can pee the furthest, it's reminiscent of O'Casey's Dublin. I mentioned this to Richard as we passed them, but he just muttered O'Casey my foot. Then pointing to a huge ad on the wall: A FUNERAL SHOULD NEVER COST MORE THAN A FAMILY SHOULD AFFORD, said it was his motto! Then Donnelly actually spoke to me for the first time, calling me Susie and saying people lay senseless in the street here and nobody gave a damn - that's a favourite expression of his. He sort of groans it constantly under his breath: "Nobody gives a damn!" Then Richard said my name was Sally and not to be scaring me about New York. Before I could say anything, we had stopped at the theatre and were crawling out the car windows.

Our theatre's imaginatively called *The Nameless*. Although small, it has wonderfully built-in props: a hole in the roof for real rain, and dampish walls for the Irish atmosphere of Richard's play. Coincidentally, the theatre's owned by a Wexford man named Sean. He has a night watchman called Solomon who lives in the basement - at least I presume he does, 'cos he's always disappearing through a hole in the floor. His only other job seems to be keeping a proprietorial eye on the ancient and empty coke machine in the lobby. You expect something from someone called Solomon, but he reminds me of Ratso Rizzo from *Midnight Cowboy*, or sometimes of Gollum blinking at the daylight. I must've been staring, 'cos the first time Richard's back was turned he winked leeringly at me and said I was a good-looking chick. God!

Well, to get back, the actors were all waiting for us, and what a talented and experienced lot they are. Stacy, the leading lady, has been an understudy for Neil Simon on Broadway in a John Osborne. Even the second lady has recently acted in an O'Casey production in Syracuse, so the street's just like home for her. The leading man's

103

Scottish and has just had his picture on the cover of *Time* as a coal-miner. I'm not sure if he's a part-time lecturer in Fordham and full-time actor, or vice-versa. He plays the moron-type lead whom Stacy eventually marries to spite her macho-type boyfriend, Tom, played by Donnelly - typecast I'm afraid. I know what the mention of marriage has you thinking, but in real life people *don't* any more. So stop worrying. Richard bought me a return ticket, but I'm hoping he'll ask me to stay when the play's over. And I hope this is OK with you and Tim.

But I was telling you about the play. I worry about my lack of experience. It's ridiculous: my only previous time backstage was when I was one daffodil and Deirdre the other. Remember our crazy costumes, Dad? Deirdre was working in a bank the last I heard. We met for a drink a few years back, but it didn't go too well. It makes me sad that I wasn't nice enough. It was my S de Beauvoir stage, so say no more. The thing is not to look back. It didn't help Orpheus and that lot. The one blessing about the passing years is one grows in wisdom and maturity. But about the play: I dreaded, just dreaded making a mistake at the theatre yesterday. But my duties consisted of just sitting listening while the actors read their parts. I asked Donnelly wasn't there anything I could do, even cleaning up. But he didn't deign to answer me. And Richard put a finger silently to his lips and pointed to a seat in the back row. Which collapsed the minute I sat on it! Which I thought howlingly funny, but which made Donnelly grit his teeth!

From the first, Donnelly's attitude made me suspect that he didn't like me. And during the meal after the rehearsal, the suspicion grew as he just talked non-stop to Richard and totally ignored my advice about his Irish accent. But back in his tiny apartment where Richard and I are staying, I knew it. As we came in, I said what a nice flat. Donnelly glared and said what did I mean? So I said it was a nice flat again, looking nervously to Richard. Then Donnelly growled couldn't I see it was an apartment, not a flat? Then Richard said they called apartments flats where I came from! That made Donnelly look chagrined OK, but he still wouldn't talk to me all night ... still, it was great listening as the two men chatted till late about the play. They also serve, as Milton rightly tells us.

At rehearsal today, Donnelly ignored me again when I commented on his terrible Irish accent - it's dreadfully phoney! And then it seemed to incense him when I had to go backstage to the loo - it's in terrible repair and there's only one for men and women. I don't know what to do to please Donnelly. He's awfully thick with Richard, which leaves me a bit in the cold. But I'm so happy otherwise. To be living in New York for the next six weeks and to be helping Richard. Even if there's no future, it'll look good on my CV to have worked in the theatre. But I'm very fond of Richard. It was just the greatest luck meeting him again. He's in bed now and I'm sitting up finishing this letter. I'd better close, as he's yelling for lights out.

Lots of love,
Sally Ann.

Hello Everyone,

I'm sitting in the back row as usual while Richard and Donnelly rehearse with the cast. They've been at it for a week now, and you've no idea how hard the actors work. I always assumed acting was only a matter of learning the lines and walking around saying them. But the actors practice with a Kamikaze dedication for long grinding hours in this dark and dankish theatre - not that I mind the cold. A few days ago, I asked Solomon could he put on the heat, but he said it was only for the Eulenspiegel Society which used the theatre on Tuesday nights. I asked if that was a cultural club. He got horribly smirky and said it was, OK, he'd bring me if I wanted. I said I might go with Richard - pointedly, so as he'd stop getting ideas. And he went off chortling hey, yeh, yeh, which is about his command of the English language. Later he came back with a smelly old coat, which I had to put on so as not to offend him!

Apart from Solomon, I can't tell you how exciting rehearsals are! I never feel redundant, just sitting in the back row. There's a wealth of knowledge and experience to be gained. My main job so far is go-for, that's getting constant coffee from the corner deli for Richard, Donnelly and the actors - once I got Stacy a sandwich. She's very nice and likes Margaret Drabble, so we talk a lot about Women's Lit. And I told her about my part as a daffodil. Another young actor called Jim is very friendly and tells me all about his problems with dominating parents who won't let him live away from home although he's twenty-two! I said what a gem you were, Dad, about letting me cross the ocean to live amid alien corn. Not that it is really; there are loads of Irish in New York, and one of our actors is from the Abbey. His name's Chris Keely and he acted there in the forties. Remember him, by any chance? He invited me down to the Irish Arts Centre where they were having a céilí of all things!

I can't say much for Donnelly's friendliness though. Yesterday I put my foot in it again. The actors were taking a break for a silent read, so while checking if Richard wanted coffee, I whispered that the Irish would never say gotten - a phrase he uses in his play. Well, Donnelly must've thought I was talking about him or something, 'cos the next thing he was yelling he could just ask me to leave. Well, Richard didn't stick up for me at all, just growled that I was to get the coffee. So I walked out to the street in a daze. Usually I go the long way by the spooky warehouse to avoid the men who might be drunk. But yesterday was so dark, I decided to pass them. Nearing them, I heard loud blood-curdling screams. Alarmed, I walked on, looking neither right nor left. Was someone being murdered? Raped? Should I interfere? Run for the police? What I'd always read about was happening to me. Then I heard a chuckle and looking into a black sea of faces on the hotel stoop heard: "Hey sweetie, who's been knockin' on your head?"

Well, I laughed too and immediately felt better. On the way back I noticed some activity in the feminist theatre, *Time and Space*, and guess

105

what they were doing? Dramatising an essay by Virginia Woolf! Needless to say I went in, and needless to say it was an unforgettable experience - you all know how I adore anything about Virginia. It's a bit difficult to describe what went on, but basically one girl read while another girl mimed. There was only one other person in the audience, and during the interval she told me the method was experimental and the theatre got its name from the difference between men's and women's thought. It seems *we* think in terms of space and *they* think in terms of time. Which is definitely true in Richard's case, 'cos when I got to our theatre the actors were all gone and he was chain-smoking in the lobby. At the sight of me, he yelled where had I gone? That Donnelly had gone back to check the apartment! I tried to explain about *The Moment*, but he shouted louder that Donnelly thought he was Kazan, but I wasn't above being told off once in my life! He looked like he was going to have a heart attack, so I explained quietly that *once* in my life would be fine, or even *twice*, but Donnelly never stopped telling me off! In fact he couldn't stand my guts, and I felt in the way etc. Well, we had it out then and there! It was our first real row. Then Richard cooled down and we took the subway home. On the way he said there was no question of me being put out of one of his plays and there'd be much more to do once the show started and I could house-manage proper. Of course, Donnelly was in the apartment gloatily clicking his tongue and growling about me runnin' round, runnin' round, and nobody givin' a damn! I ignored this, but when he said Richard should kick my tail, I explained politely that as a feminist I objected to that statement. That Richard and I had an equal relationship and didn't indulge in such barbarism. Well, that's what I wanted to say, but Richard was looking angry again and dragged me off to the tiny bedroom - to get away from Donnelly he said later. But then when I asked him if we could go to the Eulenspiegel Society Solomon was talking about, he just snored in reply.

So far I haven't clashed with Donnelly today. Solomon's been hanging round as usual wondering when Richard's bringing me to the Eulenspiegel Society. I said soon. So he went away muttering that I deserved someone better than Richard! The actors seem to be breaking up now, so I'll close.

Buckets of love to both,
SA.

Wednesday 25 April

Dear Dad and Tim,
You'll never guess, but today I was given a job. The actors now rehearse without their scripts and need a prompter who is me! I was terribly nervous about making a mistake, even though it's the actors who're supposed to make them. I just felt I'd make a mess of things and I did. Stacy was sort of stumbling, so I gave her the line. Then Donnelly snapped she'd *ask* for it if she wanted it! I went beetroot and it was a

misery sitting through the rest of the rehearsal wondering when or when not to prompt. The next thing, Donnelly was yelling line please! I've given up, just given up trying to please him. Afterwards Stacy was very nice and said I did a great job. The other actors gathered round too. Jim said he'd finally moved out of home, and Dougal explained existentialism which he teaches at Fordham. He says we're all in a void and have to take a leap of faith. I said New York wasn't exactly a void, and although I could take a leap OK, it worried me that Richard didn't believe in an after-life. He said existentialism was all about making choices like that. Then we all had to move out as the Eulenspiegel Society were dribbling in. I asked Richard couldn't we stay and see what it was like. He just glared and said absolutely not. So we wound up going to the BMT up the street. As they're doing a new play set in the Chelsea area, you'd think the place would be packed with locals! But besides us, there were only four people in the theatre. Richard, who gets gloomier and gloomier lately, remarked it was his kind of audience. I said not to be ridiculous, that more people would come to his play 'cos it was better. Still, I thoroughly enjoyed that play, and they gave us free coffee in the interval - Dad, there's something about theatre people! Their next play is going to be a premiere of Edmund Wilson's *This Room and this Gin and these Sandwiches*! - how's that for a super title?

> I'll close for the moment,
> Yours in bliss,
> SA.

<br>

Monday 1 May

Dear You Two,

Things aren't any better with Donnelly, but at least they're not worse. Yesterday he asked me to sit in his car to prevent it being stolen while he paid a fine. We drove miles and miles to a place called Queens where I had to wait, nearly melting, in a deserted car-park. Of course he was hours longer than he said he'd be. But when he came back, he at least had the grace to be apologetic and to *thank* me. So we've established a détente as there's too much to be done with getting props and arranging publicity etc for our opening night next Thursday. People in New York throw out all sorts of valuables, so we've gleaned most of our hand props and some of our furniture from dustbins. The set is being painted free by Mary Beth Mann, set designer for *Family Business*, currently running Off-Broadway at the Astor Place - a notch up from us. The lighting's being designed by Tobias Heller, a young actor and designer who has a part in *Gorey Stories*, going on Broadway in the Autumn - two notches up on us! Although neither of them would let me help, I got quite friendly with them and was greatly awed by their dedication. Their names will mean nothing to you, I know, but in future you'll see them in lights and I mean it. I said to Richard I wished I could do something special like that. He said I could be a woman of letters as I was always writing them! We also had millions of programmes printed up, and we spent hours, absolutely hours, sending out flyers to four thousand addresses we stole from the *Theatre Development Fund*. All the critics have been personally invited. Richard spends his time tinkering sort of neurotically with the lights, so I suggested we go to the Eulenspiegel Society tomorrow night to steady our nerves. He gave me a funny look and said we could go for a Guinness with Chris Keeley in the Bronx. We did and had a great time, although the Guinness here is nothing to write home about. Still it was relaxing and steadied our nerves. We met a boy called Levi from the Irish Arts Centre who offered me a job teaching Irish. I said I didn't know any and he nearly dropped dead. Then he said I could teach them Irish dancing, and when I said I hated it, he nearly dropped deader! The last time I did any Irish dancing was with Deirdre in Irish College! Still, it was an enjoyable night and, as I said, steadied our nerves for next Thursday's onslaught of customers.

     Yours in hope,
     SA.


                             Sunday 5 May

Hello Again,
    Well, the onslaught trickled in OK, all nine of them, all friends. Everything was looking great: I had picked some lilacs from the park. But just at the last minute, Solomon dragged a bag of garbage through the theatre lobby! I only just got it cleared up in time. Richard would've been really mad, but luckily he was already up his ladder and didn't see. He was too busy muttering there was a short in number two main, and he wouldn't be surprised if all the lights went out. As I frantically swept, I shouted up not to be a pessimist, and he said it was his kind of lighting. The show went OK, although the actors were a little nervous. I was nervous too, and spent the evening shuffling the programmes tidily and counting heads.

    The next night things picked up considerably and we had thirteen, mostly friends - I should know, I counted them four times. One was a critic from *The Irish Echo*, so I smiled at him a lot and gave him three programmes, which was more than he would've got at *Da* - it, by the way, has won the Drama Critics' Award for the best play of the season. Bet it never rains in their theatre! It never stops in ours! One day it was so bad, I couldn't decide whether to put buckets under the leaks in the lobby or under the leaks onstage. I decided on the lobby, as one of the scenes in the play was meant to be played in the rain. Solomon saw me and yelled what did I do down in Dublin when it rained? I explained it was over in Dublin, which really floored him, and we go to the movies. He naturally assumed I meant porn movies - the only ones he's ever seen. I said no, there weren't any in Dublin, which also really floored him, or more than floored him, 'cos he disappeared into his basement! Later, apparently touched by my cultural deprivation, he invited me to one, saying it'd be even better than the Eulenspiegel Society! I said no thanks so he gave me a free coke instead. I don't know where he got it as the coke machine still doesn't work.

We expected a crowd for today's Sunday matinee, but the only customers were Jim's parents. Thank goodness they really enjoyed themselves and seem to have accepted his decision. I'm sure things will pick up next week and we'll be booked out - luckily there's plenty of standing room.

> Yours in hope,
> Sally.

<br>

Sunday 14 May

Dear Dad and Tim,

Our review has appeared in *The Irish Echo*! It said the play was reminiscent of Clifford Odets and should not be missed *on any account*! A large portion of their 16,000 readers seem to disagree though - all actually. You'll never guess who came though? Elton John - Tim'll explain who he is. I remember someone rang and booked tickets for Mr John. Apparently he came that night and I talked to him. Can you believe I never recognised him? We'd be worth something, if only I got him to autograph the programme. Then a man came by, telling me he'd flown to Ireland especially to see *The Star Turns Red* at the Abbey. I said at least ours wasn't so far and he could take the subway! The next day an actor called Kelly Monaghan who's worked with Donnelly and Richard before, came by. And so did a few others. There's a lot to be said for a small and intimate audience of one or two or three.

Our Sunday matinee was slackish too. In fact, only two people turned up. One was Alan Simpson, the famous Irish director who's in New York directing *Androcles and the Lion*, and the other was an Irish woman from Kells who came all the way from the Bronx in a taxi. Actually they were a great audience. Alan complimented the actors, and the woman liked the play so much she promised to come back next weekend with a friend.

Richard hasn't said anything about me staying. But lately things have been getting a bit better with Donnelly. But he attacked me, just attacked me for charging Alan Simpson. I said I didn't know and why didn't he say? He snapped back that I was a stupid girl and did he have to tell me everything? I said nothing more, 'cos the strain's beginning to tell on everyone. I mean, we've all done our best and for what? While Richard never comes down from the lighting booth, Donnelly spends every afternoon tinkering with his car which is full of strange rattles. Sometimes the rattles stop when a piece falls off, but a new one always starts up. Once the police towed it away from outside the theatre which I thought improved the appearance of the place. Unfortunately we got it back though, and, to prevent it being towed again, Donnelly left me in it once when we were double-parked. Soon a cacophonous din started up outside which I tried to ignore. Then a man poked his head in the window and asked me to move on. He gaped, just gaped when I said I couldn't drive - in America that's like being paralysed! As he wouldn't go away, I finally said he could drive it but he'd have to climb in the window as the doors don't open. That made him go away pretty quick! I suppose he thought I was mad: after all, it's New York and there are all sorts.

Talking about all sorts, guess what a Cherokee Indian Chief, a white rabbit and a French poodle have in common? Do you give up? OK! They were all in the Blarney Stone, our local pub on 23rd Street tonight. Apparently they'd all drifted there after a pow-wow at the YMCA across the street. The poodle belonged to the Chief, but nobody knew who owned the rabbit. We got chatting with the Chief and ended up giving him some flyers, and he gave us some newspapers that explained the wrongs of the Indians. After the Chief went home to the New Jersey suburbs, I told Donnelly I was disappointed and expected my Indians wilder and something like Geronimo - I mean, who'd expect an Indian Chief to own a French poodle? Donnelly actually answered that I was a romantic, and Indians today are suburbanised and very peaceful. On the way, Richard fell asleep and I chatted with Donnelly. I asked him, among other things, about the Eulenspiegel Society. He said was that my thing? I said anything cultural was. He just said hmm, and that his wife had been a feminist. I said it was the first I heard he had a wife. And he said she'd left him and wouldn't let him see his kids. Which no matter how bad-tempered he is, is very high-handed of her! It made me feel sorry for Donnelly and even like him.

I must close now as Richard's yelling again about the light.

Affectionately yours,
Sally Ann.


Saturday 20 May

Dear Both of You,

To tell the truth, in terms of audience, week three hasn't been much better than week one or two. But in terms of artistic existentialism it has been marvellous. The woman from Kells came back OK, bringing her friend. And although Alan Simpson didn't, he invited us down to see his production of *Androcles* at the Perry Street theatre in the Village - I can't tell you how exciting and cosmopolitan the Village is. The show was overpowering, that is the only word. Lively and full of pizzazz with an utterly jam-packed house. It made our dingy theatre with its failing lights and scavenged props look pretty drab and I mean it. But Alan said in spite of his theatre having money and a press agent they too scraped for an audience earlier in the run. You can't imagine how difficult the artistic life is, how dedicated you have to be. The Feminists have disappeared like the Arabs into the desert, and our neighbours at BMT are having trouble with their Edmund Wilson premiere. They've even decided to scrap their next show which was to be Richard's latest

110

play. I was very gloomy about this and expected Richard to be suicidal, but he just shrugged, saying his only worry was electrocuting himself on our blasted lighting board. How lucky to love such a man, how lucky to be in his penumbra.

     Love,
     SA.

PS Something terrible has happened! Solomon gave me grisly photos of the Eulenspiegel Society in session. It's an SM club! I asked Richard why *didn't he tell me* for God's sake, and not let me natter on like an idiot! He said he thought I knew! How's that for communication! Last night I had the most terrible Anne Frank nightmare. Apart from that, everything is fine as usual.

Sunday 21 May

Dear Dad,

    I'll probably be home before you get this letter. Truthfully, until last night it was the same old three and fourpence. But guess what happened for our final performance? We got an audience! Yes! Yes! Even a critic from *Show Business*, a magazine which gave Richard and Donnelly three awards last year! It was great to see so many people. I fingered the money like Shylock and counted heads four times to make sure they were really there. Even Solomon came out of the floor and filled the coke machine for them. After the first scene, they clapped loudly, and after the second and then all through the play they clapped and clapped and laughed and laughed. And the whole thing, which I had seen millions of times came magically, just magically alive. The actors had always been super, but now that there was an audience to interact with, a magic thing happened, and there's no other word for it. And when it was over they clapped again and shouted author, author! And afterwards we had a party on the stage and Chris Keeley sang John McCormack songs and Donnelly sang Tommy Makem's "Sally-O". It was a valediction forbidding mourning. And I found myself explaining again how I had approached the part of a daffodil. Richard heard and said I was drunk, but I wasn't even remotely. I was just happy.

    But we've closed now and the next show has moved in. Uptown, *Da*'s won the Tony Award - see how right you were about that and how wrong I was. But for us our revels are now ended. And what a sad, sad line that is. Tomorrow Richard will be leaving me out to Kennedy.

     Your loving daughter,
     Sally Ann.

PS Dad, something really scary happened. But before you read on: I AM SAFE. ALL IS WELL. You know I was upset about Richard never saying anything about our future. Well, on our last night in Donnelly's apartment, I confronted him. I asked him outright was there any hope for us? He said something facetious like there's always hope if you're alive. I said no, I mean a future for us. To be specific, would he have a baby with me? He said he'd had it with children and he'd much rather have it cut off than go through that again. He has four who live with their mother. The marriage wasn't happy as you may have guessed. Well, that finished me and I cried myself to sleep. The next morning, I got up before he did and stole out of the apartment. I hate farewells, so I left a note saying I was going on out to the airport by myself. It was wrong of me, but I was under great strain. I felt I'd messed up again. That Donnelly had put him off me. That Donnelly was probably right. I was a terrible eejit who made corny jokes. And there was too much of a gap between us. Happiness would always elude me, blah, blah, blah. You know the way you feel. Well, I went to Port Authority, but there was no bus to Kennedy. They told me something about a terminal, but I couldn't take it in. I was sort of dislocated and really afraid of New York. I felt sort of paranoid. That people were following me. I walked around for a bit, stopping in an Irish bar, a Blarney Stone, to have breakfast. I ordered a big feed, hoping to make myself feel better. But sitting there on my own, I felt awkward. I thought men were staring. Well, then a young man, younger than me, came in with his grandfather. They sat near me and we struck up a conversation. He had a lovely face with a beard and jeans and a check shirt. He was so kind to his grandfather, that I thought he must be nice. I told him I was going back to Ireland and asked for directions to get to Kennedy. He told me again about the bus terminal and how to get there by subway. Then he left without the old man. As I was so nervous about travelling on the subway by myself, I followed him, asking to walk a bit of the way with him. "You're right to be careful in New York," he said. "I'll drive you over to the terminal." His Volkswagen was parked nearby. It seemed harmless, so I agreed. But as soon as we were inside and driving he said, "Why did you get into my car?" My heart stopped at the tone of his voice. I was frozen with fear. I felt like a mouse before a cat. All the time, I'd been afraid of blacks! You don't realise how racist you are. But here was a sweet-looking white college boy. "Because you offered me a lift," I said. He laughed sarcastically. "I thought you wanted to be picked up." Well, you can imagine my state of shock. "Look," I said, "I'm sorry to have given that impression, but I really do want to get to Kennedy. I'm flying home tonight." But he insisted we were going to his apartment and he produced a sharp looking knife. "Please let me out!" I begged, panicking. But he wouldn't stop. The car was going fast, so I couldn't jump out. I had to think fast. So I said cheerfully, "Of course, I'll go to your apartment. It's not a bad idea at all." He could put away his knife. But, as we had all day, could we possibly go to a book shop first? As I had just remembered I needed to buy a book for my brother who was about his age. Mention of my brother seemed to calm him, so he said there was a good bookshop with many bargains around 18th Street and 5th Avenue. We went there and I found a Karate book for Tim, mentioning that my brother was a Karate expert. All the time browsing, I kept asking if he'd read this and that. Inside I was thinking, I should run away now, somehow lose him, but I thought he'd get mad if I did. Also I was frightened of being knifed. I mean he followed me with one hand in his jeans pocket which held the knife. We went outside again and his car had a ticket for parking in the wrong place! I secretly memorised the number, while laughing aloud at the irony. I mean he's trying to commit a rape and he get's a parking ticket! My laughter angered him for a moment. So I said sorry, that I didn't mean to laugh. Then we got back into the car and drove off. On the way back downtown to his apartment, I controlled my panic by chat. "What do you do for amusement?" I asked. He shrugged. "Pick up girls in Singles Clubs". So I asked, "If you can go there, why bother with me?" Then I said I'd never been and would he please bring me to one. *Before* the apartment. Then I could at least feel as good as they were. This suggestion seemed to amuse him, so we stopped at a sleazy bar, GO-GO'S. He bought me a drink and we sat opposite each other in a booth. I asked how did he pick up the women? "Do you always use the knife?" "No," he said, "it's all eye contact." Then he demonstrated his technique of looking and then looking away. If the girl looked back it meant she was interested. Imagine? All the time, I was thinking how the hell will I get away? The irony was I'd got into the mess from being afraid. But I had to keep my head now. I asked to go to the Ladies, so he agreed to that. Miraculously there was a phone inside. So I called the operator and she got me the police. I told them he was threatening me and forcing me to have sex, but I was from Ireland and only knew roughly where I was. I told them the name of the place. So they asked for the number of the car and the phone number there. They told me to delay him as long as I could. But when I came out he grabbed me, yelling: "Bitch! You called the cops!" I screamed as he dragged me out of the bar to the car. The barman heard but barely looked up. In the street people passed and did nothing. I remembered Donnelly's groaning that "nobody gave a damn" in New York and thought I'd be killed. All the way to his apartment which was down towards the Village, I kept wondering how to get out. Once at a traffic light, I tried to open the door, but he pulled on suddenly. "Do that again and I'll kill you!" After that he kept the knife at my ribs. Well, we got there and I was crying. I thought, being raped won't be so bad. It'll be like confronting my worst fears. At least I'll be alive. The only problem is: I've seen his face. He'll kill me. He pulled me inside and up three flights of stairs, badly tearing my blouse. I tried to delay him more, saying, "There's no need for violence. I like you. Let me have a bath first." This pleased him so he said he'd get into his robe. I locked myself in the bathroom, playing for time and trying not to cry. I ran the shower, but didn't get in. Surely help would come? After a while he banged on the bathroom door, screaming, "Open up!" Then he started calling me awful names. Where were the police? Surely they could trace the car owner. He kept banging on the door and finally burst it open. Seeing I wasn't undressed he yelled furiously. "You're trying to trick me!" I sobbed, seeing an erection sort of protruding from his robe. I thought I was going to vomit. Then the phone rang, and grabbing my wrist, he went to answer it. While he was talking, the door burst open and men with guns ran in. They were dressed in plain clothes, so at first I didn't realise they were the police. I thought they were the Mafia or something. Then a women took me over to his couch, while he was grabbed and brought away handcuffed.

It was awful.

The police said I was lucky. There had been a few cases like this, and now they had a suspect. I was crying at my own stupidity, but they said I'd been smart to call them the way I did. I said it was only luck. They took me to the station to file a complaint, saying I'd have to testify later in court. I said I was flying back to Ireland that night and that disappointed them. They said he'd be let out on bail. But still, they couldn't hold me as they said I'd done nothing wrong. Finally as it was so late, they left me to the airport, saying they'd want me back to testify. I think I'm still in shock.

And there was another shock waiting for me. Richard was at the Aer Lingus booth. Mad as hell and chain-smoking. Immediately I saw him I cried. He took one look at my torn blouse and the cop carrying my case and said, "What happened?" The cop explained I was the victim of aggravated assault and attempted rape. Then he asked Richard to see me onto the plane and left. I burst out crying again, thinking Richard would be angry with me. But he said, "Why do you wear that awful muck on your eyes?" - my mascara had got messed. "He tore my blouse too," I said. "And it's a good blouse." Then he said, "Give me that return ticket!" I thought he was going to check me in, but he tore it up! So I'm still here! It was all my own fault. Of course, I told Richard everything that happened. And he agreed I was stupid to get into the car, but I trusted people and you can't these days. I never will again. Then we taxied back into the city and made the Athens bus. When we pulled out of the Lincoln Tunnel, I was glad to be out of New York. But the skyline was gold in the evening sun.

Love in buckets,
Sally.

# IX *Gracie*

Grace O'Malley certainly livened up the University of Pennsylvania, Athens Campus. For better or worse, her visit is still marvelled at by town and gown alike - town being the Tavern locals and gown the stuffy academics who employed her. Neither group had ever before met the species: Hibernicus Scriblerius Alcoholicus - which is plentiful on native soil but a merciful rarity abroad. Being Irish, I was acquainted with the breed. And luckily, when she arrived a week late for class, I was the first person she rang. It was then my third year in America, and the gravelly Northern accent was like rain on the Sahara. "Is thos Misses Sheridon?" she asked.

"Eh - no. It's Sally Ann," I said.

Mrs Sheridan, that's Dick's wife, lived in a huge house across campus, but that was too difficult to explain. That I was his current live-in girlfriend was even more so.

"Yer Dickie's daughter then?"

"No. I'm a friend. You must be Miss O'Malley?"

"Aye, It's Gracie. Reporting for action. Whur the fuck is Dickie?"

I put her language down to nerves. "He's teaching at the moment."

"The bostard said hud meet me."

"He was expecting you yesterday afternoon," I went on calmly. "We went to Philadelphia airport to meet you."

"Ye dud?"

"Yes. Your wire - "

"But I hod to see New York!"

"Yes. But - "

"Look, I'm stronded. Tell Dickie to get his arse up here!"

"Where are you?"

She coughed alarmingly, then groaned. "Oh, dear Gawd ... I feel awful!"

"Where are you?"

"Fuck knows. Some kip of a station."

"Wilmington?"

"Aye."

Her description of our nearest station was dead-on. And I knew well the panic of arriving there. "We'll be right up for you."

"How long will ye be?"

"About half an hour. Wait at the newsstand."

But she had hung up.

Dick answered his office phone, but he wasn't at all pleased about driving to Wilmington. Actually he was already very irritated with Gracie - I mean, she was late and had wasted our whole Sunday. "What happened yesterday?" he asked.

I said I didn't know.

"Why didn't you tell her to take a cab?"

"She was stranded."

"Balzac! There's a fleet outside the station."

"Maybe she hadn't the money."

"I sent her the fare!" He sighed heavily. "Oh, I suppose I'll have to go."

"Can I come?"

"Don't you have art class?"

"I can miss it."

"Well ... if you want to waste the time."

I said we'd meet at the car.

It was a yellow Volkswagen, parked as usual in the space behind our apartment building - Dick always walked to the university. He's an expert on Ireland in the nineteenth century, probably the world expert on the Famine, and had set up the University's Irish Studies programme. Last year he headed a search committee to find an Irish writer for this semester. He said he chose Grace O'Malley for a variety of reasons: she had published half a dozen novels in Penguin, some of which I'd read. And she'd known Behan and Donleavy and Co. And had an American reputation, thanks to the *New Yorker* magazine. Also she was a woman. And a friend - although I suspected there was more to their relationship. I mean, why else would he want me to stay home? He definitely had something to hide. Another thing: nobody ever called Dick, Dickie. Oh, maybe I sounded young, but an age difference of thirteen years hardly qualified me as a daughter. I was twenty-seven to Dick's forty and a half. I know it's terrible but I was always jealous of his past. Absolutely always. He had had legions of women compared to my few men. So I suspected he'd been more than just friends with Gracie. But one thing confused me: his irritation yesterday at the airport.

He looked even more irritated, coming into the car park now. He's tall, thin and handsome with thick white hair and brownish skin. As he'd been teaching, he wore his Donegal tweed jacket with jeans - even in darkest winter he never wears a coat. Odd, considering he always insists on me wearing one. He'd even bought me one for our first Christmas. And typically it was the first thing he mentioned now, frowning over the top of the car. "Don't you need a coat?"

It was February and snowy, but I wore my anorak. "This is fine."

He got in and pushed open the passenger door. I got in too, and we drove in silence through the town. It's a place that would've been idyllic in the last century. The big clapboard houses with their wonderful nineteenth century porches weren't noisy student fraternities then. The opera still hosted travelling companies. There was even a theatre. And Main Street's eighteenth century facade hadn't been ruined by fast food joints like Roy Rogers and McDonalds. There are a few remaining shops, but most have moved out to the graceless mall. Oh, they've done up the old Academy building from which the university is descended. But blight has denuded it of elms. The blight is all over, but they're planting other trees. The only other remarkable thing about Athens is it's near the Mason-Dixon line. Till about 1965 the railway track divided the town. Before that any black who wandered onto Main Street to window-shop was picked up by the cops and driven back over the track. Today that's all changed, but the cargo train still trundles evocatively through, reminding me of old films where people jumped trains on the way West. Otherwise it's dull. Take my word.

As Dick was in a mood, I didn't make conversation. I was used to his moods. I knew he was furious at the waste of time. He's a terribly hard worker. It could be the reason he went white in his twenties. Or else his unhappy marriage. I don't know. But, besides his good looks and brains, his mania for work was one of the reasons I loved him. I hoped it'd rub off on me - by osmosis or something. And since coming to America, I'd gone back to my painting and worked really hard. But despite this, I doubted my ability. I really did.

Entering the turnpike, I gripped the sides of my seat. It amazes me the way Americans are born able to drive. Even teenagers take the deadly highways so casually. I mean, you could be driving along in your little Volks when a truck the size of a house passes you out - which was the case with us now.

I tensed even more, imagining death.

"Is that necessary?" Dick broke into my thoughts.

"What?" I looked over.

He hissed through his teeth. "Breathing like that."

"I wasn't."

"You were. It's no help."

"Sorry."

Lately all the romance was going from our relationship. I missed my family and friends so much. From studying history, I'd become it. And now mostly just hung around the apartment while Dick typed on his damn book. I couldn't get a job as I had no Green Card. And we hardly went anywhere any more. In the beginning there was the play in New York. And movies. But now I went to them on my own. Dick didn't like French films, only horror or cowboy. Things like *King Kong* or *Flash Gordon*. I'm dead serious. Once we had this silly row about whether film was a literary art or not. Of course, idiotically I'd argued that it was. But lately he never talked to me. Only criticised. Like the remark just now about my breathing. And cutting class. I wanted to be a painter, but hated figure drawing. And didn't see the need for it, as my stuff was non-representational. But Dick insisted you had to have the foundation. And just smiled when I told him people didn't draw any more.

He has a terrible habit of smiling if he disagrees with me. His eyes sort of glint. It's maddening.

Now he was glowering, and he kept it up as we approached Wilmington. An interesting fact is that Wolfe Tone landed here before 1798, on his way to be a Princeton farmer. Today it's a city of vast extremes of wealth and poverty. It seems almost segregated, so it's not difficult to believe it had race riots as late as 1970. It's a place you're not tempted to visit. Or, if so, there'd be no way without a car. That's another thing about America - the lack of public transport. You can't just hop on a bus like Dublin. You're stuck in the middle of a jungle of highways. And if you take a wrong turn, you might as well be in outer space. I'm serious. We can't seem to go down the street without getting lost - it's Dick's homing pigeon streak. Once out for a short drive, we ended up deep in Amish country. But that turned out to be interesting.

There was no sign of Gracie at the station. She wasn't at the newsstand. Or in the Ladies.

Oh God, I thought, as Dick checked the platform. He came back, self-righteously scanning the waiting area. What if she meant Philadelphia? Why hadn't I got her to check? After all, I was the one who'd actually said Wilmington. Dick was right about me being vague.

He read my thoughts now. "Are you sure she said Wilmington?"

I nodded. "Nearly sure."

He jangled the change in his pocket. "You're *nearly* sure?"

There'd be a row next. But then we heard a Northern Irishwoman's voice reciting in the distance.

*There's a one-eyed yellow idol to the north of Khatmandu*
*There's a little marble cross below the town;*
*There's a broken-hearted woman tends the grave of Mad Carew,*
*And the Yellow God forever gazes down.*

It came from the bar.

Gracie sat at the counter with an old black man. She was a buxom woman of about fifty, with thick red shoulder-length hair and a weather-beaten freckled face. And worse than me in the coat line, she wore only a tarty black suit. Actually she was dressed completely in black: fishnet stockings, high heels, blouse and bag. It was very dramatic.

As we came over, she went on reciting. Later I was to judge her state of sobriety by different poems. "Twenty Golden Years Ago" or "Let the Toast Pass" meant she'd only had a few drinks. But "The Green Eye of the Little Yellow God" or "The Ballad of William Bloat" were definite danger signals. But then I was green in the ways of drink and only delighted to have found her.

Even Dick was all smiles.

Seeing us come in, she rose swayingly. "Dickie!"

118

As they embraced, her bosom collided into him.

Then she introduced her friend who nodded and smiled. She said they'd met on the train, but he looked a down-and-out to me. Was it safe to be drinking with him?

Then Dick remembered me. "This is - a friend. Sally Ann Fitzpatrick."

We shook hands. At least he'd given up calling me his secretary. He had once, in a New York bookshop - which was idiotic, considering I couldn't even type.

She eyed me curiously. "Yer the girl I spoke to?"

I nodded.

Her blue eyes were surrounded by millions of tiny wrinkles and too much eye-liner gave her a startled clownish look. "What are ye drinkin'?"

I looked at Dick.

She gripped his arm. "You're a Bourbon man, aren't ye?"

He shook his head. "It's a bit early, Gracie."

"Ah, it's not often we're out." And she waved laconically to the barman. "Here, Bob."

"We should really be getting back." Dick looked at me, saying with heavy emphasis, "Sally Ann has lunch waiting."

I blinked vaguely. "Lunch ... Oh! Yes, lunch is waiting."

"Well, let it wait! What're yes drinkin'? Fuck the begrudgers!"

I looked at Dick again.

He shrugged. "Well, all right."

"A glass of white wine," I said.

"Have something decent. And she turned to the barman, ordering the same for herself and her friend.

I insisted on wine, as it's all I ever drink. Then to Dick's exasperated look, I raised my eyebrows.

When the drinks were served, she leaned over. "Lend me a twenty, Dickie. I blew everything in New York."

He gave it to her, smiling - a bad sign.

She told the barman to keep the change.

Dick sipped his drink philosophically. "I thought you were flying into Philadelphia."

Gracie sighed heavily. "So dud I! But Aer Lingus kept serving me doubles. I woke up in consequence in the Chelsea Hotel."

I doubted Aer Lingus would do that. I really did. It was obvious Gracie was on a bender. My father had patients who regularly went on them, ending up broke in St John of God's Hospital. They came to him for certificates for work, and he gave them, saying alcohol was just another disease which got people in its grip. There were certain physical symptoms: a red face, yellow bloodshot eyes, and a sort of puffy look. All of which Gracie had.

She sat slouched over the bar now, laughing at her companion.

He requested more poetry.

She slammed down her drink, then, lowering her voice began, "In a mean abode on the Shankill Road lived a man called William Bloat!"

Dick looked desperate. He was probably already regretting Gracie.

Gracie banged the counter with her fist. "He had a wife, the curse of his life who continually got his goat!"

Her friend laughed raucously.

"So one day at dawn, with her nightdress on, he cut her bloody throat!"

They both collapsed with laughter.

Gracie got her breath. "With a razor gash, he settled her hash - "

At this, Dick downed his drink and grabbing her huge suitcase made for the door. "Come on Gracie! We're going! Sally Ann, finish your drink!"

She reddened, nudging her companion. "But I'm not finished. My old friend here wants to hear the rest of the poem, don't ye?"

He nodded into his whiskey.

Dick was halfway to the door. "Some other time. I have an afternoon class."

They eyed each other.

"I'm going now," Dick said steadily. "If you don't come, you'll have to take a taxi."

He's not a man to argue with. He has this aura of authority - from teaching I suppose.

"Oh, if ye want to spoil the party!" And muttering "Fuck the begrudgers," she exchanged telephone numbers with her friend. To my alarm, she gave him ours - I mean she'd only just met him.

Outside in the street, Gracie shiveringly hugged her skimpy jacket. "Christ! This climate'd freeze yer arse!"

"Don't you have a coat?" Dick asked typically. "It's February, after all."

She laughed. "I started out with one."

Dick smiled again.

I sat in the back and Gracie got in front with him. All the way back to Athens, she complained about the Chelsea. "I've never seen so many bugs."

Dick was concentrating on driving. "That's New York for you."

It certainly was. I knew the Chelsea area well too, from putting on our play. But if I told my cockroach story, Dick would only put me down. He always says I exaggerate things. But I swear to God once when I was waiting on 22nd Street for the lights to change I happened to look down. And a cockroach the size of a blinking mouse was beside me. The lights changed. I walked on. And so did the cockroach. Honestly.

"I had to get the manager up. They wur flyin' around the room."

Cockroaches didn't fly. Dick caught my eye in the mirror. Like me, he was probably thinking Gracie had the DTs.

She groaned shudderingly. "Gawd, when do I start giving out the wisdom, Dickie?"

"You're already a week late," he said flatly. "I've been covering your classes."

She looked puzzled. "Now how's that?"

Dick shrugged. "I sent you the dates."

"Patsy McCallow deals with everything." She turned to me. "He's my fiancé, the Mullingar poet. Have ye met him, Sally Ann?"

"No," I said.

"He must've got mixed up," she muttered.

Gracie always called her fiancé the Mullingar poet. And always blamed him when things went wrong. I suppose he was at a convenient distance.

Then I noticed her shivering. "Are you feeling all right?"

"Aye," she groaned in reply, her head in her hands.

It turned out Gracie was very sick. So Dick made her sleep in our study the first night. But the next day she insisted she was OK and taught her fiction class. Getting ready, she spent ages in the bathroom. I waited in dread.

But she came out sober and completely deflated compared to yesterday. As usual, she wore her uniform - black suit and too much eye make-up which made her look like Dracula's daughter.

"Black suits you, Gracie," I said cheerfully.

She tremblingly checked her lipstick in a small handbag mirror. "I'm in mournin' for me life. You'll help, Sally Ann. In case I dry up."

"Yes, but you won't." To learn something about writing, I had asked to sit in.

I lent her my coat. But, as we walked together across campus, she was shivering.

The class had already assembled. They were the usual mixture of younger graduate students and older women. A boy called Fred had been chosen by Dick to read his story that day. He was a Joycean, I learnt later. This is a breed of American academics who consider every Irish writer but Joyce the dregs, and spend their lives writing papers to make him seem difficult. Oh, there are Yeatsians and Beckettians too, but the Joyceans far exceed them in number and peculiarity. Fred was writing a doctoral thesis on defecation symbolism in Ulysses - "a shit man" was to be Gracie's definition of him. Also he had the weirdest notions of Dublin and of Irish history. For instance, he actually told me St Patrick had slain the armies of Chuchulain at the Hill of Tara.

Gracie said a few words of introduction to the class. Then called on him.

He was a tall, handsome boy with that healthy American vitaminy look. His fair hair and skin contrasted with studious hornrimmed glasses, reminding me of the comic-strip hero, Rip Kirby. Yet there was something fussily effeminate about Fred. And while most American students dressed

121

casually in jeans and a check shirt, he was always stiffly turned out in a suit.

His story was absolutely corny.

Rustling his papers, he began shakily, "It's called - eh - 'Love Reclaimed'." Then, clearing his throat, went on: "I'll never forget the day Bar abandoned me. It was my last year in high school. I skipped swimming and came home early to practise my guitar. The house was uncharacteristically empty, but I knew she'd be in soon. She was probably doing early Christmas shopping. Or she'd gone to the hairdresser to have that blond rinse again. Why didn't she stick to her natural grey which I preferred? I played a few numbers, then put on a Dave Bowie record. Outside the last shreds of daylight gradually disappeared. Inside a melancholy dark pervaded. 'All I have,' Bowie screeched, 'Is my love of love ...' I became more and more depressed, and finally switched off the record. Would Bar desert me without a word? Had our love meant nothing? Yes, it had. We'd had days of wine and roses. Of love and champagne. But were they over forever? No, they couldn't be. By eight I cooked a hamburger. She would surely be in any minute. Then I would surprise her by cooking her one. I would then make popcorn, and we'd look at late night TV like old times. But by nine there was no sign of her. My mind began to run away with me. She'd come to harm. Been raped, horribly mutilated. At ten I rang the police."

As Fred's voice droned on, I looked to see how Gracie was reacting. To my alarm, she held a pocket flask to her lips.

Oh God, I thought, as she rescrewed it and put it back in her handbag.

Our eyes met.

She gave me a "don't you dare tell" look. I was to become very familiar with that look. What would everyone say now? What would they think of Dick for choosing an alcoholic to be visiting professor? What would they think of the Irish? So far we'd been able to hide her in our apartment, but tonight she'd be on her own. Who would control her then? I had the most awful gloomy foreboding.

Fred read on:

"Waiting, I paced the living-room. At last the police came. I showed them a picture of Bar at the beach last summer.

'Are you a relative?' was the first thing the policewoman said.

This was the usual reaction to a young man and a grey-haired woman. So I explained we were engaged and planned to marry.

'Did you check the closets?' the policewoman asked.

'The closets?' I asked, alarmed. So they also thought she'd been murdered. 'You think there'll be a body?'

'Her clothes might be gone.'

We both went upstairs to the bedroom. Sure enough, her clothes were gone ...'"

The story got sillier and sillier. There was no question of his friend being murdered. She left him a note that she'd gone on a cruise or something. Listening, I got the most awful attack of the giggles, but managed to stop it.

At last Fred seemed to be coming to the end.

What is love, I asked myself as Fall became Winter. Christmas was on the horizon. How would I get through it alone? To cheer myself up, I went over to friends for the day. There was a huge parcel under the glimmering tree. To my amazement, my name was on it. As I approached, it started rustling. Something was moving inside the red wrapping paper. Then, to my astonishment, Bar burst through the ribbons. And fell naked into my arms.

'Honey', I sighed, 'this is love.'"

When Fred stopped reading, there was an awkward silence.

We all looked at Gracie.

She waited a minute, then coughed nervously. "Sally Ann, do ye have any comments?"

I racked my brains. "I - thought the symbolism terrific - the parcel and that."

Fred's face lit up. "You got it?"

I nodded. "The ribbons were a symbol of subjection."

Then the others joined in.

Gracie listened politely. Then, when everyone was silent, she said, "Let's talk about it in terms of structure."

Then she gave us a brilliant lecture on the Aristotelian plot: situation, complication, rising to climax, and finally dénouement. Sick or not, she really knew her stuff. The class was a great success. Everyone joined in the discussion. I asked why all stories had to have this basic formula. I mean why couldn't there be a series of small climaxes instead of one big one, like in Virginia Woolf's *The Waves*? Lately I'd become fired up about feminism and was intrigued to learn that we were a disadvantaged class, and studied in America as a separate species. So why did the male gender have to dominate a thing like plot? Locally the feminists had changed the spelling of women to wimin, and woman to womyn. So why not change in other areas?

But Gracie said I was talking rubbish.

Maybe I was.

"Virginia Woolf is caviar," she said. "But not a writer to learn from."

I was grateful for that, at least.

That night Gracie moved into her own apartment.

It was a great mistake not to tell Dick about the flask because from then on I entered into a conspiracy with her against him. While he prided himself on persuading her off the "hard stuff" and onto a maintenance dose of wine, I knew she was drinking whiskey on the sly. But she had me blackmailed that any word to Dick would involve the most awful betrayal of her.

I would be worse than Judas.

Around this time Dick got very sick. We were grocery shopping one day when he frowned as if in pain. When I asked him what it was, he said his tongue hurt. We were having people to dinner, so he wouldn't call the doctor. He kept thinking it'd go away. But all night long, it kept getting worse and swelling until he couldn't swallow or speak. He sat up, afraid to go to sleep. Although a doctor's daughter, I'd never seen anything like it. I kept getting up and asking him how he was.

But he'd only mumble, "Go back to bed."

He's a midwestern stoic and once broke an ankle without noticing. All night I dozed fretfully, dreaming he was having a heart attack downstairs. I even thought of ringing my father for advice, I felt so dreadfully lonely. And helpless.

At dawn I rang our dentist. He said to ring the doctor. I did. But, as it was the weekend, the doctor wasn't there. I left a message on an answering machine. Eventually another doctor rang me back and said to meet him at his surgery in half-an-hour. In between, I rang Gracie in desperation.

She came over immediately and peered professionally down Dick's throat. "It's a touch of quinsy."

"What's that?" I asked.

"Tonsillitis, girl."

I could've hugged her for diagnosing something so ordinary. She came with us to the doctor who said it was an allergy attack from eating cheese. Or maybe from aspirin. He didn't know. Dick was to write down everything he ate. While getting the medicine, I remembered I'd given him a vitamin B tablet for premenstrual tension - mine. I'd read they were good for it. Could he be allergic to that? I felt sick with guilt for persuading him to take it - it was just me on a health binge. And I was sick from lack of sleep.

Dick seemed to get better, but I still worried. It's silly, but I always imagine the worst. Maybe because he smokes. Or because of my mother dying, I don't know. I dreaded him eating something and bringing on another attack. Or taking aspirin. Or maybe he was allergic to something growing in the yard. Everyone in the university thought I was daft to go on so. Except Gracie. She would always listen to me with sympathy. She appeared to be doing OK in her own apartment, so I worried less about her. At first the faculty were good about inviting her to dinner, so she'd only come to us occasionally.

One evening the Athens feminist community gave a party for her. It was hosted by Anna and Sue, a lesbian couple I'd met at a series of lunchtime lectures on women. The lectures were chaired by Anna, a professor who worked with Dick in the History Department, and touched on everything from TV images of women to blocked tubes - fallopian. Sue was a lab assistant in Wilmington, who left her job to have a child. It absolutely intrigued me that they had a baby called Circe. Apparently they'd wanted to be an ordinary family, so Sue, being the younger, had got herself artificially inseminated. It'd been a struggle to find a doctor willing to inseminate single women, but they had finally. Another bonus was he used fresh and not frozen sperm - if it's anything like frozen food, I understood the preference. (Next time they are going to use two eggs.) The doctor's donors were all medical students, but the women could choose their ethnic type. To my delight they chose Irish: blue eyes, freckles and red hair. Also they'd ordered musical ability. So far Circe just smiled like any sweet little baby. I couldn't imagine her ever turning men into pigs. Or what they'd have done if she'd been a boy.

Their house was in West Main Street, one of the best areas of town. Like most American houses, it had lovely hardwood floors and oriental rugs. There were spider plants everywhere, and the kitchen was full of gadgets. Men weren't invited, so I went with Gracie who had unwittingly invited Fred. We arrived when the party was in full swing. Hordes of women chatted in the living room, while some spilled out to the kitchen and hall. Most were casually dressed à la Americaine in levis and shirts and things. So Gracie really stood out in a sexy purple dress. So did Fred in his suit. Also he was smoking - he has a habit of smoking fat cigars.

Anna met us in the hall. Although she temporarily earns the money, they're two equal women. I mean, it's not like one does the cooking, they share everything. When I mentioned this to Dick, he said "Forget it" - the trouble is, he can't cook anything but steak, although he does do the washing-up. But their arrangement is far better. They were the first lesbians I'd ever met, so I didn't know what to expect, maybe for one to be masculine. But they're not. Anna's sort of motherly with shoulder-length curly hair, bleached by the sun at the tips, and the most lovely deep-set eyes. She's always elegantly dressed. That night she was wearing floppy black evening pants and a pink blouse.

"Ah, Sally Ann," she said warmly. "And this must be Ms O'Malley."

I introduced them. They shook hands, Anna saying, "A colleague was telling me about *On Another Man's Wound*."

Gracie laughed shortly. "That's Ernie O'Malley. He's the opposition. I'm Grace."

Anna was embarrassed. "I'm sorry."

"She's called after an Irish queen," I said quickly, as Americans often mixed up Irish writers or mispronounced their names. "Gráinne Uaille - it means noble one in Irish. She was a pirate queen in the time of Elizabeth I."

Anna was interested in this, and intrigued by Gracie's accent, saying she spoke much faster than Americans. Then, as Fred was hovering, I introduced him. "This is Fred, he's Grace's student."

"Hi!" He thrust out his hand. With his cigar in the corner of his mouth, he looked like some Chicago hoodlum.

Anna didn't flinch at his grip. She looked pointedly at the cigar.

Gracie sensed the awkwardness. "He's with me."

Anna nodded understandingly. "I know. But I'm afraid he'll have to smoke on the porch. Sue worries about the baby's chest."

At the mention of the baby, Fred's tough act completely wilted and he went outside. Anna got us some cranberry punch. It was delicious. As well as being anti-smoking, they're anti-booze and coffee. And they never drink anything but a peculiar herb tea. Also they're vegetarian. They're dead right to take care of their health. I suggested to Dick that we cut out meat, but of course got the usual answer: "Forget it."

Gracie peered at the punch. "What's this? Blood?"

I kept my face straight. "It's a fruit punch."

Anna patted her shoulder. "And full of vitamin C."

Gracie looked at it sadly. "Aye, I could do with some of that."

Then we mingled with the others. Gracie was lionised. Absolutely lionised. Although no one had read her books.

Later I went in search of Sue. About three weeks earlier I'd left a toy doll for Circe in the History Department. For which they'd never thanked me. It wasn't that I expected thanks. I understood it had just slipped their minds. I just worried in case they hadn't got it. She was in the kitchen, taking a tray of snacks out of the oven. She's a small Swedish-blonde woman with her hair in a long pigtail. Now she looked red in the face and frazzled, as she took a tray of hot snacks out of the oven.

"Hi, Sally Ann," she said, looking round.

"Can I help?"

"You can put these on a plate and bring them inside."

So I arranged the snacks while Sue dashed about, doing this and that. Americans, I'd discovered, were marvellous cooks. By now I was quite good too and had learnt to make all sorts of things from a James Beard paperback. Although Dick still complained about my salads - he likes bacon bits and all sorts of funny things on it. "By the way,", I said after a few minutes. "You got that doll all right?"

Sue frowned. "Oh - yes, thanks. Didn't Anna write you?"

"No, but that's OK. I couldn't decide what to get. I thought you'd have enough clothes, so I got something for Circe."

"You never have enough clothes with a baby, Sally Ann. You'll find out!"

I was taken aback. "Well, I'll - they might change it."

"Would they? It's just that dolls are sexist."

"Oh! ... I'll change it."

Really, Sue was right to be honest. If you don't like something, why not change it? People aren't honest enough. Their outspokenness was what I liked about Anna and Sue. "Speak what you feel, not what you ought to say."

I can't remember when, but sometime in the course of that party, Anna quizzed Gracie about her classes. Anna was completely committed to women, so, on hearing about the survey course on Irish Literature, she said, "I hoped you'd be focusing on women writers."

Gracie was quite affable. "Well, I'm teaching the main ones - Maria Edgeworth, Mary Lavin, Elizabeth Bowen, Kate O'Brien, and we'll squeeze in Edna O'Brien."

"But why not teach women exclusively?"

"Well, it's a survey course. There's Yeats, Joyce, Synge, O'Casey."

"But how can we ever mainstream women?"

"Not by ghettoing them. Do you support apartheid?"

That absolutely threw Anna. "Of course not!"

"Well, you're preaching it!" Gracie hesitated, then went on.

"You could teach a course on women's fiction, but it wouldn't be what you want. Mills and Boon is a definite genre."

"I think you're being sexist."

"No I'm not. There's men's thrash too."

Anna kept her sense of humour. "You have a point there."

Luckily the baby woke up then, and Sue brought her out to the kitchen. I watched in fascination as she breast-fed her. It seemed the most wonderful thing in the world to feed a baby from your own body. Even Gracie had to admire Circe, chuckling over her name. Babies have a way of bringing out the niceness in people. It's sort of awe for a new life. An attempt to put the best face on terrible things. I forget how, but the conversation got onto marriage. I think Anna and Sue said they weren't legally bound or something. And I said I was a believer in marriage. Which brought an odd remark from Anna. "Be careful about marriage, Sally Ann."

I felt myself redden. "What do you mean?"

"Well ... by allying yourself with Richard - "

Then Gracie exploded. "Sure, who else would she ally herself with?"

I thought there'd be another personality clash, but Anna said kindly, "He certainly lucked-in in meeting someone so sensitive and beautiful."

"I was lucky too!" I knew she sparred with Dick at department meetings. I knew he could be acerbic. I knew that's what it was. Or maybe she thought Nettie and the children would cause too many complications. Still, it wounded me that she didn't like him. And I wasn't even remotely beautiful. How could I be with glasses?

I wandered off, joining another conversation.

Gracie soon followed me, whispering, "Let's be off. I need a drink."

127

I looked at her nervously. "You won't overdo it?"

She gave me her word. So we repaired to the Tavern.

Where an idiotic thing happened. Although surrounded by laughing students, I couldn't keep the tears from my eyes. Why had Anna said that about Dick? She and Sue were meant to be my friends. Probably the only friends I'd made in America - usually I was just an extension of Dick. But they had introduced me into a whole new world of feminism. And they'd taken me cycling into the country, before Circe was born. They seemed to like me. Although Sue, particularly, was always measuring me, pulling me up on what I said, as if I were some right-wing person. Like I'd once mentioned something about South Africa, saying *maybe* they shouldn't cut off all investment. That I'd read in the *New York Times* that Alan Paton thought this. But Sue had pounced on me, as if I supported the regime. She got really angry. If you ask me, there's apartheid in America. They just don't call it that. In three years, I'd only met one black, and someone told me the university had to be forced to allow them to attend. Another time Sue had attacked me for calling the loo the "Ladies Room". She asked, hadn't I read *The Women's Room*? Which, according to her, was the most brilliant novel ever written. Sometimes feminism was too dogmatic. It was just like the socialists in college. If women were oppressed, so were men, paying for all the damn washing machines. Dick always worked so hard. And for years gave most of his salary to Nettie. For no thanks. Even his children were cold to him. I knew he loved them, even if he couldn't express it. And he'd been so sick the other night. His throat wasn't entirely better. But he wouldn't give up cheese or aspirin. He said we all had a disease called mortality. That you lived till you died. But what if it happened again? What if he choked to death the next time?

I sat there staring into my beer.

Then Gracie, who'd been sitting chatting to Fred, noticed me. "What's up with you?"

Hastily, I wiped my eyes. "It's just Dick's allergy attacks."

"Allergy attacks, me eye! It's quinsy!"

I felt better. After a while, I said, trying to sound light-hearted, "Did you hear what Anna said about marriage?"

"Silly bitch!"

"You can't call her that." Although I'd used it in the past, nowadays the word took me aback. Anyway, Anna wasn't one.

"Better a silly bitch than an a sacred cow! Isn't she married herself?"

"Well, not legally. But they've taken vows to each other."

"What's that, only marriage?" Gracie downed her drink in one alarming gulp. "I don't care what anyone fucks or sucks, man, woman or goat. But I hate bad manners! A hostess shouldn't be abrasive. Fuck the begrudgers!"

I had to laugh. God, she was outspoken. Then Fred was sent for more drinks. And Gracie leant towards me. "I like Dickie. He's a good man."

I couldn't reply. It meant so much. But in retrospect, I can see I was too thin-skinned. I should've been tougher. Anna had only been concerned for me. I was a stranger in a foreign country and far from my family. And she mistrusted men. God knows what she had suffered at their hands. Sue, I know, had been in a bad marriage. Luckily, I managed to change the doll for a truck.

At spring break Gracie escaped our clutches, going North to a college she had taught at years ago. Of course, they filled her to the gills with Bourbon. One night soon afterwards we got a phone call that she was legless in the local tavern. So Dick collected her, making her move back with us. He was afraid to let her out of his sight and forbade any drink. Luckily she was too sick to disobey him.

I'd never seen anyone so poisoned with alcohol. Never. Her eyes were black circled, her pallor yellowish, and she crept around the apartment in a worn floral dressing gown. As Dick had to teach, he was out a lot. So I ended up baby-sitting her. Maybe it's my mother complex, or maybe because she was sick, but I became very fond of her. I worried about her not eating and made her eggflips - which my mother had made me.

Usually in the afternoons, I would sit in the kitchen with a book. Although it was old-fashioned, it was pleasant, the pleasantest room in our book-lined apartment. Sunlight filtered through spider plants at the windows and there was a small round white marble table. Dick had painted the antiquated fridge and walls in different greens and black frying pans and copper pots hung over the stove. Gracie would usually join me.

Once I was finishing a book of Seamus O'Shea's short stories, when she came in sipping her egg-flip and sat down opposite me. "I'd only drink this for yerself, Sally Ann."

"It's good for you."

She shuddered, huddling in her dressing gown. "It's poison."

I glanced down at my book. "You've got to eat something."

She sipped some more. "Ugh!"

I ignored this. How would she get strong without nourishment?

"Do you like America, Sally Ann?"

"It's OK." I put down my book. "I look forward to the summer a lot. We go to Dublin then."

"There's no place like Grafton Street."

I closed my book.

"Sorry, I'm interrupting you."

"No! I was just finishing a Seamus O'Shea story. What do you think of him?"

She laughed, running her fingers through her thick red hair. "He was a premature ejaculator."

"A what?" I thought it was some literary term.

"A premature ejaculator. Surely you've had selfish lovers?"

"Well ... no." I was embarrassed. I'd wanted her opinion of his writing. But I was to learn Gracie judged every man by his sexual performance.

"He was very wee," she added, sighing.

"I saw him once in Stephen's Green. He looked tall enough."

"Yes, but he was wee - in the cock."

"Oh!"

She looked smilingly into space. "He was a librarian, you know. I used to borrow books. We had an affair on the reference room table."

I laughed, picturing it.

She went on, "He was very macho. He made violent love to me. Violent. I used to be covered in bruises." She held up her arms. "Then his wife found out." She hesitated, then asked casually. "How's Dickie?"

"Fine. He should be in soon."

"No, I mean in bed."

I just looked at her, reddening.

"He looks a bit uptight."

"Oh no! He isn't! Not at all!"

She lapsed into silence. "Yer man, Freddie's hopeless."

"Is he?"

"Fuckin' hopeless, if that's not a contradiction in terms." She laughed.

So Fred was hopeless, but at least my fears about her and Dick were groundless. But why hadn't he told me? He was just like my father in the area of non-communication. Men never discussed anything. I just assumed our sex life was OK, because at last I could relate. I'd seemed to shed my hang-ups. I wasn't gay. I was just unmodern. Maybe the cliché about the right person was true. Or maybe I wanted to get pregnant.

Gracie seemed to read my thoughts. "You get on well, anyway. Are ye going to marry?"

I shrugged. "Maybe sometime. What about you and the Mullingar poet?"

"Oh, his mammy'd have a fit."

"His mammy?"

"She doesn't know about me. Although we're fifteen years at it."

It was ridiculous. Although he wanted us to marry, my father didn't object to Dick at all. I think he was relieved to be rid of me. "I suppose we'd marry if I got pregnant."

She gave me a sad look. "That doesn't go with being an artist."

I didn't see why not. "Well -"

"I had a daughter - married in London now."

"Do you see her?"

She looked past me, saying after a minute, "You're a talented painter, Sally Ann." She cupped her hands. "Talent is a little flame ... If you don't guard it, it'll go out."

I looked away. No one had ever said that to me, because it wasn't true. I was too imitative. But Gracie was kind. And full of contradictions. She really was. One minute she could be crude and the next sensitive. She was the most amazingly perceptive person. I think she knew how much it meant for a person to be something, and wanted to encourage me. Most probably, we'd hit a sore spot in her daughter, because she'd fallen into a brooding silence.

I broke it. "You haven't finished your egg-flip.

She pushed it away. "I can't ... Would you let me have a drink, Sally Ann?"

I shook my head. "No."

"Please! I need it."

"No!"

I was in a quandary. One drink and she'd be lost. That was the way with alcoholics.

"Please, Sally Ann!"

"No!"

"Yer a hard woman."

I held out. "Would you not go to AA?"

She looked outraged. "Go to AA? Are you off yer head, girl?"

"They'd help you."

"I'm not an alcoholic!" She got to her feet and stormed from the room. "An' I won't sit here and take these insults!"

But that very evening I came unexpectedly into the kitchen to find Gracie taking a swig from Dick's Bourbon bottle. Before I could say anything, she pointed an accusatory finger. "Now don't tell Dickie!"

And of course I didn't.

After Gracie moved out on her own again, I knew she wouldn't eat. So I made her promise to have dinner with us every evening. In that way I could be sure she had one decent meal a day. Also we could make sure she wasn't drinking. Well, she came for about a week. Then she came drunk one day and plonked a decanter of Paul Masson wine on the table, saying, "Let's 'ave a drink, girl."

"You know you're not meant to," I said.

"I'm OK on wine."

"Well, drink it then. I don't want any."

But she poured two drinks and pushed one towards me.

Dick wasn't in yet, so I weakly agreed.

But just then he walked in and, taking one look at Gracie's red face, grabbed the bottle and emptied it down the sink.

She watched ruefully. "Yer only wastin' good drink, Dickie."

Dick glared at me. So I poured out mine too.

We had dinner in awful silence. Afterwards, I walked Gracie home across campus. She didn't ask me in. Just yawned sleepily at the door.

131

"I'm sorry Dick got so angry," I said.

"Ah, Dick's a good man. Good night now." And she went inside, shutting her door firmly in my face.

I had never been in her apartment. I didn't know then that Fred was inside waiting for her.

Their affair was the talk of our little community, so he must've improved in the sex line. It seemed to shock everyone that he was a younger man and she an older woman. I don't know why. People accepted a young woman and an older man.

Gracie didn't come to dinner again. I missed her, but Dick was glad our life had returned to some sort of normality. It wouldn't be completely normal so long as Gracie was in town. He went back to his book, and I was thrown back on my loneliness. But I accepted this as part of our relationship. I'd made the decision to love Dick and now had to act on it. Happiness was meant to be the final end of man, but did it exist at all? And what was it? No matter how lonely I was, I couldn't go back. I couldn't admit failure. I had failed so often before - with Colm, Alastair and my terrible career. My father was only waiting for me to arrive back home. But I had to make something of my life. So I resigned myself to Dick's noisy typing and became absorbed in my own work. I worked really hard, attending every class and getting an A for the course.

We heard Gracie was drinking heavily again.

Towards the end of the semester, we were invited to a dinner party at Fred Ferris's. He lived with an older woman - a sort of patron, according to gossip - on a horse farm in the Maryland countryside. The drive down was lovely. In America they actually get a spring. I can't believe Ireland is greener than Pennsylvania. The weather was just beginning to warm up, and soon dogwoods would be out. We found the place without getting lost. It was like a movie set in an Elizabeth Taylor film. The house was a mansion at the end of a long tree-lined avenue. There were stables to one side, and the fields on the other were surrounded by white fences. There were even horses grazing. It was idyllic.

How did Fred manage to live here?

When we arrived, everyone was having drinks on the patio. There was Max Wagoner, the Chairman of the English Department and his wife, Pam. And a man called Felice who taught sculpture at the university. Gracie, looking red-faced and sexy in her purple dress. Fred and his patron, Mrs Davis.

She was a hawklike woman of about sixty with dyed gold hair and brown alligator skin. And I thought at first she must be some relation of Fred's. His grandmother - that was the answer.

While he was getting us drinks and the others chatted, Gracie whispered to me, "Try and occupy Freddie tonight. I'm angling for yer man there." And she rolled her eyes at Felice.

132

He was a smooth-looking fortyish Italian type. He had slick black hair and his shirt, open to the waist, revealed even more hair.

"But what about Fred?" I asked.

"Ah, he's her gigolo." And she nodded towards Mrs Davis.

I looked disbelievingly at the older woman, dressed too youthfully in a gold pants suit. She must be the woman in his story.

She caught my stare. "Are you a student, honey?"

I nodded. "Of painting."

She gave me a piranha smile. "I thought you might be in the English Department with Fred."

"Well, we're both taking Gracie's class."

Gracie laughed shortly. "I have some real geniuses."

Sarcasm to students was unlike her, she was always kind and supportive. So I suspected the worst.

Mrs Davis went on sociably. "Fred's doing a PhD on Joyce. He thinks there's no one like him."

"Thank God," Gracie quipped. "Wasn't one enough?"

This brought a laugh from the others.

"He was a bloody pervert," she went on.

Gracie was pissed. I knew the signs: high colour and garrulousness. But there was no way I was getting involved in her amours. So I didn't try to "occupy" Fred. What on earth did she expect me to do? Disappear with him into a cupboard? Several times she tried to chat up Felice, but he persistently ignored her. Finally, she recited "Twenty Golden Years Ago", and then fell asleep, snoring loudly.

The talk during dinner was typically boringly academic and dominated by Max Wagoner, a Joycean too. He was a big German-American with tanned ashblond good looks who had learned the English language as a teenager and ended up a professor - a suave, preppie type who always wore shirts and sweaters with little designer dragons. Anyway, during coffee, Felice casually asked him to explain the term Structuralism.

Max launched into a pompous explanation. "Well, it really comes from two sources. Saussure's lectures to his students were published as a general course in linguistics. He said you define something by its opposite - no meaning exists, except in relation to something else."

"So all works of literature could be said to be derivative?" Felice interrupted.

"Yes ... in a way. Every system needs an opposite. Twentieth century man, for instance, is only perceived as tough compared to twentieth century woman."

"And what about Deconstructionism?"

"That comes from Derrida. It means to take apart. A writer may seem to have written a comedy, but it's really a tragedy."

Then Gracie woke up shouting, "Bullshit."

There was a deadly silence.

She looked sort of deranged. "Fuckin' bloody bullshit."

Max Wagoner paled under his tan.

"It nauseates me the way you academics murder literature."

Dick smiled. "I think Gracie may have a point."

But she was really angry. "Fuckin' sure I do!"

"It's only the theorists," Dick said, trying to defuse the situation.

"All theorists, structuralists, deconstructionists! They're all the bloody same. I can't sit here talkin' gibberish." She looked directly at Felice. "Will ye give me a lift home?"

He looked alarmed. "I - I'm going in the other direction."

There is meant to be no fury like a woman scorned. At that, Gracie shouted, "Fuck the begrudgers! Yer a bum-boy, that's your direction. Gawd, give me a full-blooded man!"

There was another terrible silence.

Everyone looked glacial.

Absolutely glacial.

Just as Gracie was going to shout something else, Max Wagoner interrupted. "Miss O'Malley, there's an alcoholism treatment scheme in the university."

"What are ye sayin'?" she hissed.

"I could arrange treatment for you."

Her breast seemed to swell. "How dare you, you Nazi!"

I'm afraid I got the giggles.

"Nazi! Nazi!" Gracie screamed, walking leglessly from the room with Fred running after her.

That night when we arrived home, Dick got another allergy attack. I was sure it was from eating cheese at the party. We were up all night again and ended up going to the Emergency Centre. I told the nurse he refused to write down what he ate, so she told me to get insurance. I now became obsessed with worry about him. I even had a nightmare that he died and was buried. But I got Fred Ferris to dig him up. It was gruesome. But he still wouldn't give up things. At least for a while I stopped thinking about Gracie. Anyway, she was lost to us now. Lost.

One afternoon I was in the apartment reading when Max Wagoner rang to ask if I'd seen her.

I said no.

"She hasn't been meeting her classes. I may try again to persuade her to get treatment."

"The term's nearly over."

"Well, there are the exams to mark."

"Did you try the Tavern?"

"Yes. Lately she's met her classes there. She recites to the students. But no one has seen her for a week."

I promised to tell him if she turned up. My stomach was in a knot of anxiety. Dick said there was nothing we could do about Gracie's drinking. But was it right to leave her on her own? Why couldn't we do something about her? Force her into a hospital. After all, she wasn't really able to take care of herself. And why did she drink? What unhappiness had driven her to it? She was so talented. And the odd thing was she told me she was writing another novel. How could she do it? Two drinks and I had a hangover.

Later there was a terrible knocking on the door. I thought it was Gracie. But it was Fred Ferris.

"Sally Ann, can we talk?"

I asked him in.

He was wet with perspiration and completely winded. "Have you seen Gracie?"

I said no.

He wiped his hornrimmed glasses. "You must help me find her!"

I calmed him down. "She'll turn up."

He loosened his tie and, dabbing his forehead with a hanky, sat down. "You don't understand. She's come under the influence of very undesirable characters."

"Maybe she's gone to New York. She has friends there."

He put his head in his hands. "Oh, my God!"

I didn't really know Fred, so was surprised at his state. Apparently, it wasn't just a casual affair to him. "I'm only suggesting New York. Now, pull yourself together."

"But you don't understand. I love Gracie. I want to marry her."

"You know she's engaged to Patsy McCallow?" I said gently.

He jumped up. "She's what?"

"Oh ... Come on. Surely she told you about the Mullingar poet?"

He paced the room. "She'll have to tell him it's off, that's all."

I readjusted my glasses. I was absolutely amazed at his reaction. Gracie wasn't really my idea of an attractive woman.

He banged his fist on the palm of his hand, pacing frantically. "She'll have to tell him we're getting married."

"What does she say?"

He looked at me frantically. "You realise we've slept together!"

"You don't have to marry everyone you sleep with," I said. "Not nowadays."

"You shock me, Sally Ann."

I swallowed awkwardly. If he was shocked, I was more so to discover an innocent American. I thought they were all so sophisticated. And what about Mrs Davis?

Suddenly he went to the door. "Come with me to her apartment."

"She might be in the Tavern."

"I've looked there. She isn't." He stepped out into the hall. "Come with me! I know she's in there."

So I went.

But Gracie's apartment door was shut firmly. And there was no response to our loud knocking.

"I know she's in there," Fred insisted for the millionth time.

I tried to calm him. "She'd answer the door if - "

"Gracie, open up!"

"Look, come home and have a drink. Dick may have a suggestion."

"Gracie, come out this minute!" And he pounded again on the door. "Gracie!"

I walked down the stairs. "Come on, Fred."

But, to my amazement, at that moment the door inched open and Gracie peeped through the crack, saying in her deep voice, "I'll meet ye in the Tavern in half an hour, Freddie."

"Who's in there?" he screamed.

"I'll see you in the Tavern," she said and closed the door.

Fred tried to push it open, but was too late. "Gracie!" he sobbed. "Gracie!"

"Go to the Tavern!" she called from behind the door.

I took his arm, leading him down the stairs.

The tavern was about ten minutes away. While we were waiting, I rang Dick, asking him to tell Max Wagoner Gracie was safe.

When Gracie came over, she was dead drunk. Her hair was dishevelled, her black suit stained. She walked swayingly over to us. "What are ye havin', kids?"

We both ordered coke which reduced her to drunken giggles. "Come on now, it's not often we're out."

We stuck to coke and they brought our drinks quickly, as she was well known.

Then Fred began accusing her hysterically. "Who was in there?"

She ignored him, holding her glass up to me. "Here's to a maiden of bashful fifteen ..."

Fred banged the table. "Answer me, Gracie!"

"And here's to the widow of fifty!"

As he accused, she recited.

She was nearly finished the poem when Dick came in with Max Wagoner.

Gracie held up her glass. "And here's to the SS."

Dick went to get drinks, and Max sat down, ignoring her remark. After a few polite enquiries as to how her classes were going, he pleaded, "Ms O'Malley, would you take treatment?"

To my surprise, Gracie didn't get furious. She just patted his arm. "Ah, don't be cracked man. Sure, I'm no alcoholic."

Max looked helplessly at Dick who had come back.

"I think you should try treatment too, Gracie," he said.

Then Fred chipped in, saying fussily, "She's mixing with some very undesirable people, and the waitress here always short-changes her."

At this Gracie turned furiously on him. "How dare ye impugn the honour of my friends."

Fred was speechless.

"How dare ye!"

"We're your friends, Gracie," I said quietly.

I thought she was going to hit me. In a minute there'd be a scene. But Dick nudged me to drink up.

I did. And we left her.

I was very sad. So sad that Dick actually offered to take me to a French movie. It was the only thing on. It'd be just like old times, I thought. But we were just finished dinner and on the way out, when there was more pounding on the door.

It was Gracie.

"Stand aside!" she shouted, making down the corridor for the loo. "Stand aside!"

I ran after her. "What is it?"

"Go away!" she ordered. "I've shit me pants, Sally Ann."

"Well, take them off!" I closed the bathroom door almost crying at what drink did to people. Gracie had lost all dignity.

But worse was to follow.

As I waited outside, she called through the door, "It's all over me, Sally!"

"Well, take a bath!"

Then to my horror, she came out starkers. "Is it off me?"

I checked. It wasn't.

Then Dick came down the corridor from our sitting room, saying sternly, "Take a bath, Gracie."

She beckoned me. "Sally, will ye have a look at my suit. Is it ruined?"

Why couldn't she do it? But holding my breath, I put it under a tap. Then put it in a bag for the cleaners.

Finally we got Gracie into the bath and then back to her apartment in borrowed clothes. I learnt later she headed right back to the Tavern. Of course, it was too late for our film. So, as we were exhausted with all the drama, we went to bed. Dick was absolutely fed up. Life had become a grand opera. The term was a write-off. And Gracie had got him into real trouble with the University administrators. They'd had to employ someone else to teach her classes. He said they'd never trust him to find anyone again - and they haven't.

The next day Gracie disappeared again. I worried non-stop about her, but Dick had that male ability to detach himself. It was nearly time for us to go back to Ireland for the summer, so there was a lot of packing and that. Dick was still sick. I was afraid he'd get an allergy attack in the airplane so persuaded him to see a specialist. Gracie turned out to be right: it wasn't an allergy, but an infection. The first doctor had been prescribing the wrong thing entirely. So much for American doctors. But how had Gracie known?

It was probably her canny wisdom about life. Her enormous sympathy. You could tell her anything, and she wouldn't be shocked. There was nothing bourgeois about her. She could see through the pretentious Max Wagoners of this life. Despite everything, I liked her much better than them. She was named after an Irish pirate queen and had her own sort of grace. I'd always miss her sense of fun. But how had she made such a mess of her life? Why did she have to drink? She had so much talent.

I thought we'd never see her again.

Then Fred rang. "Sally Ann, could you help me?"

I said yes.

His voice was frantic. "I'm stranded in the Poconos. Gracie's walked out on me. I can't pay the hotel."

Then he told me they'd run away together, and he needed a hundred and fifty dollars. I was amazed that a young American could get fired up about something. I mean they were so conservative compared to us in the sixties. Not that we'd changed anything, but we'd cared about other things besides money and jobs. Oh, I was no great shakes. I never protested now. But I was different than I would've been, if I hadn't lived through those times. I knew that.

I should've asked Fred why Mrs Davis couldn't lend him the money, but didn't. As usual, Dick had to cough up.

And there was more.

We were about a week from departure to Dublin for the summer when the Irish embassy phoned to say the New York police had picked up Gracie for vagrancy and had her in protective custody. Could we come and get her? So Dick and I went to her apartment in town and packed up her things. It was a mess: there were newspapers all over the floor, and the place was strewn with empty bottles. We found her passport and air ticket in a drawer. So Dick rang Aer Lingus, changing her flight to the following day.

Then we drove to New York.

Gracie was in a terrible state. She sat behind bars on a grim prison bunk with her head in her hands. Her red hair looked grey-streaked and wildly tangled. Her stockings were torn. Her arm was bandaged, and she had a black eye and a badly grazed face.

I put an arm around her shoulder. I felt so guilty for abandoning her. "What happened, Gracie?"

"I'm a terrible person Sally Ann." Then her bloodshot eyes got angry.

"Did you see that tall cop out there?"

"I didn't notice."

"He said the Irish were all drunks, so I kicked him in the balls. Fuck the begrudgers!"

I turned to Dick. "Look at her face. Would you find out who did it!"

But she was reciting.

*There's a one-eyed yellow idol to the north of Khatmandu,*
*There's a little marble cross below the town;*
*There's a broken-hearted woman ... There's a broken- hearted woman ...*
*There's a broken-hearted woman ...*

Dick took her arm. "Come on Gracie. I'll buy you a pair of shoes."

# X  Peggy and Tony

Buying a house in Ireland is hazardous these days, especially with no money. We've just managed it, thanks to finaglings. Although I'm to blame, it was my friend Peggy who first suggested it. The occasion must be three years ago now. The four of us, Peggy and her husband Tony and Dick and I, were inhaling the convivial smoke of a Dublin pub - *The Hill* in Ranelagh, if I remember rightly. We usually met there. And the chat was probably going in the usual direction of troublesome landladies, the bane of our life then, when Peggy got her brain-wave.

"Why not buy a house?" Her words were like a stone from the sky.

Dick's pint of Guinness stopped in mid-air. "Ah - buy *what*?"

"A house!" Peggy smoothed her bleached perm. You could rent it when you're in America."

She smiled at her own brilliance - she has a beautiful smile.

I grinned nervously back, as we weren't exactly at the house-buying stage. For years we'd been sort of "unofficially engaged." At least that's what my father told people. Also that Dick was begging me to marry him, but I wouldn't. And wasn't I wise not to rush into things. The reverse was probably truer, but you have to allow fathers their pride.

In the awkward silence that followed, Tony busily knocked out his pipe. When the cards are down, I thought, the men will stick together. But Dick was lubricated enough to be taken with the idea - for a minute.

"But how?" he wailed.

Reason had returned to its throne.

"An ad in *The Irish Times*!" Peggy persisted. "You could get students."

I watched in admiration. I loved Peggy. Maybe it was some sort of mother complex, I don't know. She doesn't mind people knowing she dyes her hair, or being slightly overweight. Like Jack Spratt and wife, Tony shrinks while she gets bigger - according to Dick, the fate of all women, and one I don't relish. I just don't have Peggy's "conviction" - I think that's the word.

"I was referring to the initial difficulty." Dick sounded mildly exasperated. "Money!"

"You don't need money!" Peggy said blithely. "You need a mortgage!"

And Dick spluttered into his Guinness.

While I believe it's a free world, he thinks the opposite. So I expected him to explode about the cost of living, or the young generation. But Peggy's a seasoned mother of six and undeterred by obstacles. A steely gleam appeared in her blue eyes, and her large bosom heaved determindedly. "Sure, everyone has a mortgage."

"I know," Dick said calmly.

"Then why not get one?"

"Because I already have one. In America!" He gave her the pitying glance reserved for women and idiots, and turned appealingly to Tony.

He was still busy with his pipe.

"Rent's dead money, old son," he said between big white puffs.

Peggy waved at the smoke. "Well, get another from an Irish Building Society."

Dick frowned. "But I'm American."

"Sally's Irish!" And Peggy tore open her second packet of peanuts, offering me some.

I should explain that, although Peggy and Tony are old neighbours of Dick and his wife, Nettie, our friendship is not the less. Tony's a journalist, so I expected his tacit male acceptance of a friend's irregularity. I was, after all, the last of a line of girlfriends - or I hope the last. But Peggy was another matter. She's fifteen years my senior, and I feared her judgement as an Irish Catholic wife and mother. But she immediately took me to her bosom, "as a blasted human being, Sally!" Which is only remarkable in comparison to my relatives muttering about me "living in sin." They would whisper discretely to my father: "I didn't think Sally Ann was the type! She didn't seem interested in SEX!" But Peggy has none of the intolerance of our race and, like all the happily married, is an incurable matchmaker. So I suspected her house idea was part of a secret strategy to get Dick settled again - ie properly divorced from Nettie and properly married to me. That I had failed in this became a challenge to her. And buying a house, if not a step down the aisle, was a step in that direction.

I'd heard of building societies. I knew they were sort of banks where careful courting couples deposited their pittance, staking out a future. But the idea of joining one had never occurred to us - before I met Dick I never had a thing over, and now he had another mouth to feed.

Besides, we were suitcase people.

Still, that evening in *The Hill*, I sipped happily on my gin and tonic while Peggy explained the mechanisms of house-buying in Ireland. She's an absolute devourer of romantic fiction (Norah Hoult, Barbara Cartland, anything in Mills and Boon), but there's nothing, and I mean nothing, she doesn't know about the legal end: insurance policies, mortgages, solicitors' fees, bridging loans - topics which are Greek to me. Also, her "conviction" woos you into thinking something impossible is possible. So before the evening was lost to more drink, my house obsession had taken root, and Dick had made an appointment to view.

Peggy had already picked the house.

It was a three-bedroomed Georgian Gem in a new Bray development. The lines of redbrick boxes were all exactly the same and in perfectly ghastly taste. I prefer older houses with a bit of character, but I'm not a quibbler. I'd sacrifice my principles for stability any day. As we trooped round in the wake of the owner, a rising young banker, he pointed out the fitted wardrobe in the master bedroom, the garden shed, and the handy additions in the kitchen. And I began to settle in. The second bedroom would do for Dick's study, I thought, but I had plans for the third - a nursery. As yet there was nothing to put in it. In the meantime I could be a pied-piper aunt to the swarms of local children.

Except there weren't any.

"There are no children this end," Mrs Banker said, dangling the baby as Mr Banker poured us tea.

"All the wives work," he said. "It takes two salaries to pay a mortgage these days. The Catholic curate lives next door. It'll be quiet."

I'm a lapsed Catholic, but never in my most fervent days did I imagine living in a development with a priestly neighbour. But my training in history (BA, NUI) has taught me life is a compromise. And I wanted that tasteless little house. Like the pony when I was nine. Or the high heels when I was fifteen.

Even Dick was bitten. I knew by his gloomy look.

I said I liked the Michaelmas daisies.

"Daisies, my foot! It's in good condition." And he went inside to the owner.

If only it could be ours.

*Oh, to have a little house!*
*To own the hearth and stool and all!*
*The heaped-up sods upon the fire,*
*The pile of turf against the wall!*

All night I dreamt I was the old woman of the roads in Padraic Colum's poem. And on awakening to the world and its troubles the next morning, I reminded Dick that a motherless childhood had left me with a deep desire to be an owner. But he just said his financial need to remain a renter was equally deep.

I sat up, wide awake for once. "Well, there's no need to say it like that!"

"Now, be practical! This month's cheque is late."

Of course, he was right, but I still felt miserable.

"And there's no need to look like that! I'm still paying for the previous darling's house." And he turned gloomily into his pillow.

I kept to my side of the bed. In a minute he was nuzzling into me. Have you ever noticed the way men think making love will solve all problems? How they always feel like it when you're half asleep?

The "previous darling's" bleak Dickensian mansion was on the edge of our American university campus. As the "present darling" I avoided it on my way to a dance class at the YWCA. Nettie was nothing like Berthe Mason, the mad wife in *Jane Eyre*, but I still feared her. Which was idiotic, considering she was always perfectly kind to me. And more idiotic, considering their parting had occurred six years before I even met Dick. It was just ... oh, all those children and all that life without me. I first met

142

Dick at his UCD tutorial (Third Arts General) and then six years later at a Dublin play. Since then we've been like swallows, wintering in America for his job but as soon as the days lengthened flying home to Ireland for the summer - an arrangement which caused our difficulties with landladies. For while a cosy Main Street apartment provided an American nest, my father or some Irish friend would always be stuck with us till I found one in Dublin.

Which made Peggy very sorry for me.

Oh, I got used to all the moving. You can get used to anything. We lived in Killiney one summer, over a TD in Leeson Street another, with a cat in Herbert Park another, and with my brother in Sandymount another. For one whole half-sabbatical we shivered in squalid splendour as caretakers of a crumbling tenement in Mountjoy Square. The drawing-room was the size of a hockey field with an ineffectual fireplace situated like a goalpost at each end - handy for jogging but useless for keeping warm. An outside tap and toilet did for a bathroom, and the smell of something too impolite to mention wafted up the rickety stairs from the hall. As I had found the house, everything was naturally my fault. Probably a happily married couple would've ended that tenancy in divorce or murder, but we survived. The owner was even so delighted with our guardianship he offered us the place cheaply at two hundred thousand pounds. Wasn't it just the sort of house an American scholar would want to "do up"? In my desperation with our rootless existence, I flirted with the idea of saving a slice of vanishing Dublin, but Dick glared me into silence and politely declined.

He claims he's always right and I'm always wrong, but it evens out. Because if we were both right, it'd give us an unnatural advantage over others. He also says I complain too much about things, especially moving. So I won't here. The endless packing of books into boxes and clothes into plastic bags at the end of every summer was good for me. It was. As Dick always said, I was doing some of my almost certain purgatory on earth. And over the years we got to know Dublin well. It's a city with a great variety of accommodation. I mean, you can pay the same for a palace or a hovel. Only last year I answered an ad for a luxury executive flat and was shown round a flooded Leeson Street basement by a landlord in waders. As we splashed through the sitting-room, I said politely wasn't it dampish? And he looked at me so madly that I mumbled it was too big for us. Whereupon he showed me the door, shouting that frankly he was looking for a gang of girls. "Bankers!"

"Mermaids," was Dick's retort when I told him.

You meet all sorts renting. Our Killiney landlady rooted in our wardrobe and rearranged our furniture every time we went out. Oh, it was nice to know the place was being looked after. Our morals too. She actually evicted us because she thought my friend and her truly wedded husband were having an affair in our flat. Ironically, they were on honeymoon, we were having the affair. But for propriety I had to pass as Mrs Sheridan, making my friends address letters to her and trying not to look too startled when the same landlady, accusing me of breaking the hoover or of using the egg-beater during Dallas, addressed me as such. But it was practice for the future. It was.

I always wanted to tell her we were still 'walking out' together, but Dick says you have to consider people's feelings. In that case too, I suppose, he was right.

He also says I go on too much about psychology and that, but I'm a firm believer in self-help books: *Your Erogenous Zones* or *The Action Approach* or *How to be an Assertive Woman*. There's a wealth of knowledge to be got from them. I once read that if you imagine something you desire, it'll happen. So, as the reality of years of wandering at the mercy of capitalistic landlords stretched before me, a picture formed in my mind's eye. A picture of a whitewashed cottage set beneath a green hill with wild roses creeping through the latticed windows. Inside the huge range was always lit, and outside the old orchard always creaked with ripe apples. A place where

> I could be busy all the day
> Clearing and sweeping hearth and floor.
> And fixing on their shelf again
> My white and blue speckled store!

It was silly for a born and bred Dubliner to want to return to the land like Michael Viney. But I wanted us to be happy. To live in rural bliss like Virginia Woolf and Leonard. Or Katherine Mansfield and her man.

About a week after the Georgian Gem, we were perusing *The Irish Times* over breakfast when Dick afforded me more than his usual attention.

"What are you thinking about?"

I looked up sleepily - I often have problems with sleep. "I'm not thinking. I'm reading the paper."

"You're not. You're staring into space."

"Oh." I studied my half of the paper.

"Come on, why so pale?"

I sighed heavily. "I couldn't go to sleep. I was thinking of our house."

He rustled his paper, laughing. "I knew it! Peggy's been at her mischief again."

"She hasn't said a word."

In fact, she regarded the lost Gem as defeat in a skirmish rather than the battle, but I didn't tell him.

"The woman's a menace! She's giving the government a rest and turning her attention to me." He took my half of the paper.

I said nothing.

Peggy and Tony were always at war with someone about something:

planning permission for extensions, or people dumping, or people obstructing their view.

Dick let out a hoot of laughter. "God help the world if she were in power."

The world would be in less of a mess, but I didn't argue.

After a bit, I broke the silence. "Where'll you live when you retire?"

But he was buried in his paper.

"I can't afford to retire," he said at last. "Besides, that's years away."

"Some day you'll have to. And houses will be exorbitant."

"Then I'll take to the heath like Lear!"

Remembering no mention is ever made of Mrs Lear, I vowed to abandon all hope. Dick's children were now alarmingly producing their own children, and all expected to be supported. It was a bit like compound interest. Without knowing the bliss of motherhood, I'd become the equivalent of a grandmother. So we could barely afford a wheelbarrow, never mind a house. And I would tell Peggy this when the quartet met next.

But she'd sown her seed in good ground.

Because the next day Dick came home from the library unexpectedly early and presented me with a little blue savings book of *The Irish Permanent Building Society*.

The sum of £50 was deposited inside.

"A twig for the nest," he said laughing.

I kissed him.

"When we've got £1,000, we'll be eligible for a loan." He poured himself a Bourbon, groaning. "Then I'll have to carry you over the threshold."

By that dim and distant day, he won't be able to, I thought. I'd have attained the dignity of Peggy's proportions, and he'd be even wirier. Or else we'd both be in our graves. But the little book gave me hope. I can't describe what hope. But according to Emily Dickinson,

*Hope is the thing with feathers that*
*Perches in the soul and*
*Sings the tune without the*
*Words and never stops at all.*

From then on, househunting became our hobby. Every fine weekend we'd window-shop in parts of old Dublin like the Liberties, or one of the mucky new developments in the environs - the only two types of houses we could afford. It was a case of Scylla and Charybdis, Dick said, but he stuck to his preference for all mod cons. While I was still lured by the romance of things old. In this Peggy was surprisingly sympathetic to me. I mean for such a practical person. Still, in my obsession, even the plains of Tallaght took on charm. I lusted after a house. Any house. Unlike the birds of the air, I needed a place for my plastic bags.

Hugging me goodbye at the airport that September, Peggy whispered, "Now, come back married!"

As Dick hadn't untied his first fatal knot, I failed her in this - the failure of hope over experience, with acknowledgments to Dr Johnson. But by selling the car, depositing Dick's book royalties, and going absolutely nowhere, we did manage to save nearly £500 towards our house.

I gloated over the money like Shylock.

Back in Dublin we started our househunting again. I was content to look and lust, but Peggy had other ideas. Early that summer she saw an ad in *The Irish Times* for a Kilmainham artisan cottage at the amazing price of £7,000 - low enough for us to put a deposit on a mortgage and manage the solicitors' fees.

The little house was us.

Although I thought it was Northside, Kilmainham is south of the Liffey - the more fashionable side since the Duke of Leinster crossed the river in the eighteenth century. Our house was in a cluster of quaintly decaying cottages on low-lying land between the main road and the River Poddle. It had been painted white and looked like the child of a poor family on its First Communion day. Smoke straggled thinly from the brother and sister chimneys, but you could feel the atmosphere. Centuries of people had lived there: Danes, Saxons and Gaels. I said this to Dick on the doorstep, but he just muttered something about centuries of grime - men, I've discovered have very little soul.

"Ah, come in!" A tall, dark, moustached man opened the door. There was something sinister about his tight black jeans and high cowboy boots. And the sharp way he looked us over. "Just wander round yerselves!"

As the cottage consisted of an open-plan sitting-room with a kitchenette and bathroom at one end, this was accomplished quickly.

"It's lovely," I sighed, admiring the redbrick fireplace.

"It's new!" the owner snapped. "Everything's the very best. That's woodchip wallpaper."

I admired that too. It was sort of cream knobbly stuff. "Isn't it nice, darling?"

But Dick was looking around stuffily. "Is there a bedroom?"

"A bedroom?" The man looked puzzled.

"Yes, a place to sleep."

He opened a large cupboard door. "You could sleep in there, I suppose."

Dick peered in. "It's ah .. a little small. And there's no window."

The man bristled. "Sure, you don't need a window."

"Precisely!" I butted in. "All we need is a double bed!"

Dick grumpily counted his steps across the room.

"Look!" I opened the kitchen window. "There's a river! We can have a boat."

146

Dick came up behind me. "Smell it!"

Curds of muck floated romantically by. "It's sort of Venetian."

"Venetian my foot! It's a health hazard!"

The owner heard and glared at Dick. "I've a lot of people interested. I want cash, for a quick sale."

"Won't you wait for our mortgage?" I begged.

The man twirled his moustache, softening. "Well ... I can take a deposit ... of £50."

"Dick? We can manage that."

"It's non-returnable, mind you!"

"Just a minute, Sally Ann." And Dick turned on the owner. "We need time to think."

The man hitched up his jeans, shrugging. "Take time. Have a walk. If anyone else comes, it's first served though. I'll not keep it without a deposit!"

"Please, darling!" I whispered, as Dick pulled me towards the door.

"He's a crook!" he muttered, as we walked gloomily around the grimy cottages. "You don't sell a house like that!"

He did look like a Pirate of Penzance, but I wouldn't admit it. I only said, "It's cheap. And in good condition."

"It's a cosmetic job. God knows what's under the wallpaper. And take a good look around. Do you want to live here?"

I said I wanted to live someplace.

So Dick went back and gave the owner a cheque for £50. And he talked to the Building Society the next day.

But it seemed as if all of Dublin's fair city had the same idea. Because their doors were barred and people were queuing - like a bank-run in a cowboy film. This was caused by the society overnight changing their rules: from now on you needed 10% of your purchase price lodged for a year before you could even apply. As we had only £500, we were disqualified on two counts. Also the society said that as "Americans" our prospects weren't good.

I was cast into gloom.

Peggy suggested we try the Grafton Street bank where Dick had had an account for fifteen years. But they must never have noticed. Because after hours and hours of form-filling, the manager refused because he didn't "know" Dick. And he was "American". I was Irish, but a poor credit risk.

"Well, I suppose that's it," Dick shrugged resignedly.

"What do you mean that's it? We can't get a house?" The bottom was falling out of my stomach.

"He said it might help if I knew someone. But I don't."

My cousin's partner did, but he was on holidays in Sicily.

We were back at GO.

"Knowing" people, I've discovered, is the only way in Ireland. As someone quipped, the secret of success is on the door of every public house in the land: push and pull. And fate proved this maxim true in our case too. I know it's unbelievable, but at our darkest hour we became beneficiaries of a bloodletting. It happened that Peggy's sister donated all her blood to save the life of a dying daughter of guess who? ... A high-up official of a Building Society! And by some circuitous logic, the official would from now on refuse Peggy nothing. And she was prepared to use her influence for us.

We were saved.

So we changed societies, and by next summer had saved much more money. But, as houses were going up too, it was like running in a dream. I can't remember where we lived that year, we lived in so many places, but I know we kept up our househunting. About that time I began to suspect Dick was only humouring me about the house. I've read that there are two basic personality types: ocnophiles to whom only security matters, and philobats to whom freedom is a must. I was an ocnophile OK, but what if Dick was a philobat? I mean the spirit indeed was willing, but the flesh was weak. He showed an interest in all sorts of overpriced plastic boxes, but he wouldn't consider anything we could afford. It was Catch 22. He'd been awfully resigned about the bank loan. Awfully. He'd not even minded us losing the £50. My suspicions came to a head when Peggy found a county council cottage in Greystones. It was everything I'd always wanted. A garden. A sea view. Ivy. It even had latticed windows. As we walked around, I visualised our future life: Dick driving to the station; me painting to the distant crashing of waves; the two of us walking romantically on the beach.

But it was not to be.

"It's the wrong time, Sally Ann, " Peggy said. "Sure, you're going back to America in a week."

Knowing she'd been "got at", I refrained from asking her why she'd shown it to us. I just said, "But you could use your influence!"

"They won't give a loan in absentia. Now, don't look so miserable. I'll get you a house!"

Promises, promises, I thought, holding back tears.

"Besides, I don't like it!" Dick butted in. "There's no kitchen."

Men really only think of one thing: their stomachs. But the closest thing to their heart is their chequebook. It is. A plan began to hatch in my brain. A marvellous and courageous plan. Another half-sabbatical was due the following January. As usual, I would be dispatched ahead to make straight the way like John the Baptist - ie find a flat and pay the deposit and advance rent. For this I'd be given about £1,000. What if I bought a house with it? Our savings were enough for the downpayment balance. And Peggy'd promised to get us the mortgage. Dick might get mad, but, as we weren't married, he couldn't divorce me. It'd be a *fait accompli*.

Our university library gets Saturday's *Irish Times* two weeks late. I usually went over to read the book reviews and articles by Maeve Binchy et al. But for the next four months I secretly scoured the housing ads. There was nothing under £20,000 though. Nothing. The cheapest houses were in the developments mushrooming at Mulhuddart or Bray or Clondalkin. And I'd just resigned myself to being up to my ears in muck, when I saw an ad: "5-roomed cottage, 35 miles Dublin, central heating, telephone, £15,000."

It was for nothing.

With Christmas hangovers, it took a week for the Dublin estate agent to answer the phone. But I learnt at last that Rowley Cottage was still for sale. It was beyond Kells though, and "way off a bus route", the sleepy voice warned. Still, I was undeterred. Country life, at last! I'd always wanted it. And what was the use of all my assertiveness reading if I couldn't steer our fate? With central heating and a telephone, the cottage was a giveaway at £15,000. Tenements without bathrooms were going for double that in Dublin. With our savings, we could easily afford a deep freeze and a car. I'd learn to drive. Up to now I'd only delayed that evil hour. So I made an appointment to view with Mr Kelly, the Kells co-agent.

My first problem was getting there.

Luckily Peggy came to the rescue. She was so delighted Dick had at last agreed that I couldn't disenchant her. And I think even she would balk at what I was doing. We set out early, but by the time we saw the big Celtic Cross in Kells centre the light in the January day was waning. Kells is a bustling country town with narrow hilly streets. We grabbed some fish and chips for lunch. And on asking directions were told the estate agents was around the corner. We turned several, going up several streets the wrong way and finally happening upon it by accident in the building society's branch office. Apparently Mr Kelly wore two hats.

He was wearing slippers and a striped three-piece suit when he came out of the inner office. The combination was as odd as his red country face and badly dyed brown hair, but I stopped myself staring.

"Mrs Fitzpatrick, I presume?" He addressed me in sing-song voice as if I were Livingstone.

"*Ms* Fitzpatrick!" I tried not to flinch under his iron handshake.

"It was Rowley Cottage you wanted to see, Mrs Fitzpatrick? I'll get the keys." And he pulled on big rubber boots. Then he squeezed his burly frame into a skimpy overcoat and stomped after me to the car.

As his was laid up, we used our mini.

I made him get into the back.

"The cottage's only a stone's throw," he wheezed, squeezing in.

As we left the town again for the plains of Meath, I figured the ad was way out. It had claimed the cottage to be thirty-five miles from Dublin, but

Kells was over forty. And no sign of us arriving. Never mind. Dick usually worked at home. He only went to the National Library two or three days a week. Maybe he could stay overnight with a friend? Or we could rent a *pied à terre* with our savings?

Mr Kelly kept up a running commentary:

"Ah, yes, Mrs Fitzpatrick, ye'll like the country." He let out a melancholy sigh. "De owner o' dose fields on yer right is rooned. Rooned. Brought it on himself."

"How?" I asked.

"Mortgaged dem at a mill'on. And didn't he open de papers next day to find land fallen by a turd. Owes a turd of a mill'on."

"God!" I said.

Peggy shook her head.

But our guide chuckled chestily.

"Is Rowley Cottage much further?" I asked nervously.

"Another few miles. See dat house on yer left?"

It was a gaunt grey mansion set in lush fields.

"It's lovely." I thought it'd make a painting.

"It is! Hmm. For sale for years."

"That's hard luck!" Peggy took her eyes off the road.

"It is! Hmm." And he muttered to himself, "Serves dem right! Way over-priced ... Cromwellians ... And sure who'd want to live out here?"

I glanced uneasily over my shoulder. For some reason he was putting me off.

"Is Rowley Cottage long on the market?" Peggy looked suspiciously in the mirror.

"A time! A time!" A cautious note crept into his voice.

"It's a very good price," I said. Then, catching Peggy's glare: "Eh - I mean it's fairly good. For the country."

"Hmm ... Mind you, the owner won't take a penny less dan fourteen and a half."

Already I'd saved five hundred pounds!

We fell into silence. Hedges skimmed by, and an occasional worker saluted as we penetrated the brooding countryside. There was something odd about Mr Kelly. Something contradictory. He wasn't exactly trying the hard sell, but maybe the cottage was owned by Cromwellians too. From my historical studies I know Old Rowley was the nickname of Charles 11. But three centuries separated us from his rule. And presumably he'd been better than Cromwell? But time is nothing in Ireland. Oh, perhaps he simply had another customer in mind? This possibility filled me with dread, but at least I was on to him.

"Rowley Cottage doesn't sound very Irish," I pumped.

"Hmm. It doesn't ... It's de hunting' lodge o' Rowley House. We'll be comin' to it now."

But we drove on.

And on.

"See, through the gates!" Our guide suddenly shouted.

"Dat's Rowley House. We're round the bend."

Through massive gates, I saw a redcoated girl riding down the wide tree-lined avenue. Oh, horses are in the Irish blood, and that girl became a vision of my future life. The life which fate had deprived me of. We rounded the corner next. And there, nestling between the lowering navy sky and the green humpy fields was my whitewashed cottage.

Mine.

I slipped on the mucky path to the red front door.

Mine.

"Dis is a bit stiff." Mr Kelly heaved the door with his shoulder.

It wouldn't budge, so he tried again.

"It's probably damp!" Peggy eyed the house knowledgeably.

"Ah, it's just a bit swollen." He slapped the corners, pushing again. Reluctantly it creaked open.

"De owner bought it for his daughter, but she didn't live in it much."

"Why?" Peggy looked at him sharply.

"Ah, couldn't stand the loneliness."

I pictured an overweight suburbanite as we went in.

There was a musty smell in the hall. We followed Mr Kelly into the drawing-room. It was a biggish room with a handsome redbricked fireplace and a broken bay window. A gale force wind blew, but at least it was airier.

"Someone should repair that!" Peggy said. "It'll cause damp."

"Ah, it's only a breath of air!" Mr Kelly pulled his coat shiveringly round him.

"We'll repair it!" I turned to Mr Kelly. "Then all we have to do is turn on the heat. Eh ... where does it turn on, Mr Kelly?"

"The heat is it? Ah! Yes, the heat! The switch is out beyond." And he pointed to a couple of rickety sheds in the garden.

We walked through the two bedrooms. The cosy breakfast room, opening into a tiny kitchen with a huge old-fashioned sink.

"You can replace that with a stainless steel unit." Peggy turned on the tap. It clanked and spluttered, but no water came.

"The water's turned off," the agent admitted.

I remembered the trouble we had with no water in Mountjoy Square.

"Can you turn it on?" Peggy demanded.

"Ah, now ... well ... " He rubbed his chin worriedly. "To tell the truth, dat presents a problem. A technical problem,. Ye need a ladder -"

"It's turned on in the attic?" Peggy looked suspicious. "They should leave a ladder here."

151

"Ah, dere's one in the Big House! Dey supply the water. Eventually, ye'll have to dig a well."

"Dig a well?" we both said.

"Oh, dere's water for now. An architect has vetted everything! Eventually, I said! And by dat time the county council might've supplied mains."

That water didn't just come through the taps like magic had never before occurred to me. But now we were in the country, and different laws applied. The lack certainly explained the stench from the bathroom. But when the toilet could be flushed that would go. And the bath was fine and big. Dick likes big tubs. It's weird for a grown man, I know, but he likes to sail boats in his bath. And rubber ducks.

It was dark when we went outside. We could just see the big gate separating our garden from a picturesque barn. The garden was a jungle of thistles. But amazingly two fields were to be thrown in with the cottage. A rickety apple tree grew in one. And thistles. More thistles.

"Two fields?" Peggy tried not to look too impressed.

"Ah, sure dere's always a bit o' land trown in with a country house. Ye could build another house dere." He gave a short laugh and muttered under his breath, "If ye could get anyone to live in it!"

I looked at Peggy. He was really weird.

She gave me a hug. "We'll come and live in it!"

Mr Kelly turned on us in puzzlement.

"Where does the sun come in?" I asked. It was an important question when buying a house.

"De sun?" He looked as if he'd never heard the word. Or had forgotten what it meant. Which can happen in an Irish winter.

"Yes, where does it hit the house?"

He looked vacant.

"The sun?" I repeated.

He peered upwards at the inky sky. "No sign of it now! Ha! Or the moon!" He shivered under his coat, stamping his boots in the muck. "Come on back to town, and I'll show ye a nice semi-d."

I said if I wanted a semi-d, I'd buy one in Dublin.

We went back inside. As we lingered again in each room, he followed us, rattling his keys impatiently. I ignored him, now knowing the reason for his queer attitude. He wanted to sell us one of his own houses. More commission, probably.

"Tell ye what, girls!" he said at last. "I have to see a man down the road about a field. Lend me the car!"

I was about to comment on the idiocy of calling grown women "girls," when Peggy gave him her keys.

"I'll be right back!" And he roared off into the night.

Just then the house lights flickered and went out.

"A fuse!" Peggy diagnosed.

But we couldn't find the fuse-box. It was pitch black. Pitch. To cheer ourselves up, we lit the kindling in the breakfast room grate. It took OK, but almost immediately smoke puffed back into the room.

"The chimney's on fire!" I almost choked.

"It's only a bird's nest!" And Peggy calmly quenched the twigs with her high heel.

I was enormously grateful for her knowledge. And her presence. For in the ghostly darkness, I felt a sudden chill. It was eerie. We were miles from anywhere. Miles. And what if the rider in the avenue had been a ghost?

I asked Peggy if she'd seen her, but she said I was imagining things.

"You didn't see anything?"

"I didn't, Sally. Now, relax!" She tapped the breakfast room wall. "The first thing you do, is knock this down. You can extend into the kitchen."

I didn't answer.

For at that moment a light appeared at the window. A light with a face behind it. A bony face with mad eyes and wild wispy hair.

"Peggy!" I pointed to the window. "Look!"

But when she did, it had gone.

I was frozen with fear. It was a ghost. The ghost of a Cromwellian. Or more likely one of his victims, buried in the dumb and unforgetting ground.

"Peggy, I'm scared."

"Stop this nonsense!" She put an arm reassuringly round me. "You're suffering from nerves, Sally. Buying a house is always trau -"

The door creaked open. And a figure held a lantern torch in the door-way.

I clung to Peggy.

"Out!" screamed an Englishy voice. "Out!"

The light came towards us. I made out a thin, dishevelled woman in jodhpurs and anorak. Her bones were like sticks, but she was alive. A ghost would never use a lantern torch.

She waved it threateningly. "Out! Out""

"I'm Ms Fitzpatrick, still." I stood my ground, remembering the Duchess of Malfi. "And this is my friend, Mrs Peggy O'Mara. We've been left here by Mr Kelly of Kells."

"Oh!" The fury in her emaciated face changed to understanding. "You're viewing the cottage?"

"I'm buying it."

"You're buying it?" She fiddled nervously with her bun. "Forgive me, Mrs Fitzpatrick -"

"Ms! Sally Ann! Sally Ann Fitzpatrick."

"What a lovely name! I'm Dorothy Blake from Rowley House. I have to watch for burglars. We'll be neighbours!"

We all shook hands.

Again she held the light to my face. "You've seen everything?"

I nodded.

"Wouldn't it be wonderful if someone like you bought the cottage! Come up to the house for a drink!"

Peggy nudged me. "We wondered about the water?"

"Could you turn it on?" I asked.

"Just a minute!" And she ran into the garden shed and pulled out a ladder which the three of us lugged into the house. She positioned it under a ceiling trapdoor and disappeared up it into the attic. "Tell me when the water comes on!"

We stood by the kitchen tap.

It gurgled dryly, but nothing happened.

Then there was a loud crash.

And we ran out to find Mrs Blake dangling from a large hole in the ceiling. Her riding boots flailed wildly. And the ladder lay on the floor.

"Hold her legs!" Peggy shouted hysterically. "I'll get the ladder!"

"No! No! Stand aside!" And Mrs Blake jumped to the floor, getting up immediately and dusting herself off.

There was white plaster everywhere.

"Thank God, you're all right!" I stared in melancholy horror at the hole.

"Good Lord!" was all Peggy could say. "Good Lord!"

"That's nothing!" Mrs Blake announced cheerfully, "My husband will repair that! We'll leave the ladder. Come and have a drink."

"I certainly need one," Peggy muttered uncharacteristically.

So I left Mr Kelly a note on the door. And the three of us climbed the gate and walked up a sort of avenue between the two properties. The dark was oppressive. Mrs Blake's wobbling torch seemed the only light in the universe. The big house loomed gauntly ahead. The world of the Anglo-Irish was a foreign country to me. I only knew from books they had leaking roofs and kept drink in the bootroom. But what if Cromwellians had lived there? What if my rider had been a ghost? I shivered, unable to ask. Sometimes my imagination ran wild.

We crossed a farmyard.

Then a stableyard.

"Say hello to Rufus." Mrs Blake stopped to nuzzle a pony looking over a stable door. "He's a sweetheart."

"Do you have many ponies?" It was my chance to ask about the rider.

"Six. I run a riding school."

My rider was real then.

The pony butted her affectionately. "I couldn't manage without him!" She sighed, petting his nose again. The country can be very lonely, Sally Ann. You want to be sure you like it."

I said an artist has to be lonely. My real worry was what to do if I ran out of milk.

She waved me into silence. "I'll lend you a horse!"

I pictured Dick's face as I galloped off to Kells.

We came to the house. She led us through huge old kitchens, a hall with an antique rocking horse, into the stately drawing-room. There was a haunting elegance about everything. A sort of faded beauty. Turf smouldered wetly in the grate, so we kept our coats. Far from having supplies in a bootroom, Mrs Blake only had a nearly empty bottle of whiskey. But she insisted on sharing it. Huddling over the fire, we at last managed to warm up. Mrs Blake told us the story of her life. How she'd been born in the house. How her brother was killed in the war. How the roof had caught fire a few years ago and how the neighbours had formed a human chain from the well. How she had sold the cottage to pay for a new roof. But now she had a problem with dry rot. And she was planning to start a summer riding school to pay for that. I suggested adding English for foreigners to the curriculum. And we decided to go into business together. The evening reeked of Sommerville and Ross, my favourite writers. A neighbour "called" while we were there, returning Mrs Blake's "call" - something I thought only happened in Jane Austen. When I lived in the cottage, maybe I could "call" on someone too. Oh, it was a perfect day. The countryside. The intimacy of the drive with Peggy. Finding my house. And now stumbling on this world. By the time Mr Kelly came back, I decided that by buying the cottage I was gaining not just bricks and mortar but a way of life.

Peggy's only worry was that I'd tell someone before she could pull her strings with the building society. If it got out about the fields, someone would snap it up. She was serious about Tony and herself building a bungalow there when the children grew up. For the moment they might park a caravan for weekends.

Even Tony got infected. And took the next Saturday off from his paper and drove us down to vet it, whistling all the way.

"Much further, Sally?" He stopped in the middle of a tune, on the drab stretch beyond Kells.

"Only a few miles," I said from the back.

He looked at Peggy.

The atmosphere thickened with tension. Again it was almost dark. Oh, it was far away, but he'd fall in love with it when he saw it.

"You realise we're halfway to Enniskillen?" he said after another bit.

Peggy frowned at him. "It's not much further!"

Again we drove on.

And on.

When we got to the cottage, Peggy and I walked the land. The fields were full of thistles too. They'd be the first to go. And she'd give me plants for the garden. But Tony became preoccupied with the roof, staring oddly upwards.

"Sally Ann!" he called.

When I came over, he was still circling the cottage. He stopped to knock out his pipe. A bad sign. "Do you see that bulge in the roof?"

I noticed a sort of camel's hump.

Peggy came over. "That's nothing! An architect has vetted it!"

"I don't care who's vetted it. You'll have trouble with that roof." He shoved tobacco into his pipe. "And see that crack down the side of the house?"

"Can't we fill it?" I asked dismally,.

He went inside without answering.

I found him staring at the ceiling hole and anticipated his grumbling. "Mrs Blake's husband's fixing it."

"He'll have a job." He hunkered by the hall skirting board. "Sally, put your thumb nail into this"

I did. It was like butter. "Eh ... what's wrong?"

"Dry rot."

"It feels wet."

"It's dry rot, caused by damp. The skirting boards are riddled with it. And see that stuff!" He pointed the stem of his pipe at a white mushroomy substance growing out of the walls.

"What is it?"

"Rising damp. And there's ground damp in the kitchen,"

My father always said houses were like people, there were good houses and bad houses. But he never said that like people they had diseases. "Maybe we could turn on the heat?"

"And cause a steam bath?" he shook his head vehemently, "The place is a disaster, love. Dick'll hate it!"

I looked at the rotting boards. At the mushrooms. At the garden with its thistles and dreary sheds, the ragged fields, seeing them now through another's eyes. It was weird. Like a balloon bursting. Or falling out of love as a teenager. Suddenly you see a person, a thing for what it is. The place was a ruin. I'd been cracked to think we would live here. Dick got mad if a bulb blew. Or the toilet got stuck. But still, would I ever find another house in time? "Think what we're saving?"

"And two fields?" Peggy had come in.

"They don't want fields! They want a house on a bus route! And you'll save much more if you don't buy it, Sally. Your skin for one thing!" And he marched to the door.

I looked miserably at Peggy, but she indicated we were to follow. So I locked the door behind us, and all the way to Dublin pondered on her capitulation. She'd been so for it, but had completely caved in. I mean she'd given me the "conviction" to do what I was doing. But what if Tony was the boss all along? Oh, I suppose he was right. You can't argue with buttery skirting boards. I had rheumatism from even touching them. In a way it'd be a relief not to be always travelling in the dark. But did Tony's remark about my skin mean he suspected what I was doing? More likely it was a male way of talking. As we hit the city streets again, I felt a weird relief. The country life wasn't everything. I was a Dub. And I decided that, although the fields were lost, all was not lost. I had a week left before Dick returned.

After the Kells fiasco, Tony and Peggy applied themselves in earnest to finding a "sensible" house. It'd be too boring to describe everything I saw. Suffice it to say I'd almost bought a redone Bray bungalow when the agent sold it, after hours of haggling, over my head. I'd finally resigned myself to a cardboard box in Clondalkin when my sister heard of a Ranelagh artisan house circa 1880, going for a song.

It was built of that mellow Dublin brick and in a cul de sac behind a Victorian square. The only drawback was you had to pass a row of cottages with graffiti like "Provos OK" and "Fuck the Queen Now" to get to it. And there was no garden - the halldoor opened onto the street, and an extension had been built in the back. Usually small old Dublin houses don't have bathrooms, but it did. Although outside, through a sort of atrium - the strip of yard not built in. Oh, I admit the house needed a lick of paint, but it was great value. Artisan houses down the road were going for £35,000. And ours had a doll's house charm. And I couldn't see any evidence of disease. On the whole, its hundred years had worn well.

I had to act quickly.

And alone. The agent wanted £23,000, so I offered £22,000, and we settled for £22,750 - in retrospect, I might've got it for less, but there wasn't time. I gave him a £1,000 deposit and rang Peggy to arrange the loan. Our savings would be enough for a deposit balance. And I didn't worry about the fees.

Next I had to tell Dick.

He kissed me tiredly at the airport a couple of days later. "You found a flat OK?"

"Darling, I've a lovely surprise!"

He looked suspicious.

"I've saved you over £13,000!"

"Don't tell me you've been shopping?"

"Yes! For a house! It only cost £22,750, and houses in the next street are going for £35,000."

He looked at me dazedly. "A house!"

"I'll run for a taxi!"

He dragged his case tiredly after me,

"Don't tell me it has a bit of character," he finally groaned in the taxi.

"It has! It's over a hundred years old. We can see it on the way. I have the keys!" He had jetlag, so mightn't see the drawbacks. Also it was too dark to see the graffiti.

"Drive on!" I shouted as the taxi slowed by the sprayed cottages.

"It needs a lick of paint."

Nervously I fitted the key.

Dick said nothing. Nothing. And nothing as we walked around. Just stared at a ceiling stain and at a gaping hole in the stairway - neither of which I'd noticed.

"Well, what do you think?" I asked as he stood in the six-foot, coffin-like atrium.

"I'm looking for the back garden."

"You're in it."

He went into the bathroom. "Where's the wash-basin?"

"It's right there!"

"Where?"

There wasn't one.

And I'd never even noticed.

He faced me in the kitchen. There was a terrible look on his face. A look of terrible despair. "You actually bought this hovel?"

"I paid a deposit ... £1,000 ... I can get out of it."

"Oh, no! Oh, no! Just live in it! But I won't!" And he slammed out of the house.

The taxi roared off.

I stayed in the house.

For the second time in a week my world had collapsed. Except this time more seriously. I walked around the house, seeing it for the first time. The carpets were hideously patterned, and the wallpaper was ghastly. It must've looked even worse to Dick who as an American had no appetite for squalor. Oh, I thought I was so right, but was I? Was a house worth this? Worth loosing Dick? Had my mind lapsed. A "plank in the reason" broken? I didn't know. I just sat there dazed, for hours and hours.

Loud knocking at last aroused me.

"Honey bunch!" Dick shouted from the street. "I'm back!"

I opened the door to him and Tony. Both tipsy.

Tony looked around him. "How are ya, love? Hmm. Not bad!"

Dick let out a shriek of laughter - he always laughs when he's sad.

"I'm sorry!" I felt tears coming. "I really am. Peggy can tell them we don't want a loan."

"But then I won't be able to carry you over the threshold!" And he grabbed me, carrying me out to the street and then back into the house. "I suppose -," he gasped, sitting down on the floor. "I suppose ... this means we'll have to get married?"

"No!" I said. "No!"

But he'd fallen asleep.

I turned frantically to Tony. "Is he OK?"

"He's fine. He needs to sleep. I'll drive you over to your Dad's". And he heaved him up and out to the car.

Dick didn't back out. "Love in a hut" as the poet says, may be "cinders, ashes, dust," but it's better than renting. It is. We now have proper neighbours. Oh, I got my way. I got my little house "out of the wind and the rain's way." But my troubles were only beginning. Since we've moved in, Dick's been very gloomy. He's forgiven me all right, but there've been all sorts of fees and that. And we've no money for furniture. And there's no wash-basin. Also there's a ghastly hole in the stairway - Tony's helped with that.

I love when he comes. Then I don't feel so awful when Dick finds something else wrong. I live in dread of him finding things wrong. And hammering. Oh, we've done it up by degrees, slow degrees. But I often wonder if the whole thing wasn't an obsession. Like the Kells house, I mean. But if you can't hope, what else is there in life? And it's true if you imagine something, it can happen. Now I cheer myself up, imagining improvements. A nursery maybe. Also I'm an expert on houses. I've even learnt how to point bricks. Before I'd never notice if a house had proper gutters. Now I know if they're leaking - ours are. Oh, there's a bit of damp too, but what house is free of it in Ireland? The whole country's slowly decaying. Dick calls it a rathole of a country, but he's more committed to me now. He is. Also I'm to add a postscript: While he was pulling off a century's wallpaper, I was working on a painting. He says why couldn't I paint the house. But I told him that's man's lot.

I nearly forgot my other postscript: we're being sued for that Kells ceiling.

# XI  *Mona*

Mona opened her eyes to see a nun in white sitting by her bed. She must be living and not in eternity because the nun was humming and reading a magazine with Robert Redford on the cover.

A tube was in her arm. Her mouth was dry and she was in pain.

Terrible pain.

A minute ago she was lying on the operating table. How had she got back to the ward? What time was it? She focused on the nun again, but the white habit wavered away.

"Have you pain, pet? It's a healthy baby boy."

The nun was near, yet her voice seemed to come from the end of a long tunnel.

Mona groaned.

The next thing she felt herself being injected.

Then a tube was tied around her arm.

"Your blood pressure's nice and normal, pet. The baby's fine too. It's a boy."

Mona stared at the ceiling, drifting into a dream about her son, Danny. Danny was a good boy. He was ten now and on hard sums. Tonight's Geography was to mark the Nile on a blank map of Africa. It wiggled across the ceiling towards a peeled patch for Lake Victoria. She pointed to it, babbling excitedly. "All day, I face the barren waste," Frankie Laine's voice blared as she ran to the lakeside, "without a taste of water. Cool, clear water." She was so glad of a drink. So glad. But before she reached the edge, a wind whipped the glassy surface into a foaming tidal wave which surged towards her, getting bigger and bigger and drowning her in a great watery wall.

She awoke in the nick of time.

Slowly she took in her bandaged abdomen. The tube connecting her to an overhead bottle. The curtains drawn around her bed. The cats' chorus of crying babies from down the corridor.

The baby? Where was it? Her heart leadened. There was no cot beside her. Perhaps it had died. Someone had mentioned a baby dying. But no, the nun said it was all right. Where was the nun? There'd been talk of a cup of tea.

Mona tried to reach her bell, but couldn't. Her body felt as if it were cracking in two. If she called out, the Foxrock woman in the other bed would only want to help. She could hear her talking bossily now. "Maeve Binchy's novel was marvellous. Did you read it?"

"Not yet. I like her journalism," another voice answered. "She's the funniest person on *The Times*."

That was Sally Ann from down the corridor. Some kind of artist. She'd come in the night before and borrowed magazines from the other woman in the room. Mona remembered their conversation now. The fog was clearing. It seemed like a million years ago. She remembered the younger woman had looked in on her, asked her if she wanted anything. Oh, she meant well. Talked too much, that was all. She was having some sort of tests for infertility. The Foxrocker was called Astrid something or other - it sounded like the name of a boat. She'd had a premature baby and gave you blow by blow. A snob. Mona knew the type: Renault 4 car, meals on wheels, mohair-suited husband, nannies, children bandy from riding lessons. A life of glamour, while hers had been spent wading knee-deep in nappies. Terry's insurance had specified a ward, but they'd put her in a semi-private room. Getting out without a chequebook would be a problem. And explaining no baby clothes. She hadn't had the money to buy any. And she'd forgotten her cigarettes.

As she reached for the bell again, a glass shattered onto the floor.

"Are you all right, Mrs Reilly?" Sally Ann's head popped around the curtains.

Mona winced in pain. She didn't want to get into conversation. Not with someone who looked so disgustingly healthy. The younger woman wore a huge fluffy pink dressing gown. She had dishevelled black curly hair and, with gold granny glasses at the end of her nose, reminded Mona of a character out of *School Friend* comic. What a weird thing to think of now. It must be thirty years since she'd read that.

"I'll get Sister," the girl said.

Mona groaned in reply.

A few minutes later the nun pulled back the curtain. "So Mrs Rip Van Winkle's awake at last. Are you in pain, pet?"

Mona nodded. How long had she lain there?

"We'll get you comfortable." She checked the overhead bottle. "We'll be refilling this."

The nun went away and in a few minutes came back with a nurse carrying a syringe on a dish. The nurse injected her first. Then the nun placed a bedpan under the blanket. "Try and use this."

Mona shook her head.

"But we must get your bladder working."

"No, I'll get up!" Mona tried to haul herself up by gripping the bedhead. But the pain was like a train across her body.

"Use it, this once," the nun pleaded.

Mona gave in.

When she was finished, the nun came back with a cup of tea. Rattlingly she placed it on the bedtray which she pushed to the top of the bed. "Slowly now. Too much will sicken you. When you've finished, nurse will bring the baby. He's been in the incubator. She'll help you breastfeed."

Breastfeed? They must be crazy.

161

While in labour, Mona had been told to focus on an object in the room. Now she focused on the nun's crucifix. It rested on her bosom and was almost level with the end of the bed. A twisted body on twisted wood. "Were you here before?" she asked wearily.

"That was hours ago."

"What time is it now?"

"It's one o'clock. You've been asleep for a day and a half!"

Then a young nurse came in, carrying the baby. It was wrapped in a blanket, so Mona couldn't see it. But she had no wish to. Hysteria bubbled inside her. In a minute she was going to vomit. "Take it away."

The nurse looked at the nun in alarm. Then she started cooing at her bundle. "But he's a dote. Aren't you a dote!"

Mona turned to the wall. "Take it away!"

"Now Mrs Reilly - " The nun soothed.

"Take it away or I'll murder it!"

The nun waved the startled nurse out. "It's only normal to be depressed, pet."

"I'm not depressed!"

"But you must see your own child!"

"I won't!"

"Now, now, stop this nonsense. Nurse will bring - "

"I won't!" Frantically Mona reached for the cup on her locker and threw it at the curtains. It clattered off the floor, spilling tea everywhere. "I don't want to see it. Or you! Or anyone!"

The old nun blinked nervously.

"It was a fit of drunkenness."

"Is - your husband coming in?"

"He's left me for a whore. Why don't you give it to her!"

As the nun retrieved the cup and wiped the floor with tissues, Mona sobbed into her pillow. Her whole situation had been caused by religious people who knew nothing. "Have faith," the redfaced parish priest had said when she went to him about Terry's first affair. "Forgive us our trespasses, as we forgive others," he'd preached, ushering her out after the second. It'd always been the same. Terry just wasn't mature enough for marriage. Or children. He'd gone on a drunken binge after their first child. On another after their second. And now he was gone altogether. Good riddance. Oh, why hadn't she died? She'd lost enough blood.

It seemed years since the day before yesterday. The pains had started in the middle of breakfast. Not wanting to frighten the children, she'd hurried them out to school before dialling 999. The guards had screeched up to the house minutes before the ambulance. They waited around until she was helped into it. Arranged for her neighbour to look after the children. But when they offered to contact her husband at work, she'd lied that he was in England. On business.

It was weeks before her time, so Dr Cunningham couldn't be contacted. He was at his holiday home in the west, they'd said, leaving her to bleed. Well for some, having another home. They kept trying to contact him, but couldn't. And by that night, she knew by their worried looks, something was drastically wrong. After hours of labour there was no baby. Then at the last ounce of her strength, her own doctor had hurried into the delivery room.

After a quick examination he'd said calmly, "Mona, I'm going to do what's best for you and the baby."

"A Caesarian?"

Dr Cunningham squeezed her hand. "I believe in bringing useful citizens into the world."

Then the nurses had swarmed round her, performing the rituals. And she was whizzed down the corridor into the lift, out into another corridor, and finally into the theatre.

Bright lights shone in her face. Masked figures leant over her.

"There's no need to feel guilty," one of them had said, jabbing away the pain.

Dr Cunningham wavered away, his face like corrugated iron. "I'll give you a lovely bikini slit, love."

It had sounded like an ice-cream from Cafolla's.

Mona stared up at the cracked ceiling above her bed. The last couple of days had had the bizarre quality of a nightmare. She felt she was still in one. Maybe she'd wake to find her whole life had been a dream. Anxiety gnawed at her. Oh, God, the baby. She didn't want it. She was too weary to go through that again. Why didn't they warn you about the pain of childbirth? She hadn't known. Was it some sort of conspiracy? On the part of women too. Doctors certainly didn't give a damn. We're child fodder, that's all. Battery hens. Why did they leave her so long in labour? But at least the baby was all right. She wanted it to be all right. She just didn't want to see it. But why had she been left to suffer? Am I not a useful citizen too? Yet, I'm ripped in two. But I'm alive, aren't I? He saved my bloody life.

About an hour later the nun came back through the curtains. She was followed by another nurse, crackling with efficiency and beaming with cheerfulness. She pulled a trolley beside Mona's bed. It held a basin of water and other items of ablution.

"We're going to get you comfortable now, Mrs Reilly," the nun said.

Mona was too tired to argue.

The nun rolled up her sleeves and poked in her locker, pulling out Mona's pink nightie. "How pretty! Now sit up. That's right."

The two women helped Mona change out of her hospital gown. Then, as she lay in rigid exhaustion, the nurse sponged her. Then they helped her into the clean nightie.

As the nurse took the trolley away, the nun went back to her locker. What on earth was she looking for now? "I can't find a comb."

"In my handbag."

The nun found it, stretching wheezily for Mona's peroxided frizz. "There now ... you'll feel better when you look better."

Mona couldn't remember anyone ever combing her hair.

She watched the nun plump the pillows and tidy the bedspread. But as she started to draw the curtains, Mona panicked. "Please leave them."

"But you'll have company!"

"I don't want company!"

Then there was a clink of delf, as Sally Ann carried a tray through the curtains. "Time for tea."

The nun took it and, placing it on Mona's trolley, turned scoldingly to the girl. "You shouldn't be in here!"

"Nurse said I could give out the trays!"

The old woman sniffed. "I hear you're going down in the morning."

The younger woman grimaced. "Yeah."

"Well make sure you eat nothing after tea!"

Sally Ann nodded. "I know." She smiled nervously at Mona. "I'm having a laparoscopy."

Mona glared at the plate of bread and butter. There were two slices of plastic white and only one of brown. Anyway, she wasn't hungry. And, more than anything, she didn't want to listen to natter about operations.

"It's nothing to a hysterectomy," Sally Ann went on blithely.

Looking anxiously at Mona, the nun went away.

Mona wanted to call her back. Was she to be left with this one?

Sally Ann plonked down beside the bed. "An anaesthetic's the closest thing to death!"

Mona closed her eyes.

"They said my appendix caused an infection. I got it out at school."

Mona sipped some tea.

"Would you think that could stop you having children?"

Mona still didn't answer. She might stay longer if she got any encouragement. Why couldn't she count her blessings? She didn't know when she was well off.

There was a silence. Maybe she'd go.

"He says there's a chance." She looked at Mona. "If the infection isn't bilateral. Sorry, you don't feel like talking? I brought you something to read - *Resurrection*. She took a novel out of the pocket of her copious dressing gown.

Was she a religious nut? Trying to convert her?

"No thanks."

"Oh, but it's by Tolstoy. It's a beautiful book. It's about the noble who got a girl into trouble in his youth. Then she's convicted of murder -"

Mona looked boredly at the ceiling. If only she had a cigarette.

"And he goes to Siberia with her. The whole message is, sometimes your mistakes are the means of your salvation."

"It sounds a bit heavy."

"But you might read it. I'll leave it - in case. Can I do anything else?"

Mona hesitated. "Eh - could you get me a cigarette?"

"My husband's coming in. He'll have some."

And she went away, drawing the curtains behind her.

Mona picked up the book. It looked boring. She turned wearily into her pillow. She only wanted to be left alone. At least the curtains gave her some protection. She didn't want the Foxrocker gawking or talking about operations. Mona felt no part of the conspiracy of birth which bound women together. She could forget she ever had children - except you couldn't. That was the irony. She should ring her neighbour and find out if Danny and Lisa were all right. Lisa had just gone to school, and for the first time in ten years she had a moment to herself. And now this ... If only she could give it back.

Woozy from the injection, she dozed off. Sh didn't know how long she'd lain there when, from the edge of sleep, she heard footsteps. The scrape of a chair. Wheezy breathing.

The nun was back with her magazine. "Can I sit with you?"

"I don't care."

Mona pretended to be asleep. If only they could plug her permanently into some life-support system. She didn't want to be responsible for anyone again. Least of all herself. If only she had a cigarette now. A cigarette would help.

"If I were king," the nun murmured distinctly. "If I were king, it's a far, far better thing I do."

Mona opened her eyes. God, the woman was senile.

Suddenly she flung down the magazine. "Ah, sure, he's not in it at all!"

"Who?"

"Ronald Coleman."

"Who's he?" She had vaguely heard of the name, but couldn't place it. The nun bristled indignantly. "Who's he, indeed!"

"Well, I can't remember him."

"You remember *The Prisoner of Zenda*?"

"I - think so."

"That was where he kept saying, 'If I were king, it's a far, far better thing I do than I have ever done ...'" Her old eyes clouded as she stared dreamily into space.

Mona watched her curiously. Odd for a nun to be into films. She was obviously a bit touched, living in the past. Yet she seemed to be still working in the hospital. "Wasn't that *A Tale of Two Cities*?" she said after a while. "I saw Dirk Bogarde in that."

The nun waved her hand dismissively. "Ah, he's not in the same class! If you'd seen Ronald Coleman waiting for the guillotine, you'd never forget it. Never!" She laid her hand dramatically across her breast. "If I were king, it's a far, far better thing I do ..."

Mona turned into her pillow. She felt too sick to be listening to this. The woman was mad. Cracked. But you couldn't tell a nun to shut up.

"Surely you remember *Random Harvest* where he lost his memory?" the nun persisted. "He was the dark one, with a thin moustache."

"I don't know who you're talking about."

The old woman sighed resignedly. "Ah, no. Sure, why would you? You're too young."

Mona laughed, hurting herself.

"Is the injection working, pet?"

She nodded wearily.

The nun rolled up her magazine nervously. "Will I bring the baby, pet?"

Mona caught her breath. "Can't it wait? I need to sleep."

The nun stood up, nodding. "Well, can I get you anything else?"

Mona hesitated. "I'd give anything for a cigarette. I have some money in my bag."

"Smoking's forbidden!" Crossly, she tidied Mona's bed. "Besides, you're not well enough."

Resignedly, Mona closed her eyes. If she had a cigarette, she might be able to cope with the baby. Eventually she'd have to see it. She knew that, but now she was too tired ... Too bloody tired. She felt so old, yet the nun had called her young. Young, that was a joke. Her whole problem with Terry was age. He couldn't make love to her because she was thirty-nine and fat, and he needed someone young and slim. Oh, he tried but it never worked. And when he'd almost lost his job from the stress of sexual frustration, and starvation loomed, she'd agreed to the last affair. So long as he didn't tell her about it. But he'd moved the little bitch into the house. They were to share everything, like communists. But it got to be too much. And when Mona had threatened to leave and go to England with the children, Terry had responded by saying it was a good idea. A good idea. The ménage à trois wasn't working. Like hell! It was more like a menagerie. He'd actually driven them to the boat and bought the tickets and comics for the children. Cool as you like. What kind of man was he? Oh, God ... that crossing with the two of them vomiting. Changing to the uncomfortable train in the dark of night. Euston station in the grey morning. Porters shouting, the children crying. The café full of dead-beats queuing for tea. She thought she had the courage for it, but she hadn't. She'd never forgive Terry. Never. She'd devoured the London papers for employment, and finally got a night job in a Slough Wimpy Bar and lodgings in a guest house. They'd all got sick from the terrible food. Danny had nowhere to play and walked the streets. Only when he started sleep-walking did she wise up and come home to occupy their Clontarf bungalow. But the child was disturbed now. He still wet the bed and was backward in school. A psychologist told her his creative side was too dominant. Why the hell couldn't he learn to read properly then?

There was more muttering from the nun.

This time she was fingering her beads.

Easy enough to pray when you believed life was as simple as going to the pictures. But the nun wasn't the only one. People had the stupidest ideas. Herself included. When she first met Terry, she'd thought him the image of Marlon Brando in *The Young Lions*. Hmm ... I must've been mad.

As the nun prayed, Mona drifted back into sleep. She dreamt she was cycling with Terry. It was before the children because they were going to the Enniskerry Waterfall and he was picking wild flowers. The hedges were jewelled with blackberries, the sky a miraculous blue. "Oh, Mary, we crown thee with blossoms today," she sang lustily. "Queen of the Angels. Queen of the May." A car honked, and she discovered herself clad in the briefest of bikinis. Gaily she waved back. What did it matter when you had the figure? She raced after Terry, breathless. At the Bray turning she lost him. Where was he? Would she ever find him again? In the distance she heard a noise, and suddenly there he was. His hair was as blond as their first meeting, his shoulders as broad. He'd put the kettle on and was waiting by the waterfall for her to get the meal on. So she unpacked his favourite picnic of hard-boiled eggs (shelled), a pinch of salt in an envelope, and Jacob's Original and Best Cream Crackers (buttered). "I'm so thirsty!" she shouted, over the roaring water.

"I'll get you another cup of tea, pet."

Who was that? Terry never called her pet. Besides, his back was to her. But she knew it was him. She recognised his red woollen jumper. She tugged at the sleeve, but he refused to look at her. "You have the children! You don't need me!" he shouted at her for the millionth time. And she was left rolling unravelling wool into a ball which got bigger and bigger and too heavy to manage. At last she caught up, having ripped the whole jumper. "Look at me!" she thumped his back so hard that he turned. And she got the shock of her life to find herself staring again into Robert Redford's baby blue eyes.

"Go away!" she shouted, noticing he wore a moustache.

He arched an eyebrow and floated grinningly behind the curtains. But when she looked again he was back.

"Go away! Leave me alone!"

"Now, now, Mrs Reilly. There's no one!" A hand brushed her forehead. "Would you like some tea?"

Mona knew she was talking rubbish, but couldn't stop herself. When she awoke again, it was dark and she was alone. Where was the nun? Perhaps she'd been a dream too. No, she was real, but mad as a hatter. Praying was like believing in the pictures. They lied about love existing. Maybe your secret love could be forever with a stranger in paradise, but it didn't happen on earth. Here you got pregnant and that led to children. And they were nothing but a con trick. Little leeches bleeding you of life and youth. Even sex was a total sell, the pleasure was momentary, the position ridiculous, and the cost ... the cost.

As she painfully groped for the bell and rang it, she noticed an opened box of twenty cigarettes and a box of matches beside her hand. Who had left them? The nun? Sally Ann?

Before she had time to light one, footsteps came down the hall and into the snoring room.

"A bedpan, Mrs Reilly?" A young nurse pushed one under the blankets. "I've got an injection for you."

Mona didn't object. She wanted to be drugged, out of it.

"The baby's doing well," the nurse said casually.

Mona didn't answer.

"Are you still depressed?"

"I was never depressed."

"Bonding's the hospital policy."

"Why don't you policy off! And take this thing with you!"

Looking crest-fallen, the nurse took the bedpan and left.

"Just a minute!" Mona called into the dark.

The nurse reappeared through the curtains.

"Ah - look, I'm sorry ... I ... there was a nun. She was getting me a cup of tea."

"Sister Mercy's off duty. She can't sit up all night! We'll be giving out tea at six o'clock." She turned to go, stopping. "Can you last till then?"

Mona nodded. "What time is it now?"

The nurse glanced at her watch. "Twenty past five."

Mona lit a cigarette. Sally Ann must've left them. The nun wouldn't have. It was good of her. Especially when she hadn't been very sympathetic to her problem. She'd be having her operation sometime soon. Mona took up the novel, *Resurrection*, and read a few depressing paragraphs. It seemed to be set in a prison. And it opened with quotations from the gospel. The usual stuff about forgiving your brother. Not seven times, but seventy times seven. Impossible commands. She'd never forgive Terry. She snapped it shut, trying to sleep. But the pain was back. Gradually the injection numbed her. Nobody could understand how badly she felt. Oh, she wished the child well. She'd just never asked for it. And didn't want it now. Terry'd been drunk, that's all. After she came back from England, he'd moved out to a flat with the girl. Then one day he'd had a row with the little bitch and come home and made love to her instead. Of course, she

168

got pregnant. It was as simple as that. How would Sister Mercy like that for a slice of life? The name suited her. In school, the English teacher had been called Mother Mercy. "Girls, there's a Divinity that shapes our ends, rough hew them how we may."

Something had certainly ended her shape and rough hewed her end. Oh, she hadn't always been fat. In her dancing days she'd had a good figure. She was a culchie who came to Dublin in search of a man. It was Palmerston on Saturday nights. The Metropole or Old Belvedere on Sunday nights. The dances had been like a religion. She went on the bus, a headscarf over her curlers, smoking all the way. There was never any difficulty about getting a lift back.

But at twenty-nine she was still single.

"Mona'll get married when she finds a man who can keep her!" her father had boomed.

Money was all her family thought about. And appearances. All looked lost until she met Terry. He'd been standing at the Metropole Bar one evening and offered to buy her a drink. She'd ordered a White Lady, and he'd bought her another one to keep that one company. He was always quick with a joke. She could still see him, laughing, in a houndstooth sports jacket. Later they danced and he'd sung "The Way you Look Tonight" driving her home. It became their song. "Lovely, lovely ... never, never change. Keep that breathless charm, till you're in my arms ..." Oh, God. She'd been taken in by his Englishness and good looks. Blond hair and brown eyes were unusual. She'd bought everything. And now ... oh, he'd even been to a university, another world to her. And he worked in an advertising agency where he had loads of friends. Of course, her family hated him from the word go: London-Irish and worse - a lapsed Catholic. Was she sure he wasn't married before, they'd asked.

Her father had forecast doom. "A weak chin."

"He's mousy, Mona," said her mother.

"He's blond and we're engaged!"

"You'll regret it, Mona!"

But before she had time to, Terry was coming into the Bank to enquire if she'd got her period. She was pregnant, so they married quietly in Kildare Street Registry Office.

It was a terrible blow to her family.

Oh, why couldn't her family have accepted Terry? he was only a little different. But that was what had attracted her. Why were the Irish so insular? You were suspect if you came from the next town. Her marriage had cut her off from her family, friends, church. And now she had no one. Oh, she'd tried to go back to her religion, but the parish priest had said she'd have to go before a tribunal of bishops. She'd committed a reserved sin. When Terry left all her father could say, was had she denied him his rights? They'd done a U turn, now that she might be short of money. Terry

169

was the hero. His rights? What about her rights? Oh, it was all over between them. Terry only came home now to give her money. And if she complained, he threatened to stop paying the mortgage, After all the work she'd done on the house. That mascaraed little sexpot was too lazy to paint. Or sand floors. She couldn't cook either. Maybe she'd poison him with her wild rice.

Tears spilled down her pink nightie. She lay in the dark, crying.

"How's Mrs Reilly this morning?" The nun came in with morning tea.

Quickly Mona wiped her eyes, hauling herself up to a sitting position.

"That's the girl. Did you have a good sleep?"

Mona nodded. As she sipped her tea, the nun dug into her pockets and took out a box of matches and a packet of twenty cigarettes.

"Are Rothmans all right?"

Idiotically, Mona started crying again.

"I thought you were dying for a cigarette!"

"I am. I am." Mona ripped open the Rothmans. Luckily the other packet was hidden under the sheet. "It's very good of you. I have some change ..."

The nun waved her into silence, lighting her up. "Smoke it quickly now. I'll look out!" She disappeared behind the curtain.

Mona inhaled deeply.

"You don't mind if she has a quick cigarette, Mrs Barrett-Byrne? I'll open the window."

The other woman yawned sleepily. "Not at all!"

"We'll be getting you up to the bathroom this morning, Mrs Reilly. The nurses will be round soon." The nun was back. Furtively, she dug into her pocket again, this time taking out a photograph. "Look ... I brought this to show you."

Mona studied the faded image of a dark young man with arched eyebrows and a pencil moustache like David Niven. "Is that - ?"

"Ronald Coleman"

"Hmm ... he's sort of old-fashioned looking."

"Old-fashioned looking?" The nun snapped back the photo. She gazed at it sadly for a minute, before pocketing it again. "I suppose he is old-fashioned now."

"I - I only meant handsome - in an old-fashioned way."

The nun's eyes lit up. But before she could say anything, the day nurses breezed in and helped Mona out of bed. The few yards across the corridor to the bathroom seemed like miles. Mona thought it was a ruse to get her to see the baby, but they left her in the bathroom without comment.

The old nun waited while she did the necessaries. It nearly killed her. You always took natural functions for granted. But now it was agony. What had they done to her insides? Why didn't anybody warn you children could lead to this?

When she came out, the old nun was staring at herself in the mirror.

"Did you never want to get married?" Mona asked her reflection, as she washed her hands.

The old face wrinkled into a smile. "All girls want to get married."

"I don't know why."

"But I had a vocation."

"How did you know?"

"I was called. Everyone is."

"I wasn't."

"Of course you were. There are Rachels and Leahs, Marthas and Marys."

Mona said nothing.

The nun wagged a scolding finger. "You know the story of Martha and Mary?"

"I suppose ... One did the dishes." Mona pulled a comb through her tangled hair. "I look a sight. An absolute sight."

"We have a hairdresser who comes in."

"Oh, I do it myself."

The nun looked interested. "What do you use?"

"Polyblond. I get it in the supermarket. I can tell you one thing. You missed nothing in marriage. I've reached the end with mine."

The nun drew herself up to her full height. "Are you giving in without a fight?"

Before Mona could answer, a nurse came in to help her back to bed. When she'd gone, she lay there exhausted, cheering herself up with another cigarette. The old woman was cracked. It was hopeless to even think of winning Terry back. Anyway she didn't care any more. Still, she shouldn't have said that about the photo looking old-fashioned. The old woman must be lonely, carrying it around with her. You never thought of nuns being lonely, having no one. Bad and all as he was, she had Terry for eleven years. And they'd been all right together till the children came. And even then there were some happy times.

Waiting for breakfast, she drifted into another dream about Robert Redford running up the hospital corridor. This time he stood over her bed, suddenly producing a bunch of red roses from behind his back. The chancer had shaved his moustache, but she wasn't going to be fooled again. And why was he staring? Couldn't he see she was a woman in pain? Someone should brain him.

"Curiosity killed the cat!" she warned, lifting her arm, but just then two nurses dragged him away.

"Breakfast, Mrs Reilly? A cheerful nurse was coming through the curtains.

Afterwards they gave her another injection. She was so sore now, she had to lie on her side. Then she sneaked another cigarette, dozing at last

171

into a dream about her days in Slough. It was always the same dream. She and the children were lost in a station. It was vaulted and grimy with fetid filthy tunnels, leading nowhere. She wandered down one, looking for a timetable or a guard, but couldn't find either. Their footsteps echoed hollowly, frightening Danny and Lisa. Suddenly she came to the end, and a train screeched in front of them. Hastily she gathered the children and got on. But suddenly millions of policemen piled out of the engine and grabbed Danny. As they hauled him off, she sobbed helplessly. "He's my child! He's my child!"

"We're taking care of him, love."

Mona awoke to see Dr Cunningham standing by her bed. He frowned as he examined her stitches. "I hear you're depressed, love?"

Mona said nothing.

"I've asked the psychiatrist to see you. In the meantime, you need blood, love. Blood."

And he was gone.

They hitched her to another bottle. The rest of her day consisted of more sleep, disturbed by visits from a physiotherapist and an intern who took a blood specimen. Before lunch two nurses walked her around her bed. Then there was lunch. Then an afternoon snack which she couldn't eat. She felt only a vast indifference. It was weird. She didn't even worry about the children. She just assumed she'd hear if her neighbour had any problems. And the hospital seemed to have given up worrying her about the baby. Oh, she'd have to see it soon. Just as she'd have to face the months without sleep, the endless nappies.

In the evening Sally Ann came back. "You got the cigarettes?"

Mona smiled. "Thank you."

She sat down, grimacing painfully.

"Are you all right?"

"Sure. It's nothing."

"It's something. An operation."

"Only minor - I was worried in case you'd set yourself on fire!"

Mona reached for the Tolstoy novel. "I'm enjoying this."

"Isn't it good?" Sally Ann opened the book and leafed through it.

"He's terrific on character. Listen to this. 'One of the most widespread superstitions,' she read aloud, 'is that every man has some distinguishing quality: one is kind, another cruel, a third wise or stupid, or energetic, or apathetic. Men are not really like that. We may say of a man that he is more often kind than cruel, more often wise than stupid ... Men are like rivers: the water is the same in one and all, but every river is narrow here, more rapid there ...'"

Mona listened as she read. She was an odd girl. She was looking pale, but curiously did not want to talk about the laparoscopy.

After a few minutes, Sally Ann stopped reading. "Isn't he marvellous?"

Mona nodded. "Did the doctor say anything yet?"

"Oh, he said it didn't look very good. I've a twenty per cent chance."

"That's not bad."

"It's not very good. He advised me to adopt." The younger woman suddenly burst into tears.

Mona did not know what to say.

"I'm sorry! I'll - be all right in a minute."

"Listen, you might be as well off."

"Oh, don't say that!" She wiped her eyes, managing to stop crying. I've seen him. He's lovely."

Mona clammed up. She didn't want to talk about her baby.

Sally Ann chatted on. "I know you're feeling dreadful."

Mona pretended to be sleepy, so the younger woman finally left. Afterwards Mona lay there thinking about her. She was harmless. It was no consolation to tell her she'd be as well off. With children it was either a feast or a famine. Still, it'd be awful not to be able to have them. It was something she'd never thought of. Although she complained about her children, they were her one constant, her one blessing. Without them she'd have nothing to show for her life. Why had she gone crazy now? What had Sally Ann said about a character being like a river? Maybe she'd just hit a narrow spot. It wasn't fair to take things out on a tiny baby. But how was she going to cope with him? How?

About an hour later the old nun popped her head between the curtains. She wore a black raincoat over her habit. "You're looking better, pet." Nodding approvingly, she peeled off black woollen gloves.

Mona panicked at the word "better".

The nun took a brown paper package from her bag. "I got you this."

Mona opened the package. It was a Polyblond rinse. "You shouldn't have, I'm just a bit short now -" The truth was she had very little money.

The nun peered short-sightedly at the instructions. "It's a present. You'll feel better when you look better."

Mona felt tears coming.

"Have a cigarette!"

Mona lit up.

The nun went to open the window. "Smoke quickly now, before anyone comes. Mrs Barrett-Byrne's gone home. She left you something."

"Me?"

The nun pulled back the curtain. "You won't throw it at me?"

Mona shook her head.

The nun put a bundle of baby clothes on the bed. "Her baby died."

"Oh ... " Silently Mona fingered a white matinee coat. The matching bootees. She'd forgotten how tiny new babies were. Oh, God, what had got into her? What sort of woman was she? She inhaled deeply, looking at the nun. "You must think I'm terrible?"

"I do not!"

"Can I go down to the nursery?"

The nun busied herself, picking up the clothes. "Doctor said not till you're strong. But - we could just look at him."

Mona hauled herself out of bed. "I'd like to."

They walked slowly out to the corridor. Halfway to the nursery, Mona had to stop. She felt completely drained of strength. They went on, and at last reached the nursery. It was full of cots, but only two were occupied. Mona stopped by the first, assuming the bigger blond baby was hers. Both of her other children had been blond.

But the nun beckoned from the other cot. "No, Mrs Reilly. Over here!"

Mona went over. This baby was tiny and brown-skinned with a shock of black hair. "Are you sure?"

The nun pointed to the tag on the tiny wrist. "Yes. Reilly."

Mona studied the helpless, sleeping bundle. "He looks Spanish."

The nun bent over the crib. "He's as Irish as Sarsfield!"

Mona stared as the baby wrinkled his nose like a little old man. He made a fist with his tiny hand. Was he really her child? He was too beautiful. And how did he get so dark? And all that hair? Maybe Terry did have foreign blood, way back? She looked worriedly at the nun. "He's very small."

The nun picked up the baby. "He is. But healthy. Aren't you?"

Mona looked at her child. Poor little thing. It was a miserable world to be born into, but the only available one. And if your own mother didn't want you, who the hell would?

"Have you thought of a name, Mrs Reilly?"

A name? Of course, he'd have to have a name. She'd vaguely thought of some. She looked at the old nun, then down at the baby. "What about Ronald?" It just came to her.

## XII  Maureen and Brian

Ireland would make a feminist out of a stone. It's an absolute patriarchy.
I'm dead serious. Take Brian de Burca. He's an older friend of Dick's and
a famous modern historian. In college I used to be dazzled by his ilk. But
then I had not yet entered the groves of academe through the back door
of marriage. I only observed such luminaries from a distance: at a lecture
or on TV, where Brian had his own history programme and was always
the epitome of civilisation. So imagine my surprise last summer when he
behaved like some sort of sultan to his wife, Maureen. The six of us -
Maureen and Brian, and Peggy and Tony, and Dick and I - were in a
Galway hotel for a June weekend. And Brian's bullying started during the
very first breakfast.

He's a burly man with wire glasses, a red face, and a scholarly mane of
white hair combed carefully over a bald patch, and a Shavian beard. As
always, he presided at the top of the table. I sat on one side with Tony and
Dick on the other, while the two other women chatted obliviously at the
far end. And, as always, Brian was telling a story - this time about Parnell
and the famous Galway mutiny of the Irish Parliamentary Party. With his
captive audience, he was like some ancient Irish seanchaí - one of those
learned men who kept history alive long ago through story and lore.
Nowadays they're stuck in a university, but I digress. He was in tip-top
form that morning, but suddenly, in between the porridge and the fry,
interrupted his monologue to shout down the table, "Maureen, the Flora!"

This was margarine for his cholesterol.

Maureen is a waifish woman with wispy grey hair and a beautifully
bony face. She always wears tweeds and a twinset. She was chatting to
Peggy and did not immediately turn round. Which made Brian apoplectic.
He sort of humpfed and reddened even more.

"Maureen!"

She looked up, her forehead puckering with anxiety. "What is it, dear?"

He snorted. "You ignored me!"

"I didn't, dear."

She's a kind little woman who'd never deliberately ignore anyone.

"I didn't hear you," she pleaded.

He still glared.

She paled in agitation.

There was an awful silence. Nobody at the table knew where to look.
He was a real male chauvinist.

At last Brian relented, irritably holding up the butter dish. "You know
what the doctor said about butter."

She immediately jumped up. "The Flora! I forgot it."

He smiled patronisingly, saying with heavy emphasis, "I was trying to tell you that!" Then to Dick and Tony he had the gall to say, "You've got to keep women in line."

I watched Maureen's birdlike figure hop across the dining-room. Then looked to Peggy, silently mouthing the question, "Why didn't he go himself?"

But she just raised her eyebrows philosophically and reached for her orange juice. I wanted to protest or something. But obviously was getting no support. For all her talk, Peggy's a weak reed when it comes to any confrontation. I discovered this at the Kells house and nothing had changed since. She's still a large, comfortable woman and still dyes her hair blonde. Lately all she talked about was dieting, which was a change, but I was relieved she was at last thinking about her health.

It was Tony, the peacemaker, who broke the silence. He's even wirier now, but has a bit of grey in his thick dark hair. "You were telling us about Parnell's finaglings in Galway, Brian?"

My father would've loved to be there, as he's an expert on Parnell.

"Ah, yes!" Brian cleared his throat importantly, going on in his highish voice, "The Clare people wanted nothing to do with O'Shea for the election of '85. So he was out in the cold politically. Chamberlain's Central Boards scheme had failed - "

"What was that?" Tony interrupted.

"An early version of Home Rule," Dick said sleepily.

"Which Parnell would've nothing to do with!" Brian always pronounced the patriot's name *Par*nell instead of the more usual Par*nell* of today. He glanced irritably at Dick now - he couldn't stand anyone to interrupt him or to know more.

At that moment the waitress plonked a plate of toast onto the table. And Brian grabbed a slice, buttering it thickly.

I stared pointedly - I mean, what about his heart?

But he signalled the girl back. "I'm afraid we'll need more toast than that!"

She was young and I guessed on school holidays and had probably never seen anyone so eccentric.

"More toast!" Brian bit off a bite, munching hungrily.

"Yes, more!" Tony said.

"Toast!" echoed Dick.

As I always say, the men stick together. The girl nodded slowly then, pushing her heavy glasses up on her nose, went off. She was probably wondering how grown adults could behave in such an idiotic way. Tony and Dick were giggling moronically now. And Brian was greedily grabbing yet another slice of toast.

To show my disdain for the giggling, I said to Brian, "You were telling us about the Clare election."

Brian left his beloved toast on the plate. "Ah, yes - where was I? Yes ...

O'Shea had no intention of being fobbed off. He started to get downright nasty in '85, so Parnell had to do something to keep him quiet."

"What was he being nasty about?" Tony held him up again.

"Katharine O'Shea was Parnell's mistress," Dick said, bringing the usual glare from Brian.

"Ah, she was Kitty, the mot," Tony said.

"She was never called Kitty!" Brian snapped. "That was an invention of the Irish."

"Of the press, surely?" Dick enquired.

Brian glared at him.

"What did Parnell call her?" I asked.

"Katie," Brian said.

"Or 'my Queen' - as I call Sally Ann," Dick said with a disgusting leer. I glowered at him.

But he didn't notice, as Brian was holding up his hand for silence like a traffic policeman. When assured of our attention, he continued, "There's a lot of dispute about O'Shea's role in the affair. It's just one of those things which is impossible to pin down." He shrugged. "What is truth? Some historians claim he knew from the beginning. Others that he didn't know till '86."

"But Parnell built a cricket pitch at Katharine's house," Dick said. "He stabled his horses there. Surely, O'Shea noticed that?"

"Maybe he was short-sighted," Tony quipped, which brought a laugh from Dick.

The two of them sat there giggling. It was corny.

Brian looked irritably toward the dining-room door. "Where has that woman got to?"

There was no sign of Maureen.

Brian sighed resignedly and went on with his lecture. "Where was I? Yes ... In '85, Parnell had to get O'Shea elected somewhere - the reason will never be clear. First he tried Armagh, but the Northerners wisely wouldn't have him. Parnell, by the way, always dangerously underestimated the Northern protestant. Next, he tried one of the Liverpool seats, but the Liberals wouldn't hear of that."

Just then Maureen came back, completely out of breath and put the tub of Flora in front of him. "There you are, dear."

"You took long enough!" was all Brian could say. Then, frowning importantly, he continued holding forth,

I sat there wanting to protest. I tried to catch the other men's eyes. But received no acknowledgement. They were all the same. If Dick behaved like that he could starve for all I cared. Why hadn't he said something now in support of Maureen?

Brian was busy spreading Flora on yet another slice of toast - he'd eaten nearly the whole plate. "Finally," he was saying, "a vacancy occurred in

Galway. For which Parnell proposed O'Shea. The party was outraged, especially Healy and Biggar. But Parnell wasn't taking no. He rammed O'Shea down their throats."

"To keep him quiet?"

"Or to keep him busy. As I said, it's impossible to know."

Tony reached for the teapot. "Poor Parnell was really in O'Shea's clutches."

Brian held out his cup. "He was in Mrs O'Shea's."

"He loved her," I said.

Brian gave me an irritated look. "He did. But it was a bad day for Ireland when he met that dumpy dowager."

"It's always the woman's fault," I said. I just couldn't help it.

No one spoke.

"Tea, Sally?" Tony blithely held up the teapot.

I put my hand over my cup. "No thanks, I'm drinking coffee."

"In this case ...," Brian grabbed the milk and, pouring it into his tea, slopped it all over the table. "It was the woman's fault."

"Hmph," I sipped my coffee.

Dick soaked up the milk with his napkin, giving me a silencing glare.

Brian's breathing was short. "In fact Parnell was surrounded by mad women. His mother was highly eccentric. His two sisters, Fanny and Anna, fanatic. Emily was a constant drain on his purse."

He was definitely a misogynist. No wonder there were strident feminists.

"How come?" Tony asked.

"She married a drunk," said Dick.

"Arthur Dickinson, a roistering soldier out of Charles Lever." Brian suddenly chuckled. "He once chased Charlie out of Avondale. And when drunk was liable to burn all his clothes. Or throw crockery from the Avondale windows. Occasionally he threw the servants down the stairs. Emily tells us in her silly memoir they were so fond of him they didn't mind. Also that he drank out of love for her - he wanted to die before her! She also records her difficulty in dissuading him from strangling her because he was so fond of her. Women will persuade themselves of anything."

This brought the usual laughter from the other two men.

"What about O'Shea's affairs?" I persisted, angry.

Brian looked as if he was going to blow a fuse. The whole table was silent.

"He was a well-known philanderer," I went on.

Brian spluttered into his tea. Dick glared again, but I ignored him.

"It was all Dervorgilla's fault too," I said. "And the Normans would never have invaded us except for her."

Brian looked very put out, but I didn't care. I really didn't. Why should women always be blamed for everything that went wrong in the world?

Everything. And why couldn't I have opinions too?

I had a history degree, after all.

Then Brian said in a deadly quiet voice, "as a matter of fact, nothing is known of O'Shea's affairs. And Mrs O'Shea was no help to Ireland. The divorce put paid to Home Rule for a generation. Because of her Ireland became insular, backward, and self-centred."

"God save Ireland!" Tony suddenly sang. "God save Ireland, said the hero!"

Then Dick joined in a duet. "God save Ireland, said they all!"

A waitress carried a tray of fries to our table.

"We need more toast," Brian said.

She absolutely ignored him, slamming down a fry at every place but his.

"I ordered poached eggs." He was very aggrieved.

This brought no response.

"Maureen!" Brian shouted down the table. "My eggs haven't come! And we need more toast!"

The two women were now huddled in conversation about the benefits of porridge. "It's low in calories," Peggy was saying.

"It's meant to scrub the arteries," Maureen said.

I pictured a washing-board over a bathtub.

"Maureen!"

"What, dear?"

"My eggs haven't arrived. And we need toast!"

"They won't be long, dear." Maureen said. Then continued chatting with Peggy.

Another silence descended, during which Brian fumed, frequently looking towards the kitchen. He was furious at being left to last. But there was no sign of his eggs or toast.

Then Tony said, "Tell us what happened to O'Shea."

Brian looked slightly appeased. "Well, after all the fuss in Galway, he refused to vote on the second reading of the Home Rule Bill. And in June of '86, walked out of the House and never came back. It was the end of his public life."

Tony was hacking a rasher. "Did he give a reason?"

"Not publicly." Brian turned again to the kitchen. "Oh, there are theories - that he'd just found out about Parnell and Katie. Or that the affair was known about in high places and would make him the butt of gossip ... Where's that girl? We need more toast!"

"Toast?" echoed Dick and Tony.

"Very well," said Dick, rising. "Your health!"

"The country's!" said Tony, rising too and smashing a piece of soggy bread on Dick.

You'd never believe they were grown men. Another waitress flitted by,

179

ignoring us. They definitely had something against us. And I didn't blame them.

"I have to do everything myself," Brian finally said. Then he threw down his napkin, got up and stormed over to the kitchen, disappearing inside. He was a character. Dick told me he once forged a letter from Parnell pretending it was a great discovery to confuse a rival.

I imagined a row going on, but he came out in a few minutes, smiling and triumphantly carrying a mound of toast on one plate and his two slithery poached eggs on the other.

Dick and Tony fell on the toast, shouting "Let the toast pass!"

And the whole table broke into laughter. It was idiotic, but I had to laugh too. I just couldn't help it.

Before breakfast was over, Brian sent Maureen back to their room again - this time for his tablets. I said nothing, realising it was marriage Irish-style. Here women were nothing but servants to men. They spent their lives going on messages for them. Or else bearing children. Thank God, I'd married an American. We'd done it on the spur of the moment last year. In an American registry office. Two friends had been witnesses. I was given a mysterious brown paper package, courtesy of the State. I thought it was contraceptives but inside was a book called *Vanishing Bride*, and stain-removing products. Afterwards, we had lunch in the Hotel du Pont in Wilmington - table d'hôte. Our marriage was completely different to those of our Irish friends. I mean Dick absolutely always helped with the dishes and that. Unlike Brian who exploited his wife.

Still, Brian seemed in good form now. At least with everyone except me. He laughed at Tony and Dick who were fencing on the hotel stairs. But as we passed in the upstairs hall, on the way to brush our teeth, etc, he sort of humphed at me. And I knew an invisible gauntlet was thrown down between us. Which was to remain for nearly the whole weekend.

The hotel was on an Atlantic inlet between Galway and Mayo. The sextet planned to tour Galway one day and Mayo the next. An expedition to Renvyle strand was voted for that morning. As we had no car, Dick and I were to split up among the other two couples - as we had done on the way down. I now made sure to get into the back of the O'Maras' Fiat, leaving Dick to travel in style in the de Burcas' Mercedes.

"You'll need a cardigan. Sally love," Peggy bossed, getting into the front.

"No, I'm fine." I was wearing a shirt and jeans.

She tied a headscarf over her bleached hair. "Go and get your cardigan."

"But it isn't cold."

"Get your cardigan."

So I, a woman of thirty-two, obeyed. That weekend Maureen and Peggy bossed me about all the time. I think they forgot I wasn't their daughter, or especially young any more. So I just let them. In a way I enjoyed it, not having a mother. And I sat happily in the back of Peggy and Tony's car that morning watching the West's wild fuchsia hedges flashing past and the sheep grazing morosely. We passed a couple of woolly corpses. And several times they held us up as they stupidly crossed the road in front of us. So it was almost lunchtime when we arrived at Renvyle.

The whole weekend was dominated by food. If we weren't actually eating, we were planning meals or digesting meals. As soon as we rendezvoused on the strand, the men were hungry again. So we three women were sent in search of forage to the local shop. I would've preferred to stay and hear Brian hold forth on Oliver St John Gogarty's nearby house, now a hotel.

"Gogarty's wife sued the locals for stealing after they were burnt out," his high voice carried over the strand, as I dutifully followed the women. "She won one case and lost another. Even though the furniture was in the people's houses ..." Then he launched into another story, I couldn't hear, about Gogarty's time in the Free State Senate. Brian's knowledge was encyclopedic, and he never tired of sharing it.

The cluttered country shop sold everything from tyres to tea. I went round by myself, while Maureen and Peggy kept together, their figures reminding me of Laurel and Hardy. As they looked for stuff for club sandwiches, they were deep in chat about country prices.

"The tomatoes are cheaper here." Peggy expertly felt a couple.

Maureen picked up a lettuce. "Look, this is imported." Then she put it back. "We'd only have to wash it."

I watched an old country woman fill her basket with packet soups and biscuits. So much for country cooking. Then I put a brack in our basket. Dick really liked it.

But Peggy immediately took it out. "You can't make sandwiches with this, Sally, love."

Who would want to, for God's sake? And why was my presence required if I could make no decisions?

After lunch there was to be a swim. But this was voted unsafe for an hour, so we huddled on the soggy Irish strand waiting. I can still see us, like a modern version of that famous Monet painting - I forget the name of it - Brian in his little straw hat, with his feet bare and trousers rolled up; Dick in his plaid shirt and turned-up Levis, as usual smoking a cigarette; Tony wearing an American baseball cap with a long visor for the non-existent sun, and smoking his pipe; Peggy and Maureen discussing a knitting pattern. Nearby, children played with buckets and spades, watched over by their mothers. And down at the water's edge, bathers shrieked wildly as they dashed into the icy Atlantic.

It was a typical Irish Summer's day - miserable. A cold wind blasted us, whipping the water into vicious little waves which lashed the rocks. Dick always complained about the Irish climate, so I always stuck up for it and even pretended it wasn't cold. In a way I liked grey turfy summers. I was used to them. That day I optimistically wore my bikini under my jeans. To delude myself, I rubbed sun oil on my arms. The smell of it mingled with sea and spray brought back memories of being on a beach with my mother. Lately I thought of her all the time. I found myself staring at women whose age she'd be now, wondering what she'd look like. Her hair would be grey, she'd have wrinkles. Would she be thin like Maureen? Or heavy like Peggy? She'd got thin before her death, but that was illness. Then she went to hospital. And never came back. The beach was one of my few strong images of her. My father was always too busy working, so she would bring Tim and me to rented seaside houses - at Brittas or Donabate. One year we were poor, so she took us for a week to Butlin's Holiday Camp - where an extraordinary thing happened. There was a ventriloquist who was meant to be looking after the children, entertaining them with funny shows and that. Well, he was a child molester. A pederast. I mean he actually felt me up. Oh, I don't think it did me any damage. I was very young. One day he brought me to a variety concert and had me feel him. I thought it rather odd but never told my mother. Then another day, I was in his chalet, looking out a window. And the next thing, my mother was running up the path. She ran in and grabbed me. Or at least I think she did. Once I asked Dick if the man could've possibly molested me and I'd blocked the memory. Could that account for me being nervous about sex? But he said no. He wasn't a Freudian. And if I was screwed up, which he'd never noticed, it was probably Catholicism. That retarded people by about five years. Thank God, I was an atheist now. Still, I'd always felt inadequate. Last year, I'd gone to a sexuality workshop. I knew Dick would laugh the idea to scorn, so I told him it was a meditation group. At first I was quaking with nerves. But there were other women there. First of all we were lectured on the causes of frigidity and then did exercises to get over inhibitions. This involved studying the shape and variety of the vagina. It amazed me that they came in different sizes. We'd examined our own and each others' with the help of mirrors. It was really embarrassing. Then we were told about masturbation techniques. Also how to arouse a man. One lecturer said the trouble came from suppressing emotion. They said you had to discharge it, not bottle things up. The best thing for this was to beat a pillow. It was Balzac.

"You won't need oil today, Sally love!" Peggy interrupted my thoughts. "There's no warmth in the sun."

"It's insulation for my swim." I kept on rubbing. It was lucky people couldn't read your thoughts. Peggy would think me cracked. They all would. But you were stuck with yourself. You could change your personality but not your basic character, according to one of my self-improvement books. Tim was always quoting Popeye, "I yam what I

182

yam."

Tony looked over. "The Eskimos rub themselves with whale blubber."

I laughed. You had to accept yourself.

He shivered, gazing at the water. "It's too cold for me. Say, isn't that a Minister breasting the waves - or thinking about it?"

We all stared at the dark-haired man in his togs. He stood at the water's edge, gingerly dipping his toe in and immediately jumping back.

"It is," Brian said.

Dick laughed shortly. "A typical Irish politician."

"What's he Minister of?" I asked.

Brian peered over his glasses. "Trade and Industry. But he won't last."

The politician suddenly ran up the beach, out of the way of some shrieking, splashing girls.

Our group burst out laughing.

When we'd recovered, I asked, "Why won't he last?"

Brian stroked his beard. "He's on the outs with Haughey."

I hugged my knees. "I wish he'd do something for women."

Peggy looked up. "What do you mean, Sally?"

"I mean abortion, divorce."

She gave me a funny look.

Brian sighed. "Bread and circuses, my dear."

At least he was talking to me now.

"We're all going down the drain," Tony said. "Since the oil went up, no man is an island."

"Since Lemass," Dick said.

"Still, it was sink or swim then." Tony threw a stone at the water. "Lemass had to do something."

Brian sighed. "And now it's total immersion. We've incompetents running the country."

Dick lit a cigarette. "People are pushed by events. Look at Nixon, the cold war king, going to China. He was pushed by the times. It wasn't love of the 'heathen chinee'."

"But why is abortion bread and circuses?" I got back to the point.

"Because the country isn't ready for change. It's a smoke screen," Brian said, "to distract people from real issues."

"But it's 1982!" I argued. "Women all over the world have abortions. Why should Irish women be deprived?" I looked for support to Peggy and Maureen, but they gazed pointedly at the politician, refusing to be drawn. The Minister was slowly approaching the water again.

Tony puffed philosophically on his pipe. "Sure, we might as well have abortion here. Thanks to the British - how many women take the boat weekly?"

"I'm not sure exactly. Lots." I looked gratefully at Tony. He was always willing to discuss things. "A woman has a right to choose."

"They certainly do," he said soothingly.

Dick sighed boredly. "The government should certainly address the problem."

The politician was now dipping his fingers into the sea and making the sign of the cross. Hugging himself, he walked out a couple of steps. Then, seeing a wave, he ran quickly back. That started Dick and Tony on their duet again.

"God save Ireland, said the hero!

God save Ireland said they all!"

I had to laugh. When their noise had died down, Peggy said thoughtfully, "But what about the child being aborted, Sally Ann? Isn't it a human being with rights too?"

I was drawing on the sand with a stick. "Who says it's a human being?"

Peggy was outraged. "Of course it's a human being!"

"Why not baptise the menstrual flow?" I argued. "That's potentially a human being."

Maureen looked over. She was huddled in a rug, and her face was pinched with cold. "A human being exists from the minute the sperm penetrates the ovum."

Dick groaned. "Oh, come now. That's ridiculous. Sometimes a human being never exists. I have several children who didn't make it."

Tony laughed. "There's time yet."

"It's fast running out," Dick replied. He was like my father about his children.

Then Brian interrupted. "It's women who aren't human beings. They're heartless. A man could never have an abortion."

I thought I was hearing things. "A man wouldn't have to! And people are heartless. Not women. People!"

Even this brought no response from the women. God, they couldn't even stick up for themselves.

Just then, the politician passed our group, breathing hard and slapping himself - as if he had been in swimming. It was so silly. I mean, I'd been watching him all the time, and he'd hardly wet his feet.

"How was the water?" Tony enquired politely.

"Brutal," shivered the Minister. "Brutal!"

This again reduced our group to laughter. I sat staring out to sea. It wasn't funny really. How could there ever be any change in Ireland with the likes of him in power? If he couldn't even go for a swim, how would he bring about change? And why did men always run everything? Make decisions for women? Finally I got up and took off my jeans, saying, "I'm going for a swim."

Peggy looked at her watch. "It's not an hour yet, Sally, love. You'll get cramp."

"I won't." And I ran to the water's edge.

In a way, I didn't blame the politician. Swimming is something I don't like very much - which is probably why I've never learnt properly. It's really only a point of honour for me to get wet at least once a year, especially if I'm at the seaside. It just didn't feel right not to. The cold that day took my breath away. I plunged down, kicking wildly. And after a few strokes ran back to the edge where Dick stood shivering in his togs. His white hair and brown skin were in contrast to the pale Irish. After seven years, we were still together. Love was a mystery. The songs were right.

He cautiously dipped his big toe in. "Christ, this is awful."

"It's not bad when you're in," I lied.

His teeth were chattering. "It's not bad for the fish!"

I ran off along the strand at the edge of the water, but he called after me. "What is it?" I ran back.

He jumped out of my way. "Don't splash me! And for heaven's sake, cool down a bit!"

"I'm perfectly cool, thanks."

"Well, stop quarrelling with Brian!"

I didn't answer, just splashed off again along the water's edge to keep warm. In the distance I saw Brian undressing under copious towels. Men were all the same. They thought you were quarrelling if you expressed your ideas. Actually I don't know what I think about abortion. I could never have one. Yet I think it should exist. My mother'd been pregnant with my brother when her cancer was first discovered. She might be alive today if she'd had an abortion. Women were expected to be such saints. My American feminist friends were right about men exploiting us. They blamed us for everything - Eve, Dervorgilla, Katharine O'Shea. Dick even jokingly blamed me for the Irish climate, saying, "Your dank country," etc. And somehow the country's endless strikes were a reflection on me. I always blamed myself for the house too. If something went wrong with it, which it usually did, I got paroxysms of guilt. Also I worried constantly about Dick's health. If he got a stomach ache, it was my cooking. If he sneezed, it was somehow my doing too. Looking back along the strand, I saw he was down and swimming strongly. He'd probably get a cold now. But the Atlantic was an international ocean.

I don't know whether it's just relief at getting out of the freezing water, but you feel terrific after a swim. I did that day. My irritation at Brian was washed out of my system.

Our next stop was Kylemore Abbey, the famous Benedictine girls' boarding school. It's a chocolate-boxy castle on a lake with a Paul Henry mountain behind it. Besides the school, there's a café and pottery shop. While Dick and the others were looking around the Abbey hall, I visited the pottery with Maureen. She runs her own craft shop in Dun Laoghaire, so was interested in seeing what they had. As we stopped to admire a vase, she surprised me by saying, "Did you ever think of getting a job, Sally Ann?"

"I'm a painter."

"That's just a hobby, surely? I need someone to help in the shop."

"I'd be glad to help you. But I don't want a job."

"But wouldn't you like to earn money?"

"I do earn money - a little. From my paintings."

"But everybody should work."

"I do work! Painters paint."

She walked around the shop. I followed her small, tweedy figure, telling myself not to be annoyed. That she was only being kind to me. After all, she wasn't the only one who thought me a layabout. My father, who knew I worked five to six hours a day, was always saying, "Art is wonderful therapy, Sally Ann." Oh, he meant well. He'd just never had any faith in me. Tim, my hippy-happy brother, was doing very well now as a commercial artist, but was still the butt of my father's criticism. I would be too, if I lived at home. Except for Mother Rita, long ago, Dick was the only person in the world who believed in me. I'd never have managed without him. The only trouble was I had no real talent. I was too imitative.

As we went outside to find the others, Maureen said, "A pity you haven't your sketch-book here, Sally Ann."

I nodded agreeably. The Abbey was the last place in the world I'd want to sketch.

"Oh dear! They're waiting for us in the cars!" She wrinkled her eyes at the edges, saying as we hurried over, "why don't you display your paintings in the shop."

"Thanks." At least there was no ill-feeling between us.

She wagged a finger. "Nothing too abstract now."

"All my paintings are abstract. One is being considered for the RHA exhibition." The boast just popped out. How is it you never really grow up? You're always the same eejit inside.

She gave me a long look. "You're aiming high, aren't you?"

I shrugged. "Not particularly. Professional painters exhibit."

Just then Brian honked angrily from the car.

She hurried over. "Coming dear!"

"You're delaying us!" he shouted, flinging open the door. "Get in!"

She got into the back seat, as Dick was in the front with Brian.

And I got into the back of Peggy and Tony's.

Clifden was next, and all the way there I smarted at her remarks. It hit me, that for all my talk about women's lib, I was dependent on Dick. While she was financially independent of Brian. I'd never make a living as an artist. I wasn't good enough. I knew that now. Despite my stupid boasting. Clifden is a busy country town with two main streets converging in a V. We all had afternoon tea in one of its trendy hotels. As usual, Brian

186

entertained us with a story. This time about the death of the famous reactionary Archbishop of Dublin, John Charles McQuaid. It sounds heartless to laugh at the death of anyone, but Brian had affected a hilarious Dublin accent.

"I met a car salesman," he said, "by the name of McQuaid and asked him if he were any relation. He told me he was, so I said, 'I'm sorry to hear about your brother.' 'Ah, yes,' says he, 'poor Jack's gone and we didn't know he was going at all, at all.' 'What happened?' says I. 'Jack came out in his nightshirt and said to the sister, Treasa, 'Jaysus, I'm fucked!'"

The idea of a bishop speaking like that reduced the group to hysterics. Brian went on imitating the Archbishop's brother, "Then the sister said, 'Not at all, you're grand, Jack. Go back to bed now.' So he did. Then he came out again and said the same thing. She sent him back to bed. But he came out again in his nightshirt, shoutin' 'Jaysus, I'm really fucked!' And fell over dead."

This brought more laughter. I remembered the Archbishop. He was a stern, forbidding man who had confirmed me with a slap as a strong and perfect Christian. There was a whole row of us, waiting to be examined on our catechism, but he had to pick on me. Of course, I was too paralysed with nerves to answer. But he said it for me. He wasn't bad really.

While Dick and Tony sneaked a drink in the bar and Brian snoozed in the car, we women went foraging again. This time for fish for a picnic supper - as Brian didn't eat meat. But talk about looking for coals at Newcastle, or whatever the cliché is, there was not a fish to be had at the harbour. Or anywhere in the town. We learnt of a fish factory on the coast. So it was voted we try there.

As we waited for Tony in their car, Peggy suddenly turned to me.

"I'm surprised at your attitude to abortion, Sally Ann."

I was taken aback at her scolding tone. "Well - "

"I hope you wouldn't consider having one."

"I certainly would."

Her face blotched in anger. "Well! I'm shocked!"

I had upset her. "If I was raped, I'd take the morning after pill."

She shook her head. "But it'd be yours too."

"Not if I was raped."

She looked at me in puzzlement. "But it's very unusual for a pregnancy to occur after rape."

I was very fond of Peggy and didn't want to argue with her. Still, I couldn't help asking, "What if you were having a defective child?"

To this she had no answer.

"There has to be choice," I persisted obstinately. "Irish society discriminates against people."

"Who does it discriminate against?"

"Women, the unhappily married. Homosexuals."

She frowned in irritation. "Don't tell me you approve of homosexuality?"

"I certainly do!"

"Sally!" She picked up the folded newspaper and rustled it irritably. "Don't tell me you admire women's bodies?"

"Well, I admire ballet dancers." Now I was getting hot. "According to Freud, everyone's homosexual. If you're not active, you're latent."

This was like spitting in the holy water font.

She glared. "I've never thought much of him."

"Well, you're in the minority!"

She rustled the paper again. "If you don't mind, I'd like to read the paper."

And a silence fell like a curtain between us. Actually, I didn't know if Freud was right or not. I'd just read it somewhere. Also I read that you fell in love with your parents and spent your whole life searching for them in others. Maybe that was true, I didn't know. I only knew it was important to be loved. Then other things fell into place. I glanced over at Peggy. She was still reading. I shouldn't have argued with her. She didn't know any homosexuals. She'd never met people like Anna and Sue. If she came to America, I'd introduce her to them. Now she was really irritated with me. She was probably thinking I'd got liberal ideas in America. Had loads of abortions. Or made some sort of choice not to have children. When the opposite was the truth. I'd just never produced anything. Dick and I had tried. With Nettie, he had only to walk through the bedroom. But I always got my period. I had adhesions, the doctor had told me. And he couldn't even be sure about that, although he'd seen my insides on a TV screen. "I can't say you have blocked tubes, but I can tell you one thing: it doesn't look good." Dick was relieved when I told him, I knew. There was no one else to tell. I'd longed for my mother. Or even a sister. When I had my Irish operation, my father came to see me. For ages he just sat there looking puzzled. "Why on earth do you want children?" he asked at last. Which was a terrible reflection on Tim and me.

But I imagined this child I couldn't have. It was a boy, dark and skinny like Dick. Where was he? I knew I'd missed a great joy. Yet sometimes, I was relieved, I could do my painting. At least I told myself that.

It was hours before we ate. Absolutely hours. We drove for miles in search of the fish factory, finding it at last. They normally exported to France and were put out at having to sell to mere natives. But Peggy was persuasive, so they did. And we ended up with enough sole to feed an army.

Finding a place was next. We drove along the coast, but someone found something wrong with everywhere we stopped - no shelter or an unsuitable view. Once Peggy spotted a fat horse in a field and waved the other car down.

"It looks pregnant," she said, getting out.

Although inexperienced, I had to agree. It stood perfectly still with its feet outstretched, as if doing the splits.

Maureen looked at it worriedly. "I think we should go for help."

Peggy climbed onto the crumbly stone wall. "Yes, it's going to give birth any minute."

There was a cottage two fields away.

Brian came up. "I vote we eat here. I'm very hungry. Don't you agree, Tony? Dick?"

The other men nodded assent.

Peggy's bosom swelled. "There's an animal in need."

Brian blinked at the horse. "It looks all right to me." The horse had now lain down. Its legs stretched straight out. "Besides," said Brian, "Animals can cope. It's natural, after all."

"That's what doctors say to women! I'm going for help!" said Peggy, setting out across the field. "Are you coming, Maureen? Sally Ann?"

For solidarity I followed. And the three of us trudged across the soggy fields. But I'm afraid it was for naught. At the cottage two old men just listened to us, nodding and smiling. Then politely closed the door on us. "They probably eat children out here," Peggy raged as we all trudged back. And we left the poor horse to its fate.

After more miles of driving, we came at last to a scraggy field with rocks going down to the sea. Litter was strewn in one corner with ashes from a previous picnic. But at least the place had some shelter. So it was voted OK. Tony and Peggy immediately set up the stove, and i was given the task of chopping onions, peppers and tomatoes for frying.

To my amazement, Peggy ordered the men to set the table. Brian spread the table-cloth. And Tony and Dick put out the cutlery. They were very proud of themselves. Then Peggy pointed to a brown stain in the middle of the cloth. "Look where you've put it!"

It was a moist cow pat. I've often wondered what people see in picnics. I really do. We could've been comfortable in a restaurant. It was a miserably cold evening, and everybody was absolutely starving. Although still light, it was now quite late. Brian hovered hungrily around, and Peggy kept telling him furiously to go away. She was mad about her table-cloth. But the fish were cooked at last, and I was elected to serve it onto plates. As I did, Brian crept up behind me and snatched one.

"Brian," Peggy shouted. "Put that back!"

He ignored her.

"Brian!" She made for him with a spoon. But he ran, his white hair wild, to his car.

"Sally Ann! Get that back!"

But he had locked himself in and was eating hungrily. I shrugged at Peggy. Dammit, she could get it back herself. The rest of us were served at last. And ate our food huddled in a group near Brian's car. He had the nerve to open his window and announce, "The fish was cold!"

Peggy was quite unruffled. "Serves you right for grabbing!"

It was cold, but in that weather it was difficult to keep anything hot. I can't remember how the chat went exactly. I think we must've been talking over the career of the vacillating politician at Renvyle. Or the government or something. But just as we were finishing our coffee, Peggy said to me, "I've been thinking, Sally. In abortion, a case of assault would be an exception."

"Well, it wouldn't be the woman's fault." I was glad we were friends again.

"Of course it wouldn't," Dick said, joining in. He didn't know we were referring to a previous conversation. "Tell them your Butlin's story, Sally Ann."

Dick and I often think of the same thing. So the coincidence of me thinking of the Butlin's incident that very day didn't surprise me. It often happens with us. So I told the group my story, nervously but without trauma, because really it hadn't upset me. I was too young. They were all amazed - that the man had been looking after children.

But Brian suddenly blurted, "Nonsense. Little girls are always asking for it. My sister used to accuse a neighbouring boy of interfering with her. So I was chosen to protect her. My mother made me follow her home from school. Well, the fellow was there all right, waiting on the corner as she'd described. But assault! It was assault all right. They went down the lane together and into the garden of a deserted house. I looked over the wall, and what did I see?"

Everyone was agog.

"She was interfering with him!"

Tony shook his head gravely. "How old was she?"

"Thirteen. And she was unbuttoning his fly!" He shook his head. "They're all the same."

I was furious. For women. And for myself. So I said coldly, "I'm a liar then?"

"I didn't say that!" Brian looked violently red in the face.

"Well, I must be."

He was speechless but finally got his breath. "How do you put up with this one, Dick?"

Dick looked embarrassed. And the women, as usual, looked away.

"We'll have her shot, Brian!" Tony joked, going over to the stove. "More coffee, anyone?"

"You'll have to boil more water." And Peggy busied herself with filling it.

I went down to the rocks, pretending to go to the loo. I just had to get away from the others. They all thought me humourless or something like that. Maybe I was. But inside I was boiling. Boiling. Why had I got so upset? Because women would never speak that way about men, I told myself. Never. And Brian should know better. He was meant to be enlightened. How would things ever change for women? How? I sat on a rock for ages, hoping to imbibe some of the Connemara peace: the plopping water, the smell of turf smoke on the wind, and the swallows swooping and diving. Where had they come from? How good to be able to fly from this world's troubles.

As we drove back to the hotel through Connemara's mysterious mountains, the sky was an angry red. And I knew by his coldness Dick was angry with me. Of course, it was all my fault. Brian was only being funny. I had spoiled the day by getting angry. Why had I got so angry? I always put my foot in it. Dick travelled with Brian and was probably apologising for me now. I dozed in the back of Peggy and Tony's car. They weren't against me, I knew. Just too tired for conversation. So I wandered in my mind. All holidays turned out disastrously. My French one had ended my relationship with Alastair. For years I blamed myself. I cringe, thinking of my former selves. Sometimes they flash before me like scenes in an old-fashioned movie. I was a pain. In college I camped it up to hide my nerves. I thought I was in a Camus novel - except I didn't know any French. I remembered arguing that Jane Austen was a bore. Why didn't she write about something important, instead of who married who? God, I was thick. And so pretentious. I even fancied myself a journalist. God. Now I'm trying to be an artist. Maybe that'll be the same. I'll never know who I am. No wonder Alastair couldn't love me. In a way he'd become my Michael Furey. Did he ever think of me? Probably not. But I forgot people too. Paul Brady was dead for years. Poor Paul. And that terrible funeral. For solidarity, I didn't want a Christian burial. Actually I didn't want to be buried at all. I couldn't stand the idea of bugs crawling on me. I'd be cremated and used as an egg-timer. There was some point in that. But why had Paul done it? Life was so beautiful. "It's a great big peach, Sally Ann," Mother Rita used to say. "Take lots of bites." Then I reminded myself to ring her when I got back. It was Sister Rita now. She came from somewhere in the West. She was the kindest person I'd ever known. One of those really good people. She'd made such a difference to my life. And yet, such is human nature, I used to go round calling her names. I was so embarrassed to have feelings. I'd really shocked Deirdre once by running her down. Deirdre was from the West too. She'd never grown up, really. Lived in the past. Yet I could've helped her. The last I heard she was doing a night degree. Where was she now? Life's a journey really, the poets were right about that. And friends fell by the wayside. God, it was 1965 when I visited her. We'd cycled in those lovely fuschia-lined lanes. Seventeen years ago. Over half my life. Now I was thirty-two and still alive. Because of my mother I never expected to be old. I kept imagining diseases. Yet here I was. A brave man dies but once.

Back in our room, Dick wouldn't speak to me. He got into bed quickly and turned out the light. I knew he was angry.

I got undressed in the dark. "I'm sorry."

He didn't answer. It's typical of all men, never wanting to discuss things.

"Please say something." I could hear his thoughts ticking. He was thinking me a pain.

Finally he sighed. "It was a bit heavy."

"I didn't plan it."

He turned on his side. "Go to sleep."

I was forgiven. Still, I lay awake for hours.

Peggy called me at the crack of dawn for a sauna with her and Maureen. By the time I'd staggered sleepily downstairs in my dressing gown, the two women were sweltering in the little oven. They were both wearing bikinis so I felt awkward sitting there with nothing on.

Peggy's eldest daughter was pregnant, and the conversation focused on the event. Fragments penetrated the steam to my sleepy brain. "I tried to buy her a maternity dress, but she'll only wear jeans and a T-shirt."

"Oh, it'll be a new lease of life for you."

"Your grandchild must be two now."

"Two and a half. And a more active child you've never seen."

"Are you all right, Sally, love?"

I nodded, smiling.

"Take a shower now. We had one before you came down."

The heat seemed unbearable, so I went. I loathe showers and it was miserable, standing under that one. Yet I thought it might cool me down. The others certainly looked cool.

I went back to my perch. They were still chatting happily. And one by one went out for a shower,

"It's awfully hot," I said to Peggy.

"You'll feel marvellous afterwards, Sally."

She went for her shower. Then I went for another. Stepping out of it, I realised something was drastically wrong. I was going to faint. How had this happened when the others were completely unaffected? I managed to put on my dressing gown and stagger towards the hotel stairs. I reached them and collapsed.

I don't know how long I was there, but I opened my eyes to see Brian de Burca's red face. "My dear girl!"

I closed my eyes. Oh God, why him? He put his arm under my shoulder and hauled me to a sitting position. Then he thrust my head between my knees. "Keep your head down, that's the girl."

I felt really awful.

"What happened to you at all?"

Tears came. I couldn't help it. "I don't know. I had a sauna. Then a shower. Look, I'm sorry about yesterday."

He sat down beside me on the stairs. "Just keep quiet."

"I was humourless."

"When?"

"During the picnic."

"Oh, that! I don't know why you're sorry. I was the boor!"

In a few minutes, I felt myself recovering. This used to happen to me in boarding school years ago, but not since. What was wrong?

"Can you make it to bed?"

I nodded, and he helped me up, saying "Sitting in an oven couldn't be good for anyone."

Together we walked to the bedroom. Halfway I joked, "I'm not even a real feminist!"

"You're a passionate feminist, Sally Ann."

"I know you only like docile women."

He humpfed in reply. I was unable to say any more. Near my bedroom door he said, "Basically you were right about Katharine O'Shea."

"Well ... you're the historian."

"Don't interrupt! Katharine O'Shea was blamed for Home Rule, which many historians think would never have got through. Never. It hadn't a chance. Gladstone and Parnell were both living in fantasy."

"What was Parnell really like?"

"Now that's a silly question. What is anyone really like? There were many Parnells. There was Parnell the country gentleman, Parnell the brilliant political strategist, Parnell the mad scientist, Parnell the lover."

We came to the bedroom door. Dick had gone down to breakfast. "Get into bed." Brian looked at me over his glasses. "And I'll send Maureen up with a cup of tea. Another thing -"

"What?"

He cleared his throat, looking at me kindly. "The artist is the true historian. In a hundred years, they'll be looking at paintings to know what life was like at the end of the twentieth century."

I got into bed. "They won't be looking at mine."

He folded his arms. "That's no attitude! I thought your Christmas card showed great ability."

"You need more than ability. You need talent."

"You've got that."

I sighed tiredly. "Not enough."

"You're a stubborn woman, aren't you?"

"'Know thyself' - Plato."

"That wasn't Plato! It was written in the temple at Delphi. And you don't know anything at your age! Now get some rest. I've a surprise for you later today."

In a few minutes Dick came up. Then Peggy brought my breakfast on a tray. "Sally, love, what happened?"

"I fainted - the heat!"

She put the tray on a table and anxiously perused my face. "Can you face a little toast?"

"Maybe a cup of coffee. I'm a bit nauseous."

After Dick left, she stayed, sitting chatting on the bed. "I'm sorry I got so cross yesterday. You must think I'm right-wing."

"No - I don't."

She gave me her wonderful smile. "Well, I'm not really."

"I know ..." My mind went blank.

"Will you stay in bed?"

"No, I'm fine. Except for the nausea."

She grabbed my hand. "You're not - ?"

I laughed aloud. "Pregnant? God, no!"

She looked disappointed. "That's all right then. Children aren't everything. You have artistic gifts."

"Oh, we've tried."

Her face lit up again. "Have you?"

I sighed. "Nothing ever happens."

She thought for a moment. "Try a pillow under your hips."

"What?"

"Just try it."

I nodded, not telling her about all the tests I'd had.

Brian's surprise was a visit to Moore Hall, the ancestral home of novelist George Moore. Tony and Peggy wanted to go shopping in Louisburg instead. So Brian had only three of us to show around. Wearing his straw hat and with a huge walking stick in hand, he led us up the long ferny avenue, as usual talking all the way.

"Now the Moores were originally an English family who claimed descent from Sir Thomas Moore. The claim is unproved, but they did marry into a Spanish Catholic family and made a fortune in the wine business..."

I listened in fascination. Chauvinist or not, he was the most interesting person I'd ever met. And he'd been awfully nice to me. I was glad we'd made peace.

He hit a rambling weed with his stick. "About 1790, George Moore, the merchant, retired to Ireland and acquired about 12,000 acres in Mayo on which he built Moore Hall. Then there was Sir John Moore who was out with the French in '98. And the novelist's father who was elected to parliament in 1868."

"Before Parnell?" I queried.

"Parnell was elected in '75," Dick said.

Brian controlled his irritation at being interrupted. "That Moore was a supporter of land reform. One of the few landlords who were. Despite that, the IRA burnt the house during the Troubles."

They sure had. We came out of the green gloom of the avenue to a spectacular ruin. The big granite house was a roofless shell with bricked-in windows and weeds growing inside. Still it was hauntingly beautiful. Eerie. The four of us were like characters on a Chekhov stage set, lamenting a lost world. There was no one else about. Brian pointed out a plaque the IRA had erected in reparation for their deed.

I went up the wide steps to the non-existent door. "What a pity to burn a place like this."

Brian was following me. "That's patriotism for you."

"Vandalism," said Dick.

I wandered round the weedy gravel by myself, while Dick chatted to Brian inside the ruin. In Ireland people talked about the past, yet had no respect for it. The house was a symbol of oppression. Now its brooding presence was a scar on our country's psyche. Fanaticism got you nowhere. But it was still going on. Parnell's time was gone now, as ours would one day be. He wouldn't have wanted this destruction. It was done by the thinking of the time. People were stuck in their own rut. In the future, our Stone Age laws would seem just as ludicrous as the burning of this beautiful house. Change would come. It was only a matter of time. We still had Rome Rule, but give us another hundred years ...

Dick was waiting for me at the ruin, smoking.

"Isn't it great?" I pointed at the house.

He nodded, smiling and we followed Brian and Maureen down the avenue. They walked ahead of us arm in arm, Brian looking Churchillian with his hat and walking stick. I thought how happy I was. And how Brian was right: it was impossible to know anyone. Like heaven, marriage is a house with many mansions.

"Frankly," Brian's voice carried back, "Moore wrote like a woman."

Hmm! I thought. Hmm!

# XIII  Births, Marriages and Deaths

Two nuns were in the drab community room. Although for recreation, the floor was covered with hard lino, and the stiff Victorian furniture looked uncomfortable. By one wall a glazed bookcase held musty tomes, and there was no friendly clutter. It was early summer, so sun from the tall windows overlooking the terrace cheered things a bit, but not much.

Sister Rita sat reading the *Irish Independent* at the centre table. As usual, Sister Clement hogged "her place" by the cold storage heater. Shortsightedly she poured over *The Irish Times*, singing bits of a hymn: "Oil in my lamp ..."

"Anything in *The Times*, Clemmy?"

The older woman didn't look up. "Give me oil in my lamp ..."

"Could I have a bit of your *Times*, Clemmy?"

"I want oil in my lamp."

Resignedly, Rita tried to find something of interest in her paper. Thirty odd years in the convent had taught her patience. But Clement had had the *Times* for the last half-hour. How could anyone read and sing? And tunelessly too.

Monday was Rita's morning off from lecturing at Carysfort. And she looked forward to a quiet read of the papers. Usually she had the room to herself. But in a Mother House you could never be sure who would come out of the woodwork. The young nuns taught all day in the new building, but the old tended to wander down from the infirmary. Oh, she could take the papers to her own room, but there was a vague house rule against this. And she was meant to be the Superior. So instead she made a cup of Nescafé Blend 37 with a kettle in her room - the nearest thing to brewed coffee she could afford - and carried it downstairs. There was a house rule against this as well, but she ignored it too.

It was her prerogative as Superior to ignore petty rules.

She folded her paper, replacing it in the middle of the table. In five minutes she'd have to go and draft a letter to the Minister, protesting about delays in the secondary curriculum reform. The Conference of Secondary Sisters had appointed her as spokeswoman. And just as well too. Someone needed to shake things up. The Department had been talking about change for years now. And every year the same old excuses. Teaching sisters, she would point out, welcomed the principle of non-sexist education ... but where were the teachers of woodwork - no, woodwork *and* mechanical drawing - who would make this possible? And, more important, where were the long promised changes in the Examination Board?

A low mumble broke into her thoughts.

Clement was fingering her beads now, the paper lying unread on her lap.

"Are you finished with the Times, Clemmy?"

"Am I what?" The old woman looked comical with a brown, springy wig under her veil.

"*The Irish Times*?" Rita shouted. "Have you read it?"

"I haven't seen it."

"It's on your lap!"

"Oh!" She scrunched it up. "Have it! Good riddance!"

Rita crossed the room, catching the glare of disapproval at her jogging shoes. "How are you feeling today, Sister?"

"Terrible ... terrible."

Rita stood over her. Clemmy's health was always terrible. To be honest, she was a terrible hypochondriac. "Are you taking the new medicine?"

The old nun dragged her gaze from the jogging shoes, smiling sourly. "Ah, sure, it's useless. I'll just have to suffer. Eh ... are those shoes comfortable?"

"Yes."

"They look very queer."

Rita didn't answer. She'd given up her battle for civvies, and now always wore the short brown habit and veil like the other nuns. But nothing would persuade her to give up comfortable shoes. She was called "The Running Nun". Which is apt, she thought, because I never stop.

She returned to the table and sat down. *The Irish Times* was full of the usual alarming number of factories closing. As usual, world news was cramped characteristically onto one page. She began reading an article about Nicaragua.

"It's very near," came from across the room.

Rita didn't look up.

"I said it's very near, Sister."

Rita sighed, rustling the paper. Could she not read in peace? "What is?"

"The end of the world." And the old nun muttered worriedly, "Jesus, Lord, have mercy".

"Oh, people have always thought that."

Sister Clement shook her head. "It's coming in ten years' time. All the old prophecies are coming true."

"What prophecies?"

"Grass will grow on the railway lines ... Men will look like women ... And there'll be plagues."

"I haven't noticed any plagues."

"Look at all the cancer!"

Rita kept her patience. "There was always cancer."

The old woman laughed bitterly. "You think that because you're young."

Rita smiled to herself. To be called young at 52 was really stretching it. But there were no young nuns. And only one vocation in five years. To

197

survive at all, they'd had to sell most of their land to builders. Bit by bit. Marx was right about economics ruling everything. Things had changed unbelievably with inflation. It had been more significant than Vatican 2. With John Paul II that seemed to be almost forgotten. The winds of change were now nothing but a wheezing bellows. The church was retrenching. And the Pope certainly didn't think much of women either. Nothing. The battle was in vain.

Wearily she skipped to the leading articles. One on the Middle East. Another on the coming Abortion Amendment Referendum. People were getting hysterical about wanting to change the Constitution to forbid it, judging by the columns of letters to the editor. She glanced through them. One suggested that a "No" victory would open the door to divorce. Signed by a man, naturally. What if one of them became pregnant? Church teaching might shift then. They might stop ranting about sex and concentrate on the gospel of Christ. Oh, abortion was wrong on all counts. But she was still anti-Amendment. She'd definitely vote no. It was a woman's problem. And women were moral agents, being dictated to by celibate old men. And young men too.

She read another letter. It suggested that a pluralist society would be the death of Catholic Ireland. What rubbish. Pluralism was the only hope for such a benighted land. Divorce would eventually come. The Church would just have to accept the inevitable. Something it had never been good at. "All institutions are corrupt", a priest had once told her. "And the Church is no exception. Unholy Babylon, Dante had called it. And it was the same today. But that wasn't a reason for leaving it. No, she hadn't jumped over the wall. Unlike others, she'd won that battle. Her late thirties had been turbulent. A time she didn't think about or talk about. There had been too much pain. Her forties had been a little easier, except in the physical sense. And even now "the heyday of the blood" showed no sign of taming. Hamlet had definitely been a young man. A young prig.

She looked over at the old woman. Had she known the same sexual craving? The hunger for the love of a man? The terrible doubts? Nuns of the previous generation denied the body's existence. Accepted things. And were probably happier.

Sister Clement caught her stare. "We were warned, but we wouldn't listen."

"Stop worrying, Clemmy."

Maybe happiness wasn't everything.

Rita scanned the back page columns. No one she knew born, married or dead. She turned to the ads in the Personal Columns. Suddenly her glance darted back to a death notice.

SHERIDAN: Sally Ann (nee Fitzpatrick). 21 June 1983, at the Rotunda Hospital, Dublin. Also her infant son. Beloved wife of Richard (Dublin and Athens, Pennsylvania, USA): deeply regretted by her loving husband, father and brother. RIP. Remains arriving 5 o'clock today to Fanagan's Funeral Home, Aungier Street. Funeral tomorrow, Tuesday, 11 o'clock to Glasnevin.

It had to be Sally Ann. The age was right and the husband's name.

Rita read the ad again. No, there could be no mistake. But there was no Mass. The Rotunda probably meant childbirth. God, how awful. The poor child.

Trembling, she put down the paper. She looked over at the wigged nun. "Remember Sally Ann Fitzpatrick?"

The older woman went on mumbling the rosary.

Mechanically Rita jotted the funeral time in her pocket diary. "Remember Sally Ann Fitzpatrick, Sister?"

The mumbling stopped. "Who?"

"The Fitzer, they called her."

Sister Clement shook her head.

"Surely, you remember her? She was in the boarding school ... She left in the late sixties. 1967."

"Fitzpatrick?" the old nun mused. "Was she a daffodil?"

Rita looked worriedly at the old woman. What was she talking about? Had she gone completely senile?

The old nun suddenly looked cross. "You'll mark the table with that mug, Sister!"

Rita put her mug on the floor. "Sorry - it's cold. You taught Sally Ann Domestic Science and Art."

"Did I? ..." Sister Clement rubbed the polished mahogany table in front of her. "The table's badly marked here!"

Rita looked through the window to the garden. The grounds were at their best. In the distance she heard the hum of grass being cut. The Chestnut trees were in full glory. The white flowers always reminded her of candles on an old-fashioned Christmas tree. "She got Honours Domestic in the Leaving. Art was her other good subject."

"You've a wonderful memory, Sister."

Rita said nothing. She had a special reason for remembering Sally Ann. The girl had saved her sanity. Been her one success in a year of humility and failure. 1967, the year she'd almost left the order. The year of Maggy May's shop-lifting. Had Sally Ann heard that conversation in the hall? It was something she'd never know now. The girl had been too tactful ever to mention it. She was a problem then, but good-hearted. With a special insight. Rita used to help her with her Irish in the evenings. On one occasion Rita had been particularly blue and taken it out on Sally Ann. She had scolded her for not understanding something. "You're a very bad student!"

To her surprise, Sally Ann had got upset. "But I did my best. Irish isn't my native tongue!"

"I know it isn't!" Rita had been ashamed of her anger. "Sorry, I'm just not myself today."

Sally Ann had given her a long look, saying slowly, "I am the Duchess of Malfi, still."

The student had consoled the teacher.

But how had the old woman's shop-lifting spree leaked to the Archbishop? Only the three people involved knew of it. But that very week Rita was summoned to the Mother General and dismissed from her post as Superior. It was all her fault for being too liberal. There'd been no trial. No right of appeal. She'd been sent back into the ranks and ordered to wear the habit at all times. JC as Archbishop McQuaid was known in the Diocese, hadn't even done her the courtesy of addressing her in person. He'd followed his usual practice of writing about her to the Mother General. Oh, people claimed he was kind to the poor, considerate to ex-priests. But she'd found him a boor. An absolute boor. Rita had been made to work in the convent's kitchen. She had to accept it or leave. The next year she was sent to the Order's new Comprehensive in Tallaght. It was meant to be a further punishment, but instead it had been her salvation. There she'd met parents, women far worse off than she was. Women in the pits of depression from broken marriages. Abandoned women. Battered women. So she started night classes and a support group. Then her book came out to good reviews. And the Carysfort job came up. And ironically she was back here as Superior. She'd come full circle.

Rita looked for comfort across the bleak room. "You don't remember anything about her?"

The wigged woman looked up crossly. "About who, Sister?"

"Sally Ann Fitzpatrick."

"Oh, her? Nothing. Not a single thing."

Rita felt a sickening anger. How could she fail to remember her? Sally Ann was always in trouble with Clemmy. For talking, or acting the clown in sewing class. On one occasion Rita'd had a note slipped under her cell door, marked "Personal and Private". It turned out to be a confession from Sally Ann to the attempted murder of Sister Clement. As usual, she'd been acting up in class. And Clemmy had given out yards, saying the girl would be the death of her. Then, immediately after class, the girls had seen Clemmy getting into the Waverly Ambulance. They didn't know she was a hypochondriac who was always arranging little rests in hospital.

Sally Ann got an attack of scruples.

It was very funny. But Rita had looked sternly at the girl. "Sister is all right."

"It'll be my fault if she isn't."

And now Sally Ann was dead. And Clement was still complaining. Rita looked through the window. Tears filled her eyes.

*It is not growing like a tree*

"Why were you asking me about the Fitzpatrick child?" Clemmy suddenly shouted. "Is she in the paper?"

Rita folded *The Irish Times*. "Yes, she's in the paper."

"Why? Is she getting married?"

"She died."

"The Lord have mercy!" Sister Clement went back to her beads.

And Rita picked up her mug and left the room.

In a rented house in Sutton, Kitty Kennedy read over a letter she had just written. Around her, small children played a game of tig, while upstairs her older children quarrelled over a record. But she was used to noise and didn't hear.

Dear Alastair,

I'm writing to your old address, hoping it will find you. I have some very sad news about Sally Ann Fitzpatrick. I know you'll want to hear it. It doesn't seem possible any more, but she has just died as a result of pregnancy. I still can't believe it. I'm pinching myself all day. I don't know the details. I will never forget our college days. Her mini skirts before anyone else. And the time we liberated the library. Remember all our protests? They seem so silly now. (Of course, you were in Trinity.) And having lunch in the Country Shop - it's not there any more. So much has changed. Weren't they great old days, though? I don't know why, but I felt the Fitzer was the type to do something in life. Did you know she married an American History lecturer? He was on sabbatical in UCD in our day - Richard Sheridan. It was a surprise because she was always ranting against history. She just upped and went. They were dead opposites, I thought. Yet they seemed happy enough. A minority are, it seems.

It's selfish of me to mention my own troubles now, but I have to tell someone. Denis has left me. He was always restless, so it was bound to happen sometime. The whole trouble with him was doing Law. He always wanted to be a writer and could settle on nothing else. That was why we dragged the children to Africa. Then New Zealand. He didn't like it there either, so we came back to Ireland. By a fluke he got back into a solicitor's office. Then a vacancy came up in their Cork branch, so he volunteered and was transferred. We had to find another house. So he went ahead to look. He wanted to find one in Kinsale where he could write more easily. Well, he was there a week when he met a poet - American. He immediately threw in his job, and now she keeps him. I have a degree in French, but it's almost impossible to get a job teaching. Denis gives me nothing. So I rely on the Deserted Wives' Allowance. And my parents' help. We have six children now - Macduff, Laertes, and Banquo you'll remember. Antony Ariel and Miranda.

Write sometime and let me know what you're doing now. Are you still teaching? It seems a lifetime ago when we were all young and carefree, doesn't it?

All the best,<br>Kitty.

Deirdre Kelly sat typing in her office in UCD Belfield where she worked for Eoghan O'Connor, Professor of Modern and American Literature. A telephone rang on her desk.

"Department of American Literature. Deirdre Kelly speaking."

"Is Eoghan there, please?" an American girl asked.

Deirdre recognised the voice. "Who's speaking?"

"It's Erin Danaher, Miss Kelly." The girl was a little sheepish.

"The professor isn't in yet."

"When are you expecting him?"

Deirdre bristled with irritation. The neck of some people. "I don't know", she lied.

There was an awkward silence.

"I've got a slight problem," the student went on. "I'm booking my flight home - and need to know the date of my thesis results."

Deirdre tried to keep the irritation our of her voice. "As you're probably aware, your thesis has been sent to external examiners, and we won't know anything till we hear from them."

"Weren't they given a deadline?"

"No," Deirdre lied again.

"I thought there was a deadline."

"I'm afraid you're mistaken. Now, if you don't -"

"Will you ask Eoghan to call me?"

Infuriated, Deirdre slammed down the receiver. She dabbed her perspiring forehead with a hanky. The cheek. The absolute neck of her calling him Eoghan. Maybe you could sleep your way to success in America, but not yet, thank God, in Ireland. American students were all the same. They thought they owned the world. Oh, she noticed the professor's eyes lingering on Miss Danaher's jeaned backside. She was always "popping" in to discuss her stupid thesis. What was it called? "The Greening of the American Novel" - a discussion of the Irish influence on F Scott Fitzgerald. Deirdre had always eavesdropped on their talks. But maddeningly the professor had started taking her down to Ashton's of Clonskeagh for the tutorials. Deirdre knew what went on afterwards. They went back to Erin's Rathmines bedsit. She could see them threshing round on the narrow bed. All bedsits had narrow beds and lumpy mattresses. She knew from experience.

Deirdre had once rung Ashton's, pretending to be his wife. Then rung off before he came. She wanted to worry him, so he'd break off with Erin. But it hadn't done any good.

Then Deirdre wrote Erin a poison pen letter:

> Your filthy flirting with Eoghan O'Connor is known of. Don't think you can get away with this behaviour in Ireland. It's still a Catholic country. If this doesn't stop, you will be reported to the authorities.
>
> Signed, WITHOUT PREJUDICE

Erin had come in giggling the next day. "Will you take a look at this, Miss Kelly! Isn't it a riot? Is Eoghan in yet?"

She'd gone on giggling. The brazen bitch!

But the professor had been badly shaken.

Deirdre put a new page into her typewriter, smiling at the memory of his haggard look. Yes, she'd hit home there. At least she'd put a stop to Ashton's . There was some satisfaction in that. Now she'd better get on with the Professor's article. He'd be in soon, and she'd only typed a page. Her concentration wasn't the best this morning. On the 11 bus to work, she'd read of Sally Ann Fitzpatrick's death. She used to check the Engagement columns for news of girls from school. Now it was the Births. Then she'd seen the name Sheridan in the Death Column.

God, it boggled the mind. The Fitzer gone.

Blast it! A typo!

She corrected it and typed a few more lines. Sally Ann was only her age. Another typo! Blast!

She took out the page and wadded it. She prided herself on her typing, but today was a dead loss. The idea of going to a funeral was upsetting her. Especially with no Mass. Why the hell couldn't Sally Ann get buried in the normal way? Why did she have to go upsetting people? Even in death.

Maybe there'd be girls from school there. They'd all be looking at her, criticising what she had on. Still, maybe not, she'd never seen Sally Ann at Union Day.

She got up and poured some coffee from the Kenwood maker in the corner. It was running low, so she prepared some more. The professor needed a constant fresh supply. It was a habit he'd picked up in California. And it was her job to keep him happy. No, her privilege.

Back at her desk, she took a Mars Bar from a packet in her drawer and ate it hungrily. It was her third this morning. And she was meant to be on a diet. Lose three stone, her doctor had ordered. All very well for him. She couldn't help being fat. It was her metabolism.

And today was different.

If Sally Ann could die, she could too. When she'd never done anything. Oh, she'd scraped through a night BA degree. But she hadn't married or loved anyone. Still, she had kept her faith. While Sally Ann had married in a Registry Office, damning her soul. You wouldn't envy her that. And it isn't true that you never loved anyone. Don't you love Eoghan? Of course, the feeling between them was unspoken. Like all deep feeling. Oh, he ran around with students all right. But he always came back to her. To Miss Kelly who never misunderstood. And Eoghan was better looking and far more distinguished than Sally Ann's husband. He was too skinny and already white-haired.

Only last Christmas she'd met the Sheridans in Kildare Street. Although laden down with parcels, they invited her for a drink in Buswell's. She remembered it was crowded, and they'd had difficulty in finding seats. Then Richard had taken orders.

Deirdre daringly asked for a gin and tonic.

Sally Ann ordered orange juice.

"Oh, I'll have that too!" Deirdre was red with embarrassment.

"Have what you want!" Sally Ann said, giggling. "I'm on the dry."

"For a change," Richard had quipped, disappearing into the crowds.

The two friends look at each other awkwardly.

"Remember when you'd only drink Guinness?" Deirdre said at last. "Vin de pays, you called it."

Sally Ann giggled again. "Did I? I was an awful eejit."

Deirdre was too polite to agree.

"I only had to read someone to copy them. I think it's great we can change - sort of shed our former selves."

Deirdre sniggered. "Remember when you were a Maoist?"

Sally Ann looked at her for a long minute. "I'm not particularly ashamed of that."

"Eh - of course not! Colm Connolly is Lord Mayor now."

"I know."

Deirdre looked at her furtively. "Remember you had a crush on him."

"Yes," was all Sally Ann said.

"Do you ever hear from him?"

"I'm married to Richard."

Deirdre blushed. "Eh - of course - I know." Sally Ann was just the type to be unfaithful. She was probably an alcoholic too. "Eh - have you given up drink completely?"

"No. I'm pregnant." She patted her tummy. "Isn't it great?"

Deirdre had mumbled congratulations.

Sally Ann looked at her guiltily. "Anything can happen, Deirdre...." She held her hand on her tummy. "I mean, this after seven years."

Richard, returning with the drinks, raised his eyes upward. "You can say that again!"

Then they sat in the Christmassy smoke, discussing names for the child. Thomas, after the famous playwright Richard Sheridan's father, if it was a boy, Sally Ann had said.

"After his grandfather," interjected Richard. "His father was an idiot."

And Frances after the playwright's mother, if it was a girl. Deirdre hadn't shown her discomfort. But it was so insensitive in the presence of a single person. Married people were all the same. If they weren't going on about their babies, it was their damn house. Sally Ann had mentioned buying one in Ranelagh which they'd renovated. Richard laughed in the same good-humoured way as he'd laughed over the baby.

Deirdre drained the last of her coffee. She went over to Professor O'Connor's machine and poured more.

God, I'm light years away from a house deposit. Why do things always work out for others? What was so special about Sally Ann? She always had it easy. Never suffered. Oh, her mother died all right. But she'd got over that years ago. Her father was a wealthy doctor. Then she had a lovely husband. A jet set life. What had she done to deserve all that? I have to drag myself in here every day. Still, to work for a man of Eoghan O'Connor's calibre....Everyone didn't have that privilege. He was so dedicated to work. Yet he understood her need for an occasional day off. When he came in, she'd mention a close friend had died. A very close friend. Seeing her upset state, his brow would furrow with concern. He would pat her paternally on the shoulder. Their eyes would lock in unspoken love. His arm would remain round her, lowering to stroke her bottom...

She was having her favourite fantasy. The professor's fiery blue eyes regarded hers for the signal to go on.

She nodded assent.

He quickly locked the door.

Then, as she pulled down her tights, he pulled the rug into the centre of the room. She lay down on it. And, as usual, he lifted her loose tent-shaped dress over her hips. Deftly he stroked her breasts, between her legs.

"Oh, Eoghan," she murmured, coming immediately.

"Deirdre, my love. My dear girl!" And he penetrated her with joy.

He remained inside her.

She came again.

And again.

Deirdre took another Mars Bar from her drawer.

Night after night in bed, she imagined what life would be like if she married Eoghan. What would they say in Galway? Maybe his wife would die and make it possible. Oh, please God, let her die!

Deirdre munched hungrily.

Meanwhile the professor rezipped his trousers. "We can't go on like this, Deirdre."

She looked tragically at him. "Your wife has found out?"

He lit a cigarette, inhaling deeply. "Oh, I don't care about her. I mean, she knows all right, but it's not that."

"What is it then?"

"I have to see you in a more private place. Not here. It's too sordid."

Tears of gratitude came into Deirdre's eyes. "We could go to my flat. I'll fry you a steak."

He took her hands. "My dear girl, we can't go on like this."

She nodded, crying quietly.

Just then the office door opened, and Professor Eoghan O'Connor appeared in reality. He was a squat, balding man with the unkempt look and red face of an alcoholic.

Quickly Deirdre dabbed her eyes with a hanky. "Good morning, Professor."

"Morning, Miss Kelly," he nodded grumpily, going straight to his desk.

She could see he had a bad hangover. He usually did.

He flicked through his post. "Any phone messages?"

"Eh, no!"

Flustered, she put a page in her typewriter. It was nearly twelve, and she'd done nothing. Wearily she began typing the article. It was the same old thing day after day. What was the point? When the one man she loved never even noticed her? Oh, who slaved for him? Covered up his drinking? His affairs? For what? What?

"You're sure no one rang, Miss Kelly?"

She stopped typing. "I'm sure."

He most probably was with Erin last night. And they'd parted fighting. That was why he wanted to know if she'd rung to make up. The thought of them together was too much. Just too much. She started crying again, not caring if he saw.

At last he looked over. "What - what is it, Miss Kelly?"

Deirdre's shoulders shook. "A - a school friend has died."

He came over to her. "I'm very sorry. Were you close?"

Deirdre nodded through her tears. "I'll need tomorrow morning off for the funeral."

"Of course. Take today off too. You look very distraught."

Deirdre managed to stop crying. "But there's your article to be typed."

"There's no hurry with that."

"Well, maybe I'll go home then."

"Do, Miss Kelly." He went back to his desk, forcing a smile at her.

Deirdre gathered her things and left. Halfway down the corridor, she remembered she'd forgotten to wash her coffee cup. She couldn't leave it there all night. It might attract bugs. She'd slip back now and get it, casually mentioning the coffee was fresh.

She reached the door, pausing for a minute as the professor's voice came from inside.

"Erin, darling? ... I knew you'd ring me. Your thesis results?...I told you not to worry. You're a straight first....Of course not. The expert in sour grapes wouldn't give me a message. I've got rid of the tub of lard for the day, and hopefully for tomorrow. Some friend has done me a favour and died."

Deirdre slunk back down the corridor.


Colm Connolly was at a Monday afternoon committee meeting. He was still handsome. His brown skin was deeply tanned from a recent holiday in Portugal. And if anything, he looked more distinguished with greying hair. He had perfected a frown of concentration, which he wore now, for the endless meetings he'd had to attend since his inauguration as Lord Mayor of Dublin. Oh, there were other functions too: receptions, prizegivings, charity events. But this meeting today was an endless discussion on the government's recent introduction of water rates. As a Labour Lord Mayor, he was against them, but he'd have to vote to retain them. Dammit, they were in a coalition now. But the people were refusing to pay. And a politician should please the people. Stringent economic policies were fine, but they didn't get votes. Fianna Fail would only reap the benefits at the next election. Fine Gael would be out, and what would happen to Labour then?

He was on a sinking ship.

"These penal rates are another dishonest ruse of a conservative government," an opposition councillor's voice droned on.

Colm re-adjusted his chain, looking at the speaker with intense interest. But he was thinking of Sally Ann Fitzpatrick. All morning, since reading of her death in the paper, he'd been trying to summon the courage to phone his wife, Una. It wasn't that he was upset. God no. He'd only seen Sally once in Ranelagh since college, and then he couldn't be sure it was her. It was all too long ago. When was it? 1969? No, '68. Just after the Gentle Revolution. God, they'd all been mad. And that den of internationalists in Sandymount. She'd been so damn intense. And so sexually uptight. Pity she was caught in the raid. God, that had been a near thing for him. A drugs charge would've hurt him politically. You didn't realise these things when you were young. It hadn't done her any damage. Ah no, she had nothing to lose. And now she was gone. It was amazing. But you couldn't live in the past. No, he was just curious to know if a woman could still die in childbirth. It looked like that from *The Irish Times*. Also, he wanted Una to come to the funeral with him. It'd look good to be seen together. Old college friends might be there. Potential voters.

But he hadn't yet rung home.

"The Labour Party are insensitive to the people who elected them."

He just couldn't bring himself to forget last weekend's row. Lately they'd been getting on better. Even talked of ending their trial separation.

But when he'd brought the kids back from Dawson Street to their home in Mount Pleasant Square on Sunday night, there'd been a pregnant girl sitting in the comfortable basement kitchen. Cool as you like, she'd offered him a cup of tea. Then Una had come in, blithely informing him that the stranger was to occupy the top floor.

Indefinitely, it seemed.

His study, dammit. Personally painted and soundproofed against the children's noise. Oh, he could work in the Mansion House all right, but he wouldn't always be Lord Mayor. And anyway he'd decided to move home again. For the weekends at least. He felt lonely in these huge rooms. The view of Dawson Street was great, but it was like living in a museum. Even the private living apartments were full of heavy antique furniture. And the kitchen was most inadequate. There was nothing homely about it. But when he'd admitted all this to Una, she'd shouted, "It's too late now!"

The one word led to another. He stormed out of the house. And hadn't rung since. Neither had she.

Colm shifted in his chair. He flicked a piece of lint off his dark suit. The councillor's voice was giving him a headache. Una had over-reacted about his last affair. Couldn't she accept it was over? Her whole trouble was a refusal to grow up. Philanthropy was fine in college. It went with all the protest. Oh, it was acceptable to be idealistic when you were young. It was good for your image later. But to be still collecting stray cats in your thirties was too much. And last month she'd really embarrassed him by picketing the Dáil with a group of women against the Referendum. Oh, he was against abortion being illegal too. For God's sake, it was a woman's right to decide about her own body. Hadn't he paid for two abortions? Of course, Una didn't know that. But it wasn't the thing for the Lord Mayor's wife to appear on the front page of *The Irish Times*.

In jeans, for God's sake.

This blasted feminism incensed him. It had driven him from his home. Why did he seek the company of other women? Because Una was obsessed. She could talk of nothing but women's lib. She knew he had to approach these things cautiously. Ireland was still predominantly rural. And rural values prevailed, except for a minority in Dublin. Mainly the media. Besides he had his career to think of. And especially now when the party was thinking of him for the vacant seat in Dublin South. He had a good track record. As a councillor, he'd done solid work for housing in the inner city, and now might reap the benefits. If he wasn't picked, he might try for the Senate at the next election. Senator Colm Connolly sounded all right...not too bad at all.

"I sincerely hope my resolution will be passed unanimously."

The councillor sat down.

There was coughing and shuffling as someone else got up to speak. Just then Eddie Nolan, the small, bald Labour Party secretary, leaned over, whispering to Colm, "It looks like we'll be here all day. Remember, there's a meeting tomorrow at ten, Colm."

Colm frowned. "I'm afraid that's bad for me. I've a funeral."

"But you can't miss the meeting. We're discussing the by-election. This is your chance, boy."

Colm didn't hesitate. "Ok, I'll be there."


Across town in Westmoreland Street, Mona sat in Bewley's Café, waiting for her friend Barbara. All around her was friendly noise and chatter. Across the table a man read *The Irish Times* with the Death notices visible. But Mona didn't notice them. She was too busy hoping the man would go. Then she'd have the table for herself and Barbara. They always met here on Tuesday afternoon. At least, ever since Ronnie was born. It was a definite ill wind that blew some good. Poor little fellow. To be responsible for another person's happiness at that age! But Terry had literally taken one look at him and come home. He said it was easier financially. He was sick of mess. But Mona knew it was more. It was the power of the old nun's prayers. The important thing was now they both tried. She could cope much better because of co-counselling. And she'd heard of it in hospital from that girl. What was her name? It slipped her mind. But she had told her, "Mona, there's a group of people who can help you. They all advise each other. I'll ring you."

Mona had been sceptical. But sure enough, the girl phoned with the number. "Ring them, Mona!"

She agreed, but did nothing for weeks. Then one day she dialled and asked for information. There was an introductory meeting in a house in Clontarf that very night, so she went.

Mona smiled, remembering her nerves.

They had all sat in a circle.

Each person was asked to say something they were happy about.

Mona had quaked, and when her turn came had said simply, "I'm happy to be here."

Then they had separated into twos. She had spoken to Barbara for ten minutes, pouring out her troubles. Then Barbara had done the same.

It was like confession.

Next they had sat in another circle. Each person was asked how they had found counselling and how they had liked being counselled.

Then they had sung a song and gone home.

Mona had thought the song idiotic. It was "Pack up your troubles." But the next morning she'd felt so much better. So she agreed to do an introductory course. Terry had been rather amazed at the change in her. And now if she got too sensitive about anything, Barbara helped her discharge her emotion. So she didn't bottle things up. That had been her trouble in the past. Also expecting too much of marriage. Now she was into meditation.

"Hello, Mona!" A tall, thin woman with red hair interrupted her thoughts.

"Barbara!"

"Sorry I'm late."


At 5.30 that evening, tall and stately Brian de Burca waited outside Fanagan's of Aungier Street. It was the rush hour, and a handful of people stood about awkwardly, awaiting the hearse. No one knew quite what to do. He, for one, had never attended a funeral like this. Wasn't Sally Ann a Catholic? Good Christ, it was awful. Poor Dick. The girl had been a handful on that holiday, but you had to admire her guts. Luckily Maureen had seen it in the paper at lunchtime and they could be here.

Maureen stood beside him, dressed in a suit and sensible brogues. Her wispy grey hair was hidden by a hat.

Brian paced up and down the pavement. Then whispered to her, "I wonder what's keeping them?"

"It's the rush hour, dear."

He cleared his throat and stuck his lower jaw out. "I can tell you one thing. I know how I'm going to vote in the abortion referendum."

"How, dear?"

"As Sally Ann would've wanted."

She looked sadly down the street. "That's against it, I'm sure. Remember Connemara? Sally Ann got quite worked up."

Brian paced again. He could see her sitting on that beach, arguing with them all. She was too young to die. What had happened?

A large woman stopped him, smiling sychophanticly. "Hello, Professor de Burca."

Brian recognised her from somewhere. "Where have we met?"

"In UCD"

"Ah, you were a student?"

"Yes, but I work there now. I'm Eoghan O'Connor's secretary."

"Of course! That's where I've seen you. How's Professor O'Connor? We used to meet at the Abbey, but I haven't seen him for a while."

"He's been working hard on a new book."

"Hmm!" Brian despised the man. An alcoholic and philanderer of the worst sort.

Her face lit up. "Belfield isn't as personal as Earlsfort Terrace."

"No, but the students prefer it." God, he hated making small talk. "Isn't this a terrible business?"

The woman nodded lugubriously. "How do you know Sally Ann?"

Brian stuck his chin out. "I'm a friend."

"Of her husband? Of course, he's a historian ..."

"Of both."

The woman dabbed her eyes with a lacey hanky. "We were best friends in school. She was so delighted about the baby."

Brian perused her irritably. Why did she pick on him to talk to? He didn't want to talk about it. And surely they weren't contemporaries? You could never tell age with women.

Maureen tugged his sleeve. "Here they are, dear."

A huge black hearse pulled up with a coffin inside.

Then another limousine. Dick, a tall young man, and an older man piled out. Hmm...That was Dr Jack Fitzpatrick, the amateur historian. He had met him at a reception in the National Library. Must be her father. It was a small world. Then Peggy and Tony O'Mara drove up in their old Fiat. Thank God, they were here.

Brian went over to shake his friend's hand. "Dick, my poor fellow."


In London on the morning of Sally Ann's funeral, Alastair Macbeth heard the postman. He grabbed his glasses and ran downstairs. He had aged very little. His woolly hair was a bit thinner, but he wore the same thick hornrimmed glasses. Usually he was gone to the University of London, where he taught French literature, by this time but today he was waiting for a letter. He was expecting to hear from his girlfriend, Penny, who had gone to a kibbutz for three months.

On the hall floor there was a letter from the bank. And one with an Irish stamp. Nothing from Penny.

He turned over the Irish letter. No address on the back. Who could it be from? He hadn't been in Dublin for nearly ten years. Could it be from Sally Ann? If so, he wouldn't reply. Christ. What was the point? The past was the past. Oh, he thought of her now and again. But the whole affair had been a mistake from the word go. The bloody woman had clung to him like someone drowning.

Still, he was curious.

He ripped open the letter and read the signature - Kitty.

What was she wanting?

Slowly he read the letter. Sally Ann dead. Good grief. He stood there, stunned. What had gone wrong? He wadded it and stuffed it into his jacket pocket. He was already late. Today there was a department meeting, and he had to be in top form for it. He couldn't afford to get upset about someone from the past.

Running down the path to the road, he thought it just as well Penny hadn't written. Maybe she'd changed her mind about marriage. Become more independent. How many times had he told her he wasn't the marrying sort? He didn't want to settle down. Why couldn't he meet the independent type you were always hearing about? A woman's libber. The new junior lecturer looked independent. Maybe he'd ask her for a date this weekend.

But as he waited on for his train, Alastair thought of Sally Ann. He saw her on that platform in France. Somehow she'd always be Ireland to him. She was so damn daft ... She'd hugged him so tightly that last time. He'd wanted to see her again. But had thought it best to end it. It had gone on too long already. He'd meant to finish with her when he left Dublin, but never had the strength. She kept hanging on. He should never have agreed to that holiday. But having agreed he should've gone to Paris with her. He could have done that at least. But what was the use of regretting things now?

The train screeched up and he got on.


Grace O'Malley was on her second double gin and tonic in the Palace Bar in Fleet Street. For years it had been her breakfast haunt. They knew her here and contacted Pat if necessary. Also it was private in the back room, and they let her in early if she needed a cure. God, she needed something this morning. You couldn't go to a funeral on an empty stomach.

Poor Sally Ann.

What had happened?

All morning Grace had thought of nothing but Athens, Pennsylvania. Dick could be a right intolerant shite, always calling her an alcoholic, but Sally Ann was all right. She'd cooked her so many meals. And those disgusting eggflips. Grace smiled at the memory. It seemed so long ago now. But it was only a few years. She'd never cross the Atlantic again. Although it had been money for talk. And good money. Freddie Ferris still wrote to her. The fellow was cracked. He'd come over to visit her once, and she'd had a terrible time hiding him from Pat. She giggled, remembering the ducking in and out of doors. God, she'd had a hell of a time in bed with him. But it had certainly pissed Pat off. Their relationship almost didn't survive it.

The door opened and a journalist from *The Independent* came in.

"Gracie! What are you drinking?"

Grace gathered her bag. "No, thanks, Jim. I'm off to a wee girl's funeral."

"Well, have one for the road."

Grace hesitated. If she didn't go now, she'd be there all day. But then she wouldn't have to face Dickie. All those people.

"What're you drinking, Gracie?"

"Ah, fuck the begrudgers! A double gin and tonic."


Tony and Peggy were finishing breakfast.

Peggy poured herself more tea. She sipped it, staring through the window to their well-tended garden. It was early summer, so the geraniums

212

had come out in pink and red flowers. And this year the apples would be good. She must weed the vegetable garden this weekend. Sally Ann had shown an interest in the garden. That was why she wanted to live in the country. "Remember that house in Kells Sally nearly bought."

Tony was behind the paper. "Sally was a dear girl, but cracked."

"It was a good idea basically."

"You're cracked too."

"There was land going with it."

Tony rustled his paper. "I couldn't see them growing cabbages."

Peggy stared sadly into her cup. It was hard to imagine Sally gone. Now they could have no more arguments. She smiled to herself at the memory of their heated discussions. Perhaps she'd been too intolerant of her. But no, Sally really liked an argument. She needed someone to bounce opinions off. A mother figure. Poor pet. There was no harm to her. And she'd made a good job of things really. "They did all right in the end."

Tony looked up puzzled. "What?"

"I mean, the Ranelagh house was fine."

"It's fine now. The bookcases made a difference." He folded his paper with sigh. "All things are basically tragic."

"Cheer up!" Peggy gripped his arm.

He shook his head. "It's not good. It's not -"

She got up and started clearing the table. "I think we should call and see if Dick's all right."

Tony stood up too. He looked at the garden. The grass needed to be cut. He'd keep busy all weekend. "Let's not intrude. He'll be with her family."

Peggy went into the kitchen. That was unlikely. Sally Ann had told her she didn't communicate much with her father. There was only a much younger brother. Dick would need company. He'd looked dreadful at the funeral home yesterday evening. She'd tried to get him to talk about it, but he wouldn't be drawn. But she certainly didn't blame him for that.

"I'm going to call before the funeral." She called. "Come with me if you like."

Tony sighed. "Grief is a private thing."

Slowly Jim Nolan backed his Post Office Toyota van into the narrow cul de sac of small nineteenth century Dublin houses. These days he worked full-time delivering parcels. He now looked completely Mod and wore an earring in one ear. He still read and attended a "Writing for Pleasure" class in the Adult Institute in Mountjoy Square on a Tuesday evening. But, as yet, he hadn't had anything published.

He stopped to avoid a child playing ball in the street. It was always a bitch to get out of here. Already this summer, he'd delivered umpteen sacks of books to the Americans in the corner. Sheridan was the name. Must be terrible bookworms. Where did they fit them all in, in that tiny terraced house? Must remember to collect the empty bags this time. The mot usually answered the door. Sleepily. Still in her dressing gown. Thank God, she didn't recognise him. At first he didn't remember where he'd met her. But then it clicked. That pub in Greystones. Must be well over ten years ago now, he knew by his eldest's age, since he left her there to pay for the drinks. It was something yours truly wasn't particularly proud of. He remembered the gold granny glasses. Those dark Afro curls. He still fancied her. Last week he'd given her the eye, but she'd just giggled at him. Giggled. Very funny. Some would be glad. Anyway she was pregnant. And the husband was usually hovering in the background. Just his luck.

He hopped out and rang the bell. Then dragged the heavy canvas sack from the van.

No one in. That was unusual.

He banged the brass knocker.

Still no answer.

Jaysus, it wasn't his day.

He scribbled out a note on a delivery docket and popped it in the letter box. Just then the husband yanked open the door. He was tall, thin and white-haired, and held a glass of whiskey in one hand.

"Who are y-y-you? Another c-c-country c-c-cousin?" He stared groggily at the sack. "T-t-travelling light? C-come on in."

Plastered. At ten in the morning. So much for the intellectual classes.

"I'm from the post office, mate. Delivering your books."

"The p-post office. Oh..." The man gulped his drink, swaying dangerously. "Well, d-do me a favour."

"Sure." Jim heaved the sack forward.

"Dump them in the canal."

God, he was really crocked. "What?"

"Dump them!" The drunk made to slam the door, but Jim put his foot in it. He knew the type. Down to Rathmines first thing tomorrow, claiming his property.

"Look, let me leave them in the hall. There! Good man! I'll get the bag later."

Obstinately the man held the door shut. "Take them away."

"Listen, mate! I'm not bringing them back!"

"Well...g-give them away then."

"OK, I'll leave them on the pavement."

The man hiccuped from behind the door. "D-d-do that!"

Angrily Jim looked at his watch. Christ, it really wasn't his day. If he left them, they'd be stolen. And yours truly would get blamed. The only thing was to haul them back.

The American peered out, his brown eyes oddly blinking.

Jim pushed the door further. "Look, mate! I'm only doing my job."

214

Slowly the eyes comprehended,. "Y-y-your job? Of course, Y-your job."

He opened the door and stretched to help with the sack. Instead he took a header onto the pavement and lay face-down. There was broken glass and whiskey everywhere.

Christ, he was out cold.

Gently Jim rolled the man onto his back. Blood oozed from his grazed forehead. "Are you all right, mate?"

The man opened one eye, nodding.

Jim gripped his armpits and hauled him up. Together they staggered into the sitting room. As Jim got him onto the couch, the man took out a hanky and dabbed his forehand. "M-must've missed my step."

Jim watched to make sure he'd stay put. He looked around the little room. It was full of pictures and had been recently done up. "I'll just get the books off the street."

He dragged the sack in, then carefully picked up the scattered pieces of glass. When he came back, the American had his head in his hands. "Is there a bin?"

"What?"

"A bin. For the broken glass."

The man pointed to a wastebasket in the corner.

"Don't worry about the sack. I'll be back for it." He crossed the room. "Eh, is the wife out?"

The man didn't answer.

Jim lingered in the doorway. "She's out shopping?"

The American looked up, suddenly soberer. "My wife is dead."

His voice was cold.

Jim shifted awkwardly,. "God, I'm sorry!"

"She died," the man said savagely, "She died in fucking childbirth."

Jim came back to him. "Look, I'm sorry, mate. Can I make you a cup of tea?"

The man looked amazed. "Tea? Tea? I'm going to plant her in an hour."

"Coffee then?"

The man staggered up and swayed towards the door. "I can't go to a funeral on coffee. I'll pour us both a Bourbon. If...you'll join me."

Jim eased him back onto the couch. "Let me make you a cup of coffee. You definitely can't go like this."

"OK"

Jim went out to the kitchen. The floor was red-tiled like the rest of the downstairs. A long pine table took up a wall, and there was a pine dresser with neat rows of white cups. Hanging spider plants and pictures on the wall added to the cosiness. It was hard to believe she wouldn't be coming back. He found the coffee and put on the kettle. Then went to the pantry for cups. The sink was full of dirty dishes, and an opened packed of cream crackers littered the draining board. God, what if Nora died? He took her, the children, their life, so much for granted. Yet was unfaithful if he could. Oh, most of the time he went round resenting her. Accusing her of nagging him. Only this morning they'd had a row about money. And he left their Bray semi-d at seven in the morning and wasn't home till seven in the evening.

When he came back, the American was wiping his eyes.

"Now...listen, old son..." Awkwardly Jim held out the cup.

The man took it. "They lost the baby too."

Jim sipped his coffee. "I didn't know it still happened."

The man laughed shortly. "Anything can happen. That's what she used to say. Well, she was damn right!"

Jim didn't know what to say. "Was it the labour?"

"No. Christ, she had a headache. A bad headache. So I said, take aspirin."

"What else could you say?"

"But it was a bad headache. And it got worse."

"A headache isn't usually serious."

"This one was. It got worse and worse. Finally I rang her father - he's a doctor."

"What did he say?"

The American looked at him dazedly. "What? Oh, he...sent an ambulance immediately. I went with her. I held her hand. When we were at Portobello, she said, "Oh, Dick." Then had some sort of fit and passed out. She was dead on arrival."

Jim didn't know what to say.

The man went on dully. "They said to leave everything to them. So I did. But they couldn't save the baby. They were both gone."

"I'm sorry. The kid too -."

"What would I do with a kid? Do you have any?"

"Four."

The man put down his coffee cup. "I have four too. By another marriage. I didn't want another. But she did. And now -." He put his head in his hands, sighing wearily. "I wish we'd never met."

"You can't say that!" Jim felt completely at a loss.

Dammit, he was only the postman. "You know what they say, "Better to have loved and ... lost -.""

The man's hands were still on his face. "Yes...yes."

Suddenly he jumped up. "Now go! Please go!"

"I'm on my way!"

Luckily the doorbell rang.

Jim went to answer it.

A middle-aged couple stood on the pavement. "We're Tony and Peggy O'Mara. We wondered if Dick needed a lift."

216

Jim ushered them in. "He needs something. He's in the sitting-room."

"Are you Sally Ann's brother?" The woman asked cheerfully.

"No, I'm the postman. And I should be gone!" And Jim slipped quickly out to finish delivering his parcels.

It wasn't a big funeral. Dr Fitzpatrick, his son-in-law, and son followed the hearse in a large, rented limousine. They were followed by a couple of cars. No one spoke in the rented car. Dr Fitzpatrick's thoughts were slow and mechanical. He looked worriedly at the man who had married his daughter. Although they were both very private, they'd always got on well. By keeping their distance. Now the younger man looked out of it. He just stared blankly ahead of him. As if he'd imbibed a bit. Which was no harm, the doctor thought. Yesterday he'd refused tranquillisers. The doctor had tried to explain to him that Sally Ann's death had been a fluke. Although eclampsia was one of the three major hazards of pregnancy it was usually preceded by pre-eclampsia which could be controlled. As far as he could determine she'd had no early symptoms like oedema or albumen in her urine. At seven months her blood pressure had suddenly shot up, bringing on toxaemia and causing fulminating eclampsia. Which had killed both mother and child. He knew her husband blamed him. People always blamed doctors. As if they were the Almighty. Maybe if she'd been in hospital, they could've saved one of them. But she wasn't. And there was nothing to indicate she should've been. It had happened. It was a fact. You had to deal with facts. And death was a fact of life. He was always telling people this.

As they passed Christ Church, a man blessed himself. Dr Fitzpatrick was consoled by it. People had done it all along the route. And, at least, it wasn't raining. There was nothing worse than a wet funeral. Dick had surprised him by insisting Sally Ann hadn't wanted a Christian burial. He'd got quite worked up about respecting her wishes. But the doctor had argued that it was only some passing whim. He knew his daughter. She was always getting crazy whims. She'd got married in a Registry Office, without even consulting him. But she was still a baptised Catholic and entitled to the consolations of the Church. He didn't really care about the marriage, but he wanted her buried properly - with her mother. At last they'd compromised, the husband agreeing to a priest at the graveside. A mass could always be said later, the doctor thought. Now he was grateful for the funeral. For things to do. He had a déjà vu feeling. Everything seemed external to him. Like he was witnessing someone else's tragedy. Not burying his child.

He knew he was in deep shock.

He'd sat up all night reading poetry. It was all he could do. He looked at his red-eyed son. Poor Tim had taken it badly. At least he'd had a haircut and wore a suit. He'd shown some respect for his sister.

Tim caught his glance, frowning worriedly. "You OK, Doc?"

The doctor nodded. His children were such a puzzle to him. What sort of people were they? Since they became teenagers, they were strangers. Did he really know either of them? You walked into a room one day, and your child glared at you. They called it adolescence. Although from the Latin, a modern word. For a modern generation. Who spoke a different language. He'd tried to instill a love of poetry into them, but had failed. Still, they'd been such sweet little children. Gogarty had some good poems about children. "Golden stockings you had on..."

Dr Fitzpatrick blew his nose noisily.

His son looked at him anxiously. "Are you all right, Doc?"

"We're lucky with the traffic, Tim." He had to reassure him he was coping.

Tim looked abruptly away. "Yeah."

The boy was crying but the doctor could think of nothing to say. He, at least, had to carry on. He'd done it all his life. God, this was monstrous. Monstrous. You knew not the day nor the hour. But he expected to see his daughter again. God's will be done. And his wife. A doctor had to believe.

He'd never expected to have children. Then Sally Ann had come...and she was so clever, reading at five. He'd brought her everywhere, showing her off. Crabbit, Maeve had called her. And then Maeve's death. He hadn't expected that either. After all he'd married a much younger woman. Sally Ann, child though she was, had tried to console him then, but he wouldn't let her. He shut his children out. It had been wrong, but he couldn't help it. He was too old. Had not the nuns thought him Sally Ann's grandfather? They were right. He was old..old.. "You are old Father William."

At Glasnevin a small group had assembled at the graveside with a priest. It was sunny, but there was a slight wind. It caught a woman's hat and Richard's white hair as he stood with one hand over his face. The priest held his prayerbook as its pages blew. The men who brought the coffin and were lowering it into the earth. But the grave wasn't big enough, and it got stuck, lurching queerly to one side.

Richard laughed. "She was always awkward."

There was an embarrassed ripple of not exactly laughter.

The men huffed and puffed, trying to get the coffin in again. Finally they gave up, leaving it standing up at one end.

"Since Almighty God has called our sister, Sally Ann, from this life to himself, we commit her body to the earth from which it was made."

Rita watched Dr Fitzpatrick. He looked so lonely, standing here. What could you say to console him? Somehow he reminded her of her own father. She had made her peace with him at last. It was one thing she was grateful for. And it had come about because of the trouble she'd got into with the Order. To her amazement he'd taken her side, advising her to leave. "Bad cess to them, child."

Rita smiled at the memory. His reaction was so unexpected.

The priest scattered dust on the coffin. "Dust you are, and unto dust you shall return..."

The people bowed their heads.

"Let us pray for our sister to our Lord Jesus Christ, who said, 'I am the resurrection and the life, the man who believes in me will live even if he dies ...'"


Afterwards Rita went back through labyrinthine convent corridors to her own room. Her shoes squeaked eerily on the waxed floors. Ghosts seemed to follow her. Thousands of children had walked these corridors. And where were they now? Names came into her head, names she couldn't put a face on. And faces without names. It was like that at the funeral. She'd recognised one or two, but couldn't put a name to them until they'd introduced themselves. It was amazing they way you forget.

She reached her room and sat weakly on her narrow bed. Then got up and poured a brandy into a tooth mug from the bottle in her cupboard. A cousin had brought it from America. And now she needed a drink. The funeral had been heartbreaking. That poor husband. She had shaken hands with him, mentioning that she had taught Sally Ann. He'd seemed interested in this, grasping at any detail about her. But then someone else had come up and Rita had offered her sympathy to the father and brother. The brother was a nice young man. She could see Sally Ann in him. Suddenly she'd come to life again as a schoolgirl. Untidy. Her skirt too short. Unruly hair and vague, short-sighted eyes. The girl was blind as a bat and always losing her glasses. Or breaking them. It was maddening. And now ... What did it all mean?

I am the Resurrection and the Life.

Because of that promise, she stayed in a Church she often had no time for. A Church which had forgotten about love and the personality of Christ. It was Maggy May who taught her how to live in the spirit. How to love. She had been the first to comfort her after the demotion and disgrace. Had stuck to her when the others had shunned her. If only she had her now. But the old nun was gone. One night in the summer of 1967, she'd knocked on Rita's door for a chat. And later, when Rita had indicated it was time to go, the old nun had pleaded, "Can I stay the night. I'm frightened." Against all rules, Rita had let her sleep in an armchair. And in the middle of the night she awoke to find the old woman dead.

Her heart had stopped.

Just stopped.

Rita got up and went to her desk. She had work to do. It had always helped her in the past. And it would now.